CRITICS PRAISE COLBY HODGE!

SHOOTING STAR

"This action-packed story picks up after the events of Hodge's previous novel, *Stargazer*…Hodge is definitely on a roll, and it is a great pleasure to revisit her thrilling world. Entertainment galore!"

—*RT BOOKreviews*

"*Shooting Star* is an exciting tale featuring high-tech adventure and showcasing a fun side with the author's humor…Ms. Hodge has created an exiting new world of good and evil with characters I want to hear more about."

—Romance Reviews Today

STARGAZER

"Talented Colby Hodge delivers space adventure at a breathtaking clip! Fans of *Star Wars* and Riddick will love *Stargazer*."

—*New York Times* Bestselling Author Susan Grant

"A pulse-pounding futuristic thriller. Hodge has created a genuinely engaging new world. Her characters are absorbing and the story is intriguing."

—*RT BOOKreviews*

"*Stargazer* is a rousing space adventure set in a fascinating universe brought vividly to life. Exciting and action-packed, it's one of the most purely fun books I've read this year…a real thrill ride and an easy book to recommend."

—All About Romance

"Colby Hodge gives us a romping good time across the stars with this futuristic tale of romance, revenge, and renewal.…*Stargazer* _____ the reader along for _____ everyday world."

CLAIMED

"You forget how well I know you, Elle."

And I don't know you at all.

Where was Boone? Where was the boy she had played with and teased? This Boone was serious. This Boone smoldered with something that she was not sure she wanted to know.

"You're scaring me, Boone," Elle finally said.

"You scare me," Boone said. "You don't know the power you have...over me."

"I would never use my powers on you."

"You could hurt me without them," he said.

"Boone?" Elle asked.

His head moved quickly. His lips touched hers and suddenly she was crushed against him.

This was dangerous. This was out of control. This was Boone plundering her lips as if he possessed her. This was Boone branding her as his own.

Other *Love Spell* books by Colby Hodge:

SHOOTING STAR
STARGAZER

COLBY HODGE

Star
Shadows

LOVE SPELL NEW YORK CITY

LOVE SPELL®

November 2007

Published by

Dorchester Publishing Co., Inc.
200 Madison Avenue
New York, NY 10016

ISBN 10: 0-505-52629-8
ISBN 13: 978-0-505-52629-8

The name "Love Spell" and its logo are trademarks of Dorchester Publishing Co., Inc.

Printed in the United States of America.

10 9 8 7 6 5 4 3 2

Visit us on the web at www.dorchesterpub.com.

ACKNOWLEDGEMENTS

To my husband Rob who understands what a deadline is and everything that goes with it.

To Candy Halliday who said, "Why don't you have those two dudes fight each other."

And to my wonderful friends who get me through each day. Alesia Holliday, Barbara Ferrer, and Marianne Mancusi.

Star
Shadows

PROLOGUE
BALI CIRCE

"Sagan?" the woman asked. She thoroughly enjoyed the sound of her husband's name on her lips, the way she felt when she said it, the knowledge that he would reply. "What did the sky look like before?"

"I never saw it before," he said. "My mother told me that at sunset there would be yellows and oranges and pinks along with all the shades of blue. And stars. More than you could count."

"I wonder what the stars look like," she said as she looked up at the gaseous cloud that stained the sky.

"My mother said they were tiny pinpricks of light. Like jewels that were scattered on a black cloth."

"It's a shame we ruined it." She settled back against his strength and his hands splayed across the growing mound of her belly.

"It wasn't you. You weren't a part of it."

"Aren't I? I am one of them."

"Not in your heart. Not where it matters." He placed

his cheek next to hers. "And don't forget, my mother was one of them also."

The wind off the water tossed her pale blond hair around her face and she pushed it back, only to have it come out again, teased by the strong breeze.

"Let it go," Sagan said. "I love to watch it."

"Look," she said and pointed to the water. A cloud scudded before the moon, darkening the vista, then moved on, allowing the magenta light to dance atop the waves.

Dolphins appeared at the surface and tossed their heads in greeting.

"Do you think they see the moon?" she asked. "Do you think they know that the sky used to be different?"

"They know," he said.

"They always seem so happy," she said.

"Because they know they'll play a part."

"A part of the legend?"

"Yes."

"Tell it to me again." She never tired of hearing it. The hope. The part of her planet's history that was forbidden by the evil and greedy women who controlled everything and everyone. But they could not control her. They could not control who she loved any more than they could control Sagan's mother when she chose to love.

How many others were there like her on the planet? Other women who were blessed with the inherited abilities but not the greed or desire for unlimited power. Women who were not interested in clawing and fighting their way to the top. Other women who just wanted to live and love and experience the happiness that came with it.

"There will come, someday, a man with forbidden eyes who will have more power than the Circe women," he began, quoting the legend that had been passed down from generation to generation of the common people.

"Eyes like mine?" she asked.

He kissed the top of her head. "Yes. Eyes the same color as yours."

"Imagine," she said. "Imagine the looks on their faces when they see him, the Aberrant, in the flesh."

"The legend calls him the Empowered One," Sagan corrected her, using the legendary name for their savior, instead of the Circe curse. "The Empowered One will come from the sea escorted by the dolphins. They'll join him in battling the Circe Witches and when it is over all people on the planet, woman and man alike, will finally be equal."

"Was it ever so?" She knew that part of the history better than he since she had trained to be a Circe.

"No. The balance has never been equal."

"They don't know that it is the only way to be happy," she said. "The equality." She placed her hands over his, then laughed when the baby still inside her kicked hard. "Did you feel it?" she asked.

"Yes."

"Wouldn't it be wonderful if she could see it happen? If our daughter could be a part of it?"

"It would," he said. "I would like for her to know happiness such as ours."

"You will keep her safe," she said. "You will watch over her."

"I will," he said. But the lights showing off in the distance worried him. Ships were coming, flying low over the water to cut off their escape by boat. Their hiding place had been found.

"We should move," he said.

"Do we have to?" she asked. She settled against him as if she wanted to get closer and his arms tightened around her, just for a moment, before reality set in.

"We have to warn the others," he said and pointed to the lights.

He helped her to her feet but she stopped suddenly as he sought to guide her off the beach.

"I love you," she said. "Don't ever doubt it."

"I won't," he said. "I don't." He gave her a quick kiss. "You sound like you're afraid we'll never see each other again."

She placed her hand over her stomach. "It's the baby," she said. "She makes me worry."

"Everything will be fine," he said. "We've got plenty of time."

"I know."

But she couldn't help but look over her shoulder at the approaching lights as they made their way off the beach.

CHAPTER ONE

It was one of those days that hurt to be alive. The beauty of it inspired you to live life to the fullest. But it also made you feel as if you could die from it.

At least on the inside.

Arielle Phoenix, one day short of her eighteenth birthday, looked at her twin brother, Alexander, and grinned.

"How long before they figure out we've escaped?" she asked.

Zander shrugged as if to say he didn't care and flashed a grin of his own. Elle grabbed the back of their friend Boone's shirt with a shriek as he kicked the jet cycle off the ground and set off over the waves.

Zander was right behind them as they headed straight out to sea and hopefully out of sight of the villa that hung on the side of the dormant volcano. The "borrowed" jet cycles hovered just over the top of the waves, kicking up spray as the ocean rolled beneath them, revealing swirling colors of bright blues, shimmering greens, and the purest aqua.

A pod of dolphins joined them as they headed toward a small spit of sand and coral that only appeared at low tide. It was another remnant of a volcano, one that had long ago caved into the sea, leaving behind a veritable garden beneath the glasslike surface.

Elle moved her arm up and down as if she were skimming it over the waves. The dolphins swam closer, racing beside them. The animals jumped over the wake, fanning out behind the jet cycles and then diving beneath the surface, only to come up again in a race against the humans.

Elle didn't understand how she could *speak* to the dolphins. She just knew that they, somehow, understood each other. The dolphins tossed their heads with a smile and agreed to join them in their getaway.

It seemed there were no limits to what she could do with her mind.

Zander couldn't do anything with his. At least not anything extraordinary. Their parents seemed to think that he should be capable of great things. Their parents were both telepaths, and their father could move large objects with his mind and had the ability to see in the dark.

Yet no matter how hard their mother probed into Zander's mind, there was nothing there. At least nothing that answered back to her. After countless attempts and endless frustration he begged her to stop wishing for something that obviously was not going to happen and she did, reluctantly. Not that she had much choice. Zander might not have the ability to project into minds but he knew how to protect himself with the litany their parents taught them.

Elle knew that he felt like a disappointment to their parents. All she had to do was look inside his mind to know how he felt.

She looked because he wouldn't talk about it. But in

the past year or so it was harder to see what was inside him. His mind was not able to reach out as Elle could do with hers, but it was very good at keeping things hidden. And Zander kept a lot of things hidden from his sister and his parents.

The truth was that Zander was normal. Like Boone. Boone's mother had some of the psychic abilities, and his sister showed some promise, but his father, Ruben, and the twins' grandfather, Michael, and the servants, were all just normal, everyday people.

Elle wondered what it would be like to be normal. To live a normal life and not live under constant security and scrutiny. She also wondered what it was that made her so special.

Elle did not understand the fear that consumed their parents. Both of the twins chafed against it. They felt as if they were prisoners in their own home. In their entire lifetime they had never left the villa, except for short jaunts down to the beach, and only under the watchful eyes of unseen yet heavily armed guards. The guards whose jet cycles they were now riding across the waves at breakneck speeds.

If only they knew why they were so protected.

Their parents were very good at shielding their thoughts from their children. At least Zander had inherited that talent, or else he wouldn't be so good at hiding things from his sister.

And Elle was very good at convincing their parents that she and Zander were completely innocent.

Until they found out they were missing from the villa.

But until then, they were free.

The wind poured through Elle's waist-length hair, spreading the ash-brown locks behind her like a banner. Her strangely pale gray eyes, identical to her brother's, crinkled against the salt spray and the bright sun reflecting off the top of the water.

"Faster," she said into Boone's ear. He stole a quick look over his shoulder at Elle and her heart did the little flip that always resulted when his bright green eyes were on her.

"Hold on," he replied and the jet cycle jerked forward as his thumb pressed a button on the handle.

Elle shrieked with joy as they sped up and the dolphins raced beside them.

Zander, up to the challenge, flew by on his craft and leaned sideways, spraying Boone and Elle with water.

"No!" Elle screamed as Boone went after him. Her protest was halfhearted at best. She knew she'd get the wettest when the two started battling but she didn't care. She'd be soaked through soon enough when they dove into the coral garden that grew beneath the surface of the water.

Zander's cycle moved directly in front of them and Boone bent low over his. Elle moved with him but still got a faceful of spray. She felt Boone's lean, muscular frame move with laughter as she held on tight. She tried to pinch his abdomen, but could not find enough loose skin to grab. His years at Academy had erased any softness left over from his boyhood.

"Get him!" Elle yelled.

"I will," Boone said. The velocity of the wind snatched the words from him but Elle recognized the intent in his eyes. She had seen that look many a time in the past. They had grown up together, and mischief was not a new concept for any of them.

The dolphins moved away, content to follow along at a distance as they realized the play was getting serious. Zander's cycle sped away, hopping waves, and Boone moved even lower over the engine.

Elle, pressed against his back, was sure she felt the pounding of his heart against her cheek. He moved his hand from the control to brush against hers and she knew that he was allowing her to enter inside his mind.

"We're carrying more weight." The words formed inside him. *"It will be hard to catch him."*

"You will."

The craft skipped across the wake, zooming behind Zander as they gave pursuit. Zander toyed with them, veering across from left to right and then back again, knowing they would be slower, knowing they would have to fight the chop, hoping that they would . . .

Elle felt her body fly through the air as the nose of their hovercycle got caught in a wave and stalled against it. The craft flipped up on its end and both of them were dumped into the water.

Elle immediately kicked to the surface and a dolphin nudged her side with the tip of its nose as she rose.

I can do it. . . .

The dolphin responded in kind, its smiling face inches from her own as she broke through into the warmth of the sunshine that danced across the water.

Zander circled them and waved cheerfully when he saw that she was safe. Elle was tempted to send him a blazing, torturous thought but lost it when she was jerked back under from below.

She twisted and found herself caught in Boone's arms as he moved up from below. Even though the water was cold, her insides warmed as their bodies slid together beneath the water. Strange sensations coursed through her as his eyes moved level with hers.

"We might drown." She sent the thought into his mind as they bobbed just below the surface.

"I could . . . easily . . . or . . . we could try this."

His lips touched hers, tentatively, then more forcefully as she opened her mouth against his and closed her eyes. Elle's stomach gave a sudden lurch and she realized that she needed to breathe but didn't really care.

This was better than breathing.

It wasn't the first time Boone had kissed her. They had shared a few awkward, embarrassing moments when he was home on his breaks.

But this was different. It was almost as if he'd been . . . practicing?

Her eyes flew open and she shoved him down and

away as she kicked toward the surface. Zander was waiting on his cycle, a concerned look on his face.

"What happened?" he asked.

"Nothing." Elle spat out the word with the water she had swallowed after her quick trip into Boone's mind.

"That wasn't fair," Boone yelled as he came up beside her.

Elle splashed water in his face and swam toward Zander.

"What's wrong with you?" he asked.

"Nothing," she said as she held her hand up. "Help me up."

Zander looked over her head toward Boone, who was trying to right the craft in the water.

"Zander," Elle hissed. "Pull. Me. Up." Her words were threatening and he knew better than to toy with her when she was angry. Zander jerked her up and she settled herself onto the seat behind him.

"You're soaked," he said.

"Shut. Up."

"Did he kiss you?"

"Yes."

"Isn't that what you wanted?"

"Yes."

"Then why are you so mad?"

Elle looked over her shoulder at Boone, who had righted the craft and was now following them. It wouldn't take him long to catch up since they were now the heavier ones.

Why was she angry?

Because Boone had kissed a lot of girls. She had seen their faces in his mind as if she were watching a parade, and each one had been more beautiful, more mature, more self-assured than she was. He had practiced. A lot. And more than kissing.

Boone was no longer the boy they had played with in the dark tunnels beneath the villa. He was a man. A man who had the capability of traveling the universe. Her father admitted that he was already the best pilot he had ever seen. He processed numbers and equations in his head as if he were a machine. He had been to more planets than she could count and had the type of freedom that she and Zander dreamed of.

And he's here . . . with you. . . .

Elle felt her anger dissipate a bit. After all, if all those girls were so wonderful why wasn't he with one of them?

And the kiss had been nice.

She glanced his way and quickly recognized the stubborn tilt to Boone's chin. He was looking straight ahead. The sandbar was in sight. The dolphins swam merrily between them.

He was right. She shouldn't have looked inside. It was an unspoken agreement among the three of them and something her mother had pounded into her head since she began her training.

She should never use her abilities to take advantage of her family and friends.

But it was always so tempting. And easy.

Zander cut the engine back to idle and they coasted in to the narrow curve of sand. Boone pulled in beside them and jumped from his cycle with a quick, jerky, motion. His green eyes rounded on Elle and sparks seemed to fly from them as he stared down at her.

"I think you two need to talk," Zander said. He got his pack from beneath the seat and walked toward the opposite end of the spit.

Elle turned to watch him go. She was avoiding Boone, which despite the open spaces around them was hard to do. The spit was barely wide enough for them to stretch out on but was long enough that Zander's body diminished in size as he moved away.

It suddenly struck Elle that her brother seemed lonely as she watched him shrink against the horizon.

Her heart ached with a strange emptiness as she watched him jump up and down three times and move his neck from side to side as he always did when warming up his muscles.

Elle felt Boone move up behind her and dismissed the thought of Zander's feelings from her mind as other strange and bewildering things flooded in.

"It's hard to be away from you, Elle," he said. "And it's lonely at Academy."

She was surprised. She had expected a fight, not this strange gentleness.

He was so close that she felt the rise of his hand, as if he were about to touch her. Elle crossed her arms and kept her eyes on her brother as he peeled off most of his clothes and sliced into the water.

"I have no claim on you, Boone," she said. "We're friends, nothing more."

"What if I want it to be more?" he said.

Elle's heart pounded and she turned to face him. "What do you mean?"

His hair, a warm rich brown shade, was already dry from the wind. The academy required that he keep it short, but Elle could remember a time when it hung over his eyes and flipped wildly around his ears. His eyes, all the greener against the vivid blues that surrounded them, looked down at her with a strange yet familiar glow.

"You know what I mean. You're all I ever think about."

"Strange way to prove it," Elle said defensively.

His hands gripped her upper arms and pulled her a step closer. Elle placed a hand on his chest to stop him and Boone looked down at where it rested gracefully against his chest. A slow smile spread over his face.

"My heart has always been yours, Elle. Since the first time I saw you."

"You were only six," she said with a wry smile. "And I was four."

"It doesn't matter," he said. "I love you. I always have and I always will."

Elle looked up at him, her pale gray eyes searching his. "How can you know that?"

"I just do." He lifted her hand from his chest and placed it against his temple. "Look inside and you'll see."

Her hair whipped around them as the wind picked up. She closed her eyes and let her mind flow into his.

She saw the girls again and quickly dismissed them. She saw the pranks he pulled at Academy. She saw him studying with his comrades and she saw him practicing the fighting skills that his father and hers had taught him alongside Zander.

She saw shared memories from their childhood and she saw the places he had been with his father and with his uncle Stefan. She saw the love he felt for his mother, Tess, and his sister, Zoey, who was several years younger than Elle.

But there were some places he would not allow her to search. He knew the litany that her mother had taught them. He knew how to protect his mind. Elle wondered what he kept hidden but quickly dismissed it because of the surprise she felt as she realized that with all the memories she saw there was one constant.

She saw her own face staring back at her.

Elle felt Boone's forehead touch hers as her mind floated with his. He truly loved her. But how did she feel? She had nothing to compare her feelings with. Boone was the only boy besides her brother whom she had ever known. What if there was someone else out there whom she was supposed to love?

But all thoughts of anyone else left her as Boone kissed her. She couldn't imagine kissing anyone else. Kissing Boone was all she ever dreamed about. All she ever thought about. And there was more than kissing; she had seen that very clearly in his mind.

She wanted that too. She wanted Boone to show her

what it felt like. Her arms snaked around him and she felt his sudden intake of breath as she pressed against him.

"Elle." He groaned her name and moved the lower half of his body away from her.

"What?" she asked. She felt dazed, breathless, and warm yet twisted up inside.

His hand smoothed the wild tendrils of her hair back into place. "Maybe we should go for a swim," he said. He tossed his head toward the water. "Zander."

"Zander," Elle sighed. For the first time in her life she wished that she didn't have a brother.

Boone quickly turned away as she looked at Zander, who was playing in the water with the dolphins. He handed her pack to her and moved to the other side of the cycle and turned his back to her as he pulled off his shirt.

Elle couldn't help but admire the contours of muscle in his back as she wondered at his sudden shyness around her.

She skinned off her shirt and kicked away the baggy pants that she wore. She adjusted the hem of her short top, checked the tie around her neck, and made sure that her bottom half was properly if not scantily covered.

Her father would certainly raise his eyebrows at the cut of her attire but she didn't care. What could he do to her? Lock her away from the world?

"Ready?" she asked Boone as she adjusted a set of shields over her eyes.

"Right behind you," he said, settling his own shields into place.

Elle took off at a run for the water and flattened herself out to dive beneath the gentle lap of waves with Boone close behind her.

The sandbar ended suddenly as the rim gave way to the ancient crater, and a world of bright colors and exotic plants opened up beneath them.

The water felt warmer, as if the volcano that had

once been here still burned down in the deep. Elle was certain parts of it were inside her. She felt the brush of Boone's body as they swam side by side and was certain that the water around them would boil.

Boone pointed out a pair of brightly colored fish that darted from behind a trumpeting piece of coral. From below a ray moved up as if it were part of the water and barely missed their heads with its tail.

They turned and grinned at each other and as one moved to the surface for air. The dolphins quickly circled them and chattered as Zander joined them.

"I see you two made up," he said.

Elle pushed her goggles up and looked at Boone.

"Kissed and made up," Zander added.

Elle splashed water at his face and Boone rose up with a yell, placed his hands on Zander's head, and pushed him under. The dolphins headed for cover as the three of them splashed, wrestled, and dunked each other as they had done for years.

But it was different now. Zander knew it and he swam away as Boone pulled Elle under again.

He's lonely.

The thought once again faded as Boone's lip's found hers and they twisted away from Zander, moving as one beneath the surface, breathing air into each other's lungs.

They kissed until Elle thought she would pass out from lack of oxygen. Her ears roared as she felt the blood rushing to her head. She pulled her head away and opened her eyes to look at Boone but saw that he was looking up.

A shadow fell across the water and as they swam to the surface Elle knew they were in trouble.

Her father had come looking for them.

CHAPTER TWO

His body was cramped but he kept his place. When he was a boy he had fit easily into the space. Now that he was supposed to be a man . . .

"When are you going to start acting like a man, Zander?" his father had yelled at him in anger after they landed from their silent trip back from the coral.

"When are you going to start treating me like one?" Zander had yelled back, his own frustration pouring forth in an uncontrollable eruption. It was the first time in his life that he had raised his voice to his father. He had stalked off into the tunnels, shaking with shock and rage, leaving Boone and Elle to face the lecture that was sure to follow.

If only he knew why they weren't allowed to leave the villa. If only he knew what it was his parents were so afraid of.

If only he knew why he was so . . . lacking . . . in their eyes.

In all the years of listening, he never found out any of

the answers to his questions. And every morning he woke, feeling as if every day of his life was one big question.

What were they protecting them from? What dangers lay waiting for them? What were they preparing them for? What was it he was supposed to be able to do?

He kept his ear pressed against the thin sheet of metal that was part of the ventilation system. He had discovered quite by accident that he could hear everything said in his father's study by just lying in the small niche off one of the main tunnels and keeping his ear pressed to the vent. It was one of his favorite hiding places when he, Elle, and Boone played seeker in the tunnels. There was a slight curve to it so it was easy for him to disappear. Now he was as long as the alcove and had to pull his legs up so they wouldn't hang out for everyone to see.

He felt somewhat guilty for leaving Elle and Boone to face the punishment that was sure to come.

And he also wondered if Boone would even stick around for it. He knew his friend had great respect for their father but he was a second year at Academy. Shouldn't that mean that he was now part of the adult world?

Boone's father certainly treated him like one. Ruben was with Zander's father when they found them and had flown them back to the villa without a word to his own son. Zander knew them well enough to know that there probably wouldn't be a lecture. Ruben treated his son with respect. He treated him as if he knew something. And Boone had earned his father's respect. He excelled at Academy although in private he said he hated the constrictions. He had piloted ships all over the galaxy with either his father or his uncle Stefan at his side. He had seen things Zander could only imagine. He had been places Zander could only dream about. Boone was allowed to experience life.

That was another thing Zander heard when he hid in the tunnels. His father and Ruben talking late into the night about the past, about the present, about the future. They talked about their adventures. They talked about their families. They even talked about the unknown threat, wondering about it, if it were still there, what they would do if and when it happened.

It was from these talks that he had eventually learned that apparently he was supposed to take over the reins of government someday. He knew everything there was to know about Oasis. His grandfather, Michael, was one of his teachers. He knew there had been a war and his parents had saved their planet from being taken over by another planet. He knew his father had instituted a thing called Democracy that let the people elect their own leaders. And those elected had a say in the governing of the planet, and if there was ever a tie, the deciding vote was cast by his father, known to Oasis as the Sovereign Nicholas.

Yet he, Prince Alexander of Oasis, had never been past the coral.

His weapons training and fighting skills were the best. He could even beat his father, sometimes, when they sparred and he and Boone had long ago quit taking their practice battles seriously because they always ended up in a tie.

But he was tired of shooting at targets, tired of training in the large room that took up the entire top floor of the villa.

He had spent untold time in simulators learning how to fly every craft there was.

Yet he had never done anything more than pilot small ships around the Crater Lake. And as much as he had overheard, he had never caught even a whisper about *why*. Why were his parents so overprotective?

Perhaps the bigger question about his life shouldn't be what, or why, but when? When would he be considered a man and thus privy to all this unknown and un-

speakable information that controlled every aspect of
his life?

What was taking them so long to get to the study?
So far he had heard nothing, although he knew his father was below. He could hear him pacing as his boots
went back and forth on the smooth stone of the floor to
the softer tread of the large rug woven by Boone's
mother, Tess.

"How did it go, Lilly?" He finally heard his father,
Shaun, speak. His mother must have entered the room.

"The usual," his mother replied. "Why can't we go
there? Why are we being punished?"

"They aren't being punished," his father said.
"They're being protected."

"Do you ever think that perhaps we've protected
them too much?" he heard his mother ask.

Yes. Yes. Yes . . . Zander wanted to scream the words,
but he also wanted to hear more of what his parents had
to say.

"I remember how it was for you," Shaun said. His
voice sound muffled and Zander could easily imagine
his father holding Lilly in his arms. She brought that
out in a man. The willingness to protect and to sacrifice. "When we met, it was as if you bore the weight of
the universe on your shoulders."

"Because I had my duties and responsibilities laid
out before me as soon as I was able to walk and talk."

"Your childhood wasn't happy."

"No. It wasn't." His mother sighed and Zander
wondered what made her childhood so sad. Was it because her mother died giving birth to her? Her own
father adored her as he did his grandchildren. She
spoke again. "But ignorance isn't bliss either. Don't
you remember how frustrated you were when you
were trying to figure out what was going on inside
your mind?"

What are they talking about? Zander's ears ached with

the thought that he might finally find something out. He'd never heard his parents speak so specifically about the past before.

"Two extremes," his father said. "Perhaps we should have found the middle ground."

"Perhaps," Lilly said. Zander smiled in his privacy. His mother possessed a great talent for diplomacy that was sorely lacking in his father. "It's a bit late for regrets in that matter. And we have something else to worry about now."

"What?"

"Boone and Elle."

"What about them?"

"Haven't you noticed that he's in love with her?"

"Er . . . um . . . what?"

Zander buried his face in his arm and allowed himself a silent laugh at his father's complete discomposure.

"How do you know?" Shaun was finally able to ask.

"I looked at them," Lilly said. "He's always loved her but now, since he's been gone, he wants her."

"You looked inside?"

"I didn't have to. It's obvious."

"And when you say wants her . . ."

"I'm saying that he's just like his father. And just like you."

The vent echoed with the sound of something shattering against it, along with a string of words that Zander knew well, but would never dare say in the presence of his parents.

"Do you think they've . . ."

"No. But I think it won't be long until something happens."

"But they're so young."

"He's the same age I was when I met you."

"I'll kill him," Shaun said.

Lilly laughed. "No, you won't. You'll give Elle time to figure out how she feels about him."

"Damn," Shaun said.

"You act like this is a bad thing," Lilly said. "Who better for Elle than Boone?"

"I just never thought . . . Damn."

"You just can't stand to think about her with any man."

Zander was pretty sure he didn't want to think about it either. Elle and Boone . . . doing things.

Another part of his education that was thorough but also frustrating. He knew all about sex. He knew all about procreation. He even knew what it felt like to wake up in the mornings in an embarrassing predicament.

Especially when he had the dreams. . . .

"Zander," Elle whispered. "What are you doing?"

Zander jerked as Elle stuck her head into the space next to his legs. His head crashed against the top of the tunnel and he saw stars and felt something wet and sticky ooze from his temple.

"Do you mind?" he whispered angrily as he touched his fingers to his temple and then looked at the blood that stained his hand.

"Sorry," Elle said. "Are you hurt?"

"Bleeding to death," he said sullenly and turned back to the vent.

"Move over," Elle said and wiggled her way in beside him.

"Go away," Zander hissed.

"What is your problem?" Elle whispered back as she slid in beside him. The quarters were close and she continually jabbed him with her elbow so he'd make room. She looked at the wound on his head. "Ouch," she said. "You're bleeding."

"Thanks for noticing and asking," Zander whispered forcefully. "I'm surprised you just didn't look in my head and find out what my problem was. Besides the blood, that is. Which is all your fault."

"Zander," Elle started, then stopped as he quickly moved his hand over her mouth.

"They're going to hear us," he mouthed and pointed down.

Elle froze into place and tilted her head toward the vent. Sure enough, voices could be heard.

"Where are we?" she asked inside Zander's mind.

"Over Father's office."

"So we are agreed?" Lilly asked.

"Great, you made me miss something."

"Are they talking about us?"

"More like you and Boone."

"I just want them to be happy," Lilly continued. "But I also would like to keep them young a bit longer. And safe."

"All that worry . . . over nothing really," Shaun said.

"Zander?" His mother's question. Always the question.

Here it came again. The disappointment. If only he knew what it was they expected of him. What exactly was it that he was supposed to be able to do? Be like Elle? Read people's minds? See in the dark? Slam doors and make things fly across rooms?

"They wouldn't believe us even if we told them," Lilly said. "They'd still take him if they had a chance."

"Who are they talking about?" Elle asked in his mind.

Zander shrugged. All the years of listening and he still didn't know the answer. He didn't feel guilty about it either. He wasn't doing anything that Elle couldn't or wouldn't do. He was just doing it in a different way.

"Physically," Shaun said. "He's amazing. I have no doubt that he could protect himself. And he's only going to get stronger, quicker, as he matures."

"Not against the Circe," Lilly said. "Even with the mind training."

Elle grabbed Zander's arm.

"What are the Circe?"

"I don't know." It was the first time he had ever heard his parents mention the word.

"Even after all this time, I find it hard to believe that

he can't do it," Shaun said. "Could he be that stubborn? Could he be hiding it, even from you?"

"He could be that stubborn," Lilly said. "After all, he is your son."

Shaun laughed.

"And he has shown signs," Lilly continued.

"But he was so small."

"And he was right," Lilly said. "At least the one time. I guess we'll never know about the other."

"What are they talking about?"

Zander ignored her. He didn't want to miss anything that his parents said.

"It was so obscure, how could we even know?" Shaun said.

"I wondered about that myself," Lilly said. "Until he did the same thing with Ruben. For some reason he knew he was in danger."

"When has Ruben not been in danger?" Shaun laughed.

"Since he married Tess," Lilly answered. "But you still have to admit that it had to be more than a coincidence."

"If only there'd been more . . . signs."

"I don't know. I wish I did. But I don't."

It was strange to hear his mother sound uncertain. The silence from below made him realize how strange. He didn't have to be in the room to know that his parents were worrying over something. If only he knew what it was.

They heard a knock on the door and then Ruben's voice. "Well, I've beaten my son into a bloody mass. Do you need any help with yours?"

"I haven't seen Zander since he stormed off," Shaun said.

"Boone thinks you should tell them," Ruben said. "He thinks it's not fair that he knows and they don't."

"That's your fault," Shaun said. "I'm just amazed that he's kept it from them."

"Boone gave his word," Ruben said quietly.

"I meant Elle," Shaun said quickly. "She could have found out, even by mistake. His mind is strong."

"Yes, it is."

"I knew he knew something. I saw that he was blocking."

"He let you in?"

"Yes."

"Do you love him?"

Elle didn't answer. Instead she squirmed her way out of the tunnel.

"Coward," Zander threw after her. He turned to listen again but heard the sound of the door closing below. They had left the study. Zander pushed his way out and ran after Elle.

"Wait," he said. He wiped at the blood on his face and was surprised that the gash didn't hurt. It had throbbed when he first did it but he had forgotten the pain when he was listening to his parents talk.

"I don't want to talk about it right now, Zander," Elle said when he caught up to her. "I'm still trying to figure things out."

"Where is Boone?"

"Ruben sent him to get Tess and Zoey at the vineyard and bring them back. Apparently they didn't know he was home from Academy."

"You mean he came here first?"

"Yes."

"He really does love you."

"I know. But he's had something to compare it with. He's met a lot of girls."

"Jealous?"

Elle made a face. "How do I know if I love Boone or if it's just because he's the only boy I've ever known? Don't I need something to compare it with?"

"At least you know someone else besides me. You're the only girl I've ever seen, besides the servants, and they're all old."

"Thanks," Elle said. "I think."

"You know what I mean."

"I know," she agreed. "And I don't know. Aren't you tired of not knowing?"

Their feet followed a familiar path along a dark tunnel that led to an opening overlooking the lake and the hidden landing bay. From there they would be able to see Boone return.

And it was the one place they were allowed to go where they felt a bit of freedom.

"Maybe there is one thing we could know," Zander said as they walked out into the afternoon sun. The light dazzled the water until it was a pure silver and they both blinked against the brightness.

"What do you mean?"

"Mother said I knew Ruben was in danger when I was little."

"As in you showed some of the psychic abilities," Elle said. "I don't remember it happening. I just remember Ruben coming back with Tess, Boone, and Ky and saying that you were really the one who saved his life."

"Ky," Zander said, recalling the huge newf that had been Boone's shadow for years. Ky had died of old age the summer before Boone went to Academy. It was surely a good thing he died then. He would have died of loneliness had Boone left him behind.

"Boone misses him."

"I know. I miss him too," Zander said. "But Mother also said there was another time."

"And you want me to help you remember it."

"You can, can't you?"

"I've never done it."

"But you know how."

"Yes. I know how."

"Then do it."

Elle chewed on her lip for a moment as she looked out over the lake. Zander saw a vision of their mother doing the same thing. She did look just like Lilly, who was still young and beautiful.

Too bad he wasn't more like their father. He looked

like him but he wasn't like him. Maybe he would have been trusted with some knowledge, the way Boone had been.

And just maybe it was time he figured some stuff out on his own.

"Sit down," Elle said. "And make sure you open your mind."

They sat down facing each other with their ankles propped on their knees in the meditation position that their mother had taught them. As one they closed their eyes and took a deep breath, clearing their minds of any errant thoughts that would interrupt Elle's concentration.

"Are you ready?" She didn't have to ask permission. She could have just looked.

"Yes."

Elle placed her fingertips on Zander's temple and then just as suddenly jerked them away.

"Zander," she said. "Where did the blood come from?"

"From my head. I hit it when you snuck up on me."

"Where's the cut?"

Zander touched his fingertips to his temple. The blood was dry on his cheek but he felt no cut. He wet his fingers with his tongue and scrubbed against the blood.

"There's nothing there," Elle said. She searched the dark locks of his hair. "Nothing. It's gone."

"You mean it healed?"

"Or disappeared. What do you think?"

"I don't know." He rubbed his temple again, wondering if he possibly could have imagined it.

The blood was still there, drying on his cheek.

"Has this ever happened before?"

"Maybe. I don't remember."

"Well, either it has or it hasn't."

"Or maybe it's just not important enough to think about." He was irritated. It seemed to be a permanent condition for him. "How quick do you heal?"

"I've never been hurt like that. I don't know."

Elle had missed most of the scrapes and falls that he had when they were young. She was born with a natural grace. Zander tried to recall the last time he'd been injured.

"I remember falling down sometimes, scraping my knees. Maybe I do heal fast."

"It's strange," Elle said. She seemed worried.

"Don't worry about it," Zander said. "You can catalog all my injuries while you're inside."

"We should tell them," Elle said. "Maybe it's a sign of something."

"Like what? Your son is more of a disappointment than you thought?"

"Zander. They are not disappointed in you. They just don't understand why I can do things and you can't."

"Says the daughter who can do anything."

"It you're going to be a gank, then I'm not going to help you." Elle jumped to her feet and stalked to the entrance to the tunnels.

"Elle, wait." Zander went after her. "I'm sorry. Please help. You're the only one I can trust."

He felt as if he were looking in a mirror when he stared earnestly into her eyes. They were identical in shape, in color, even down to the dark shade of their lashes. It was confusing sometimes, to look into her eyes. He felt as if he were almost looking inside himself.

And then he realized that she could look inside him and the frustration would come forth again.

There had been a time, when they were small, when it didn't matter what she could do and he couldn't. They shared everything through her powers. But then their bodies had changed and with that their attitudes and they started keeping secrets from each other.

He needed to make sure that Elle didn't see the dreams.

"We need to hurry," Elle said as she stared back at him. "They might think we ran off again."

Zander nodded and they moved back to their positions.

"If there's someplace you don't want me to go, just tell me," she said.

Resentment flared that she even knew that he kept secrets, but he quickly tamped it down, using the litany that their mother had taught them.

I'm ready.

Elle's fingers touched his temples and he felt her slide into his mind with a gentleness that he never truly noticed before.

It was almost comforting.

"Our memories are shared, Zander."

"Not all of them. Not my—"

"I have dreams too. Relax."

Zander willed his worries and frustrations into submission. He felt the warmth of the sunshine on the side of his face. He felt the heat radiating from the stone cliff they sat on. He felt the kiss of the breeze as it whipped across the lake. He heard the sigh of the trees that grew miraculously from fissures and cracks in the mountainside.

His life opened before him as if he were watching a dige, except that it moved backward, as if he were winding up a ball of the thread that Tess used in her weavings.

Backward they went until they were children, small, and innocent, comforted just by being with their parents. They were adored.

Suddenly he wasn't with his parents or his sister. He was with Ruben. He was piloting his ship and was under attack. He saw the blasts that rocked the ship. He felt the panic. Sheer terror overcame him as the ship careened toward the ground and crashed.

"Elle?"

"Wait."

Was it a memory of his? Or was it something he imagined from listening to the stories that were told about Ruben's adventures. Boone had seen the crash. Was it one of his memories mixed up with his own?

"You saw it, Zander. Boone saw it coming, but you saw it as if you were there, inside the ship."

"How?"

"There's more."

He saw himself once again as a small boy, playing with a brightly colored starship on a plush rug. Elle was beside him with one of her beloved dolls. His father and grandfather were inside, discussing the politics of the planet. His mother and Ruben were on the balcony and his mother was searching Ruben's memories, exactly the way Elle was searching his.

Suddenly his mind saw a dark and dreary place. Not like the tunnels that they walked with their father as he encouraged them to try to see in the dark.

This place was dim, dingy, and dirty. There were bars and there were chains. The only light came from a torch that tried gallantly to fight back the darkness.

Three women were gathered around a narrow plank attached to a wall. Two of the women were dressed in dark robes and wore strange hats decorated with beads and crystals. The third woman was dressed in simple clothes and held a squirming bundle in her arms. Another woman with pale blond hair lay on the plank in a ragged and bloody gown and she was pleading with the other three.

"Give me my baby," she cried. "Please."

The other women ignored her. They looked at a baby that cried loudly in protest against the arms that held her.

"What color are her eyes?" one woman asked. She seemed older than the others. Much older.

The woman holding the baby moved the child around so that the torchlight reflected in her eyes.

"Violet," she said.

"Tsk," the older woman said. "I thought perhaps we

might be on to something with the breeding. Her father did have the bloodline, even if he is a rebel." The woman gathered her robes and turned away from the crying baby.

"What about the mother?" the woman holding the baby asked. "She needs a healer."

The younger woman paused at the entrance to the cell. "Let her die," she said. "She has been tainted by the rebels and is of no further use to us."

The women left. The one holding the child looked with sympathy down on the woman bleeding to death before her eyes. "At least your daughter will live," she said. "We will find a place for her to serve."

"No," the woman cried weakly. "Please," and then she sighed. "Sagan."

The child screamed as her mother's life faded away and as she screamed Zander felt her pain and he screamed also.

"Zander!"

His eyes flew open. He was lying on his side and his hands were clenched against his face as if he were battling something inside. Something trying to get out. Elle held on to him and he realized that he was extremely close to the edge of the cliff.

"What was it?" she asked. "What did you see?"

He pushed himself backward until he rested against the solid foundation of the mountain.

Elle's eyes were on him, intently serious as if she were searching for a wound.

"Didn't you see it?" His heart pounded in his chest. He felt as if he had just run a race. And his life had been the prize.

"No. It was as if a door closed. But I felt something . . . sadness . . . terror . . . then you started screaming. What was it?"

"A baby. I saw a baby. There were women. The baby's mother died."

"That's it?"

"The baby was a girl," he added. "What do you think it means?"

Violet eyes.

"I don't know." Elle chewed on her lip again. "Maybe Mother can see it."

"No."

"Zander."

"I don't want her inside my head. I don't want either of them inside my head."

"You're being ridiculous."

He climbed to his feet. Why did he feel so weak? "Boone's back," he said, pointing toward the sky.

Elle reached up and he took her hand, pulling her to her feet. They stood on the cliff, side by side, as they watched the sleek craft circle the crater and then come in, skimming over the water until it reached the landing bay below.

"Let's go see how much trouble we're in," he said and they turned into the tunnels as one.

CHAPTER THREE

It never failed to amaze him how well the Firebird handled. Every time he held the yoke in his hands he felt the thrill.

I did this.

It couldn't have anything to do with the fact that he designed her. Well, adapted her. Boone used the Falcon's sleek design as his starting point, modified the cabin to hold four comfortably into deep space travel but kept the same sleek shape that made for faster transport. To top things off he added the same red flames on the side of the ship that had been on a toy starship he had as a boy. The very toy that sat in a small indentation on the com before him.

Ruben, impressed with Boone's design, then commissioned the ship to be built and was pleased with the results. So pleased that he gave Boone sole ownership of her when he went to Academy. His father was thinking about going into the fleet business now but Boone wasn't sure if he liked that idea. It was a great feeling to know that he possessed and designed the best starship in the galaxy. The only Firebird in the galaxy.

"I see Elle and Zander," his little sister, Zoey, said. Her blue eyes danced with excitement as she pointed to the overhang above the bay.

"I see them too, short stuff," Boone said. She stood in between his seat and their mother's, watching everything with rapt attention. "Strap in," he said. "We're on final."

Zoey edged back into her seat and cinched the belt but still managed to sit on the edge and closely watch everything Boone did in preparation for landing. Kyp, one of Ky's shaggy offspring, sat beside her on the floor, patiently waiting until he'd be able to step out onto solid ground.

The flight from their home was just a short hop in the Firebird. They didn't even leave the atmosphere, just skimmed over the ocean. Ruben owned a winery in the soft rolling hills above the equator, overlooking a cerulean sea. It seemed worlds away on a map, opposite side of the planet actually, but in the Firebird it was nominal.

He cut back the engines and the Firebird floated into the bay as if she were carried on a breeze. There wasn't even a jolt when the gear went down and she settled into place. He felt the smooth hum of the platform as it turned the ship to be ready for takeoff.

"Perfect as usual," Tess said with pride.

Boone grinned at her. He must have inherited his engineering talents from his biological father. And as far as he was concerned, that was all of the man he wanted. Boone had been no more than two when he died and didn't remember anything about him, but he knew he had been cruel to his mother. He also knew that he was a result of that cruelty.

Which made him love Tess all the more. She could have hated him when he came along. Instead she made it her purpose to make sure he was happy, even if she wasn't.

And then Ruben came along. Ben. His father in heart and spirit and soul. Ruben who saved his mother and thus saved him.

"System shut down," Boone instructed ELSie. Ruben still laughed every time he talked to his Encrypted Language System. Especially since Boone called it ELSie.

"Hatch open," ELSie informed him in a somewhat feminine monotone.

Zoey was gone with Kyp at her heels.

"She reminds me a lot of you at that age," Tess said.

Boone watched as one of the guards smiled at Zoey and waved her into the tunnel that led up to the villa. "I was never that innocent," he said. "No matter how much you pretended I was."

"Did I do that poor a job?" Tess asked, her eyes smiling at him.

He knew she was teasing but he kept on. There was something he was trying to work out in his mind. "You did a good job of pretending, Mema," he said, using his childhood name for her. "But pretending everything is perfect isn't always a good thing."

"Why do I get the feeling you're not talking about you and me?" Tess said. She looked through the Plexi at Elle and Zander as they arrived in the bay.

"They should know why they live this way," Boone said.

"You sound like they live in a horrible prison."

Boone shrugged. "Don't they? It's not right that they don't know what is out there. It's their lives, after all."

"I don't think Shaun and Lilly meant it to last this long. I think they just kept waiting for the right time to tell them. And the right time just never came. They wanted them to be happy and innocent awhile longer. Would you have wanted to live your childhood knowing there was a death sentence on your head?"

"I remember what it was like before. Even without

you telling me, I knew things weren't right. And I wanted to do something to fix it."

"Boone, you were only six."

"And Zander will be eighteen tomorrow. Practically a man. If they don't tell them soon, Zander is going to do something foolish."

"Has he said anything?" His mother seemed fearful of the notion.

"No," Boone said. He leaned over and gave his mother a quick kiss on her forehead to reassure her. "And I wouldn't tell you if he had."

"I'm sorry it was so bad for you," his mother said.

"It was worse for you. You've never said anything about it but I know it was horrible. If Ruben hadn't showed up when he did . . ."

Zander stuck his head in the hatch. "Can I take her out?"

"Clear it with your father," Boone said, feeling older, wiser, more mature than his best friend. He knew he had gotten off light earlier in the day. Ruben was of the same mind he was where Elle and Boone were concerned. He didn't think their parents had done them any favors by sheltering them for all these years. And there was no need to tempt Shaun's wrath. Not when he needed to be in the man's good graces.

Zander made a face. Boone knew he'd rather cut his arm off than ask his father for anything right now. He'd just have to decide which he wanted more. The temptation to fly was always greater.

"Hi, Elle," Tess said as Elle entered the craft. She gave Boone a knowing look.

"Welcome, Tess," Elle said. Her smile for Boone seemed shy.

Maybe he should work on not being so obvious. But he couldn't help but grin when Elle stepped into the Firebird.

She slid into the seat Tess vacated and rubbed her

hand across the com. "I can't believe you've still got this thing," she said, picking up the toy.

"Hey," Boone said. "Put it back."

"I thought you were supposed to share your toys," Elle teased.

Boone took the ship from her and put it back on the com. "That's not a toy. It's an essential part of the design."

"Oh, really?" Elle asked doubtfully. "What part is that?"

"If it doesn't move, then I'm flying her right." He grinned at her.

"Do they teach that at Academy?" Elle asked.

"It's not exactly a part of engineering," Boone said. "But I did get Es in all my courses."

"I see that they teach modesty there also," Elle continued teasing.

"I've learned all kind of things there," Boone said, suddenly serious. "Things I'd love to teach you."

I burn for you, Elle. I can't stop thinking about you.

Elle's gaze, so striking and intense because of the paleness of her eyes, turned quickly away and she focused her attention on the com as if suddenly curious about the purpose of each light that blinked reassuringly in the dim ship.

You scared her. Slow down.

"So, what are the plans for the celebration?" Boone asked, quickly changing the subject. "Something spectacular, I guess?"

"You mean because we're coming of age?" Elle said, turning back to him. "Not that they'd notice." She seemed anxious for an argument. Boone wasn't sure if it was because he had come on too strong or if she felt the same frustration as Zander.

"They're just protecting you," Boone said. "Their intentions are good."

"You know what it is they're hiding from us," Elle

said. She turned the coseat to face him and tentatively took his hands into hers. "I saw it . . . before."

"What did you see?" Boone asked. His mind raced through arguments that he knew so well. It wasn't his place to tell them. He swore an oath to Ruben that he wouldn't. He had been trusted with the secret. He didn't agree with it but he had still promised.

"I saw that you were protecting something. I saw that you have a secret that I can't know."

"I'm sorry, Elle. I swore on my honor not to tell."

"It's the Circe, isn't it?"

Boone pulled his hand away from Elle's and looked through the Plexi. Zander and Tess had gone into the tunnels. He wondered briefly if Zander would ask Shaun for permission to fly the Firebird. He was also waiting to see if Elle would dare try to search his mind without his permission. He hoped she wouldn't. It was a dishonorable thing to do. But he wouldn't put it past her. He knew her that well.

"Where did you hear that?" he asked after a long silent moment.

"It doesn't matter," Elle said. "What is the Circe?"

She didn't know anything beyond the word.

"Ask your parents."

"Why would they tell us?" she exploded. "They like us not knowing anything. They like keeping us prisoners in our home."

"Elle," Boone said, this time taking her hands into his. He waited a moment until she calmed and her gaze fell steady upon him. "Have the two of you ever just sat down and asked them? I know Zander broods about stuff and he's so stiff-necked with pride that he wouldn't ask for help if it meant his life, but you're a bit more diplomatic. Why don't you just ask them to tell you instead of moping around like a couple of spoiled brats?"

Suddenly his hands felt as if he had stuck them in a

reactor coil. He jerked them away involuntarily as Elle crossed her arms and looked at him in satisfaction.

"Kind of proves my point, don't you think?" Boone said, leaning back and giving her his own green-eyed perusal. "You just proved that you aren't mature enough to know the truth."

My mind is my own. He started the litany in his head in order to thwart any torture Elle had in mind for him.

Elle jumped from the seat with a curse. Boone was impressed. He wondered where she had heard the word since it was one that was vulgar even by Academy standards. He admired the curve of her back as she stalked through the hatch and stormed from the bay.

"You're just mad because you know I'm right," Boone yelled through the Plexi with a certain amount of satisfaction. A very small amount of satisfaction. He might be right but it had cost him Elle's company. He didn't have much time before he went back to Academy. He wanted to make sure she was his before he left again.

What if you are right?

What if Shaun and Lilly told Elle and Zander about the Circe? How much would that change things? He felt pretty confident this past year at Academy, when he realized that Elle was the only one he wanted. Every other girl he met came up lacking. None were as pretty, none as graceful, none as sweet, or driven, or any other comparison he could think of. There were none like Elle. He made sure of it.

Boone had to grin at Elle's reaction when she saw that he had been with girls. In the physical sense. But it had all been nothing as far as he was concerned. Just physical. After all, he was at Academy and he was supposed to be learning . . . things.

What if it was the other way and Elle was the one . . . learning things?

He didn't like that idea at all.

It was easy to remember the first time he'd seen Elle. He had come to Oasis with Shaun and Lilly, along with Ky. When they arrived the twins were waiting with their grandfather in the bay and upon seeing Elle he was struck by her wild hair, her intense eyes, her welcoming smile. He had never been around other children, had never known he could feel so welcomed.

Ruben soon found a place for his new family and they had gone to their own villa to create a vineyard. Boone attended a regular school and made friends but special times were reserved to spend with his father's best friend and his family. It wasn't until Boone reached the end of his education on Oasis that he realized that Shaun and the Sovereign Nicholas of Oasis were the same man.

And yet there were shadows around this wonderful family. Elle and Zander never came to visit him. Zander could never go with him on trips with his uncle Stefan. And Boone was never allowed to speak to outsiders about Zander and Elle, or the special things Elle could do.

He knew about the Circe. Lilly had tested and trained his mother when she discovered that she was from the planet. Tess did not have the great capabilities that were characterized by the strange pale gray eyes. Her eyes were more of a clear gray green. But her mother, his grandmother, had been one. One who apparently rebelled and ran off with an unacceptable mate. Tess's memories were vague since they had been erased. Lilly pulled as many of them to the surface as she could. Tess did remember that her father had the same bright green eyes as Boone, and that she had a brother. She could not recall her brother's name.

Boone knew the Circe were evil. He had seen that firsthand in his own life. Yet at Academy they were referred to as great counselors to the Senate. It was as if even the scholars did not want to get on their bad side. They had spies everywhere. Thus the danger to Zander and Elle.

Male children were not allowed to have the power that the Circe possessed. Shaun's mother sacrificed herself so that her son would live when the law demanded that he be killed. His powers did not come into being until after he met Lilly. The Circe would still pay anything to have him killed.

And the children of such a union would terrify the race of psychic women.

Lilly had triggered Shaun's powers.

Suddenly it was so clear, as if Boone himself had suddenly inherited the powers.

Maybe that's why Zander isn't like Elle. Maybe he has to have his mind triggered by a woman . . . a woman he loves.

"Is it possible that I . . ." He stopped himself before he finished. Even though he had Circe blood, his bright green eyes were a sign that the powers did not run inside him. His mother's eyes were gray green. She had healing powers and a psychic link with Ruben and nothing more.

Only those with the pale gray eyes held the true powers. Which is why any male child born to a Circe woman was killed immediately if he had gray eyes. There was no way of telling in the womb what color eyes a child had. The child had to be born. The women of Circe, who had spent generations under the rule of their men, would no longer be enslaved. Now they were the power. And they would kill any threat to it.

They would consider Zander to be the biggest threat of all because he was a true Circe on both sides.

Yet Zander held no powers at all. At least none that were evident.

Was it possible that there was a Circe woman somewhere who would trigger Zander's powers? And if there were, what were the chances that she was of a good heart, like Lilly?

Boone did the final check on the Firebird and went in search of his father.

Had it ever even occurred to them?

His footsteps echoed on the stone floor of the tunnel.

Or was it a foolish and wishful thought? There was only one way to know.

The time of secrets was over.

CHAPTER FOUR

Flying was his favorite thing. But flying around Crater Lake was not enough.

It was never enough.

Zander felt guilt at his own frustration. He possessed anything and everything he could ever ask for.

Except freedom.

He knew his parents loved him.

And he hated them for it. Their love was suffocating him.

If only he could go to Academy with Boone. If only he could visit the Senate planet with his father. Or even the capital city on his home planet.

If only he could take off screaming for the stars and never look back.

He kicked off the sheets and padded on silent feet to his balcony. Trying to distract his mind from his dreams had resulted in failure.

What a surprise.

The sky was cloudless, the stars too many to count.

They pricked the sky like diamonds. They called to him, whispered his name, and made him promises they could not keep. Zander gripped the rail as if to keep himself from hurtling out into the darkness.

Tomorrow I am a man.

What difference would one day make in his life? Would the rising of the sun suddenly change how he looked at things? Would it change how his parents looked at him?

Would he finally be privy to the truth? Would he be able to handle it? Would one day's passage make the difference in how his life would be led?

What was the secret? What was out there that was so horrible that they couldn't even know about it?

And why did it only apply to him and Elle?

It had something to do with Elle's abilities. And since he did not have any abilities, surely it had nothing to do with him.

He had researched the Circe as soon as he had the privacy of his room. He had checked every resource that he had access to. He had even tried to plot the Circe, as if it were a planet, while flying the Firebird. ELSie did not seem to know about it. And when she had tried to question him Boone had shut her down.

"Ask your parents," he said.

He had no doubt that there was information about the Circe in his father's office. Information he wasn't allowed to access. The lack of information was just another way to *protect* them.

The protection would end tomorrow. He would have answers or he would leave.

Somehow.

Where he would go or what he would do was a mystery. But no matter what, he was not long for this place.

The soft kiss of the breeze that wafted from the falls on the side of the villa gave the promise of another beautiful day to come.

If only the answers would come with the dawn.

It was late. He would seek his bed.

But he knew it would hold no rest. The dreams had become more real of late. The things he felt more painful.

There was nothing to give him peace. Not even his sleep.

Elle balanced gracefully on the rail of her balcony. One slip and she would tumble into the darkness below. She didn't even blink. She heard the water roaring over the falls that ran along the side of their villa.

The waterfall usually lured her to sleep. Tonight the sound would cover her movements.

Somehow her decision to punish Boone by ignoring him had backfired as the day progressed into evening. At dinner she had felt herself in the role of petulant child instead of the center of attention.

The center of Boone's attention.

Add to that the fact that her father had been watching her like a hawk. Everyone had been, although at least her mother, Ruben, and Tess had been a bit more casual about the entire thing.

And Boone had laughed at her. Not outwardly but on the inside. She could see the hilarity dancing in his vivid green eyes.

At least Zoey was oblivious of the internal strife around the table. And much better company than Zander, who hadn't even tried to hide his bad mood. The shadows under his eyes were darker . . . deeper.

There was something troubling him, something beyond the usual frustration.

Elle took a moment to peek over the wall that divided their balconies. The breeze lifted the curtains and they spun an ethereal dance around the entrance to his room.

Zander? she questioned with her mind but there was no answer beyond a twist of his body beneath the sheets.

No need to disturb him. He'd just try to stop her anyway. She kept on walking on the rail, her toes out-stretched and her arms raised elegantly over her head. Her short gown swirled around her thighs as her feet gripped the rail instinctively and she did not falter as she reached the end of Zander's balcony.

She looked up. Boone's room hooked over and to the right of Zander's. His balcony stretched out deeper as it was over a room that was used for storage.

Was he asleep? She hoped so. She planned to plant some sort of torment into his mind. Something to make his sleep miserable and his morning horrible.

Some sort of revenge for making her feel childish and temperamental.

Elle leaned out and grabbed a protruding curl in the carved beam that decorated the underside of the balcony. She pulled herself up far enough to hook her foot into another curl and then found herself crawling, upside down, using the curls until she was able to hook an arm over the ledge.

Not a modest approach, especially with what she was wearing, but it got her there.

Elle stood quietly on the balcony, silently willing her pounding pulse to slow down. She reached out with her mind to see if Boone was sleeping.

Nothing out of the ordinary came back to her. Just the steady sound of restful breathing.

Not for long.

She adjusted the hem of her gown. Perhaps she should have grabbed a robe first. Still, she wore more now than when they were swimming. She flipped her hair over her shoulder and smoothed it into place.

Prepare to suffer.

She stood for a moment, in between the entrance, half in, half out, letting her eyes adjust to the room's shadows. The bed was cast in darkness but she was sure she saw a form within it.

She had no more than stepped into the room when a

hand covered her mouth and she felt her back slammed up against a firm chest.

"My mind is my own, Elle," Boone breathed in her ear. "None other may possess it. I will keep my mind and use it to overcome my enemies."

Elle squirmed against him and then froze when she felt something hard pressing against her back.

"Are you my enemy, Elle?"

She shook her head no. She was confused, thrown off center. This was not the Boone she expected to find.

He pushed her away, quickly, as if he suddenly could not stand her touch, and she stumbled.

She never stumbled.

Boone grabbed her arm as she regained her balance. When he was sure she was safe from falling he dropped it and leaned back into the shadows so that he was nothing more than a disembodied voice.

"What games are you playing tonight?" he asked.

Elle rubbed her arms, suddenly chilled.

"Children should be asleep now," he continued.

"I am not a child."

"Then quit acting like one," Boone said.

"I'm not," Elle spluttered.

He took a step toward her. "Then why did you come here?" He took another step and Elle backed up two. She looked around nervously. Somehow Boone had maneuvered himself between her body and the opening to the balcony.

He took another step and she did the same, away from him.

His teeth flashed in the darkness.

"Why are you here?" Another step.

Elle moved and stopped as the back of her legs hit the edge of his bed. For some reason this was not going as planned.

"You went to all this trouble," Boone said, waving his hand in the direction of the balcony.

"I . . . I wanted to talk to you," Elle said.

Just plant something and go.

"Then talk." Boone's long finger tapped his temple. "Or were you planning on doing your talking inside my head?"

"I would never do that," Elle said, attempting to look shocked. She glanced around and wondered if she could hop over his bed and make the door. Of course then she'd have to explain to her parents what she was doing on the floor above her room in the middle of the night.

Suddenly Boone grabbed her upper arms and jerked her up. "Yes, you would," he said. "If you were angry enough." He leaned in and looked into her eyes.

His were unfathomable in the shadows.

"You forget how well I know you, Elle."

And I don't know you at all.

Where was Boone? Where was the boy she had played with and teased? Where was the companion she had studied and trained with? Who was this man who stood before her, gripping her arms so tightly that she was sure there would be marks when he pulled his hands away.

This Boone was serious. This Boone smoldered with something that she was not sure she wanted to know.

This Boone frightened her.

"You're scaring me, Boone," Elle finally said.

"You scare me," Boone said. "You don't know the power you have . . . over me."

"I would never use my powers on you."

"You could hurt me without them," he said. His voice was hoarse, no more than a whisper.

"Boone?" Elle asked.

His head moved, quickly. His lips touched hers and suddenly she was crushed against him.

She knew the kisses from the morning had been different from the ones in their past. But they had been nothing compared to this.

This was dangerous. This was out of control. This was Boone plundering her lips as if he possessed her. This was Boone branding her as his own.

She wasn't ready. She didn't know this feeling. She had no control. None.

Her body was betraying her.

My mind is my own. She tried the litany because she wanted to know more. She wanted to know what was happening.

She knew he wanted her. She could feel his want pressing against her abdomen.

My mind is my own.

But her body wanted to be Boone's.

No. No. No. No. No.

Why couldn't she control this?

"Elle," he breathed, tearing his mouth away from hers.

Her legs were weak. Trembling.

And as if she was the very air that he breathed, he began his assault again. His hands roamed her back, then lower. He gripped her thighs and lifted her, wrapping her legs around his waist as his hands moved up her legs, under her gown, and to the bare skin of her back.

Elle felt the shock of his lust pressed against a part of her that wanted him just as badly.

Too fast . . . this is too fast.

"Boone . . . Stop."

She felt his body move and realized they were falling to his bed.

His hands were everywhere and her body betrayed her, arching and seeking his touch.

She pushed against his chest. "Boone . . . we can't . . . I . . ."

His lips moved down her cheek to her neck as his hands roamed around her stomach, making the muscles jerk in anticipation, or fear. She didn't know which.

Elle arched her neck as his progress moved lower, to the neck of her gown. His hands moved up, reaching, searching.

Panic overcame her. She couldn't breathe. This was too fast, too much, too confusing. She wasn't ready. Not for this.

No!

Boone flew upward and off. He landed on the floor, sprawled on his back.

Elle wrapped her arms around herself and rose to her knees.

"Boone?" she said with a voice that did not sound quite normal.

"You should go," he said. "Now."

"Are you hurt?"

He rolled to his hands and knees and then stood, slowly, as if he were in pain.

"No," he said finally. "Can you get back?"

"Yes."

"Then go." His voice cracked. "Please." He wouldn't look at her. His face in the darkness was hidden, lost.

"Boone."

He put up a hand as if to silence her. Elle slid from the bed and padded to the balcony on silent feet.

"I'm sorry," she heard him say as she passed through the entrance.

She kept going.

Her legs shook as she stood on his railing. For a quick instant she thought she might fall but a deep breath brought her under control.

What just happened?

"Concentrate," she reminded herself.

It was an easy drop to Zander's balcony. The addition of a flip made the landing softer.

She was freezing. The air had quickly cooled her and she shivered violently.

She would take a bath. That would settle her.

Their bathing chambers were connected. Elle dashed into Zander's room.

"No!" Zander called out.

Elle froze in her tracks.

"Her eyes . . ." he said.

"Zander?" Elle whispered. Was he dreaming?

"Who . . . who is she?"

Elle peered at the bed. The light trickled in from outside. Starlight, just enough to illuminate his face.

His eyes were closed and he twisted the sheets between his fists.

Peace, brother.

She went on her way.

Peace . . . Zander felt the word enter his dream and knew he would have no peace. Not as long as the woman haunted him.

Every time he closed his eyes he saw her sweet face. She stood on a shore and called out to him. Her pale blond hair flew out around her and her eyes—deep amethyst eyes—begged him to come for her. To take her. To save her.

Who was she? Where was she? His mind struggled for answers as each night she came to him and left his body longing for her.

If only he could find her. If only his dreams would let him go to her, or let her come to him.

If only he knew where to look for her.

If only he could touch her.

Her eyes. He would know her eyes anywhere. They were the most extraordinary color. Deep. Intense. The color of the sky just before the moonrise.

Amethyst. The deepest purple. Violet.

Zander rose from his struggles with a gasp. Fully awake. Every bit of his body erect and throbbing. He ran to the balcony and gripped the rail once again and stared out into the vastness of space.

The memory Elle summoned overwhelmed him. The women, gathered round the newborn child.

What color are her eyes?

Violet.

CHAPTER FIVE

Perhaps he should have let Elle torture him instead of the other way around. Boone was pretty sure he wouldn't feel any worse. What little sleep he captured last night was haunted by alternating dreams of Elle flaying him alive or Elle willing and eager beside him.

Boone scrubbed his hands through his hair and blearily greeted the day.

What were you thinking?

That was easy. He was thinking about Elle. Dreaming about her, and in such a state that he only had one thought when he realized that she was coming to him.

How did you know she was coming?

Boone looked around the room, dappled now in sunlight, as if to find an answer to the question.

He had spent a sleepless night, heavy in regret and longing. And he still wasn't sure what he regretted more, his assault on Elle, or stopping his assault on Elle.

He wanted to make her his. But he shouldn't have

pushed her. She should come to him willingly. She was still so young.

And is what you did any worse than her intentions?

Yes, it was. Her intention was for temporary discomfort.

His intentions were for a lifetime.

How did you know?

He sensed her presence last night as if she called out to him. He surely called out to her. And she came. She had mischief on her mind, but she came.

Elle. Could she hear him now? Did she know he was thinking of her?

He was breathing, wasn't he?

Maybe it was a mistake to let her know his feelings. Maybe it was too soon.

But why hide them? It wasn't as if she couldn't just look inside his mind and find out.

If only he could look inside her mind and see how she felt about him.

There had to be something there. She wasn't exactly unresponsive to him last night. She had seemed most willing, eager, and also frightened.

He frightened her because he went too fast.

He came very near to losing his control last night.

How did he know she was coming to him?

Was it because she was Circe? Was it because he had Circe blood?

His mother knew when Ruben was near. She knew almost instinctively, even though she had none of the psychic abilities.

And after years of observing Shaun and Lilly he had realized that they practically shared a mind, instead of being two separate entities.

Was there a connection between soul mates? Was there something in the Circe blood that made it so?

He had never heard of anything like it. There wasn't any written history on the Circe race available. Everything that was known was legend. The planet, Bali

Circe, was off-limits. Traders were not permitted to land, but did all their dealings on satellites in the airspace above. He had never heard of anyone who actually set foot on the planet, although he sometimes wondered whether Uncle Stefan, with all his adventures, didn't know more.

He would ask Lilly about it.

And then be prepared to explain his feelings for Elle, who most likely would make him pay for his sins.

What frame of mind would Elle be in today? It was her birthday. A day of celebration. Boone found her gift among his things and slipped the silver velvet bag into his pocket. His choice for her was one that he had agonized over for a long time. It was important that he pick exactly the right thing.

She most likely hated him.

Boone realized he slept through breakfast but was able to make up for it when he gave the cook his most charming smile. He ate as he made his way to the training room, which was on the entire top floor of the villa. The room was airy and sunny, with a series of curved arches that led to another balcony.

As he expected, everyone was there. Zander hopped up and down on the mat and moved his neck from side to side as he always did when preparing to spar. Shaun tested an Escrima Stick for speed while Ruben and Lilly practiced with their knives. Tess, who saw no need to learn weaponry when it was obvious that she was well protected, sat on a chaise overlooking the ocean. She flipped through the pages of a book, Kyp at her side.

"Boone!" Zoey called as soon as he walked in. "Watch what I can do." Zoey extended her leg and pointed her toe, then took off at a run toward Elle, who was crouched by a mat. Zoey performed a handspring with Elle ready to spot her, in case she ran into difficulties.

"Did you see me?" she said when she finished with a graceful flourish. "Elle taught me how."

"That was magnificent," Boone said. He looked over Zoey's smiling face at Elle, who quickly looked away.

She hates me.

"I can do a back one too," Zoey said, chattering away in her excitement. "Elle has to help me more."

"Maybe she can show me what to do so I can help you practice," Boone said, and crouched down near the mat opposite Elle.

"Just put your hand under my back when I go by and push if I get stuck," Zoey explained.

She moved to the end of the mat, struck a graceful pose, and ran down the mat. She did a handspring, then twisted her body to go over backward.

Boone and Elle both shot their hands out toward Zoey at the same time as she appeared to falter in midflip.

The jolt Boone felt as their hands connected had nothing to do with Elle's mind torture. He knew she felt it too. Her cheeks flamed and she gave him a quick look before turning her head to watch Zoey continue on down the mat with a series of cartwheels.

Zoey started talking again the instant she landed. "And if I keep on practicing I can do one with no hands."

"Why don't you practice," Boone said, "while Elle and I go for a walk?"

"I don't think she should be left alone," Elle quickly protested. She kept her eyes on Zoey. "She might get hurt."

Boone gave Zoey a quick wink and she immediately went to where Elle was still crouching and whispered in her ear.

"You have to go because he's going to give you your birthday present." Zoey had yet to learn the art of talking quietly. Boone heard every word she said, which was fine with him since that was his plan. "I've seen it and it's very special," she added, just to make sure Elle fell in with her brother's wishes. "And I have to go make sure Kyp isn't bothering mother."

Elle looked doubtfully at Kyp, who was lying in a sunny spot on the balcony.

"Please?" Boone said as he held his hand out. "We need to talk."

"As long as that's *all* we do," Elle said.

"I'll leave that up to you," Boone answered. She looked up at him, her eyes dazzling in the morning sun, as if she were taking his measure. Behind him he heard the heavy grunts of Zander and Shaun as they sparred and the occasional twang of a knife hitting a target. Boone's hand felt heavy as he held it out toward Elle. He willed it not to shake as he started the litany in his mind.

She could hurt him. It would be so easy for her to do. And after last night he couldn't blame her at all.

Elle took his hand and allowed him to pull her up. He felt everyone's eyes on his back as they walked toward the tunnels, even though the noise of Zander and Shaun sparring did not cease.

"Where are we going?" Elle asked. "I thought you wanted to talk," she continued with a suspicious note in her voice.

"We are going to talk," Boone said. He heard the familiar click of claws on the floor and realized that Kyp was following them. His heart panged as it always did when he thought of Ky. There would never be another one like him. He had lost a piece of himself when Ky died.

See how easy I hurt, Elle? Can you see how much I love?

Things would change for his friends now that they had reached adulthood. Shaun and Lilly would have to expose them to the world, especially if Zander were to take over the reins of government. Then they would experience new things. They would meet new people.

He needed to make sure that Elle's heart belonged to him before others could take his place.

He led her to the overlook. He didn't want her to feel

trapped. The sun, still on its upward climb, teased the rim of the ancient volcano while bright rays of light danced through the craggy cuts in the rock.

The wind moved across the lake, making it restless with whitecaps. Boone swallowed hard. His insides felt as churned up as the surface of the water.

Elle stood with her arms crossed, looking at him as if she were waiting for something. Kyp lay down with a grunt. He probably was hoping for a place to run and play instead of more confinement. Boone promised in his mind to take him down to the beach later on.

Elle was waiting.

"I've decided not to apologize for last night," Boone said.

"What?" Elle asked. Her tone led him to think that she thought he was insane. Boone resisted the urge to flinch from her sure to be coming wrath.

"I won't apologize for letting you know how I feel," Boone said. He took both her hands into his. "I will apologize for frightening you."

"What makes you think I was frightened?" Elle said.

"The fact that you threw me across the room and just about knocked me unconscious," Boone said, grinning down at her.

Elle's cheeks blushed bright red and she turned away.

"You could have just said no," Boone said.

"I'm pretty sure I did," Elle said.

Boone had the decency to blush this time. "So I got carried away. Do you understand now what you do to me?"

"I didn't *do* anything, Boone—" Elle began.

"All you've got to do is look at me," Boone interrupted.

He bit back a laugh when he saw her eyes dip down to the front of his pants.

"I'm not that out of control," he said and laughed out loud when he saw the shocked look of embarrassment chase across her face.

Elle's eyes flashed and Boone prepared himself to receive a bit of her mind torture.

But she didn't do anything, except look up at him.

"I'm not sure I'm ready to give you what you want," she said finally. "I'm not sure that I know what it is that I'm feeling."

"Tell me what you feel," Boone said. "Maybe I can help."

Elle looked up and Boone's eyes followed hers. The sky was so blue that it was blinding. The air so clean and clear that they could practically see the deepening colors of the atmosphere.

"I feel like there is a universe out there that I haven't seen yet. I feel like there are people, places, things I want to experience. I feel like there are so many things that I don't know about, so how do I know what I feel for you is real?"

Boone felt his dreams slipping away as Elle spoke.

"Do you feel anything for me at all?" he asked finally, when she stopped. His eyes bored into hers and he wished that he had the power. That he could see inside her mind as she could see into his. He had, after all, shown her, let her walk inside so she could see that all he thought of, dreamed of, was Elle.

"I do, Boone. Really I do. When you touch me"—she squeezed his hands—"I get shivery inside. When you kiss me I feel like I'm melting. Last night . . ." She looked away, suddenly shy, but then brought her eyes back to his. "I miss you dreadfully when you're gone and count the days until you come back. I even dream about you at night."

"Good dreams, I hope?"

"Good dreams," Elle said with a smile. "But . . ."

"But?"

"How do I know if it's enough? If it's forever? You've been with other girls . . ."

"And you don't know if it's just because I'm the only man you know?"

"Yes," Elle said. She let out a sigh as if she were letting go of a heavy burden.

"So you need time?" Boone asked.

"Yes . . . time." Elle's eyes dazzled him as she looked up at him. "Can you give me some time?"

"Elle, I will give you anything that's in my power to give you. Time is something we have. An entire lifetime stretching before us. Forever if you want. I hope that's what you want."

"I like the way that sounds," Elle said with a sweet smile. "You have a year left at Academy. I promise that this time, next year, I'll know. I'll tell you how I feel."

"Agreed," Boone said. He could wait a year. It would be hard, but he was in this for forever. A year was nothing compared to eternity.

He pulled the bag from his pocket. "And so you don't forget about me, while you're—"

Elle snatched the bag from his hand. "Quit being such a gank," she said.

Boone clutched his hands to his chest as if he were wounded. "I give you a gift and I'm being a gank?" he asked incredulously, while grinning at her.

Elle rolled her eyes in mock disgust and pulled the strings loose on the velvet bag. A silver chain pooled in her hand as she poured the contents out.

"Oh . . ." she said as she held the chain up. The sun, now at the tip of the crater, caught the pale color of the glimmering star's gemstone and cast rainbow reflections upon their bodies and the stone behind them. "What is that gem?" Elle asked in awe.

"White tanzanite. It's the rarest gemstone in the universe."

"How did you get it?"

"Stefan," Boone said simply. His uncle had taken over the smuggling end of his father's business. "That shape is extraordinary also," he added proudly.

"It's a star," Elle said. "How?"

"A master cutter is all I know. I told Stefan what I was looking for and he found it."

"Remind me to get him a list," Elle said. She handed the chain to Boone, turned her back, and lifted her hair.

Boone's knuckles rubbed against the soft skin of her neck as he fastened the chain. She spun back around to face him, her fingers caressing the star that lay in the valley right at the top of her breasts.

"It's beautiful," Elle exclaimed.

Boone's hand touched her cheek. "Yes, you are," he said.

She chewed on her lip. Boone grinned at her as he leaned down and covered her lips with his own.

He kissed her gently, his hands barely skimming her arms, his body held back and away until she melted against him. She kept her hands on his shoulders and Boone placed his arms around her back, but held her loosely.

He didn't want her to feel trapped. He didn't want her to feel pressured. He wanted her to know that he would be patient. He would wait.

Their lips finally broke apart and Elle placed her head on his shoulder as they both looked out over the lake. Boone kissed the top of her head.

He could wait. This moment would carry him through.

Elle pulled away and turned her eyes toward the villa, as if she were trying to see through the tunnels that separated her from her family.

"Something's wrong," she said. She took off at a run.

"What is it?" Boone asked. He knew her abilities well enough not to doubt her instincts. He took off after her with Kyp at his heels.

"Zander."

CHAPTER SIX

Zander watched his father's eyes follow Elle and Boone as they slipped into the tunnels and allowed himself the luxury of an inward smile. How many times had his father told him to watch his opponent's eyes for an opportunity to press his own attack?

For once Zander did not chafe under his father's guidance. He swung his Escrima Stick and was rewarded with the impact of flesh and a grunt from his father.

Shaun arched an eyebrow in surprise. Whether it was at the force of the blow or just the fact that Zander had gotten through his defenses, Zander could not tell.

Zander took it as a challenge and swung with his other arm.

Shaun met his blow with a block and because of his greater strength pushed Zander back.

Zander feinted with his right arm and when Shaun moved to block he swung with his left. The blow hit Shaun in the upper arm.

Zander knew it stung his father. He felt the impact of it in his hand. He saw the pain flash across Shaun's face.

He didn't care.

It was the first time he had ever seen a weakness in his father. The first time he seemed less than perfect. The first time Zander felt justified in his anger. His parents were hiding something from him. They didn't trust him. They had no confidence in him. They thought he was a child. They thought he needed protection.

Now was the time for him to prove to them that he was capable. He was of age today. It was time for him to make his move. It was time for him to prove himself.

Zander's rage and frustration rose to the surface and boiled over into his blood. Without thought he struck again. And again. And again.

He felt the blows hit against his father's blocks. He was moving so fast that his father could only block. Zander felt the force vibrate into his arms. He felt sweat roll down his face as his hair dampened and fell into his eyes. Blood dripped from a cut on his cheek.

He felt rage and a burning hatred. It blinded him.

Zander moved as if possessed. He was aware that he was fighting his father, but the thought that he could hurt him or be hurt didn't enter his mind. All that mattered was the fight itself.

He had to win. He had to prove it to himself and to his father. He had to beat his father down to the ground and have him yield. No matter that his father was bigger and stronger. He was quicker and he was younger. He would outlast him. He would outmaneuver him. He would beat him. Fairly. Finally.

Then he would know what the secret was. He would know what it was they kept from him. He would know what it was they feared. And then he would know how to beat it so it no longer held him captive.

He would be free. All he had to do was beat his father. He continued to rain blows until one of his sticks flew from his hands and landed on the tile floor with a clatter. Shaun had managed to disarm him.

Zander made as if to dive for it but instead spun his body sideways in the air toward the weapons rack and picked up a pair of Kamas. He dropped the other stick he held, slid the loops attached to the handles of the hooked blades around his wrists, and dropped into the ready position. His chest rose and fell with the effort to breathe and he willed his body to relax, using the techniques his mother taught him.

Zander noticed his father was breathing hard too as he walked to the weapons rack and carefully dropped his Escrimas into place and picked up his Kamas. His movements were slow and methodical, as if he was thinking about the fight to come, or else he was being deliberate to catch his breath.

Zander watched him closely and said the litany in his mind.

My mind is my own.

He would not allow his father to distract his mind. He would use every tactic he possessed.

"Stop this right now," Lilly said. Her voice seemed to come from a distance and Zander saw her as if she were on the edge of a nightmare. She stood at the side of the mat with a horrified look on her beautiful face. Ruben stood beside her, his blade in his hand. Tess was behind them, her hand on Zoey's hair. Zoey had her arms wrapped around her mother's waist and tears streamed from her bright blue eyes.

"He started it," Shaun said with a grin on his face.

Zander's gut exploded as if a terrifying creature was seeking to claw its way out. His father saw this as a game. He was toying with him.

Zander swung the Kamas. He would show his father. He would show both of them. He was tired of being treated like a child. He was tired of the games. It would stop today.

Zander bellowed in anger when he felt his body fly backward. He landed against a pillar and instantly scrambled to his feet.

Lilly walked toward him with eyes narrowed. The handles of the Kamas burned his hands but he refused to let go.

His mother was in his mind.

"Why?" she said. Her voice was in his mind but she also spoke the word.

"Where did this hate come from?"

"My mind is my own." Zander ground the words out between clenched teeth. He battled his mother's mind with his own. All he had was the litany and sheer force of will. He would not drop the Kamas. He would not.

"You know we love you. Why are you doing this?"

Zander felt hot tears well behind his eyes and he blinked them away.

"Your love is killing me."

"Alexander," Shaun said. He stood beside Lilly. "Stop this now."

Zander closed his eyes. He would not look at them. The look on their faces was too much. He would not submit. He would not.

Against his will his fists opened and the Kamas slipped from his grip.

His father had done it. His father could do anything when he set his mind to it. Just like Elle.

And he couldn't. He couldn't even hold on to his weapons. He was useless.

They expected him to run a world. Yet they didn't trust him enough to tell him the truth. When would they trust him?

He opened his eyes and saw the look on their faces.

Not now. Not after today. He was still a child in their eyes. They wanted his trust yet they would not give him theirs.

My mind is my own.

Ruben left, taking Tess and Zoey with him. This was no place for them. Not now.

No other may possess it.

"We should all take a break," Shaun said. He rubbed his upper arm where Zander was sure he landed a blow. "Get cleaned up before the celebration."

His mother looked at him. Zander knew she wanted inside his mind but he kept up the litany. She was worried about him. He didn't have to be a telepath to know it.

I will keep my mind . . . it's too late, Mother . . . and use it to overcome my enemies.

Zander . . . He felt her on the edge, searching for a way in. He would not allow it. That was one thing he could do. He could block. He would block all of them. They had secrets. He had secrets.

Her eyes bored into his as his father picked up his Kamas and put them away in the rack.

"We'll talk after dinner," Lilly said, vocally admitting her defeat. "We have some things to tell you. Things you should know."

"You mean about the Circe?" Zander said.

Lilly's eyes widened in shock and Shaun turned as if a proton blast had rocked the room.

Zander felt pleased with himself for the first time in a long while. He had finally done something that impressed his parents. The look on their faces said it all. They were too surprised to speak.

Zander turned without a word and walked away.

His mind tumbled in confusion. He felt vindicated and guilt-ridden at the same time. He knew he hurt his parents. The look on his mother's face was enough to tear his heart in two.

But they also had to know that he was no longer a child. They expected him to act the part of a man but they did not allow him the considerations that a man deserved.

Zander heard the fast approach of Elle and Boone. He ducked into a room off the staircase and went into a rapid repeat of the litany, willing his mind to rest and his heart to stop pounding out of his chest.

Elle must have sensed the turmoil. He hoped she would be concentrating on their parents now and would not sense the thing he was about to do.

Zander waited until he heard their footsteps fade away. He ran down the stairs and into the tunnels.

They were empty. No one questioned him as he ran. No servants, no guards, no messengers from the capital. He saw no one until he got to the bay. The guard was there, as usual.

Zander stopped and went through the litany again until his breathing returned to normal. He had every right to be here. There should be no questions. He was the heir. The guard wasn't there to keep him in, just to keep unwanted guests out.

Keep the Circe out . . .

Zander walked by the guard, gave him a slight nod, and headed straight for the Firebird. The sleek ship sat in the same spot where he had landed her yesterday, turned and ready to take off once again. The same guard had seen him take her out. Of course Boone was with him then but it was not the guard's place to question him.

There was nothing on Oasis that could catch the Firebird. If he made it to the hyperport, then he would be free. He would find his own answers. He would learn all there was to know about the Circe. And then he would show his parents there was nothing to fear.

"Welcome, Zander," ElSie said when he placed his hands on the yoke. Boone had programmed ElSie to accept his commands and Zander was grateful that he had seen no need to remove it.

"Make for hyperport, ELSie," Zander said.

"Where is Boone?" ELSie asked.

"Not here," Zander said.

He held his breath for a moment, hoping that ELSie wouldn't question him any further. There was a small blip on the com and a green light flashed.

"Destination?" ELSie asked.

"The Senate," Zander said. He powered up the engines and waited for ELSie.

"Coordinates found," ELSie reported. "You have the com."

"Thank you, ELSie," Zander said. He strapped in and placed his hands once again upon the yoke. Without hesitation he gave the ship full throttle and joy overcame him as they blasted out of the bay. He felt a thrill as he guided the Firebird in a turn and they screamed over the crater and into the clear blue sky. He felt as if he had waited his entire life for this moment. Never had he dared to fly so fast. There wasn't enough room before. But now he had the entire universe before him.

"Sorry, Boone," he said, hoping his friend would understand. Surely he would.

In the next breath he was in the stratosphere and two Falcons from the Oasian Fleet were shadowing him.

"Incoming message," ELSie reported.

"Respond," Zander said. He knew the Firebird was a familiar ship to the members of the fleet.

Let me pass.

"Solar flare is breaking up the transmission," ELSie reported.

"Open the com," Zander said.

". . . back to the Academy?" one of the pilots said over the com among the static.

Zander punched the communicator. "Yes," he said, hoping he sounded like Boone. "Too much work, not enough break." The flare should help distort his voice enough.

The pilot laughed. "I remember," he said. "Safe stars." The Falcons peeled off and Zander saw the blinking lights of the hyperport up ahead.

"Entering hyperport," ELSie said.

Zander felt the pull from the hyperport and the engines shifted up for the jump. The next instant he felt the impact of the g-forces throw him back against the seat. He let out a whoop as the stars turned into blurs and the ship was sucked into hyperdrive.

He was free.

CHAPTER SEVEN

The tension on the top floor of the villa was thick even though the room was deserted. Elle and Boone found Lilly on the balcony.

In Boone's mind it could have been Elle standing there. Lilly's hair was shorter but the slender body was the same, along with the set of her shoulders.

"Mother?" Elle said as they approached Lilly. "What happened?"

Boone saw Lilly quickly hide her tears as she turned to her daughter. "I'm not really sure," she said. "Zander . . ." Her hands gripped the railing on the balcony. "It seems your brother hates us. With a passion that I didn't know he possessed."

Boone wasn't surprised at the words. But it wasn't his place to speak.

"He doesn't hate you," Elle said as she moved next to her mother. "He's just . . . frustrated."

"He tried to kill your father," Lilly said.

"What?" Elle looked over her shoulder at Boone.

"Should I leave?" His mouth formed the words.

"*No*," she said in his mind. "*Stay*."

"What happened?" Boone asked Lilly. He moved to her opposite side, not really sure if he should stay but willing to because Elle asked him to.

"They were sparring and suddenly Zander turned vicious. Shaun disarmed him and Zander went for the Kamas. He was going after your father and I had to throw him."

"Which reinforced his feelings of inadequacy," Boone said.

"Feelings of inadequacy?" Lilly asked as she turned toward Boone. "Zander feels inadequate?"

"Doesn't everyone next to you three?" Boone said. "You can do these amazing things and Zander can't."

"But we've never said—"

"You didn't have to, Mother," Elle said. "You didn't mean to but you were always wondering why Zander couldn't do what I can. You've always wondered when, or if, he'd ever develop the abilities. Even when you didn't say anything the worry was always there. That and the other things. The things you never told us about. The reason why we are prisoners in our home."

"You aren't prisoners," Lilly said. "Why would you say that?"

"Mother," Elle said. Boone sensed her frustration but to his surprise she changed tactics. "What is it that frightens you so? What are you protecting us from? Why aren't we allowed to go to the beach, or the capital, or to Boone's? Why can't Zander go to Academy? What is it?"

Elle's eyes once again found Boone. "And why does Boone know about it and we don't?"

Lilly turned from the balcony to look at both of them. "Boone knows because it's just as much a part of him as it is a part of you and Zander. The threat is there for all of you."

"What threat, Mother? What is out there that is so horrible? What is the Circe?"

Lilly did not seem surprised when Elle mentioned it. She sighed as if she'd been expecting it.

"We are the Circe," Lilly said. "We all are. Except for Ruben. We are part of the race."

Elle looked between her mother and Boone, her face showing confusion and frustration.

"Find Zander," Lilly said. "I'm going for your father. It's time you knew everything."

"How bad is it?" Elle asked Boone when Lilly was gone.

Boone put his arms around her. Elle melted into his chest, her head resting under his chin. It felt so right to rest his cheek against the top of her head, to smell the fragrance of her hair, to feel her at home in his arms. It was where she belonged. If only she knew it the way he did.

"Sometimes I think a secret is scarier when it is a secret," he said. "When you know the facts and know the enemy, you can meet it head-on. You know what to expect. You know how to deal with it."

"Did you learn that at Academy?" Elle's voice was muffled against his chest.

"No. I learned that from my father," he said. "Just remember, Elle, everything they did, they did to protect you. They wanted your happiness to come before everything."

"Tell that to Zander," Elle said. "If he'll listen."

Boone felt the buzz of the remote in his pocket.

"What is that?" Elle asked as he reached for the small device that he always kept close.

"ELSie," he said. "It's my link to the Firebird. Someone is on board and whoever it is has initiated her systems."

"Zander," Elle said. "He's leaving."

"He wouldn't," Boone said as a cold feeling washed over him. "He wouldn't steal my ship."

He would. You would.

"Can you shut it down from here?" Elle asked.

"No. She's programmed for Zander. I left it on since I figured we'd take her out again today. ELSie will follow his instructions since that's what I told her to do."

"Hurry," Elle said. They were already down the stairs.

"Can you reach him?"

"He's blocking. That's one thing he's very good at."

They ran into the tunnels. "Contact your father," Boone said. "Tell him to have the fleet stop him."

"I'm trying," Elle said. "I can't concentrate."

Boone grabbed Elle's arm and they both stopped. "We'll never reach him in time. Take a deep breath and concentrate."

Boone was glad she was concentrating on her parents. He didn't want her to see the fear in his mind. Zander had no idea what was out there, just waiting for him to appear.

Elle closed her eyes to clear her mind. Before she could take a cleansing breath the tunnels rumbled with the sound of engines. Boone recognized the whine of the Firebird. He knew she was airborne.

Boone looked toward the bay and then back at Elle. "Concentrate," he urged her.

"Mother," Elle said. She looked at Boone. "They know. They can't get through the com links. There are solar flares in the upper atmosphere."

A curse exploded from Boone's lips. "Come on. We can track him if we stay close enough. But we've got to be on his tail when he hits the hyperport or we'll never find him. The Firebird is too fast."

"What should we do?"

"We'll take my father's ship," Boone said. "We won't be able to catch him, but we should be able to stay close enough to figure out where he's going."

The bay was empty just as they expected. The guard looked at their faces and panic spread over his.

"Was Zander authorized to leave?" he asked. "I

thought he was taking your ship out, like yesterday, but when he took off, I knew he was going for upper atmosphere."

"Don't worry about it," Boone said over his shoulder as they made for Ruben's ship. "You didn't do anything wrong."

Boone quickly punched the code on the door and the hatch slid open. He dived into the seat and fired up the engine.

"Strap in," he said to Elle. She stood in the hatch with a strange look on her face.

"Maybe I shouldn't go," she said. She sounded like a little girl who was afraid she would get into trouble, but Boone didn't have time to worry about her feelings.

"Either come in or get out," he said. "But be quick about it." His hands flew over the com as he programmed the onboard computer to link with his remote.

Boone heard the hatch close with its familiar swoosh as it pressurized and Elle slid into the coseat. Her hands fumbled with the belt but she managed to strap in as Boone took the yoke and guided his father's ship out of the bay.

"Boone?" Ruben's voice came over the com.

"This is the only way I can track Zander," Boone said. He knew his father well enough to know that he didn't need to go into long explanations.

"We know," Ruben said. "Is Elle with you?"

"Yes."

"We're coming right behind," Ruben said. "As soon as you get a heading, let us know."

"I will," Boone said.

"Boone?" Boone heard the concern in his father's voice. "Safe stars."

"Safe stars," Boone replied. He gave Elle's hand a quick squeeze as the ship nosed into the sky. In just a few simple words Ruben conveyed his complete trust in what he was doing.

If only Zander could know that feeling. There was such a thing as protecting your children too much. Something he would remember when it came his time to be a parent. If that time ever came. With Elle. He refused to even consider it with any other woman.

Elle's eyes were as wide as the sky outside. Whether it was fear or excitement she was feeling, Boone had no way of knowing. She had not spoken a word since his challenge.

If she was mad at him she was hiding it well. Was it just yesterday that he told her to grow up?

"Hailing Star Shooter," a voice said over the com.

Boone looked both ways to see the Fleet escort on either side. "This is Firebird," he said. "Anybody seen my ship?"

"Sorry, Firebird, it just went into the hyperport. We thought it was you."

"Any indication of destination?" Boone asked. The last thing he wanted to do was let anyone know that Zander had stolen his ship. He wondered if the fleet even knew of Zander's and Elle's existence.

"Whoever it was said he was going back to Academy," the pilot said. "We had no orders to stop him. Probably lost them in the flare."

"No problem," Boone said. "It's just a friend who thinks he's being funny. Be on the lookout for the real Star Shooter coming behind me."

"Glad I'm not the one on the Firebird," the pilot said. "Safe stars."

"Safe stars and out," Boone said. "Hang on," he said to Elle. "We're going into hyperspeed."

"Do you know where he's going?" Elle asked.

"I'm waiting for ELSie," Boone said. "I know he's not going to Academy. And I know where I hope he's not going."

"Circe?" Elle asked.

"Bali Circe," Boone said. "Hyperspeed in five, four, three, two, one."

Boone felt the familiar rush as the g-forces kicked in. He couldn't blame Zander for what he had done. Who was to say he wouldn't have done the same thing? Zander had never experienced the rush of deep space travel.

Would you ever give it up?

He knew the answer as soon as he voiced the question in his mind. As long as he could remember he longed for the stars. Once he'd experienced it, he knew that's where he belonged.

As much as he wanted Elle he knew that he couldn't give it up. Not now. There was too much to see, too many new places to discover.

Boone stole a look at Elle. Her face glowed with excitement.

Maybe the two of us . . . together . . .

Maybe he wasn't being fair to her. He expected her to make a commitment to him, yet he wasn't ready to stay put.

They both had some growing up to do.

The com beeped and a set of coordinates appeared on the screen.

"He's heading for the Senate," Boone said. "And he picked the best time to go there."

"Why?" Elle asked as he programmed the ship for autopilot.

"It's Carnival. The anniversary of the alliance. That's why I'm on break. Academy cancels classes during Carnival. All my friends are there. It's one big party. It will be very easy for Zander to disappear there."

"If all your friends are there, why did you come home?" Elle asked.

"I came home to be with you, Elle."

Once more his heart was out there waiting for her to show her own. Her gaze was on him, steady and clear, her worry for her brother evident on her exquisite features.

"Tell me about the Circe," she said.

Too much . . . too fast . . .

Boone checked the course once again. It would take them two solar days to get to the Senate. They should enter cryo. They had no idea what they would find when they got there. He knew Zander was intelligent enough to figure the procedure out on the Firebird. And ELSie could instruct him.

He suddenly wanted to gather Elle into his arms and hold her for the duration of the trip. Especially if he could assure her that Zander would be found, that he would be safe.

He knew what he was about to tell her would take that thought away.

"The Circe are a race of women who are telepaths," he began.

"Like me?"

Boome nodded.

Elle swiveled the coseat around so she faced him and settled back, her pale gray eyes intense and excited.

Boone couldn't blame her. She'd waited her entire life for this.

"Circe was settled eons ago by a religious sect that believed that women were lesser beings and at the mercy of their husbands," Boone began. "The women were under complete control. They could not eat, drink, or even speak unless their husbands said so. They hardly ever went out in public and when they did, they were completely covered, except for their eyes. The daughters were sold off in marriage to men they never met until the ceremony. The control was so oppressive that some men even cut out their women's tongues so they would not embarrass them in public by speaking without permission."

"Where did you hear this from?" Elle asked in disbelief.

"Your mother told my mother. My mother is a Circe, as is yours. My mother was born there but she has no memory of it. Your mother was born on Oasis of a Circe woman.

"As the generations passed something began to happen," Boone continued. "At first it was told that the women could communicate with their eyes and then they began to reach out to each other with their minds. They did so until they were able to control the men by suggestion. My father said it was because the men became complacent and lazy and the women found an alternate way to communicate. Eventually the women became stronger and took control."

"But what does that have to do with us?" Elle asked. "If all the women are telepaths like me, then why do we fear them?"

"Because they don't allow the male telepaths to live," Boone said. "Your father is the only one who ever survived them. And only after a remarkable set of circumstances. Did you know that his birth name was Nicholas? That he never knew his real mother?"

"What? How?" Elle's face showed her confusion.

"Your father was born on Oasis, a direct descendant of its sovereign ruler. But he was born during a time of terrible conflict, when the Circe tried to take over Oasis. His mother, Arielle, hid with him aboard a cargo ship and got off on a planet called Pristo. It was a mining colony at that time. The entire surface was covered with gas and everyone lived underground in these huge chambers. Arielle died and your father, who was too young to remember any of it, wandered around until he was discovered by a miner named Ryan Phoenix. Before she died Arielle carved the emblems of the Oasian creedo on the back of his neck. It looked like it spelled Shaun so that's what they called him."

"Strength, Honor, Obedience, Unity, Nobility. They thought the O was an A. Her hand must have slipped." Elle's face showed her horror at the thought of anyone being desperate enough to harm a child in that manner. "She must have known she was dying and she wanted to make sure my father was safe but could be found." She knew there were scars on the back of her father's neck but never knew where they came from or what they stood for.

"The Phoenixes raised him as their son. And while he was growing up underground, your father's eyes evolved so that he could see in the dark."

"His Circe heritage," Elle concluded. "But didn't they notice his other abilities?"

"No," Boone said. "Because they did not develop until he met your mother. She was the key to his mental awakening."

"I don't understand," Elle said. "Father had no abilities until he met Mother? How did they meet? Did he learn them or could he just do them? What happened?"

"I don't know that part of the story," Boone said. "But I do know that the Circe went crazy when they realized that your father was alive. They demanded his death. They called him an Aberrant. At the same time there was a war going on because another planet was trying to conquer Oasis and the Circe were involved in that also. Somehow your father and mother were a part of the victory but they had to go into hiding because the Circe would never rest until your father was dead."

"And they would kill us, especially Zander, because they fear our powers would be greater than the Circe because we inherited it from both our parents," Elle said. "They fear my father the most because they assume he is stronger because he is a man."

"Exactly," Boone said. "And they fear Zander more because of his parentage."

"But he has no powers," Elle said.

"They don't know that. They would just think he was shielding them if they did find him."

"How do they even know about us?" Elle asked. "No one has ever even seen us except for a trusted few."

"Remember when my mother and I came to Oasis?" Boone asked. "Your parents helped us. They saved us."

"Because Zander sent them. He was the one who

told our parents Ruben was in trouble. One of two times that he showed any telepathic abilities."

"There was a Circe there. She saw inside your mother's mind during the fight. Our fathers went after the ship she escaped on. They said some pods got away so your parents erred on the side of safety. They knew the Circe would be looking for you and would stop at nothing to get their hands on both of you."

"To kill Zander and control me," Elle concluded. "That explains why we were so protected. But I still don't know why they never told us any of this."

"How would you feel if you had to live with that fear every day?" Boone asked. "I remember what it was like before Ruben came. I remember worrying every day if Joah was going to beat my mother or worse, or if she would be taken away by this man who wanted her. I was only six but I remember the way he looked at her. I also remember how happy I was when Ruben killed him."

Boone's hand tightened on the yoke, even though the craft was on autopilot. As a boy he was unable to protect his mother and he well recalled the frustration he felt at his inadequacy. "My mother tried to hide it from me but I knew she lived with a constant fear. And I also knew that her first and only thought was to protect me." Boone looked at Elle. "They wanted you to be happy. They wanted you to have a normal childhood, without the fear."

"And Zander has no idea what's out there. If they see him, see his eyes, they'll know immediately who he is, and they'll take him."

"Yes. And he won't know to fear them."

"They should have told us," Elle said. "So we would be prepared."

"It's too late to worry about that now," Boone said. "The Circe will be present at the Senate. There'll be hundreds of them there. Maybe thousands. Everyone fears them. And whichever one finds Zander will be rewarded. If they think he's there they won't stop until they capture him."

"Doesn't Oasis have people there?" Elle asked. "Can't our father alert them?"

"He can. But you've got to understand, Elle. During Carnival there are millions of people on the planet. The traffic is unbelievable. He'll get cycled into a landing pattern."

"But the Firebird has Oasian markings. They can look for him and stop him if they know he's coming."

"They can try," Boone said. "One thing you've got to understand about the Senate and the planet it's on. Everything is for sale and everyone has a price. Oasis can ask the Senate Guard to be on the lookout for the Firebird. But if they think they can get a price for him from the Circe, they would turn Zander over before he'd have time to fire the engines."

"No wonder Father hates it so," Elle said. "I've never heard him say anything good about it at all."

"The Senate sat on the fence when Oasis was at war," Boone said. "They were waiting to see who would come out on top. And that's something I learned at Academy. From what I studied I'm fairly certain they weren't cheering for Oasis."

"Maybe I can reach him," Elle said.

"We're in hyperspace," Boone said. "And he's probably in cryo, like we should be."

"I can at least try," Elle said. She pulled her legs up onto the seat and folded herself into her meditation position. Boone watched as she closed her eyes and took a deep cleansing breath. Her forehead furrowed into a frown as she concentrated, her mind seeking and searching for her brother.

"Nothing," she said finally. "I felt Mother and Father searching too." She looked at Boone. "Do you think the Circe will be able to sense his presence?"

Boone shrugged. "Not if he's not a telepath. You would know more about it than I would."

"Do you have any abilities, Boone? Does Tess?"

"Lilly says she's a healer, which is obvious. And I know there's some sort of mental connection between her and Ruben."

"Boone." Her voice trembled slightly. "How did you know I was coming to your room last night?"

Boone felt as if he'd been punched in the gut. He still wasn't sure how she felt about what had happened last night. So how did he know she was coming? Her eyes seemed to pierce right through him and he recalled the fear he had seen in them when he almost lost control.

"I just knew. I was thinking about you. Dreaming about you. And I sensed that you were coming. I didn't even think about it, I just got up and waited for you to appear because I figured you were up to no good."

"I was," Elle said with a slight smile. "Do you think it's because . . ." She stopped in midsentence and turned away suddenly shy.

What is she thinking?

"Do you think that Zander has to meet his life mate before his abilities will appear?" she said finally.

"It could happen. No one knows. Your father was the first Circe male with abilities, so no one knows."

"What if Zander finds her? Or she finds him? I wonder what will happen."

"The chances of that happening are too much to think about," Boone said. "And it's all just a big what-if right now." He checked the com again. They were on course but losing time against the Firebird's greater speed. Zander would have a good head start once he hit the planet. And the odds of finding him were slim, especially if he was blocking. "We best get some rest," he said. He pulled a lever on the side of Elle's seat and it slowly reclined.

"What are you doing?" she said.

"Putting you in cryo," he replied. "Unless you've got another idea on how we should pass the time."

Once again, her eyes seemed to pierce right through him and Boone felt the familiar punch in his gut.

"I know . . . too much . . . too soon. But you can't blame me for trying," he said with a grin. He clamped the vise over her wrist that initiated the sleep state.

"No. I'll never blame you for that," she replied with a smile.

Boone gently bent and kissed her forehead as her eyes fluttered shut.

CHAPTER EIGHT

She called to him. She stood on a shore with a magenta sky deepening behind her. Her pale blond hair tossed in the wind and her amethyst eyes were full of tears. She called his name over and over again and he didn't know where to find her.

If only he knew where she was. In his dream it seemed as if she were closer but that wasn't much help. If he could just concentrate hard enough he knew he could find her, but the strange buzzing in his ears did nothing to help his concentration.

Zander blinked sleep-filled eyes open and swallowed, fighting a strange dryness in his throat as he moved his seat into an upright position. He had set the alarm to bring him out of cryo in plenty of time to do some research before he landed on Senate.

He was fortunate in that he only had to see something one time in order to know how to do it and Boone had shown him how to operate everything on the Firebird, including the cryo. He took the band off his wrist and stood up for a good long stretch to get his blood pumping again.

Who is she? And why do I keep dreaming about her?

There was no answer to be had. Zander shook off the dream, and the guilt he felt for the fight with his father and stealing Boone's ship, as he took a shower in the well-equipped lav and put on the Academy uniform he found stored in a locker. Since he and Boone were close to the same size it fit rather well and he couldn't help but wish that it belonged to him.

Maybe I can convince them to let me go.

As he looked at himself in the mirror over the small tuck-away sink he knew the answer to that. His hand brushed across his cheek where he was sure there had been a cut from his fight with his father. Or maybe he had imagined it. Regardless, it was gone now and there was no need to waste time dwelling on it. If only his transgressions could be erased as easily as the wound.

Zander was fairly certain that his punishment for running off would put Academy out of reach for good. So why not take advantage of the time before him? There was so much to learn. So much to see. So many things he wanted to do.

The first think he did after digging into Boone's store of snacks and having a long drink of water was have ELSie show him the coordinates for Bali Circe. It didn't take him long to find the correct name for the planet once he let ELSie know what he was looking for.

ELSie was only able to give him the facts: location, size, geology, geography, population, which seemed rather small for the size of the planet. Its natural resources seemed limited as well. Bali Circe imported more than it exported. It had no surface technology. All of its food stores came from Oasis. From what Zander surmised, Bali Circe was entirely dependent upon outside sources to support its population.

So where did the credits come from to buy all the resources to support an entire planet? There had to be something else. Something that wasn't common knowledge. Was that why his parents were afraid of them? Did they know their secrets?

Who were these people? What did they do? And most importantly, why were his parents so afraid of them?

Unfortunately ELSie reported nothing beyond the basic facts. But he was sure he could find the answers he needed on Senate. There had to be a central source of information on the planet.

The Firebird was close enough to catch a broadcast from the Senate News Network. Something else that he'd never seen. It was amazing how much he'd missed. He had a lot to learn and a lot of time to make up for. The monitor showed a celebration. People dancing in the streets beneath large Plexi tunnels covered with brightly colored streamers.

A quick check with ELSie told him that Senate's atmosphere was inhospitable. The planet had been chosen to house the governing body of the universe due to its central location. Everything was built beneath giant domes of the thickest Plexi. Underground tunnels connected the domes along with covered walkways that hung in between. The domes simulated the atmosphere of a normal oxygen-based planet and each one was powered by a generator buried beneath the surface.

The energy needed to keep the domes habitable had to be enormous.

SNN reported that Carnival was in progress. The Anniversary of the Alliance. The Senate was one giant party right now and he had scored an invitation.

Zander kept one eye on the monitor as the pretty newscaster talked about the championship match to be held that night. Something called the Murlaca. Before he could figure out what that was ELSie interrupted the broadcast.

"Coming out of hyperspeed in five, four, three, two, one," ELSie counted down. "Senate fleet has fed coordinates for landing," she continued. "Turning off auto-pilot."

"What do I do?" Zander asked.

"Senate has us on tractor beam," ELSie said. "Hailing now."

"Oasian ship, identify," came over the com.

"This is Firebird," Zander said. "Where do I land?"

"Are you going directly on-planet or to your Embassy Satellite?"

Zander knew about the embassy. He knew the political operations of the universe. The embassy was one place he wanted to avoid. His father probably had alerted them to his escape and they would be looking for him.

"On-planet," Zander said.

"You'll be taken into a docking station where you can get transport to the ground," the voice said. "So sit back and enjoy the ride."

"That's my plan," Zander said. "Out."

It would have been nice to land the Firebird on his own, but since he didn't want to draw any attention to himself he allowed the tractor beam to take hold and watched the traffic outside the Plexi.

Starships of every size, designation, and quality floated in holding patterns in the space above Senate. Zander made a game of identifying the markings on each ship and checked with ELSie to see if he was correct in determining their home planets.

His education was excellent, if incomplete in the things his parents excluded, and his memory did not fail him. It also helped him pass the time until the Firebird was pulled into orbit around a giant space station that in Zander's mind could have passed for a small planet.

Control was given back to Zander at this point and he guided the Firebird into a landing bay that was similar to the one he was used to back on Oasis.

"Nice landing," the tech said when he opened the hatch.

Zander couldn't help but grin. He knew he handled the Firebird well but it was nice to hear a complete stranger compliment him.

"You can catch the shuttle to the planet in Bay Nine," the tech added and pointed him in the right direction. "Want to refuel?"

"Yeah," Zander said, then immediately wished he hadn't. "Um . . ."

"I'll scan your code and it goes against your planetary account," the tech explained. "Oasis."

"Er . . . fine," Zander said. His hand closed around the credits in his pocket. He had found them on the Firebird. Something else he owed Boone. His list of crimes was getting longer and longer and at this rate his father would probably throw him into the deepest caverns on Oasis.

He would worry about that later, when and if it happened. For now he was free. And he was pretty sure Boone would understand why he did it. Under the circumstances, he was sure Boone would do the same thing.

The corridors were busy and Zander fell into the traffic, all headed toward Bay Nine. He noticed a pair of girls staring at him and he immediately became self-conscious and wondering about his appearance until he heard one of them whisper to her friend.

"Look at his eyes," she said. "Have you ever seen anything like them?"

"No," the other said. "They're beautiful. I've never seen that color before. At least not on a man. Wish I had lashes like that."

Zander grinned at them and the girls immediately blushed and laughed self-consciously.

This is fun.

He had never been around girls before. His stomach

did a little flip as the crowd became thicker and the girls moved in closer to him, each of them trying to outmaneuver the other one to get beside him.

"So you go to Academy?" one asked as they approached the shuttle hatch.

"What? Er . . . yes," Zander said as he looked self-consciously at his uniform. "Second year," he added.

"My brother's there," the other said. "He's second year too. His name is Phillip Vanderpelt. Do you know him?"

"Um, no . . . but the name sounds familiar." Zander's mind scrambled. Should he know everyone there? Boone never really mentioned anyone's names but did share a lot of pranks that happened.

"Is he the one that put the worrat inside the simulator?" Zander said, remembering a story Boone had mentioned.

"No," the girl laughed. "But his bunkmate was the one that was testing when it woke up. I'm surprised you don't know him," she added.

"I spend most of my time studying," Zander said. Which wasn't a lie. "My friend probably knows him. Boone Monaco."

"I think I've heard him mention him," she said. "My brother's already on-planet . . . maybe you could carnival with us?" Both girls looked at him expectantly.

Zander tried not to let his panic show. The last thing he needed was someone to identify him as an imposter. He needed to keep a low profile since he was sure the Oasian delegation would be looking for him.

"Er . . . I'm meeting someone," he said. "Sorry."

The crowd was on the shuttle now and people maneuvered for the best seats for the jump down to the planet. Zander regretfully let the crowd separate him from the two girls.

His ego enjoyed their attention but his conscience reminded him of why he was here. His purpose was to find information about the Circe.

But if he could enjoy the spectacle of Carnival also, then so be it.

In a matter of moments the shuttle touched down on-planet and the crowd shuffled from the shuttle, through a platform, and out into a huge dome. Zander let the people carry him along and made sure he kept plenty of space between himself and the two girls who kept looking toward him.

The height of the dome astounded him. Zander couldn't help but look up. He knew the blue sky was artificial, nothing more than a trick of the light, but it was still amazing to see the technology at work.

He came from a planet that used natural materials and recycled its waste. The buildings on Oasis were carved from stone or built from trees that fell to earth in the great forests.

Zander was amazed at all he saw.

He followed the crowd along, marveling at the brightly colored pennants that hung in the archways of the tunnels. Loud pulsing music pounded the Plexi, and he felt as if were inside a huge drum.

They entered another enormous dome, this one so big he could not see where it ended. There was nothing above him but blue skies and the great height of buildings. Brightly colored streamers and confetti poured so thick from the windows that it looked like rain and small pieces of it stuck to his skin and clothing.

There was a parade on the street. As far as the eye could see was a stream of hoverpods, each one bearing several people dressed in strange costumes and masks who flung beads and treats at the people lining the boulevard.

A lot of the people he saw in the crowd along the street were masked also and it seemed that the masks freed their inhibitions. As the crowd carried him down the street several soft bodies pressed up against him, draped beads around his neck, and took his hand to pull him into a dance.

The music was contagious. Hypnotic. Freeing. Zander couldn't help himself. Whatever he had to do could wait. He let himself be carried along with the crowd.

The sheer numbers could have been frightening. As far as he could see, there were people. Women of indeterminable age pressed against him. They touched him in places no stranger should touch him. They kissed him full on the mouth, some even slipping their tongues inside.

Strange sensations coursed through Zander's body. He even took a moment to wonder if he could possibly have been drugged. Maybe there was something in the air, some sort of aphrodisiac or hallucinogenic that made everyone lose their inhibitions.

Zander didn't care. He didn't care that he had run away from home. He didn't care that his parents were most likely chasing after him. He didn't care that there was a race called Circe that his parents feared or that their fear affected him somehow.

All he wanted was to *be*. He wanted to feel, to touch. He wanted more of the wild release that filled his mind and body. He was totally without thought. His body took over.

A girl fell into his arms. Young, fresh, soft, her mask torn away, her bright red hair streaming around her in wild abandon. Zander kissed her and she kissed him back, her arms snaking around his neck as she pressed against him.

In the next moment he sprawled into the street, pushed by someone. Years of training took over and Zander rolled back on his shoulders and arched onto his feet, instantly ready to fight.

"She's taken," a man, considerably larger and considerably older, growled at him as he pushed the redhead behind him.

Zander responded with a wheelhouse kick that staggered the man and followed up with a sweep kick that took his legs out from under him.

Someone jumped him from behind and he had no trouble flipping his assailant over his shoulder and onto the other man.

Zander bounced on the balls of his feet three times. He tilted his neck to the side until he heard the familiar pop. He was invincible. He wanted to fight. He was ready for anyone, anything.

"*Zander?*"

"*Leave me be, Elle.*"

She was far enough away that he wasn't worried about her finding him just yet. Boone must have tracked the Firebird. Which meant his parents would be close behind.

The redheaded girl was on the ground on her knees, concern evident for the man Zander had dropped. Maybe she was taken. Zander didn't care. There were plenty of other girls around. Right now his blood was boiling for the fight, just like it had been on Oasis, when his father thought it was all a game.

The two men clambered to their feet and Zander grinned.

This is fun.

"Protectors!" someone yelled. Suddenly the crowd around them turned away, their attention once more on the parade. The two men looked at each other and a red light flashed across their faces. Zander turned and saw a hoverpod headed toward them.

"Cease and desist," one of the uniformed men on the pod said through a voice enhancer.

"Best run," the redheaded girl said as she looked at Zander with a sly smile.

Zander didn't wait. He dashed into the crowd. The last thing he wanted was for his father to find him in a security station.

He heard the shouts of the security detail but he ignored them. He still felt invincible. The crowd seemed to be thickening as a mob gathered in front of a kiosk. It was covered with several huge dige screens and a hologram of the word Murlaca hung in the air over the top of the kiosk. Zander caught a glimpse of three-dimensional blood coming from the screen as curved blades slashed. The crowd squealed and shouted as if they were actually splattered with the blood and he turned to look.

Zander threw a quick look over his shoulder to check if he was still being chased, and when he saw no one after him he went closer to the kiosk. Diges played over and over, each one featuring either men or women, all clad in close-fitting armor with gauntlets on their arms covered with several hooked blades running down the underside from their elbows to their wrists.

Words ran on the bottoms of the screen proclaiming the names and records of the fighters and how many kills each one had. That was followed by an invitation to the matches and the times.

Zander even flinched when the image of blood came toward him. He was disgusted by it and quickly turned and crashed into a woman dressed entirely in robes of black.

"I'm sorry," he said quickly as the woman staggered back.

She let out a hiss of disgust and shook off the hands of the two men, also masked and in black, who attempted to steady her. Two more men stood behind her dressed as the others and ready to do battle.

Zander suppressed a grin at the sight of her poufy hat, which he had set askew when he bumped into her. It was covered with beads and sparkles and seemed a bit ornate, even for the Carnival atmosphere.

"Fool." She spat the word out, viciously, as if he were contaminated with some disgusting disease. Then suddenly she stared at him.

As soon as her eyes caught his Zander felt as if he were caught in a trap. As if he were staring death in the face and could do nothing to stop it. A strange feeling started in his spine and moved up into his mind, as if a snake slithered up his back.

"Aberrant," the woman said as she looked closely at Zander's face.

She acted as if she smelled something horrible. A strange consuming fear overcame Zander as he looked into eyes the same exact color as his own. He was used to seeing eyes that color, everyone in his family had eyes like his, but these were different. They were flat. They were lifeless. They were evil.

My mind is my own.

He turned and ran, not even conscious of starting the litany.

Suddenly he doubled over in pain and he knew it came from the woman. The same way it could come from Elle. And his mother and father.

No other may possess it.

"You fools. He's getting away."

He heard her voice in his mind and he heard it shouted on the streets. The pain was horrible but he kept running. He had to. He suddenly knew what it was his parents feared. He knew what it was they were hiding him from. He now knew what the Circe was. And he knew that his family was part of them.

But he didn't know why they were after him.

Aberrant. . . .

The word rang in his mind. The pain he felt coursing throughout his body told him to stop but he knew better.

I will keep my mind and use it to overcome my enemies.

Why was this woman his enemy?

Zander saw steps, leading downward. A tunnel, one that led to the transports. If only he could make it.

He almost fell down the steps. She was trying harder to stop him. He could feel her desperation.

The crowd protested as he jumped over the rail and

shoved people out of his way in his haste to escape. There was a line leading into a scanner, and though he had no idea what it was there for he burst through it to the protests of several transportation workers.

Zander ignored them and ran toward the transport. He jumped inside and the door slid shut behind him. His sides heaved from the exertion as he scanned the people milling about on the platform for any sign of the woman in black.

He saw nothing, but he knew she was out there somewhere. He could feel her in his mind.

CHAPTER NINE

"Wake up."

Elle shook her head. She was dreaming. Horrible visions of haggard women with eyes that showed nothing but white. She was nothing more than a babe in her mother's arms and the women took her away as Lilly's screams joined hers.

"Let her die," one of the women said and Elle cried because she knew they were talking about her mother.

"Elle," the voice insisted. She opened her eyes and saw Boone staring down at her, a look of concern on his handsome face. "Drink this," he said. He handed her a bottle of water and gently moved the coseat back into an upright position.

She felt groggy. The inside of her mouth felt like a freshly plowed field and her body was lethargic.

"Don't worry, it's normal," Boone said.

"Where are we?"

"In space above Senate."

Elle looked through the Plexi as she willed her mind to focus on Zander.

"I've got a lock on Firebird," Boone said. "It's in orbit on one of the space stations. We're heading there now so I can lock ELSie down."

"And keep Zander on-planet," Elle concluded.

"Hopefully."

"Do you think he's already on-planet?"

"Wouldn't you be?" Boone motioned to the monitor on the com. It showed what looked like a party going on in the streets of the planet-wide city.

"You could have been," Elle reminded him.

"Maybe if I had, this wouldn't have happened," Boone said.

"Zander would have found a way," Elle said. "It was something he had to do."

Boone nodded. Elle knew he couldn't help but feel guilty since he'd left the Firebird totally accessible to Zander.

"Where . . ."

"Still behind us. They're going to the embassy first to coordinate a search."

"They trust us to go on-planet by ourselves?" Elle asked in disbelief.

"Why shouldn't they? You should be able to find Zander and then we just wait for reinforcements to show up."

"You think he's going to fight?"

"I would," Boone said. "Or I'd run."

"Why do I feel like I'm betraying him?"

"He's got to know what is out there, Elle. After that your family can deal with what's happened."

Elle let out a sigh. She was not looking forward to that.

"Let's just find him," Boone said.

The tractor beam released the ship and Boone guided it into the landing bay. They quickly found the Firebird and Boone locked her down so Zander would be unable to use her to run. Then they made their way to Bay Nine for the shuttle down to the planet. Elle couldn't help but look around in wonder at the mass of people all crowding into the narrow hatch. She stayed close to Boone, her fist clutched in the back of his shirt as they entered the shuttle.

Boone immediately cursed as soon as the doors slid shut with a whoosh.

"What's wrong?" Elle asked.

"Keep your eyes down," he said. "One of my classmates from Academy is on board."

"Are you embarrassed to be seen with me?" Elle asked in his mind.

"Your eyes give you away and will draw too much attention to us." As he formed the words in his mind he circled an arm around Elle and pulled her against his chest. He turned his back to the crowd so she was between him and the hull.

"We've got to find you a mask," he said against the top of her hair.

"Am I that different?"

"Your eyes brand you a Circe. Most people are terrified of them and curse them as witches."

Elle shuddered within Boone's arms, as the realization of how much her parents sheltered her sank in.

Cursed as a witch? The worst she had ever heard was teasing from Zander and Boone.

"Hey, Boone," someone said.

Elle's heart pounded in her chest. What should she do? She kept her head down and pulled her hair around so that it hid the sides of her face.

Boone turned halfway around. "Hey, Kent," he said.

"Thought you were passing on Carnival," Kent said.

"We changed our minds," Boone said. "Can I catch up with you later? My girl just got some bad news."

Elle kept her face buried in Boone's chest.

"Yeah, sure," Kent said. "Sorry about your news," he said, leaning around Boone.

"Thank you," Elle said with her voice muffled

against Boone's chest. It really wasn't a bad place to be. His arms felt strong and secure around her. He held on to her so tightly that the gem from the necklace he gave her felt crushed against her skin. He smelled wonderful, a cinnamon, clove mix from the natural soap made on Oasis. When she was in his arms she felt as if things really were going to be fine. Was this what it meant to love someone? To be loved?

She'd think about that after they found Zander.

"Can you find him?" Boone asked. Strange that *he* seemed to know what she was thinking a lot of the time.

"I'll try," she said.

Elle took a deep breath, centered her being, and concentrated with all her strength. It was hard to concentrate on Zander when Boone smelled so good, but she forced her mind down to the planet below as she reached out for her brother.

"Leave me be, Elle."

She saw two men sprawled on the street and a redhaired girl kneeling beside one of them before Zander shut her out.

"He's in a fight," Elle said when she came back to Boone. "I don't see any Circe, just some men who look like workers of some kind." Her mind went back to recapture everything she had seen and heard through Zander. "They were on the ground." What was Zander feeling when she'd entered his mind? "He's not frightened. He's happy."

"Did he feel you?"

"He told me to leave him alone." She looked up at Boone. He seemed to think what she had seen was funny.

"Then he's safe . . . so far."

"But he's in a fight," Elle protested.

"You said he was happy," Boone explained. His green eyes danced.

"Men are just stupid," Elle snapped back. "You think fighting is fun."

"Well, sometimes it is," Boone said with a wry grin. "Zander's on his own for the first time in his life. And if the men are on the ground, then he's winning the fight. So he's proven that he can take care of himself."

"But he doesn't—"

"That's why we have to find him," Boone said. "So he'll know."

The shuttle landed and they fell into line to disembark. Elle walked in front of Boone with her head bent and her waist-length hair covering the sides of her face. They followed the chattering throng through a small tunnel and out into a huge dome.

The noise was deafening. Elle couldn't help but shudder as the cacophony of sound pounded against her ears. She fought the urge to clamp her hands to her head to block out the horrible mix of pounding music and screeching voices. There was too much noise, too much space, and way too many people crowded around them. Thoughts and voices from the others started an assault on her mind and she wondered if she'd be able to breathe.

She realized that Boone felt her panic when his hands grasped her upper arms from behind and gave a gentle squeeze.

"Just relax," he said against her ear. He guided her toward a building and once again sheltered her from the crowd by placing her between the wall and his body. "Take a deep breath," he said. "Center yourself."

Elle nodded and did as she was told. There was nothing to fear. Boone would protect her. Her parents were probably already on the satellite above and her father was at this very moment issuing orders and making plans to find Zander.

She could help. All she had to do was concentrate on her brother.

And avoid a horde of murderous telepaths with eyes the same color as hers who would probably know the instant she communicated with Zander.

She took a deep breath and went to her center.

"Better?" Boone asked.

"Yes," she said, looking up at him.

"Put this on." He handed her a set of eye shields that had feathers going up both sides and brightly colored spangles around the frames.

Elle made a face. "Do I have to?'

"Yes, you do."

"Where did you get these?"

Boone made a motion with his head back over his shoulder. "They're everywhere."

Elle felt a moment of panic when she realized that she had not been aware of Boone even picking up the shields. She steadied herself once again and slid them into place. "What now?" she asked.

Boone suppressed a funny sound as she looked around the boulevard with sudden interest. She felt well protected with her eyes covered behind the shields and her curiosity was piqued after she'd gotten over the initial shock of being in the middle of the huge celebration.

"I hope you're not laughing at me or the way I look in these ridiculous shields," Elle said coolly without turning to look at him. "Because you know that would be a big mistake on your part."

"I would never dream of laughing at you," Boone said with a hint of a grin as they stepped into the street. There was a parade going on and the people along the route were fighting to catch strands of beads that were thrown from the wildly decorated hoverpods.

Elle gave him a sideways look and saw that he had trouble keeping his lips in a serious line. She debated throwing a quick searing pain his way but decided against it. The Carnival atmosphere certainly made one feel carefree and forgetful of one's task.

Was there something in the atmosphere? Something added?

The thought was fleeting as she was overcome with a sudden uncontrollable urge to kiss Boone. He certainly looked kissable with the way his lips quirked from trying not to laugh at her. His eyes seemed greener, if that was possible, and the shadow of a beard that covered his jaw made him appear dangerous, in a way that excited her.

The look he gave her sent a shiver down her spine. It was full of longing, but also full of promise. It made her think of things she was sure she wasn't ready for. But it also made her want to be impetuous, wild, free. To experience things. To feel things.

She knew, without the mind connection, exactly what Zander had felt inside when he ran off. He had acted on his feelings. Why shouldn't she do the same?

And why shouldn't she act right now when a woman from the crowd was looking at Boone like he was a special prize that she was destined to win? The woman moved toward him with several strands of beads dangling in her hands as if she was about to place them around his neck.

Before she could touch him the woman stumbled to the curb, her hands clenched over her head as she wailed in pain. Her beads fell to the street and some onlookers scrambled to grab them in what seemed to be a contest to collect the most strands.

"Did you do that?" Boone asked. He took Elle's arm and guided her away from the screaming woman.

"Yes," Elle said as the crowd separated them from her victim. "I didn't like the way she was looking at you." She jerked her arm away indignantly but Boone took it again, this time commanding her attention as he pressed her up against the wall.

Boone *was* dangerous. Why was it she never noticed it before?

Or perhaps she had. She certainly noticed it the last night on Oasis when she came to his room. And she couldn't help but notice it now as his eyes moved over her face, searing into her, branding her.

She looked into his eyes through the dark hue of the

shields and saw the raw hunger simmering, beneath his usual self-confident facade. His body pressed up against hers in a way that felt achingly familiar yet strange as she felt her gut tighten and a strange longing fill her body.

"How about the way I'm looking at you, Elle?" Boone said, his voice low and husky. It made her tremble, just to hear it and to see the way his mouth moved with the words. His eyes once again roamed over her, as if he were deciding exactly where to kiss her.

Please kiss me.

His lips brushed against hers in a passive manner, as if he was teasing her, which surprised her. She had expected Boone to be more urgent and demanding once again. Instead he placed his hands on the wall on either side of her head and moved away from her. She tried to lean into him but found she couldn't since his lower body was at an impossible angle. His legs were spread apart and his arms braced as if he were sheltering her. He pulled his head away as he caught her lips deliciously between his teeth, gently tugging the full part of her bottom lip toward him.

Elle whimpered in frustration.

The crowds swelled around them but Boone's arms remained steady against the wall as he leaned in, his palms and forearms pressed against the solid surface and his body so tantalizing close yet too far away.

She didn't care about the people. She didn't care who could see what they were doing. She just knew she wanted Boone, all of Boone, in a way that she had never felt before. She was desperate for him.

Desperate enough to move him with her mind. She pushed the ridiculous shields up on her forehead and looked into his eyes.

"Elle," he said in a hoarse whisper as she forced his will to her own and made his lips come toward her again. "What are you doing?" His body followed until he was pressed up against the length of her from head to toe.

His eyes narrowed as if he would fight her and she knew what she was doing was wrong. But she couldn't help stop.

He didn't fight her. He kissed her as if his life depended on it.

Elle was vaguely aware that they were in a very public place. She felt the impact of bodies bumping into Boone yet none touched her. He would not allow it.

They should go someplace, any place, private. Desire coursed through her. Her blood boiled with it. And she knew Boone felt it too. His breathing was ragged as he tore his lips away from hers to draw a breath before he began an assault upon the tender skin of her cheek and neck.

Yet something nagged at the corner of her mind.

"Elle?"

She ignored it. Probably her mother or father . . .

"Please hear me, Elle."

"Zander?"

"Help me, Elle."

Her eyes flew open and she pushed Boone away. He blinked as if coming awake from a long sleep.

"Zander," she gasped. "He's trying to communicate with me."

"Can he?" Boone looked around as if suddenly realizing their location.

"Only if I'm listening for him," she said.

"Zander? Where are you?" Elle cast her mind out, searching for her brother. She felt as if she were flying over the crowds of people as they grew smaller and smaller until it seemed as if they were all grains of sand on the beach back home. So many faces, all unrecognizable, separated the two of them.

"Show me," she said in her mind.

"I can't. They'll find me."

"Say the litany," she said. *"Try to send me something."*

She caught a quick image. All she recognized was what looked like sunlight reflecting off a curved blade.

"Hur—"

"Zander?"

Nothing.

"Zander?" She said his name aloud, as if he were standing beside her.

"What is it?" Boone asked, his concern clearly evident. "Where is he?"

"He's frightened. He couldn't tell me because he's afraid they'll find him. I think he's in trouble. I think they may have him. He was interrupted."

"The Circe are after him?"

"Who else could it be? He sent me an image. It looked like knives of some kind. Short, curved, I've never seen anything like them."

"The Murlaca," Boone said. "He must be near the pits."

"The what?"

"Come on," he said. Boone grabbed her hand and they took off at a run toward the tunnels.

CHAPTER TEN

"Anything?" Boone asked.

Elle shook her head. He knew she'd been concentrating as hard as she could on Zander the entire time they were on the transport.

How could he have been so foolish? He was supposed to find Zander and bring him home, not seduce his sister in the middle of Carnival. He couldn't stand to think about what could have happened.

What exactly did happen? What was it about Carnival that made people act without regard for the consequences?

"I'm frightened, Boone."

She spoke so quietly that he almost missed it in the excited chatter of the crowd around them.

"We'll find him."

"What if we don't? What if they find him first?"

"Elle . . ." What could he say? If only they had not wasted so much time. What was he . . . were they . . . thinking?

"I'll never forgive myself," Elle said. "We shouldn't have—"

"Don't ever say that. Don't even think it."

He wanted to grab her and hold her tight. He wanted to tell her everything would be fine, but how could he when he didn't know for sure? For the first time since he had come to Oasis as a child, he was truly terrified.

He was terrified of losing Elle.

Boone's eyes scanned the stops listed on the holi above their heads. One more stop until the pits. Diges flashed on the walls, battles were being fought as they traveled, and the crowd watched in morbid fascination.

One visit to the pits had been enough for Boone. He'd gone during the last Carnival and immediately regretted it. It was nothing more than an excuse for assassination. When he mentioned it to his father Ruben told him of Shaun's experience there and how lucky he'd been to come through it alive. If not for the fact that he was Circe, he never would have survived it.

What a strange twist of fate that Zander was in peril at the same place Shaun had been.

He felt the vibration in his pocket and pulled out his com link.

"Boone?" He could barely make out his father's voice. The reception was horrible because of the transport and the noise around them.

"We think we know where he is," Boone said. "Elle's been in contact with him."

He heard nothing but static.

"Go to the pits," he said in hope that they could hear him.

The link went dead. Not a good sign.

Elle felt it too. He could tell by the look on her face. They were Zander's only hope at the moment.

"Next stop," Boone said as if that would make everything all right. "Hopefully we can link again when we get out of the tunnel."

Elle nodded in agreement but her face was pale beneath the ridiculous mask.

She was trying to find Zander.

Of course the crowd moved even slower now. Or maybe it was their fear that made it seem as if the entire population came to a complete stop right in their path. Boone had the benefit of being able to see over most of the heads in front of them. He kept a tight hold on Elle's arm, not willing to risk the possibility of becoming separated from her.

Everyone was pouring into the pits. Everyone. Boone was doubtful they would be able to move, much less find Zander. He could hear the roar of the crowd and the amplified voice of the announcer from the transport station.

"Anything?" he asked.

Elle shook her head.

"We've got to know if he's in there," Boone said.

"Don't you think I know that?"

Boone looked around for a place, any place where she could center her mind. A fountain built into a wall caught his attention and he dragged Elle through the crowd, much as if he were swimming against a tide, until they were next to the wall.

Water trickled down a rippled piece of metal and into a low-ledged depression that was around knee high and barely as wide as his palm. Artificial trees stood on either side of it.

It wasn't Oasis but it was the closest thing to it in the madness that surrounded them.

"Concentrate on the water," he said as he once again placed himself between Elle and the crowd.

Elle pulled off her shields and took a deep cleansing breath. Boone stared at the water trickling down and tried to imagine himself on Oasis, as if he could help Elle put herself there. He stood as close as he could without touching her, his spine rigid to keep the jostling crowd from distracting her. He saw her shoulders relax and knew that she had achieved a deep level of concentration.

"Zander." Elle whispered her brother's name. To Boone's ears it sounded like a sigh. She was silent for a long moment, so still that he wondered if she was breathing. Then her body trembled.

"Run," she said in a strangled voice.

Then she screamed. *"Run!"*

Elle turned into him as if she was preparing to run and Boone grabbed her as she screamed again.

"What is it?" He was aware that people stopped to look as she fought against his arms. He needed to quiet her before someone misunderstood what was going on and decided to get involved.

Tears streamed from her eyes. "They found him," she said.

CHAPTER ELEVEN

They were there. Everywhere he turned. He could feel them in his mind and he saw the men in black advancing on him through the crowd.

It was almost as if they knew what he was thinking. But how could they?

Zander knew the woman with the dead eyes was out there, somewhere. He felt her search. He knew she was attempting to enter his mind. Somehow he kept moving because he knew that if he could keep her from seeing him, then she could not hurt him.

My mind is my own.

He repeated the litany, over and over again. He barreled his way through the crowds, not caring that he knocked people aside. He ran down a long flight of steps that were set in a carved-out depression in the ground.

The crowd roared, ignoring his desperation. The multitude's attention was on the center, where a huge cage stood. Zander quickly surmised that he was in some type of arena. He scanned ahead in hopes of finding an escape route.

The people he crashed into in his haste cursed him and some even threw things at him: food, half-empty cups; he felt the wet on the back of his shirt and occasionally threw up an arm to fend off some of the more dangerous missiles that came his way.

He reached the bottom of the long staircase and was immediately pushed back by a security guard. Zander threw a quick palm strike to the man's chin and bolted by as he staggered back.

A woman screamed and he unconsciously looked her way and saw that her face was sprayed with blood. And she seemed to be enjoying it. She jumped up and down and her tongue flicked out to lick the droplets.

Zander quickened his pace as he saw an opening on the opposite side and his feet slid, throwing him temporarily off balance. He realized that it was blood. The entire area around the bottom of the arena was covered with it and with horror he looked toward the cage and saw that it dripped from the sides.

Zander looked up as he scrambled for his footing. A man stood in the center of the ring. He wore leather armor and his chest heaved up and down with exertion. His forearms were covered with a series of long hooked blades. At his feet lay a body that dripped blood from a gaping wound across the throat.

Zander was barely conscious of the frenzied screaming around him as his mind tried to absorb the horror, the confusion, and the fear.

Why did I ever leave home?

"Zander?"

"Elle . . ."

"Where are you?"

"I don't know. An arena. Murlaca. They're after me."

Then he felt it. The creepy, slithery sensation, as if his mind was invaded by a horrible, evil creature.

The woman was in his mind. Somehow, through Elle, she found him.

Zander felt Elle's awareness of the woman. Her mind recoiled in fear and he felt her pull away. The fear in his mind grew stronger.

"Run, Zander. Run." She didn't leave him. She should. She should be far away from his place. He deserved whatever happened for his stupidity, but not Elle. If only he could tell Boone to take her away. If only . . .

"Stay away, Elle." He made for the steps. He sensed the presence of the black-uniformed men. The evil in his mind directed them to his location. His only hope was to outrun them.

"Run. We're coming."

Zander felt the rush of thrill run through the evil that was connected to his mind. He had to protect Elle.

"No! Stay away. They'll get you. I don't want them to get you."

The evil chortled in glee. His mind filled with an obscene cackling noise and he once again felt the pain begin. His throat began to close and he choked. He knew it for a mind trick and he said the litany as he bolted up the steps.

How long could he outrun them? He couldn't breathe but he also couldn't stop. He put his shoulder down as he reached the top and barreled through. Bodies flew aside, crashed into one another, and Zander ran on, headed for the gate.

He felt them. They were right behind him. If he could just make the gate.

"Run, Zander. Run. We're coming."

CHAPTER TWELVE

"We've got to find him," Elle said.

"I know," Boone said. He held her hand in his as they fought their way through the line toward the entrance to the pits. "This place is so big, he could be anywhere."

"He was running up steps," Elle said. "I think he's coming out."

"Which side? There are four exits."

"I don't know."

Boone punched his link. "Are you there?"

"We're on-planet." Ruben's voice came back and Elle immediately felt a sense of relief. Surely with their parents here they could save Zander. "We're coming toward the pits but the crowd is slowing us down."

"Hurry," Boone said. "They're after him."

"What do you know?" It was her father's voice.

"Elle connected with him," Boone explained. "He's running. We know he's trying to get out of the pits but we don't know which side."

"Where exactly are you?"

Elle looked around, totally lost, as Boone glanced up at the holi over the entrance. "We're on the east side."

"Circle it," Shaun instructed. "We'll come at it from the other side."

"Yes, sir," Boone said and slid the link back in his pocket. Boone led her out of the line and she saw the relief on his face. "We'll find him," he said.

Elle looked into his eyes. She trusted him. She knew he wouldn't stop until Zander was safe.

Boone's eyes scanned the crowd and Elle darted her head back and forth, trying to see over or around the heads and shoulders that blocked their way. The going wasn't so difficult now since most of the people were stationary and watching the pits from the railing that surrounded it. But it was still crowded.

Where did all these people come from? Elle never dreamed there were so many people in the universe, much less so many gathered together on one planet.

And Boone seemed totally in control. Even with all the frustration she sensed in his mind, he didn't panic. He knew what needed to be done and he did it.

He was the same boy she knew since childhood but now she saw him as a man. How could she have doubted her feelings for him? Boone had seen plenty and he still chose her. Why did she have to hesitate when the best was right beside her, with her hand in his? He protected her without smothering her. He respected her abilities and trusted her instincts.

Elle studied Boone's profile as his attention was caught by something in the distance.

Was there something in the atmosphere that was distracting her as before? Was she caught up in the moment of Carnival?

She took a deep breath to center herself. Her mind was clear. They needed to find Zander, and quickly.

And she loved Boone.

"Can you see anything?" Boone asked.

Yes. Elle felt her heart take a great leap as her mind voiced what she just realized. She loved Boone. But now was not the time to tell him. She'd tell him later. When this was over. When Zander was safe. Where there was time.

"Zander?"

She didn't want to go there again. When she realized the Circe witch was in Zander's mind she had felt a horrible evil. She didn't know such a terrible thing existed until she saw it all so clearly in Zander's mind.

Somehow the witch had used her mind to find Zander. She thought such a thing impossible until she felt it and with it came all the knowledge of the Circe intent. Zander was a rare prize, and whoever captured him would be greatly rewarded with more power. That was the thing the Circe desired more than anything. Power over each other.

How could it be that her mother came from this race? And her father? There was no evil in them, none that she ever sensed, and there certainly was no evil in her and Zander.

What drove these women to be this way?

Did she put Zander at more risk by trying to contact him? She knew he was using the litany. Zander had always been good at blocking; perhaps that would help him now. But how could he concentrate when he was running for his life?

Use the witch.

Could she? Dare she? She never attempted it before. How did you contact someone you did not know?

You know her . . . You saw her.

Elle wanted to block the image. She wanted to lose it forever. The pure glee that the woman felt when she centered on Zander. There was no compassion inside her. No pity. Just a never-ending greed. The witch considered Zander nothing more than an instrument for her own end. A prize. The fact that he was a person did not move her. The fact that he was terrified was nothing more than an added bonus.

"This way," Boone said. Something caught his attention and he moved with a purpose. Elle couldn't see where they were going but trusted him to lead her.

Do it.

Could she concentrate enough while they were moving? She didn't want to risk stopping. Especially if Boone thought he knew where Zander was.

Just concentrate on the evil.

It was tangible enough. Like a person it breathed and it bent to the will of the one who created it. It was a powerful force.

It was waiting for her.

Elle gasped as she felt it take hold in her mind. She was not prepared for this. She was not strong enough. She squeezed Boone's hand as if he would give her strength. He spared a moment to look at her, then turned once again to the movement that caught his attention and pulled Elle after him.

The evil entered her mind and gleefully went after all her secrets.

My mind is my own. She began the litany as she fought against the slimy, slithering, snakelike feeling that penetrated the nerve endings in her brain. Her skin crawled. The vessels that carried the blood beneath her skin felt as if they were turning into live creatures that wanted nothing more than to break through the fragile covering that contained them.

"Foolish child. You cannot fight me."

My mind is my own . . . Elle began again. She tried to will her mind into submission. Into a peaceful place. She willed her mind to fight.

"I know what frightens you, child. I know your secrets now."

"No." Elle said the word aloud, as if it would stop the demon in her mind.

It laughed at her.

Then it showed her its power.

"Zander." He was before her. Did Boone not see him? Why didn't he stop? Elle jerked to a stop.

Zander smiled at her. There was nothing wrong with him. No one was after him. It was all a joke, a game he played. There was no danger here. It was all a fabrication, a lie that their parents made up because they hated them and wanted to keep them prisoner for the rest of their lives. Zander told her so. He told her with his mind and Elle was amazed because he'd never been able to initiate communication before.

Elle knew that everything she saw and felt was not true yet the thoughts in her mind were so powerful that she could not help but listen to them.

Then, just when she realized that perhaps, just possibly, it could be true, Zander's face contorted and he let out a horrific scream. He raised his hands in horror and Elle saw that they were on fire. His hands were torches and the flames traveled up his arms and down his sides until his entire body was a conflagration. And through the inferno she saw the pain and horror on his face.

"Help me, Elle!" he screamed. And Elle screamed too. She knew she was screaming because she heard herself, but it seemed as if she were so very far away.

And Boone even farther. She saw him look at her in confusion and terror but he was so small she felt as if she were at the bottom of a long narrow shaft looking up.

She was conscious of all the people who looked at her as if she were insane. Why were they looking at her when her brother was burning up? He was still alive, she could hear him, yet no one made a move to help him. Not even Boone, who seemed dumbstruck. What was wrong with everyone? Elle felt as if the entire planet of people had gone daft and she was the only one who saw what was real. Was it real? Her mind tried to focus but all she felt was the evil. The despair. The glee.

But most confusing of all was when she saw Zander burst through the flames. How could he be running toward her when he was on fire? Why was he telling her to run when he was dying?

And why was Boone's fist coming at her face? She watched it come, slowly, as if it were all a dream, yet she knew that it was coming fast. So fast that she could not block it.

The last thing she saw before the darkness came was Boone's face. Why was he crying? Was it because Zander was dead? It was all his fault. He'd done nothing to stop it.

The evil laughed gleefully as she slid into oblivion.

CHAPTER THIRTEEN

Boone caught Elle before she fell to the ground. He scooped her up into his arms and turned in time to see Zander stumble as two men clad entirely in black dived at his legs.

The crowd, who just moments earlier were fascinated by Elle's hysteria, now turned to watch Zander struggle against the men as they hauled him to his feet. He managed to get one arm free and landed a sound blow directly to where a nose should be under the mask and the man staggered back, his hands clutched to his black-covered face. Before Zander could press his attack, two more men jumped into the fray.

It looked as if Zander was choking, or else in some sort of pain. His face was contorted and Boone could see his gasps from where he stood with Elle sheltered safely in his arms.

A Circe witch moved in behind Zander, her pale eyes and face a sharp contrast to the stark black of her robes and ridiculously decorated hat.

Boone knew what would come next. The minions finally subdued Zander enough for one of them to snap a collar around his neck. The white circle started blinking immediately and Zander's face went blank as his body stilled and his will submitted.

The witch looked beyond her prisoner. Her eyes scanned the crowd, back and forth, the pale eyes darting as the people turned away in fear.

None would dare interfere with a Circe.

The witch was searching for Elle. She used her mental powers to try to make the connection with her mind.

Boone hated the fact that he hit Elle. But it was the only way he could protect her. Elle was unconscious and the witch could not tap into her mind. He knew he was no match for a Circe, especially one who had four armed guards at her command. And he'd seen the effect the witch had on Elle. He didn't know what she saw but it was horrible. The look on her face told the tale.

Boone disappeared into the crowd with Elle safe in his arms and headed toward the transport. He needed to get Elle as far away from the Circe as possible.

He felt the link vibrate in his pocket but he didn't dare stop long enough to take it out until he was sure he was far enough away from the Circe. Now that they had Zander under their control it would be a small matter to search the surrounding crowd.

No one stopped him as he made his way back to the station. It was a common occurrence during Carnival for the revelers to succumb to the food, drink, and assorted other offerings. To the assembled Elle was nothing more than a weak spirit with little or no self-control.

Boone was glad for the anonymity. It wasn't until they were safely on a transport that he realized he was shaking. He fell into a seat on the surprisingly empty transport and held Elle on his lap with one arm while he pulled out the link with the other.

And got nothing but static. He forgot it wouldn't work on the transport. How could he forget something that simple when lives were at stake?

Their parents were out there, somewhere, looking for Zander. And he had just walked away from him. He left him. He couldn't tell them where he was. He couldn't help him. All he could do was get Elle away from there. Away from the Circe.

He sacrificed Zander to protect Elle.

Maybe Lilly and Shaun were able to link with Zander like Elle had. Couldn't they? Certainly they were stronger than Elle.

But Elle had said nothing about communicating with her parents. Had Zander's blocking of the witch kept Lilly and Shaun out too? And Elle did have the benefit of having had a response from Zander.

Boone's mind whirled with all the possibilities and none of his conclusions satisfied him. The truth was he'd abandoned his best friend. He sacrificed him to keep Elle safe.

Boone knew in his heart that Zander would have wanted it that way, but he still couldn't help but feel as if he'd failed. He let him down. He had also failed his parents and Zander's and most importantly in his mind, he had failed Elle.

Even though he sought to protect her she would not care about that. All she cared about was saving her brother.

And he would have to be the one to tell her that Zander was gone. The Circe had him. He had no way to fight them because he now wore the collar.

Boone looked down at Elle. Her hair covered her face and he smoothed it back to reveal a bruise darkening her face where he'd struck her.

She would most likely be extremely angry with him when she woke up. But Boone wasn't sure there was anything else he could have done. He kept replaying

the scene over and over in his mind and he came up
with the same results.

He should have done something to save Zander.

"I'm sorry," he said, knowing that she could not hear
him. Her face remained impassive. He dreaded to see
the tears that would surely come. "I'm so sorry." Boone
pulled her close, his arms tight as if he feared that she
too would be taken.

He should have done something.

CHAPTER FOURTEEN

"This is the son." The woman's nails dug into Zander's cheek as she gripped his jaw, turning his head from side to side as if to get a better look at him. "He is the image of the father."

"I knew as soon as I saw him." The woman who captured him agreed.

"How fortunate, Arleta, that you just happened to find him," the woman with the sharp nails said.

There was hidden meaning in those words. Zander's mind scrambled. It was the only thing about him that was capable of functioning at the moment. His body was totally under the control of the one who captured him, due to the blinking collar they placed around his neck. His body had submitted to their commands but his mind was screaming against the constraints.

He tried to fight them as they led him to a building close to where he'd been captured. He was surprised by the look of the place; he'd expected them to take

him to some sort of palace instead of what appeared to
be a warehouse or storage facility.

In spite of his desire to escape, his feet felt obliged to
follow along and even his head stayed bowed in a submissive pose, even though his anger boiled and raged
on the inside.

He sensed the evil around him as they led him into
the presence of a woman wearing a hat more extreme
than that of the one who captured him, if that was possible. And the fact that she seemed vaguely familiar to
him disturbed him more than her distasteful perusal of
his looks. She was younger than the one who captured
him and his mind saw her as younger still. Was it a trick?

"What of the sister?"

"She escaped," the one called Arleta said. "She was
aware of us."

The woman lifted an eyebrow as if in admiration of
Elle. Zander felt his mind swell with pride. He knew
Boone would do whatever necessary to protect his sister.

If only he had the luxury of being forewarned as
Elle was.

If only he'd stayed on Oasis where he was safe.

I'm sorry. . . .

The woman released his jaw and walked around
him as if he were a beast of burden being offered at an
auction.

He wanted to jerk away from her. He wanted to run.
He wanted to beat the men stationed on either side of
him into the floor. But mostly he wanted to wipe the
smug look off the face of the woman who was now considering him as if he were something she had on the
bottom of her shoe.

He couldn't even make a sound. The thing they had
put around his neck kept him immobile, waiting on the
will of the woman. And he knew her will. He felt her
slithering around inside his head like a snake.

"What is your name?" she asked.

Don't tell her. Don't tell her. Don't tell her.

"I already know it, boy. Don't you realize that I've already found out everything I need to know?"

She had. She knew everything about him. Or nearly everything.

My mind is my own.

"Tell me your name." Her nostrils flared, disgustingly close, and her eyes narrowed.

"Al . . . ex . . . ander . . . Phoe . . . nix."

Was that his voice? It didn't even sound like his own. How could he speak without wanting to?

"Named after your grandfather. How touching."

I hate you.

Zander felt the hatred bubbling up from deep within him and an image formed in his mind, one of his hands around her throat, choking the life from her until her pale eyes rolled up into her head.

She laughed. "How amusing," she said. "He wants to kill me." She stepped back to consider him. "You can't, can you?"

Let me loose and I'll show you.

"The best breeding and there's nothing there." She sneered at him.

Her words and tone disgusted him. She spoke of his parents as if they were nothing. And yet it sounded vaguely familiar.

I thought we might be on to something with the breeding.

"No powers. No abilities. Nothing," she continued.

"Are you sure?" Arleta asked.

"You dare to question me?"

"I recall how his father tricked Honora," Arleta said.

"And his mother tricked her also," the woman said. "Which led to your present status, I believe."

Zander sensed the resentment in Arleta.

Good. I hope you're miserable.

The witch snorted in contempt. "*I* was aware of his father's abilities."

Arleta opened her mouth as if to speak and then snapped it shut.

They know my father. What happened? Why? How?

"Yes, I know of your father," the witch said. "I witnessed the full force of your father's power. And Arleta herself was the victim of your mother's treachery and betrayal of her race."

My mind is my own. Whatever his parents had done, he was glad for it. Glad they had put these women in their place.

"His mother has trained him," Arleta said. "He knows the litany. He knows how to use it."

The other woman stepped away from him. "Take off the collar," she commanded the men. "Let us see how well his mother has trained him."

One of the guards moved to take the collar off. As soon as he unsnapped it, Zander felt his will return. But he waited. Waited until the man had turned away before he exploded.

With his father's training.

A side kick put down the man with the collar in his hand. He stumbled sideways into a pillar. Zander followed with a spinning side kick to the opposite guard. He moved so fast that they were both caught off guard, but it did not matter.

Zander fell to the floor with a scream. Every cell in his body had exploded into a blazing pain. His back arched against it then he went into uncontrollable spasms, jerking against the cold marble.

"Tsk," the witch said. "You disappoint me, Alexander. I know your mother would be appalled to see how easily I have conquered you."

She released her hold. He knew it wasn't real. Yet he felt as if his body had exploded into innumerable molecules and then come back together in the wrong form.

Zander rolled to his hands and knees and tried to catch his breath.

My mind is my own.

He couldn't breathe. His hand went to his throat as

he fell once again to the floor, clutching at nothing, grasping for the mental hold that choked him.

She walked toward him as he struggled to draw a breath.

It's not real . . . you can fight this . . . my mind is my own . . . my mind is my own . . .

"Your mind is mine." She spat the words in disgust. "And I will take it."

He was choking. He was dying. And she was taking his mind?

Just let me breathe. Just fight me fair.

The guards dragged him to his feet. He hung between them, trying to breathe, but the noose around his neck seemed tighter. His throat rattled dryly as she placed her hands on either side of his face. Her eyes, pale, lifeless, evil, bored into his as darkness circled around him.

"Give me your memories and you will breathe again." His teeth clenched against her hands on his face. It was as if she meant to squeeze his mind from his skull. "Give them to me and you will live."

Elle escaped. Elle escaped.

If only I could breathe. . . .

Father . . . if only I had known.

CHAPTER FIFTEEN

Boone carried Elle into the embassy palace. Tess met him at the door as a servant let him in, worry plainly written on her face.

"What happened?" she asked.

"They got him," Boone said. He carried Elle to an overstuffed chaise and gently placed her on it, then smoothed her hair back from its wild disarray.

"I know," Tess said. "Lilly sensed it. She couldn't locate Zander because he was blocking the Circe out, but she sensed the victory in the woman who captured him. It was an old enemy of hers. One who lost power when Shaun and Lilly fought against the Circe."

"I couldn't help him, Mema," Boone said. "I was afraid they would take Elle too." He looked helplessly toward the chaise and Elle's bruised cheek. "I hit her. She was linked to the witch so I knocked her out."

"You did what you had to do to protect her," Tess said.

Boone collapsed into a chair and put his hands over his face. "I saw him go down. I watched when they put

the collar on him. I should have done something."
Once more the anguish rose in his throat like bile. He
swallowed it back. He couldn't fall apart now. There
was still a chance they could find Zander.

"Boone." Tess knelt in front of him and took his
hands into hers. "You can't fight them. You don't have
the power. You saved Elle. Be grateful for that."

"But, Zander . . . I had to choose. I couldn't save him."

"You aren't responsible for the choices Zander
made." Tears filled his mother's eyes and trickled
down her cheek. Were they for Zander or for her son?
"It's not your fault."

"But he didn't know, Mema. He didn't know. I
should have told him. They should have told him."

Boone felt his mother's arms come around his neck.
She pulled him close as if he were still a child.

I can't cry . . . I have to be strong. How easy it would be
to break down and cry on his mother's shoulder. How
easy it would be to let her comfort him, to make the
pain go away. If only it would all go away.

"Zander!"

Boone jumped up as Tess stumbled away.

Elle sat upright on the chaise, her eyes wild as she
screamed her brother's name.

"Elle!" Boone ran to her.

"He's gone, Boone. He's gone."

"I know." His hand trailed up her arm and wrapped
around her biceps. "They took him."

"No." She shook her head. "He's gone. I can't feel
him anymore." Tears filled her eyes as she looked up at
him. "He's dead."

CHAPTER SIXTEEN

There was awareness. There was a huge room. A cold floor. Hands that pulled him to his feet. Nothing there that he knew. And then he realized that he knew nothing.

"Send him to the pits." A woman spoke. A woman with cold, vacant eyes. Who was she?

"To be killed?" another one asked as the first one turned away.

The woman paused and turned back to look at him. She ran a long nail up his arm and over his chest, which was heaving with exertion. He felt as if he had suffocated and the feeling of fear made him tremble as his mind whirled in panic, trying to land on something familiar.

Who am I?

He dared not voice his fears. That would be a weakness. He wrapped himself around the concept. *Don't show them weakness.*

"No," she said decisively. "I have decided to make

an investment in this one. Tell them to train him. Tell him I think he has great potential at the Murlaca."

"A fitting punishment," the other woman said. "And a tribute to his father."

"Tell them to keep his face covered," she added. "I'd hate to have it . . . scarred . . . in any way."

The men holding his arms turned him toward the door. His feet stumbled. Pits? Murlaca? Where was he going? Why? His mind scrambled, searching, seeking; there was nothing.

He didn't even know his own name.

CHAPTER SEVENTEEN

Her father refused to believe it. "He's not dead," he said when he, her mother, and Ruben returned, white-faced and desperate, after Tess called them back on her link.

Lilly shook her head. "I can't feel him either," she said, her face showing her disbelief. "There's nothing there." Elle watched as Tess wrapped her arms around Lilly's shoulders that seemed suddenly fragile, hollow, as if her mother was empty.

"He is not dead!" Shaun's anger shook the foundation of the embassy and one of the servants screamed in terror in the hallway as glass shattered in the wide-paned doors.

There was no doubting the raw power of her father's rage. Elle had never seen it before. Never. She tried to swallow the sobs that trembled in her body but was unsuccessful and let a desperate gasp escape.

Boone stood across from her, his lips tightly compressed in a stern line, his face set in a mask. He'd been that way since she pushed him away with her hands and with her mind. The realization of what his actions cost them were more than she could stand.

She hated him. She felt it emanating from her body with a life of its own. She should learn how to use it. It should come easily to her since she was a Circe. She knew the feel of such raw power. It had been inside her.

It was his fault. All of it. He should have told them about the Circe before. As soon as he knew about it. He was supposed to be their friend; he knew what the secret was. He knew what it meant. He knew the danger.

And when they were on-planet he was more worried about seducing her than finding her brother. He wasted time that could have been used to catch up with Zander. Time to make sure he was safe.

When Zander was right in front of them, desperate for salvation, he ran and made sure she couldn't do anything to help. The side of her face showed the results of that. Tess had tried to heal the bruise but Elle brushed her away. She wanted Boone to see what he had done.

She wanted Boone to suffer as she was suffering now.

You played a part too.

Her conscience nibbled at her brain as the memory surged of the lust she felt for Boone on-planet. She quickly beat it back into submission. It was a result of Carnival, nothing more. Probably an aphrodisiac of some sort that was piped into the atmosphere beneath the domes.

But what of the night in his room?

It was nothing because she desired it to be nothing. She was a Circe. She was born with the ability to control minds. She would start with hers. She would show control. She would show how strong she was.

She did not love Boone. She did not want Boone. She never wanted to see him again. Seeing him reminded her of Zander. Of her failure. Of Boone's betrayal. Of her brother's lonely death.

Seeing Boone reminded her of pain, and pain was something she never wanted to feel again.

This gut-wrenching, searing emptiness was more than she could stand. Her heart felt as if it were shattered into a million pieces and scattered across the universe, never to be whole again.

She *would* never be whole again. Her brother was gone, dead, because of the evil desires and greed of her own race. They desired power. She would show them power. She would become so strong that the Circe would tremble before her.

And she would never love again. Love meant betrayal. Love meant loss. Love was a weakness she could no longer have.

"Elle!"

She blinked, unaware that her father was talking to her.

"Change your clothes. We're going to see the prefect."

"What?" she said. She looked around the room as if she'd just awakened from a long sleep. Her father was already moving through the door, the wide panels swinging back on their hinges at his mental command. She saw her mother coming toward her and behind that Ruben talking on a link.

"We must find you something suitable to wear," Lilly said as she reached for Elle's hand.

Elle wrenched her arm away from her mother. "Clothing? You're thinking of clothing at a time like this? Don't you know, Mother? Zander is dead. Can't you feel it? There's nothing there." Was that her voice? Was she screaming? Inside she was. Inside her body was a long horrific scream that choked her in its effort to escape.

"We have to make sure. We have to let them know," Lilly said calmly, although her voice trembled.

"Let them know? Why didn't you let us know?" Elle felt her anger boiling inside her. She needed an outlet for it. She needed to share it. She needed to make someone suffer as she was suffering.

Your brother. Her son. Is there a difference in the intensity of the pain?

Her conscience warned her and she listened to it. But she still felt the need to get rid of the pain.

"We should have told you," Lilly said quietly. "We thought there was time."

Elle looked past her mother's apology to Boone. He had not spoken to her since she told him Zander was gone. She saw the remorse in his eyes, the sadness, and the despair. Did he believe her? Or was he simply feeling sorry for himself?

He had no right to feel that way. After all, he was the one responsible for it. For all of it.

"You should have told us," she said to him, forcing her anger across the wide expanse of the room. "You were supposed to be our friend." Boone's vivid green eyes changed from despair to shock. Elle felt some satisfaction at how easily she read him. Without using her abilities she knew just what he was thinking.

"It's not his fault, Elle," Ruben said. "I made him give me his word that he wouldn't tell."

"You said you loved me," Elle continued as she ignored Ruben. She reveled in the pain that she caused him. "Yet you let my brother die."

"Stop it, Elle," Lilly interrupted. "You don't know what you're saying."

"Yes, I do, Mother. Look at my face. Don't you see where he struck me? Zander was right in front of us and he knocked me unconscious so I couldn't help him."

"He saved your life," Tess said. She moved to stand by her son. "They would have taken you too."

"He ran from them."

"Because they would have killed both of you,"

Ruben shouted in anger. "You have no idea what these women are capable of."

"I know *now* what they are capable of," Elle sneered. "I saw it. I felt it. They murdered my brother and *he* let it happen."

"That is enough!" The quiet calm of Lilly's voice held more impact than Ruben's shouts. Or perhaps it was the force of her will that quieted Elle. All she knew was that she was suddenly afraid of her mother.

I want that kind of power.

"Elle, go to my chambers now."

"You forget, Mother, I've never been here. I don't know where your chambers are."

Elle suddenly found herself flung onto a chaise. The piece skidded across the room with the impact of her body and crashed against a pillar. Lilly stood before her, her face inches from hers as she grabbed Elle's face between her hands.

"You are acting like a spoiled child who has lost its toy," Lilly said into her mind. *"And until you act like a grown-up woman you will be confined to my chambers, which you have enough sense to find on your own."*

Elle let out a whimper. The force of her mother's will was painful. She could not even attempt to fight it. She felt her face flush with embarrassment as her mother showed her how trite and spoiled her tirade had been.

"We need you to be the proof of Zander's existence before the prefect. You will go and make yourself presentable. You will represent your family and your planet. You are Princess Arielle of Oasis and you will not show pain or emotion when you are presented. Have I made myself clear?"

Elle realized that her mother allowed her enough room to respond and she slowly nodded her head in agreement.

"Go," Lilly said and Elle scrambled from the chaise and fled the room.

Boone watched her go and felt as if his life was going with her.

What just happened? It feels as if she hates me.

He dropped into a chair and put his hands over his face.

Be strong. Be strong. Be strong.

"Boone," Lilly said. He felt the gentle touch of her hand on top of his head. "We don't blame you for any of this."

"I should have tried—"

"You saved Elle. There was no way you could have saved Zander."

"But . . ."

The tips of her fingers touched his temples.

"Be at peace, Boone. You followed the only path open to you."

Boone felt Lilly's mind enter his and knew she spoke the truth. But still the recriminations, both his and Elle's, haunted him. Lilly chased each one of them down and tried to soothe his conscience.

"We are responsible. We should have told them. We should have warned them. We should have prepared them. We thought there was time. We are grateful that you had the presence of mind to stop Elle. We would have lost her too. Be at peace, Boone."

Lilly answered each and every one of his doubts about what he should have done for Zander.

However, she had no answer for Elle's feelings. His mind tumbled and swirled over her words and the vicious meaning behind them.

"She knows not what she says."

Boone knew better. She knew exactly what she said. She blamed him for Zander's death.

He felt his mother's hand on his shoulder just as Lilly pulled hers away and broke contact with his mind. Boone kept his head down. He was grateful for Lilly taking the time to soothe his fears but questions still spun in his head.

Was Zander really, truly dead? Could Elle tell without actually seeing it happen? What if he wasn't? What could they do to help him? To find him?

"I'll stay here in case there's word," Tess said.

"Stefan is waiting on me," Ruben said. "He's already got his contacts watching the shipping ports."

"The Circe would have immunity for transport," Lilly said. "There's no one with authority to search their crafts."

"He's got that covered too," Ruben explained. "Everything on this chunk of jetsam can be bought, including loyalty."

"Thank you, Ruben," Lilly said.

"You'd do the same," Ruben said. "Boone? Are you coming?"

Boone looked up at his stepfather, who was already on his way out the door.

"Yes," he said. He had to do whatever he could to find his friend. He had to do whatever he could to regain Elle's trust.

"Don't worry too much about Elle," Ruben said as they made their way through the city. The crowd was less now. Many of the partiers were resting up for the evening activities. "She's young. She's grieving."

"We all are," Boone said. He appreciated the fact that even though Zander was gone, their parents were also worried about him. "I just wish she would let me help her."

Ruben stopped and placed his hand on Boone's shoulder. Once again Boone was struck by the fact that Zoey had her father's eyes. "She's in shock, Boone. She's trying to blame someone and blaming Shaun and Lilly is too painful."

"Maybe we should all share in the blame."

"We all make mistakes. But if you want to blame someone, if you want to hate someone, then hate the Circe. They will stop at nothing to get what they want. The lives they destroy are of no consequence to them."

"Yet Lilly is kind. And Shaun. As is Mother, although she doesn't have the abilities."

"It's not the abilities that corrupt them. It's the power that goes with it. Lilly learned control and the value of helping others from Michael. Shaun had parents that loved him and his powers did not come until after he met Lilly. And your mother—your mother is good through the core."

"She is," Boone said as they resumed their pace. They were to meet Stefan in one of the pubs close to the spaceport.

"You knew Shaun awhile before he met Lilly?" Boone asked.

"Seven solars," Rubén said. "He dropped out of Academy, much to his father's disgust, and we partnered up."

"And he showed no abilities whatsoever?"

"None. Except for his eyes. Why?"

"If Shaun's powers didn't show up until he met Lilly, then maybe it will be the same for Zander."

Zander is dead. He refused to believe it. Elle said he was gone. She had a connection, not only because of her abilities, but because he was her twin. But wouldn't he feel it too? Zander was his best friend since childhood. They shared everything.

Almost everything.

"What if a male Circe has to meet his soul mate for his powers to materialize?" Boone asked.

Ruben stopped as if he were startled, then got a faraway look in his eyes.

"Ben?" Boone asked.

"I don't know," he said. He seemed to be thinking about something. "It's strange."

"If Shaun is the only male Circe to live . . ." Boone began.

"Even with your mother," Ruben said.

"What?"

"I know this is not something you want to hear, but

the first time your mother and I made love it was almost as if I was inside her mind. I had never experienced anything like that before."

He was right. Boone didn't want to hear about it. Yet he knew there had always been some sort of mental link between his mother and Ruben.

"She doesn't have the powers but she is a Circe. Maybe there is a trigger of some kind."

"So you think it's possible?"

"I think we've got to find Zander first. Then we'll wonder about the possibilities," Ruben said.

"Do you think he could be alive?"

"Boone, it doesn't matter what I think. It doesn't even matter what Elle thinks she knows or feels. All that matters is what the Circe were thinking when they captured him. And I think the Circe want Shaun and Lilly to suffer."

"But wouldn't that mean they would taunt them? That they would prove it to them?"

"I guess Shaun and Lilly will find out as soon as they meet with the prefect."

CHAPTER EIGHTEEN

Elle knew her father hated the Senate. But she never knew how much until they were waiting to be presented to the prefect.

She felt his hatred radiating from his mind and wondered what had happened in the past to make him feel this way. Boone had referred to a war fought over Oasis and her parents being part of the victory but it all happened before they were born. Could this hatred still be lingering over a war fought a lifetime ago?

Elle sensed the same feelings in her mother, who nonetheless sought to calm her husband with her mind.

How could her mother remain so strong? How could she stay so focused with everything that happened? Elle found herself looking at her parents in a new way, and it had nothing to do with the ornate uniform of office that they wore.

She had never seen them in full Oasian regalia. She never even imagined that she would wear the uniform of her office.

Her mother's words rang in her mind.

"You are Princess Arielle of Oasis and you will not show pain or emotion when you are presented."

"Remember it's all a game of one-upmanship," her father warned her as they were escorted to the outer offices of the prefect by the Oasian ambassador, his secretary, and four Oasian soldiers.

She felt all their eyes on her and knew without delving into their minds that they were curious about her.

They didn't even know I existed until today.

The things her parents did to protect them. And all of it useless because Zander refused to be protected. Did she blame him for running away? Would she have done the same thing?

You wanted to.

Did Zander run away because he possessed more courage than she did? Or was he more foolish than she was? Would he have run had he known the threat? Would she?

If only Boone had told them.

It's not Boone's fault.

Elle refused to listen to her conscience because she desperately wanted to blame someone for what happened.

Shouldn't you share the blame, then?

She willed her trembling body into submission as the lust she felt for Boone came back to remind her of her part in their failure to save Zander.

She had wanted him. She wanted him so much that she used her abilities to move him toward her. Even though she knew it was wrong and that deep down, it hurt Boone that she did it.

She still wanted him.

No . . . I will not go there.

Elle saw her mother give her a glance as they waited silently in the antechambers. She fidgeted with the robe she wore as if that were her only concern.

My mind is my own.

No one would ever know about what had almost happened with Boone.

Never again would she feel that way. Never.

"Show no fear," her father said as the doors opened to the prefect's chambers.

"*Protect your mind,*" her mother added internally as they were escorted in by four Senate guards.

One could almost think they were fighting a war by all the show of power. Then she felt the evil that was present in the room, and realized this was a war.

Elle knew that the older of the two women who stood to the side and behind the prefect was the one who captured Zander. Her mind instantly recognized the malice that visited her mind earlier in the day.

Both women smiled benignly as the introductions were made and a proclamation was read by the Oasian ambassador. The prefect introduced the younger Circe as Bella, Sacrosanct Mistress of Circe and his closest adviser.

"*Keep your friends close and your enemies closer.*" Her father's voice spoke in her mind. "*They still wear those ridiculous hats,*" he added.

The slight flaring of the nostrils of the women dressed in the ornate hats gave indication that they heard his thoughts.

But only because he allowed it. A new appreciation for her father swelled through Elle. He was the leader of a planet. He was strong. He would find Zander and bring him home.

The younger one's abilities were more potent. She stared at Elle with her pale eyes and phony smile and Elle knew she was trying to penetrate her mind.

"*Show no fear,*" her father said in her mind

My mind is my own.

"To what do I owe the honor of this visit after all these solars?" the prefect said to Shaun. His voice was controlled yet Elle sensed the hostility in the man.

I wonder exactly what it was that Father did to him.

"They have taught you well." It was the younger one. *"You sense the prefect's true feelings."*

Elle had let her guard down for an instant and the Circe sensed it immediately and began her attack.

"Shield your mind, Elle," her mother warned her. *"I cannot protect you and find out what we need to know."*

My mind is my own. Elle realized there was so much to learn. So much about her abilities that she did not understand yet.

"I came here to find my son," Shaun said.

"You have a son?" The prefect raised an eyebrow questioningly. "Congratulations on his birth."

"I have not come here to play games with you," Shaun continued. "You knew of his birth eighteen solars ago. You also know of his disappearance on this planet earlier today."

The prefect raised an eyebrow in evident amusement. "I have not been informed of either of these circumstances," he began, then instantly stopped.

Her father was in his mind. Elle sensed the struggle in the prefect. Her father dared much.

He loves us. He loves Zander.

"Your advisers only allow you limited knowledge," Shaun said when the prefect was subdued. "As usual they are only worried about their agenda."

"I will not stand here and be insulted by this Aberrant," Bella said. Her words were meant only for the prefect. Her eyes stayed on Elle.

"You want the power," Bella said in her mind. *"I can feel your desire for it."*

My mind is my own.

No wonder her father hated the Senate. It was all a pretense. All an act. Posturing and protests and machinations. All for power. All for control.

"Just imagine what we could teach you. What we could show you. Imagine what you could do. Imagine the power."

"Leave my daughter alone," her father said. His voice commanded attention yet his features remained calm as if he spoke without effort. The sound of it echoed into the upper arches of the chamber and the ambassador's secretary jumped.

Imagine what my father can do.

"*Aberrant.*"

"Arleta," Lilly said. Her eyes remained on the older woman. "I see you've managed to work your way back into the good graces of the Sacrosanct. How fortunate for you after your disgrace all those years ago."

"I have never forgotten who caused my temporary circumstances," Arleta said. Her upper lip trembled, as if speaking the words pained her, and she firmly tucked it into a straight line when she was done, her eyes resting on Lilly.

Arleta's anger was a tangible thing. It reached out and touched everyone in the chamber.

A chamber full of hatred and vengeance. A chamber full of evil desires. Elle fought the desire to run. If only she was home, if only Zander was home. The villa that just a few days ago she had thought a prison now seemed suddenly desirable, a safe haven.

I want to go home.

The ambassador cleared his throat.

"Was this your reward, Arleta?" Lilly continued. "Was my son the prize that put you back into a position of power?"

"We have yet to establish that your son even exists much less has been . . . trifled with," the prefect said.

It's all a struggle for control. Elle's mind quickly grasped the intrigues of Senate life. The prefect was nothing more than a puppet for the Circe. Yet he thought himself the center of the government. His words certainly made him the center of attention in the chamber, which was what he wanted.

He is a fool. Is that why they allow him to be in power? Do they protect him because he is so foolish?

"*Lesson learned, Elle,*" her father said in her mind.

"My son exists. As does my daughter. Twins born

eighteen solars ago and kept hidden to protect their lives."

"Kept hidden," the prefect said with an amused smile on his face. "And you've lost him? Did you perhaps forget where you *hid* him?"

Elle waited for her father's anger to explode. Instead she watched as her mother placed her hand upon his arm. Whatever passed between them was enough to keep him on course.

"I knew exactly where my son was," Shaun continued. "Until that witch found him here." He pointed to Arleta.

Her face remained impassive.

They're enjoying his frustration.

"Revenge is sweet." Bella agreed with her.

"Which one of you killed my brother?" Elle ventured forth with her mind. She caught a glimpse of something in Bella's mind. Was it surprise?

"What proof do you have?" the prefect asked her father. "Besides what you say you see in each other's minds."

The prefect enjoys pitting us against each other.

"Only to see which of us is strongest," her father said in her mind.

"My daughter witnessed his capture," Shaun replied.

How did they do that? Talk to her and talk to each other. There was so much to learn. So much power to be had.

"His death is just the beginning of your pain," Bella said inside her mind. *"We could take the pain away. If you join us."*

"I will never join you. Never."

"What did you see, girl?" the prefect asked.

"You shall address her as Princess Arielle," her father said.

"Tell us what you saw, Princess," the prefect said condescendingly.

"Very well, then . . ." Bella said.

It didn't matter what he called her or how he said it. Elle found she could not speak. An image filled her mind. The same one she had seen earlier in the day. Zander burning alive.

Elle shook her head. She didn't want to see that. She didn't want to relive the moment. She opened her mouth to speak and nothing came out.

"Perhaps I could help her," Bella said. "I could look inside her mind and tell you what she sees." She smiled eagerly for the prefect.

"You will not touch her," Shaun roared.

"But how else would the prefect know the truth?" Bella said, her voice a sickeningly sweet contrast to her father's anger.

"It is the truth because she speaks it," Shaun replied.

Zander was burning alive before her eyes and her father talked as if nothing was happening.

"*It's a trick, Elle,*" her mother said. "*Protect your mind.*"

But Zander was dying.

Zander was dead.

She saw it. She felt it. She knew it in her mind. She knew it in her heart.

When she thought of Zander, when she wished for Zander, when she sought for Zander, there was nothing there.

"*Your brother is dead and you were betrayed,*" the voice said in her mind.

"Tell them what you saw, Elle," her father said.

Elle looked at him. Tears welled in her eyes. He did not understand. None of them understood.

"He is dead," she said. "Don't you understand? He is dead." She felt a tear trickle down her cheek and saw the same appear on her mother's face.

"Tell him who is responsible," Shaun said. He looked at Elle desperately but she could only shake her head.

"I did not see them. I only saw Zander. Because of Boone. Boone kept me from seeing. Boone kept me from helping. Zander is dead. If you need to blame someone, blame Boone."

"Elle," her mother said.

Elle put her hands over her ears. "No more," she said. "No more." She felt her legs tremble. She felt faint. The image would not leave her mind.

"His death is just the beginning," Bella reminded her.

"I want to go home," Elle said before the darkness overcame her.

CHAPTER NINETEEN

"They've gone back to Oasis," Tess said. Boone looked at his mother in disbelief. They had spent most of the night with Stefan, tracking down useless leads, bribing officials, watching the Circe hideaways. He was exhausted, Ruben was exhausted, and he could tell his mother was too.

"Elle?" Boone asked. "How is she?"

"I don't know." Tess shrugged wearily. "She's convinced that Zander is dead. Lilly can't say for sure whether he is or not. She knows that a Circe named Arleta is the one who captured Zander but beyond that they don't know what happened. They were worried about Elle. Something happened to her in the prefect's chambers. And I think they just don't want to admit that he could be dead."

"He's not dead," Boone said. He could not believe that Elle and her family had left the planet. How could they go when Zander was still missing? How could they leave when there was so much to do, so much to say, so much to explain?

How could Elle leave when he hadn't had a chance to tell her what happened? She had to know how much it tore his gut out when she screamed because he knew he couldn't change what she saw in her mind. How could she go before she forgave him for what he did?

"Arleta," Ruben said. "That old bitch is still around?" He poured a tall glass of juice from the table that the servants were setting for breakfast.

"Who is she?" Tess asked.

"She's the one who had me drugged and put a collar on me to find out about Shaun," he said. "Fortunately I was pretty out of it when they had me collared. The Circe who drugged me used too much and I wasn't making much sense." Boone was amazed to see his stepfather's face turn a brilliant shade of red as if he were remembering something funny. "If Shaun hadn't come along when he did they probably would have killed me." He drained his glass and filled it again. "When the power struggle was going on for Oasis, Lilly managed to plant the suggestion in the Sacrosanct of the time that Arleta had betrayed her. Arleta was next in line to be Mistress so she got her silly hat handed to her. I figured as mean as those women are that they had her killed or threw her in a hole or something along those lines."

"Too bad for us they didn't," Tess said.

"Could she be the one who left for Bali Circe?" Boone asked.

"Don't jump to conclusions," Ruben said after he drained his glass. His face had returned to its normal color.

"What is it?" Tess asked as she looked between the two of them.

"Stefan found out a transport is scheduled to depart for Bali Circe," Ruben explained. "A witch is on it and several crates were loaded on. At least that's what Stefan's spies told him. He said the witch in charge was in a big hurry and got extremely angry when one of the crates got dropped."

"It could be Zander," Boone said. "They could be taking him off-planet."

"We came back to tell Shaun," Ruben said. "We figured he could stop it before it took off or at least block it before hyperport."

Tess shook her head. "They were devastated when they left. Shaun wouldn't talk. Lilly seemed numb. She said Elle broke down in the prefect's chambers and told everyone that Zander was dead. They think Bella got to her."

"Bella?"

"The current Sacrosanct," Tess explained. "They thought Elle could tell the prefect about Zander's capture, but she said she didn't see anything because you hit her."

"I saw it," Boone said. "I saw the witch and her minions take Zander. He was alive the last time I saw him."

Ruben placed his hand on Boone's shoulder. "Unfortunately what you saw won't be enough for the prefect," he said.

"There were hundreds of people there," Boone protested as he moved away from his stepfather's hand. "They all saw what happened."

"Could any of them go up against a Circe?" Ruben said. "Could you?"

"I know the litany," Boone said.

"As I do. Yet it's not enough. Not when they can find your secrets. Not when they know exactly what it is that will pain you the most. It doesn't matter what you saw. All that matters is what they can make you say. They can make you say or do anything with their minds. They can control your will."

As Elle controlled my will when she made me kiss her.

"If they could do it to Elle, what makes you think they couldn't do the same to you?" Ruben finished.

"What if Zander is on that transport?" Boone asked as he shook off the haunting thought. "What if they're taking him to Bali Circe?"

"What if he's already dead?" Ruben said. "We might have to accept that fact." He sat down at the table and rubbed his hands over his face. His tiredness showed in the lines of his body.

"How can you say that?" Boone said. "We don't know. We haven't seen his . . . body."

"Don't you think Elle would know?" Ruben said. "Son, I know Zander was your best friend but Elle was connected to him. And she is a Circe."

"I don't believe it," Boone said.

Ruben's link beeped and he pulled it from his pocket. "It's Stef," he said.

Boone paced the length of the room impatiently as Ruben talked to his brother. The chaise Elle had landed on earlier was moved into a different place as if the servants were afraid to put it back. As if it was cursed. Boone felt much the same way. Out of place. Cursed. "I won't believe it," he said. "Not until I see his body will I believe it."

"The transport took off," Ruben said as he slid the link back in his pocket.

"So what happens now?" Tess asked.

"We might have to accept the fact that we will never find out what happened to Zander," Ruben said. "They have no reason to keep him alive. He's the very thing they fear most."

"*No!*" Boone said.

"Boone," Tess said. "It's not your fault. No one blames you."

"Elle does."

"She's young, Boone. She's had a shock. She needs time to think about things."

"She hates me, Mema."

"She doesn't."

"Yes. She does. She believes Zander is dead and she believes that it is my fault."

"You did . . ."

Boone held up his hand. "I did what I thought was best for Elle. I made the same decisions for her for the same reasons her parents did. I'm older, I'm wiser, and I knew the dangers." He knew the routine by heart. His mother, his father, his uncle Stefan, and even Lilly had assured him that he'd done the right thing. "But what if she could have helped him? What if she could have stopped them?"

"If she couldn't handle being in the prefect's chambers with the Circe, then there is no way she could have engaged in a life-and-death battle with them," Ruben said.

"We'll never know, will we?" Boone said. "It's one of those things that I'll have to wonder about for the rest of my life."

"Boone, it is not your fault."

"Yes, it is. In Elle's mind it is and that is all that matters because she is all that matters. To me."

"You need to give her time," Tess said. Boone saw the pain in her eyes. Pain for him. Yet Elle's pain was greater. He had to do something to make that pain go away.

"I'll see if I can raise Shaun," Ruben said. "Maybe the ambassador can file an injunction against the Circe and have the transport searched when it reaches the Bali Circe hyperport."

"I don't think the prefect is of a mind to do anything to help Shaun," Tess said. "Especially since they believe Zander is dead."

"*Don't say that!*"

Ruben and Tess both stopped and looked at Boone. He didn't realize he had shouted at them until he saw the look on his mother's face.

How could he convince them that Zander wasn't dead?

Or was he just fooling himself? If Zander wasn't dead, then Elle would have no reason to hate him. He had to do something. He couldn't just give up on his friend. And he couldn't, wouldn't, give up on Elle. Not after he had loved her for all these years.

He had loved her his entire life.

"I've got to do something," he said.

His mother looked at him imploringly. She didn't understand and he realized that he could not make her understand.

He walked out of the room.

"Let him go," he heard Ruben say. "He's got to work things out on his own."

The streets were deserted. The planetary clock said dawn and the artificial light that came with it pinked the dome that contained the higher-ranking embassies.

Sanitation workers rode hoverpods over the streets, stopping occasionally to pick up some of the larger pieces of trash that the vacubots had missed.

Cleaning up after the party.

It was amazing how quiet the streets were. Especially when it was so easy to recall the madness from the day before.

The wild thumping of the music. The glitter of the confetti. The mad crush of bodies. The overwhelming lust for Elle that still caused a tightening in his groin.

Stefan would recommend a visit to the nearest pleasure house. A quick warming of the sheets would be just what he needed to get his mind back on track.

But Elle's reaction when she found out was enough to keep him from pursuing that end. He had pledged his undying love. He had promised to wait for her to make up her mind.

But that was before Zander was taken.

Would she ever forgive him?

Could she ever forgive him?

Could he forgive himself?

The transport up to the space station was as empty

as the streets. Boone was grateful for the solitude. It gave him time to think.

He couldn't tell anyone what he was about to do. They'd stop him. His only chance was to get through the hyperports before anyone figured out where he'd gone. And then he would need an incredible amount of luck.

The Firebird still sat where last he saw it.

"Welcome, Boone," ELSie said when he fired up her engines.

"We've got a big trip ahead of us ELSie," he said. "Plot a course for Bali Circe."

"Plotting," ELSie responded. "Landing on Bali Circe is strictly forbidden by law 1737A of Senate Treaty."

"I know, ELSie," Boone said as he piloted the Firebird out of the space station. "Which is why we have to keep this on the down low."

"Not computing down low," ELSie said.

"We'll be flying off the radar," Boone explained. "I need you to send out a false signal to anyone who may be tracking us. Also when we get there we need to muck up the system so it looks like we're limping."

"Muck up?"

"Falsify our status. Pretend we're broke so they'll allow us to land."

"Understood," ELSie replied.

"I want you to send a communiqué to Academy. Addressed to my parents."

"Understood," ELSie said. "Recording when ready."

Boone looked at the blinking green light on the dige screen. What should he say? He knew what he was doing was foolish. But someone had to do something. If there was a chance Zander was alive . . .

"Mema. Ben." The thought that they would see his face on the dige almost unnerved him. He had to show confidence so they would not worry about him. "By the time you receive this I will be . . ." Should he tell them where he was going? What if they got it too soon and tried to stop him? "I've gone to find Zander. Tell Elle . . ." Boone had to look away. He had to show them that he knew what he was doing. He couldn't show fear. "Tell Elle that I'm bringing Zander home. Tell her that I love her."

"Hyperport in five," ELSie began.

"Tell Zoey to take care of Kyp," Boone added. "And don't worry about me. I'll be fine."

"Two, one," ELSie continued.

"Safe stars," Boone said. "Out."

"Communiqué sent," ELSie informed him.

"How long to Bali Circe?"

"Five solars," ELSie said.

"Might as well get some rest." And if he was in cryo he wouldn't be thinking about what he was doing.

He was weary. He felt as if he'd lived a lifetime in the past week. Was it just a few days ago that his biggest concern was how much trouble he'd get into for sneaking off to the spit with Elle and Zander?

Boone picked up the toy spaceship that had its own place on the com. His mother had bought it for him right before they met Ruben. The day she bought it they saw Stefan as a prisoner of the Circe and somehow, because of her Circe blood, a link was created between her and Ruben that brought Ruben to their planet.

And changed his life for the better.

Ruben had followed a hunch. A belief that his brother needed him.

Couldn't he do the same for his best friend? Didn't the same Circe blood that ran in his mother's veins run in his?

But it runs in Elle's too. And she's certain he's dead.

If there's a chance Zander is alive . . .

What? What would he do? No one else was doing anything. They all believed Zander to be dead. They had all given up.

Boone stuck the toy in his pocket. He'd never give up on Zander. And he certainly would never give up on Elle.

Boone placed his cryo pack on his wrist. "Wake me at the hyperport, ELSie," he said before he slid into sleep.

CHAPTER TWENTY

Fear comes from the unexpected.

He knew what to expect now. The screaming crowds. The smell of fear. The blood. He knew it better than he knew himself.

And all he knew of himself was that he was a glorified assassin.

Blood dripped from the arena above. He held his arms out to his sides to protect his body from the blades that hooked down the gauntlets he wore. His eyes did not move beneath his mask to look at the droplets that spattered upon the vicious metal. Instead they turned inward, as they always did before a battle, to the first thing he remembered.

A woman with eyes the color of his. The woman who condemned him to fight in the pits as a tribute to his father.

The woman who condemned him to never know himself.

Who was he? Who was the woman who sent him

here? Who was his father? Did he fight in the pits? Did the woman hate him? Was that why he was sent here?

What horrible crime did he commit to deserve his sentence?

And why, after six solar years, was he still alive?

At least that question he could answer on his own.

It is hard to die when your wounds heal overnight.

"Phoenix. Phoenix." The crowd began the chant. The lift would not move until the people were whipped into a frenzy.

Like the fabled Phoenix his wounds healed and he arose once again to fight.

And since he had no name to speak of, that was what he was called.

Could not the woman who sent him here tell them his name?

What difference did it make after all this time?

He focused on Laylon. The woman who trained him. The one who counseled him. The only person he knew. The only one he trusted spoke as the lift began its ascent.

"You know what to expect," she said.

"Did you expect them to take your eyes?" he asked as he rose above her.

He saw her head tilt in confusion. In all these years it was the first time he spoke of her blindness.

He couldn't help but grin wolfishly as the floor to the arena parted above him. At least now he was guaranteed some interesting conversation after the battle. As soon as he was done with the latest victim.

He had ceased a long time ago to worry about the men he killed. When Laylon first began his training he had several questions, but she could answer none of them except for the ones that dealt with the Murlaca. Her life outside the pits had ended long ago when she was blinded in a battle. But she taught him one thing.

Kill or be killed.

He soon learned that some of the men and women in the rings were professional fighters. And some were prisoners, sent there for assassination. The professionals were treated like celebrities. They wore special armor, had trainers, medics, entitlements.

The prisoners were different. They weren't there long. Some of them were good fighters, some of them survived to fight another day, but they all died eventually.

The rules were simple enough. You were thrown into a ring and you fought. The winner moved on. The losers were carted off. Some of them died in the ring. Some of them bled to death as they were waiting for their bodies to be incinerated. If they were lucky.

He was the only prisoner to survive this long. He had beaten all the champions. They did not have to die, although some did of their injuries. Now there was none who even challenged him.

And after each battle he returned to his cell because he had no choice but to do so. At first he rebelled against the handlers who were all selected for their size and cruelty. But they had ways of controlling him.

They stunned him with their long prods.

They kicked him viciously when he collapsed. More so when they found out how quickly he healed.

He hated them for it.

He hated the crowd that erupted into screams and more chants as he rose to floor level in the caged arena where he was supposed to fight.

He hated the lights that flashed in his eyes, and whoever controlled them. He was certain that one day an opponent awaiting him in the ring would take advantage of his temporary blindness when he appeared through the floor and use that instant to kill him.

Even though he couldn't die.

He still felt pain. He knew it when his flesh was ripped open by the blades. He felt it when his ribs broke from the violent kicks of his handlers.

He felt everything.

Yet he had no scars.

He quickly found his opponent once the light left his eyes.

His blood quickened as he turned his head to where the man stood, his sides heaving in anticipation. Tonight he would have a challenge. The man had some size on him, a wide chest, thick muscular arms, and sturdy legs. There was intelligence in his face, more so than the usual fear. And it seemed as if he was used to the blades. His arms were relaxed at his sides instead of clenched. Clenching them just made the muscles weary. Made the blades heavier. The match shorter. He was also wearing the armor of the champions. Thick leather covered most of the man's body as it did his own. But it wasn't thick enough to stop the blades. Nothing could stop the blades.

He wondered briefly what his challenger's crime was. Or maybe he just crossed the wrong person. The man waiting to fight him must have done something to someone to be sent here. Just as he had. Was it the woman with the pale eyes?

He knew the mask made him look more intimidating. Heartless. Cruel. The hooked crest that arched over his forehead and covered the bridge of his nose gave him the appearance of a predator.

For some reason the woman who gave him his sentence to this place did not want his face to be seen. And since he did not recognize himself, it made no difference to him whatsoever. It gave him an advantage so he took it.

And it wasn't as if anyone would claim him. He was nothing more than a glorified assassin.

As usual he raised his arms above his head in a show of strength, watching his challenger to make sure he didn't attempt to attack him. Then he crossed them in a slashing motion as he brought them down.

The crowd screamed louder.

He hated them. All of them.

He heard the announcer amplify his name over the screams of the crowd.

He hated the announcer. He was the one who had first called him Phoenix. And since he had no other name it became his title.

He rose from the ashes of his blood and the blood of his victims to fight again another day. Just like the fabled bird of ancient times.

But the bird was able to fly away eventually. And death would be an easy flight to take.

Too bad he couldn't die.

He bounced up on the balls of his feet three times. Then he leaned his head to one side until he heard the familiar pop.

The crowd screamed in anticipation.

His challenger was not as intelligent as he first thought. His came at him as if he thought to overwhelm him with his greater strength.

Phoenix moved aside gracefully and watched in amusement as his challenger waved his arms in an attempt to stop himself from careening into the side of the cage.

Should he prolong it? Or simply put the man away so he could return to his cell?

His cold, lonely cell.

He was bored, so he decided to make it last.

Make him bleed.

Maybe he'd get a reward for his trouble.

Sometimes they allowed him a woman. And the luxury of the baths.

His challenger realized that his greater strength wouldn't work. Not when Phoenix had speed and agility on his side.

The challenger circled him. Phoenix kept his eyes trained on him, turning with him in an almost casual manner. He held his arms out at his sides, the blades ready.

The challenger grinned, as if he suddenly saw a weakness, but Phoenix knew it was nothing more than a ruse.

He had no weaknesses in the ring.

But he might let him think so, just to make it interesting.

The floor was wet from the cleaning it received between matches. The blood was sprayed into the crowd to keep the next combatants from sticking and slipping. The crowd loved it.

Phoenix took a step back as the challenger circled. As if he was afraid. His foot moved awkwardly. As if he slipped.

The challenger came at him. As he expected. He raised his right forearm up to slash downward at Phoenix.

Who ducked under the strike and slashed his left forearm across the challenger's belly.

The man was softer than he first thought. What he thought was solid muscle was nothing more than thick layers of fat that oozed a thick stream of blood.

He seemed surprised that he was injured. But no more so than Phoenix, who saw rather than felt the blood on his hip.

Phoenix realized that there hadn't been a mark on his opponent until now. He must have fought well to get to this level without injury. Or else this was his first battle of the day.

It made no difference. It would soon be over.

The wound wasn't deep for either of them. Nothing more than an annoyance.

But it sent a clear message. Neither of them was to be trifled with. Or easily dismissed.

Phoenix saw the impact of it in the challenger's eyes.

"What are you hiding under that mask?" the man said.

It was the first time, in the solars. In all the matches.

In all the deaths. That anyone had ever said anything to him beyond please.

He was not prepared for it.

And his challenger knew it.

The man saw the doubt in his face and came at him with a roar. Phoenix threw his left arm up in defense just in time and heard the crowd's intake of breath as the two arms collided in midair, the blades tangling as the combatants tested each other's strength.

The challenger's was greater. But Phoenix had not survived this long on strength alone.

He bent backward under the pressure. He used his right arm to block the slashes aimed at his thigh.

As soon as he felt his attacker shift his balance Phoenix kicked upward with his legs. His armor-plated boots struck the man in his chest as Phoenix flipped backward. He landed in a squat and slashed with his right arm along his opponent's thigh. His aim was for the back of the knee but the man knew it was coming and managed to turn his leg in time to take it on the armor.

Phoenix did not expect his blow to be deflected. Every other time he struck in that manner he crippled his opponent and it was just a matter of time to finish him off.

He knew he was vulnerable in his crouched position so he swung his leg out in a sweep kick, hit his opponent in the ankles, and sent the man toppling as he rose to his feet.

The impact of the man hitting the mat bounced the floor. Phoenix flexed his legs to absorb the vibration and looked down at the man. He should finish him now. Just a strike across the exposed throat and it would be over, but he was curious.

The crowd roared for him to strike a death blow but he ignored them, as he usually did. "Why are you here?" Phoenix asked. "What was your crime?"

"I have to admit you are as good as they said you are," his opponent said as he moved to his feet, his eyes on Phoenix the entire time.

"They?" Phoenix said. "Who are they?"

The man swung his arm out to encompass the crowd. "Everyone. You're a legend of the universe. Unbeatable. Indestructible. A slave who's the master of the game. Until now."

He feinted with his right, and swung with his left. Phoenix saw it coming and blocked with his right, then swung his left straight up. The blade on his wrist buried itself in the soft skin beneath the man's chin and pierced through to his tongue.

The man gagged and staggered back as Phoenix wrenched his blade free.

He had missed the artery.

"Who are you?" Phoenix asked.

The man spat out a gob of blood. Phoenix saw the slice in his tongue; saw the hole in the bottom of his mouth as he worked to speak.

He couldn't form a word but his eyes spoke volumes. He meant to kill him and he meant to kill him now.

With a cry from deep in his belly he came at Phoenix. Arms slashed as he sought to run over him and overpower him with his strength.

Phoenix met him head-on, his own blades slashing. Blood poured from the man's chin and down his front, slicking both of them, covering them, making them slide as it spilled onto the floor.

Was it possible that the screams of the crowd were even louder?

Phoenix strained against his opponent as their arms locked into each other, the blades capturing them and keeping them attached as they fought for balance, for a superior position.

But Phoenix was flexible. He pushed against the man with one leg planted and was able to open enough room between them to bring his knee up into a snap kick as he pried his opponent's arms open wide. The toe of his boot hit the gash and his head snapped back, exposing the vulnerable throat.

With a roar from his gut Phoenix slashed the man's throat. Blood gushed forth in a heavy shower. Phoenix caught the man as he toppled and turned his body toward one side of the arena so that the blood spouted out upon a dark-haired woman who looked at him in fear but screamed in absolute ecstasy.

He hated her too. For a very good reason.

He looked down and saw the life leave the man's eyes, along with his unanswered questions. He dropped the body to the floor and went back to the center of the ring where the lift would take him down to the cells.

He didn't even bother to lift his arms in victory. He had too much on his mind.

CHAPTER TWENTY-ONE

"Mother," Elle said, "why is it you and Father never had more children?" She met her mother's eyes with her own through the reflection of the mirror that hung over her dressing table.

She saw the pain that her mother carried reflected back to her. Was it worse for her mother knowing the mistakes that she made contributed to Zander's death? The pain and guilt that Lilly carried was still obvious, even after the passage of so many solars.

It seemed to Elle as if Lilly needed time to gather her thoughts. Her mother's fingers trailed across the tattoo that now decorated her shoulder, her coming-of-age mark, the design chosen by Elle herself that signified her as Oasian Royalty. Elle shook off her touch.

"Your father and I thought it too much of a risk," Lilly said. "We didn't know what kind of world . . ." Her voice trailed off and Elle knew she was thinking of Zander.

Always Zander.

"We were frightened," Lilly said finally.

If her mother had made that statement before Zander's death she would not have believed it. There was a time when she thought her father feared nothing. But now she knew better. He feared the worst and it had happened.

"If you had known the results would you have still had us?" Elle asked. In all the years it was the first time they had spoken aloud of Zander's death even though it was always present in their minds. Always between them.

Lilly turned away and walked to the wide arched portal that led to Elle's balcony. Elle watched as her mother looked to the right, to where Zander's room was and where it remained, just as he left it. Did she imagine him to be there?

Sometimes I do.

"Would I have traded never knowing the joy of having you and Zander or the years we were together?" Lilly said. Through the mirror Elle saw her mother's hand clench the brush. "No. I would not." She turned and looked once again at Elle. "Do I wish I could have spared you the pain of losing your brother?"

"It wasn't just my pain, Mother," Elle felt the familiar burn in her throat, the swell behind her eyes. Why did it still hurt so much? "We all had pain."

We all have pain. It was a constant companion. Pain that was ever present. Everlasting. First Zander. Then Boone. Then the emptiness of lost friendships as unspoken words and grief came between her family and Boone's. She blamed him for Zander's death. They blamed her for Boone's disappearance. All that was left was emptiness and grief and questions that never went away. Like the pain.

Did Zander suffer pain as he died? Did he feel alone? Was he frightened? Did he know his death was coming? Did he meet it with courage?

And what of Boone? He disappeared just as Zander

did. No trace, no answers, just a vague message as to his intentions that left a nothingness that filled all their lives.

I shouldn't have blamed him.

Elle's hand went to the necklace she still wore around her neck. The star-shaped stoned nestled between her breasts upon its silver chain. For some reason she could not bring herself to take it off.

"The pain fades, Elle," Lilly said. "The memories remain." Her mother saw her hand on the jewel of the necklace. Elle dropped it as if it burned her and felt it fall back into place.

"Has your pain faded, Mother?"

A sad smile crossed her mother's face. The years had finally caught up with Lilly. The lines around her eyes, at the corner of her mouth, were proof of it. Or maybe it was the grief that aged her.

"Why all these questions? Or are they just your doubts about the path you are about to take coming to the surface?"

"I have no doubts, Mother."

Lilly let loose with an unladylike snort. "You forget I've seen what's inside your mind."

"You haven't seen everything," Elle assured her. "I have my secrets. As do you."

"I know why you're doing this, Elle," Lilly said. "I fear your motives will bring nothing but trouble."

"As yours did?"

Elle knew her tone was less than respectful. But at her age she didn't much care anymore. She was an adult woman now. Twenty-four solar years. She was entitled to her opinion. Especially when she saw what her parents' motives had done to so many lives.

At least Elle's motives were obvious, although her true plans were not. And her motives were not wrapped up in what was best for her happiness and safety. She wanted power. Plain and simple. In the years since the disaster on Senate her one desire was to acquire power. Power over her own mind and power over the minds of others. She well remembered how Bella had tortured her with visions of Zander that still haunted her. She would never allow that to happen again. No one would ever enter her mind. No one.

His death was just the beginning.

If only she could remove the memories too.

She studied hard. She trained her mind and her body. She trained with weapons and was unbeatable with the Sai. Where once before she threw Boone across the room in panic she could now hold someone dangling in the air on a whim, a trick that angered her parents when she first discovered she could do it. Of course the suitor who hoped to make an engagement with her did not appreciate it either.

He was a gank who only wanted her because she was heir to Oasis. Not that it mattered to her what the suitors wanted. All that matter was what she wanted.

Elle wanted power.

The discovery of her existence had brought a long line of suitors to plead for her hand. She turned them all away. Except for one.

"I don't want to fight with you, Elle," Lilly said. It seemed that was all they ever did. Either fought or did not speak at all except for inconsequential things. It was just easier that way. They had lived with secrets their entire life as a family.

"It's just that I've been down this path you're about to take," Lilly continued.

Her mother's words turned Elle around to face her. It was the first time her mother ever spoke of her youth. For her mother it was always in the here and now. Where her father was.

"What path?"

"Marrying for the wrong reasons," Lilly said.

"I'm marrying to protect Oasis," Elle said simply. "I'm not pretending about why I'm marrying."

"At one time I was to marry for the same reason," Lilly said.

"But you met Father instead."

"Something like that," Lilly said. The smile on her face was reminiscent of something from the past. Sweet, youthful, full of longing.

"What happened?" Elle asked. She tried to imagine her parents young, in love, full of passion instead of empty souls. Or maybe it was her own soul that was empty. They did have each other. She had no one. It was better that way. No pain.

"We were at war with Raviga. My uncle agreed with the prefect that the best course for peace would be an arranged marriage between myself and Ramelah, who was the heir to the Ravigan throne. Meeting your father put a twist in the plan that no one counted on."

"Because he was the true heir to Oasis?"

"Yes. But I had no way of knowing that at the time. And that had nothing to do with why I fell in love with him. As a matter of fact, finding out he was the heir almost put an end to us."

"How did you meet Father?"

"I met your father during a crash of the ship we were traveling on."

"What?" Elle said in disbelief and was rewarded by a seldom-seen smile from her mother. Elle moved over to her bed and sat back against the pile of pillows, prepared to listen to the story she thought she would never hear. Lilly joined her, her hand smoothing out the thick silk of the coverlet before she sat down. The peace of the moment felt precious but Elle quickly tamped the feeling away. It would only lead to pain.

"I was traveling on a common freighter. Your father was imprisoned in a cryo tube when I came onto the ship."

"Wait," Elle said. "Father was a prisoner? What did he do?"

"He was convicted of murder," Lilly said. "But he was justified in doing it."

"I can see that," Elle said in a matter-of-fact tone. She wrapped her arms around her legs and settled her chin on her knees. She well recalled her father's outburst on the day of Zander's disappearance. He refused to believe he was dead. He still refused to believe it. And the results of his disbelief affected every aspect of his life and his reign on Oasis.

"I felt a mental connection to your father as soon as I was in his presence. And for him it was like an awakening of some sort."

"Boo . . . Boone told me once that Father had no abilities until he met you. Is that true?" When would she be able to speak his name without hesitation? Without guilt?

"Yes. His eyes developed the ability to see in the dark because he was raised underground. But his telepathic abilities did not come into being until we met."

"You were the trigger," Elle said. "Maybe that's why Zander never . . ."

Lilly's eyes widened in realization. "I never thought of it," she said finally. She looked at Elle and Elle saw the tears glistening behind her dark lashes. "Maybe—"

"Don't, Mother," Elle said. "Don't." She didn't want the pain to come back. Never the pain. Never again. "So you felt a telepathic link with Father."

"Yes." Lilly swallowed and continued. "The ship was attacked. It turns out my uncle, your grandfather, tried to have me killed so he could blame it on the Ravigans. All those innocent people killed . . ."

"So what happened?"

"I awoke from cryo to find my bodyguard dead and your father in a fight with his guard. For some unexplainable reason I knew your father was the only one I could trust with my life, so I knocked out the guard and we escaped."

"Just like that?" Elle asked, amazed that her mother could be so impetuous, so foolish.

"I followed my heart."

Following his heart got Zander killed.

"But what about the man you were to marry? The prince?"

"Your father killed him."

"Why not?" Elle said sarcastically. "After all it wasn't his first time."

Elle felt her mother's anger flare but Lilly kept it in check. "It was kill or be killed. They were fighting the Murlaca."

Elle arched an eyebrow in surprise but kept quiet. There was so much about her parents' history that she didn't know. She really shouldn't judge. And she really shouldn't be so hostile. But sometimes it was hard. It was hard to forget the price they all paid.

"Your father was convicted on murder charges because he killed the soldiers who brutally murdered his adoptive parents on Senate orders. The Senate kept moving the settlers around whenever riches were discovered and your father's family refused to comply. They were merciless in what they did to his family and he, in turn, did the same. If not for that, I never would have met him."

"If not for your mother he never would have been in that position," Elle said. "Boone told me that part of the story," she explained when Lilly looked at her in confusion. "Why the Circe hate you and Father." She said his name without stuttering over it for once.

"The Circe need no reason to hate. It's bred into them."

"Was it bred into you?" Elle asked.

"No. I was never exposed to their brand of hatred. Only my uncle's. And the Senate's."

"Who was not really your uncle at all."

"Yes. Michael kept me sane." Zander's death had

nearly been the end of Michael, Elle's true grandfather. And it had aged him more so than both her parents. It was as if the light was gone from his life. "Michael always loved me," Lilly continued. "He loved me enough to not claim me as his own because he knew it would be the death of me."

"How did you feel when you found out the truth?" Elle felt her anger at what keeping secrets had cost them.

"Michael did it to protect me," Lilly said. "Just as we were trying to do."

"Luckily for you it worked," Elle said. "Too bad Zander can't say the same."

Lilly sighed. Her eyes burned into Elle's until Elle, unable to stand it, had to look away. "If I could undo the past, I would, for all our sakes. Which is why I'm asking you not to take this path you're set upon."

"It's too late to turn back," Elle said with a shrug.

"It is not." The emotion in her mother's voice surprised her. Perhaps because Elle had successfully voided it from her life. Almost.

Lilly reached across the bed and grabbed Elle's hands. "I want your happiness. And I fear you will never find it. Not if you continue on this path."

"Are you happy, Mother?"

Lilly dropped her hands and Elle moved back and away from her. "I love your father," she said. "That love has given me great joy and gotten me through great sadness. But my happiness has nothing to do with yours."

"As mine has nothing to do with yours," Elle said.

"Don't you want to be happy? Don't you want to know love?"

Elle moved from the bed in one graceful motion and went to her balcony.

Love means pain. Love means loss. Love killed Zander.

"No, I don't." Elle gripped the carved stone of the railing as Lilly came up behind her.

"Why?"

"Because love hurts too much."

"How can you say that?"

"It was your love for us that made Zander run away. And it was my love for Boone that killed both of them."

"Elle." Her mother's arms reached for her. Elle put her hand up protectively and her mother stopped. Elle turned and walked away.

CHAPTER TWENTY-TWO

The dolphins always made him think of Elle. He well recalled the last good day they spent together. The day they stole away, he, Elle, and Zander. The day they played with the dolphins.

The dolphins were what saved him. When the Firebird crashed into the sea the dolphins found him and brought him ashore. At least that was what he remembered of it after he fell from the sky, shot down by the Circe Sky Guard.

The impact of the ship hitting the water, his head hitting the com, the Plexi losing its seal and then floating away as the water rushed in. Then he saw the dolphins as he sank toward the bottom of the sea. They rescued him.

Or so the people who found him said. He couldn't remember much about his first years on Bali Circe.

The moonlight dappled the surface of the water with magenta, fuchsia, and lavender hues that gave the dolphins a surreal look as they frolicked beyond the gen-

tle lap of the waves. The strange colors were caused by
the gases that escaped from the mines beneath the surface of the planet. Mines that had long ago been emp-
tied of their resources. The gases hung in the upper
atmosphere and gave the entire planet a pinkish hue in
broad daylight. He could not see the stars because of
the gases. It was hard to say which he missed more, the
stars or Elle.

Elle . . .

Sagan had told him once, long ago, that the mines
could be purged and the atmosphere cleaned and con-
ditioned if only those in power would do it. But they
had no interest in taking care of their planet. Their interests lay elsewhere. To the Circe who held the power,
Bali Circe was nothing more than a supply depot. A
source of income. A breeding farm for slaves. And the
stars were nothing more than a temptation to those
who could not travel them. Perhaps it was best that he
could not see them. Could you really miss something
you could not see?

Elle . . .

Yes, you could miss something you could not see.
Would never see again.

"Beautiful night," Sagan said. Boone turned to the
older man, whose coming had been lost in the sound
of the waves. Or maybe it was just his memories that
blocked out the normal sounds.

"You're back," Boone said as he turned his eyes back
to the water. Sagan came and went like the wind, moving about the planet without notice of the authorities.
He was lucky to still be alive after all these years. The
man knew how to move in the shadows.

The Circe in power hated him. The rebels worshiped
him. Boone was grateful for his existence. It helped
him from feeling so alone.

Everyone who knew them both always remarked
upon how much he looked like Sagan. Both had long,
lean frames, dark brown hair, and vivid green eyes, a

rare color on Bali Circe. Their faces even resembled each other's, except for the long scar that sliced through Boone's left eyebrow and down his cheek.

It was a souvenir from his crash. He was lucky he didn't lose his eye. He lost everything else. Everything but his toy spaceship, which he still carried with him. Everything except his life.

"Any luck?" Boone asked.

Sagan had a daughter that he had never seen. A child born twenty solars past when his wife, a Circe, was imprisoned for joining the rebellion and allowed to die after delivering their child. Sagan's spies told him the child had the palest blond hair, like her mother, and amethyst eyes, as intense a purple as his was green. She disappeared after the birth, likely given over to a trade house to be raised for servitude. His life since then was a constant search for her and his sudden disappearances and appearances were usually related to a sighting.

"Yes and no," Sagan said. Every time there was a rumor of a girl who fit his daughter's description he went to see if the girl remotely resembled the wife he still loved passionately. "The girl in question was sold to the slavers. Whether or not she was my daughter I'll never know."

"Just like my mother," Boone said, as he recalled a conversation he'd had with Sagan on the beach years earlier when he told him his history.

"So other planets sell their people?" Sagan had asked.

"She was from Circe," Boone said. "I guess I never mentioned it before since it still pains me to talk of her. It was just the two of us for the first six years of my life. I can't imagine the pain I've put her through. The not knowing what happened to me."

"Not knowing is the hardest," Sagan agreed.

"Her memories were erased before they sold her. The only memories she has of this place were those that Lilly brought to the surface."

"Your friend's mother?" Sagan knew about Boone's reasons for coming to Circe, as foolish as they now seemed. He knew better now than to think Zander would be alive on the planet. He was the thing they dreaded. He was the legend they told him brought to life. Yes, he was dead and Boone was a fool for thinking otherwise.

"Yes, she was able to retrieve some things from her past. Her mother and father's faces, and she recalled a brother but she could not put a name to him."

"Is your mother's name Tess?" Sagan had asked.

Boone looked at the older man, his face so familiar. "You're my uncle."

"Our father's name was Boone," Sagan said. "He was the one who started all this."

"The rebellion?" Boone had quickly realized he was lucky to have been found by the freedom fighters instead of the Circe Guards. He would have been killed or, worse, sold off as a slave if Sagan's followers had not found him on the beach with a pod of dolphins just offshore.

"Yes. He was trained to be a Guard. Protector of the planet. In those days they weren't controlled by the collars. Fear was enough to keep them in line. But my father had a mind of his own. As did my mother."

"She was a Circe?"

"Yes. The women in charge are very particular about their breeding program. My father was not on their approved list, so their joining was forbidden. They escaped, along with some others with the same mind-set. It was the first time anyone had publicly gone against the controlling body; the first time a high-profile Circe had ever rebelled."

"Your mother?" Boone asked.

"Your grandmother," Sagan said. "She was directly descended from one of the most powerful witches to ever rule. Our ancestor was the one who ingratiated the line with the Senate and brought power to the planet. You could say you are of royal blood where Bali Circe is concerned."

Boone let loose with a wry smile. "A lot of good that's doing me," he said. "Perhaps I could use that as a ticket off this place."

"There's only one way off-planet for people such as us," Sagan said. "And that's on a slave ship."

It was some time later when Boone learned the rest—that Sagan's family had been captured, his mother executed, his father condemned to the Murlaca. Sagan himself had survived when the Circe chose him to be a breeder. And now he wondered about the fate of his own daughter.

If his daughter was even alive. How hard would that be to live with? Not knowing if your loved one was alive.

As hard as it was to live knowing that you would never again see the ones you loved.

As Sagan told him time and time again, there was no way for him to get off the planet. There was no way for him to send a message to let his family know he was alive. He was trapped on Bali Circe and as good as dead to his family.

Yet he couldn't help thinking of them. And thinking of Elle.

The two men took a seat on the same boulder as they had on a night similar to this one. The dolphins continued their frolic as the moon turned and cast its light toward the shore.

"So what deep thoughts trouble you, nephew?" Sagan asked.

Boone shrugged.

The same thoughts that always haunt me.

Sagan was concerned for him, so out of respect for his uncle he spoke.

"I was thinking of my sister, Zoey. I wonder what she looks like. She'd be twelve solars by now."

"On the edge of change," Sagan contributed.

Boone smiled into the darkness. "I imagine she's a handful. She's a lot like her father."

"Your stepfather? Ruben?"

"Yes." It was hard to speak. Boone nudged a shell out of the sand with the toe of his boot and bent to pick it up.

"I thought perhaps you were thinking about the woman."

Boone looked at him questioningly.

"The woman you never speak of," Sagan said in answer to his silence. "The one you still mourn. The one who keeps you from considering the women who would warm your sheets were you to give them any indication you were interested."

"The woman," Boone said, smiling softly.

Elle . . .

"It is the curse of the Circe men," Sagan said.

Boone looked at his uncle in confusion.

"When we love, we love forever," Sagan explained. He looked out over the ocean, and then closed his eyes as if he were in pain. "Once our hearts choose our life mates, then we can love no other. Even after death our hearts long for our mates. None other can take their place."

"That's why you search so hard for your daughter," Boone said.

"She's all I have left of my wife," Sagan said in agreement.

A moment passed, one in which Boone did not move or speak out of respect for Sagan's memories.

It was the first time he'd ever spoken of his dead wife, other than to acknowledge that she had existed and was gone.

"I can still see her face before me when I close my eyes," the older man finally said.

Elle . . .

Boone nodded in agreement.

"Thank the stars," Sagan said as he placed his hand on Boone's shoulder, "that there is a woman."

"Why?" Boone asked.

"I was worried that perhaps you might prefer—"

"No!" Boone said quickly. "Er, no, never, I . . ."

"The women wonder," Sagan explained with a smile. "You've never given any indication. And you have been here a long while."

"A lifetime, it seems." Boone flung the shell into the water. "So the women talk about me?" He felt somewhat flattered. And he had not missed the looks they gave him.

"Yes," Sagan said. "There is nothing wrong with seeking physical release, especially when it is freely given."

Boone nodded. But somehow the thought of it was a betrayal.

To what? She made it clear how she felt.

"Memories are a cold companion," Sagan said. "I hope yours can give you some comfort."

Did they?

No . . . there was none. Nothing but regret and loneliness. Perhaps he should find a woman to warm his sheets. Maybe then for a moment he could forget.

"At least now I know your secret," Sagan said. "It makes it easier now."

"Makes what easier?" Boone looked at his uncle in confusion.

"Do you trust me, Boone?" Sagan asked.

"I trust you," Boone said. "Have I given you a reason to think otherwise?"

"What if I told you I know a way to get you off Bali Circe?"

"That's a moot point," Boone said. "According to you there is no way off Bali Circe for someone like me."

"I've recently seen something that makes me think differently," Sagan said. "I've seen a change."

"In what?"

"The collars."

Boone looked at him in confusion. He'd been spared the indignity of the collar, but he well recalled the vacant look on Zander's face when he was captured.

"The collars contain liquid Perazine," Sagan began.

"Perazine?"

"The mines. Perazine was a low-cost fuel source. One small chunk would burn for hours and create enough energy to run one household for a day. It was especially needed by the outlying settlements. It was light and efficient and easily transported and there was no waste when it burned."

"Sounds as if Perazine was a great resource for the planet," Boone said.

"It was until the Circe found out that when it is mixed with Aeon and boiled down it acts as a neuron blocker."

"So they take over giving the body orders because whoever wears the collar can't," Boone concluded.

"Exactly," Sagan said. "The mind commands but the body can't respond because of the liquid Perazine."

"The Aeon is what gives it the glow," Boone said.

"Yes," Sagan said. "When the Circe in power realized the control they would have they used all the Perazine to make the liquid. Which meant we had no resources to send out to other planets."

"Which led to the slave trade because the Circe have a need to represent themselves well to the Senate. They cannot show a weakness."

Sagan smiled at Boone's quick comprehension of the politics of Bali Circe.

"You said you noticed a weakness?" Boone asked.

"I said I noticed a change," Sagan said. "Whether it is a weakness or not we will need to discover."

"What is it?"

"The collars blink with the white light when activated," Sagan said. "But lately I have noticed that some are turning colors."

"Such as?" Boone asked.

"Magenta. Lavender. Pink."

Boone laughed. "Hard to imagine running in fear from a guard with a blinking pink circle around his neck."

"Do you not see the connection?" Sagan asked as he smiled in agreement.

Boone stopped a moment, his mind whirling.

"The liquid is turning to gas?" he said finally.

"That was my first thought," Sagan said. He waved a hand toward the sky that was too dark now to reveal its strange hues. "We know that in gaseous form the mineral is harmless."

"The collars are breaking down," Boone said and a grin spread across his face.

"We shall see," Sagan said. "Come, nephew. We have plans to make."

The two men turned toward camp. The dolphins paused in their play and watched them go before they slid beneath the waves.

CHAPTER TWENTY-THREE

The wind moved over his face. Had he ever actually felt the wind? Not that he could recall. Not in the memories he had. The new memories. The after memories. Yet he knew it was wind even though it never blew in the arena, covered as it was by the dome. He turned his cheek toward it, grateful for its caress.

The woman felt it too. Her white-blond hair tumbled with it, lifting and swirling, making pale streaks across the magenta skies.

Her arms reached for him and he fell into them, suddenly overcome by their welcoming strength. Tears gathered behind his lids and he blinked them back as her hands ran over the aching muscles of his back.

"Let them go," she said. "You are safe here. You are safe with me."

"Who are you?" he asked. His arms wrapped around her waist and he buried his face against her welcoming breast. "Do I know you?"

"I am your sanctuary," she said. Her fingers moved

to his hair, caressing the dark locks as if he were a child. "As you are mine."

He looked up into her deep amethyst eyes. Eyes he recognized from his dreams but eyes he could not recall seeing. Did he know her? Had he seen her face in the years he could not remember?

"How can I save you when I can't even save myself?" he asked. "I don't know who I am. How is it you know me?"

"We have always known each other," she said.

"Then who am I?"

"You are the Empowered One."

Her answers were not the answer he sought, yet they were more than he ever heard before in the visions that came to him night after night. He looked at her, wishing for more. Wanting more. There had to be more. There had to be answers. There had to be a reason.

"What is my name?" he said. He thought that this time there might be hope. There might be an answer.

She smiled at him and suddenly her pale locks turned to black and the sweetness of her face was lost in an evil grin.

He felt the familiar tightening in his loins and he panicked as he fought his way up from the dream.

Never again.

He hated her. The woman who used him.

Phoenix rolled off his narrow bunk in one fluid motion and prowled the narrow confines of his cell. It was early, too soon to prepare for his match.

He was ready to kill. And he knew she would be there, watching, as she always did. But she would never come to him again. He made sure of that.

It happened after his first victory. Laylon had prepared him well for his match. He was lucky that they, whoever they might be, chose him as a warrior instead of just sentencing him and throwing him into the fray. He received training. He knew what to expect. He knew that to succeed he had to kill.

He didn't know what to expect after the match. Maybe his freedom? There had to be some prize for victory. Some prize beyond surviving. Something beyond the chance to be killed again another day.

He breathed deeply as the lift took him down. The crowd still screamed, amazed at his quick and merciless kill of the current champion.

There was a long deep gash in his leg. He was lucky the blow didn't cripple him. Luckily he had turned in time to take it on the front of his thigh instead of the back of his knee, where he was vulnerable.

"This way," the guard said when he got to the floor below the arena. The man swung his prod in a way that suggested he was prepared to use it.

He was surprised. He expected Laylon to be there, waiting to disarm him. She couldn't see the match, but she would have listened. She would know he won. She was the only person who cared about him, the only person he even knew although there was no name she called him by. He had none that he knew.

He wished to celebrate his victory with her.

He assumed they were taking him to be stitched up so he followed the guard, limping slightly while he held the bloody blades out and away from his body. Walking was awkward, especially with the trail of blood that oozed from the wound on his thigh. The mask bothered him too. He was glad for it during the match, as it made him seem less vulnerable, but now it stuck to his sweaty skin. He wanted to take it off but didn't dare while he wore the blades for fear of injuring himself.

The guard led him to a cell that held nothing more than a metal table formed in the shape of a cross. There were chains on it. Another guard stood at a door on the opposite side of the room.

"What is this?" he asked. "Where's the med tech?"

"She's waiting on the other side," the new guard said with a disgusting smile. "We have to prepare you first."

"Prepare me for what?" he asked suspiciously.

The prod touched his temple, paralyzing him as a current shot through his nervous system. He dropped to his knees and clenched his fists in the heavy black leather gloves he wore.

The two men grabbed him by his upper arms and dragged him to the table before he could react. As he started to come around, another prod hit his chest and the impact of it slammed his back against the unforgiving hardness of the table. They quickly wrapped the chains around his arms as they spread them on the table.

He kicked against the guards and the prod hit his side. One man lay over his thigh, putting painful pressure on his wound, which brought forth a groan.

"What are you doing to me?" he asked from between gritted teeth.

"You won," said the man who wrapped the chains around his ankles. "You get a reward."

The other one rubbed his hand on the top of his head, forcing the mask against his head so that it pulled his hair. He jerked against it, recognizing it for the insult it was meant to be.

The door was behind him. He heard it open and turned to see but it was out of his sight line. He heard the distinctive clink of credits hitting a palm and a malicious laugh.

"Try not to hurt him," one of the guards said. "After all, you might want to ride again sometime."

His body tensed. He checked the chains, pulling against them, but they would not budge. The blades screeched against the metal of the table and a strange metallic odor filled the air.

It was blood. His blood.

A hand touched the top of his head. A gentle hand. Or so he thought until long fingers splayed over his forehead and forced him back so his neck arched and he saw the woman's face that stared down at him.

Her hair was black as night and pulled back tight from her face before it cascaded down her back in a high tail. Her eyes were as black as her hair and heavily colored with deep red shadow on the lids. Her lips were also deep red, almost black in comparison to the brighter red droplets of blood that spattered the pale white skin of her face.

Her tongue flicked out and tasted a drop.

"Who are you?" he asked.

"Shhhh," she said. She placed a sharpened nail over his lips and dragged it down over his chin.

If her intent was to cause him pain, she succeeded. Her nail bit into the tender flesh of his neck and raked across the stubble of beard.

He jerked his head away and she laughed.

She walked around the cross of the table, teasing her fingers against the blades as she moved as if he were about to cut her.

He couldn't move his arms.

She was mocking him.

When she came into his line of sight he realized that her dress was transparent. It was black and filmy and two silver rings hung in her nipples that were barely covered by the deep V of a neckline that reached down to her navel.

He watched her from beneath the hood, his eyes following her hands as they touched his cheeks, came down his neck, then moved over the breastplate he wore. She stopped when she got to the waist of his pants and looked at him with a crooked smile.

He didn't dare speak. Speaking would mean weakness. He was sure she meant him harm and he was in no position to move.

Her nail dug into his navel, pushing against the skin as if she meant to break through and touch his internal organs. He tightened his abdominal muscles, making a solid wall against the pressure, but there was nothing he could do to protect the fragile skin she sought to pierce.

She stopped as if she changed her mind; then her fingers dipped beneath his waistband and she laughed again.

Gleefully she unfastened his pants.

What was she doing? He had thought himself weak, helpless, before, when they brought him to the pits. When he did not know his name. When he did not know who he was or *where he came from. When he did not know why. He chafed against his imprisonment, roaring his frustration in his cell after exhausting his body in the training, day after day.*

He had thought himself afraid when he was shoved into the arena for his first battle. He was sure he would die. But he won his first match, and then the next one, and he kept on fighting, letting his body take over with skills he did not recall ever learning. He fought until he was exhausted and the pain kept the fear at bay as each movement became an effort. He was afraid until he realized he won. And for one brief moment he thought part of the fear and frustration might be over.

But he realized he did not know what fear was until now.

She spread his pants wide and slid them down over his hips.

He hissed in shock and embarrassment as she looked at him, inspected him.

He was hard. He could not control it. It was a result of the battle. A sign of triumph.

She touched him. Placed her hand around him and pulled. His back came off the table as she pulled him up, leading him with her hand. Her nails dug at him and he gritted his teeth against the scream that gathered in his throat.

Was that her intent, then? To unman him?

She swung her leg onto the table. Her ascent was less than graceful but he was too scared to notice and she was too intent on her purpose to care. She lifted the hem of her dress and straddled him.

She was naked beneath it.

Then he slid into something wet and tight and his eyes widened as sensations coursed through his body.

She opened her dress and her hands ran over her breasts and pulled on the rings in her nipples.

He shuddered as she moved on top of him. Her pace quickened and she moaned.

He jerked against the chains as his mind left him and instinct took over. His hips rose to meet her downward thrusts and her movements became more frantic.

He wanted to scream. He knew the sensation but he did

not recognize it and his mind whirled around it as she gasped with each downward thrust and then let loose with a long deep moan.

His spine stiffened. He felt as if he were about to explode and then he did. She moved off him as he quickened and he felt the result moistening his pants where they hung open below his manhood.

"I take it I was your first," she said as she straightened her dress. "How did you stay pure for so long?"

Her fingers trailed through the blood on his thigh and she stuck them in her mouth, relishing the taste.

"At least you'll never forget me," she said as she walked to the door, leaving him exposed. Vulnerable. Weak.

He didn't know how long he lay there in his own sweat, blood, wetness, until Laylon came. He knew he was there long enough to fight back the tears that he did not dare cry. He was there long enough to well with hatred. He was there long enough to decide that he would kill her if he ever got the chance.

Phoenix looked in the small mirror that hung over the sink in his cell. Eyes, pale and cold as ice, stared back at him. One day he would kill her. One day the chains would break or she could come too close to the blades or the fence that surrounded the arena would dissolve and he would go into the crowd, slash her neck, and watch as her blood soaked her and everyone around her.

The next time she came he told her he would kill her. She laughed and had her way with him. It happened repeatedly. But one match the fence was weakened. Repeated hits from misses with the blades made it bend outward toward her seat. He saw it, recognized it, and when he was victorious that day went straight for it in an attempt to claw his way through. The guards enjoyed the beating they gave him that night. Especially with the knowledge that he would heal quickly.

She believed him then and never came again.

But other women came. Some paid for the privilege

to be with him. Some were rapture whores, sent as gifts. The whores taught him how to please a woman. Not that he cared to, but he was curious.

None gave him relief from the woman in his dreams.

He splashed cold water on his face to chase away the visions. He stretched his arms over his head, and checked the skin on his chest for the wound he'd received in the last battle.

It was gone, as he knew it would be. But the wounds were coming more frequently now as his challengers kept getting better and better.

It was if they were determined to kill him in one manner or another. Either in the arena, or by sheer exhaustion, as the times between matches was now closer together.

It did not matter. He was always ready to fight and if he died, then so be it.

Just let it be quick. Merciful. As he usually was.

Usually.

"You did not sleep long," Laylon said. Her entrance was quiet, as usual, even with the clang of the key in the lock.

"I slept long enough," he said. "How long?"

"Time enough for a meal," she said. "Time to prepare."

"Time for a bath afterward?" he asked. The large pool was his one privilege, the one thing he enjoyed and looked forward to. It was a place he could relax without worry or the eyes of the guard on him. Laylon always stood watch with her sightless eyes, acting as a barrier between him and the world when he was in the pool.

She smiled. "Yes," she said. "The powers-that-be said if he survives he may have the bath." She said it lightly, as if it were a joke, or a treat. They both knew the powers-that-be wanted him dead.

"Another challenger?" he asked as he pulled a loose shirt over his head.

"Another champion," she said casually. "From another planet in the known galaxy. He will soon learn there is only one true champion."

"I would gladly give it to him, would they just leave me in peace," Phoenix said.

"If only life were that easy," Laylon replied. They moved down the corridor to the room he prepared in. A meal awaited him on the table and his armor and weapons lay out, cleaned of all blood and gore by Laylon.

She went to his armor as soon as she heard the scrape of the chair that meant he sat down to eat.

The meal before him was nourishing, as always, but not tempting. He looked at it as if he'd never seen the food on the table before.

What do I like to eat?

He never considered it before. Surely he had acquired a taste for something in his lifetime, but as usual there was nothing there but a blank.

He wanted to slam the plates against the wall in his frustration, but out of consideration for Laylon he channeled his rage to the inside, to save for the match.

Laylon's fingers moved over his chest protector to assure herself that there were no weaknesses in the armor.

"How long have you been here?" Phoenix asked.

She tilted her head toward him in the funny way she had. He watched her closely as she considered the question. It was hard to know what she thought since her eyes were gone and the shields she wore hid that part of her face. He knew the blades had taken her eyes. The scar ran from one side of her head to the other, right across the bridge of her nose.

He knew her to be older, old enough to be a parent to him from the lines on her face. Her hair was close cropped, shorter than his, and it showed gray scattered throughout. More so in the past few solars.

"All my life," she said finally. "My mother served here. I was born here. My father was one of the champions although my mother could not say which one.

They decided when I was young that it would be entertaining to have women fight the Murlaca, so I was chosen to be a warrior." Her voice showed the pride she felt. "I was fortunate they allowed me to stay when this happened."

"So your entire life had been the Murlaca?"

"Yes. But it wasn't always like this. I was a champion. I walked the streets of Senate with pride. The people treated me like I was somebody."

"You are somebody," Phoenix said.

"I was, once upon a time," Laylon said wistfully.

"So you actually lived a life outside the pits?"

"Yes." She smiled. "I even tweaked the nose of the Circe one time."

"The Circe?" Phoenix asked.

"The ones who sent you here."

"Do you know why I was sent here?" He had asked her that before and he knew the answer but he couldn't help but ask again.

"They have power. Others don't. Obviously you didn't so they sent you here," she said simply.

"Tell me about tweaking their noses," Phoenix said. It was the first time in all the years together that she had ever said anything about her past.

"There was one that they hated more than anything. They feared him because of what he was. He had powers like them. They tried to kill him but he got away and then he came to fight the champion in a match of honor. To win the hand of the woman he loved, who was also a Circe. But she wasn't like the witches. She was kind and good."

Phoenix smiled even though Laylon could not see it. Her face had a look of contentment on it and it gave him satisfaction to see it.

"The Circe wanted him dead so they used their mind tricks against him. The man had a friend, Ruben . . ." She smiled at the memory.

"What did you do?" Phoenix asked. He was on the edge of his seat with the story. It carried him away from the monotony of his life.

"The same thing I do for you," she said. "I prepared him for battle. I checked his armor. Which was a good thing because what they sent him was a piece of ish. Instead I gave him good armor, armor that was worn by one of the champions. One who retired undefeated."

"They allow that?"

"It has happened," she said. "A few times."

"So what happened next?"

"Ruben and I snuck up on the witches when they were using their mind tricks. I grabbed one and knocked her out and Ruben took out the old bitch with the big hat."

He laughed then. A sound so foreign that he wasn't sure if it even sounded correct. Laylon laughed too. "If those witches only knew how foolish they look. I remember Ruben saying that he wanted to just pull their hats down over their heads and stuff their bodies up inside and drop-kick them out his hatch."

He remembered the ridiculous hat on the woman who had condemned him to the pits. It was the first memory he had. He felt the anger again and refused to dwell on it, for Laylon's sake.

"Ahhh, Ruben," she sighed.

Phoenix looked at her. She wiped her fingers beneath her eyes and then the back of her hand over her nose. Was she crying?

"You were in love with him, weren't you?" he asked.

Laylon turned her head in her peculiar twist, then smiled gently. "I was. But for him it was nothing more than a convenient friendship," she said.

"Sounds nice."

"It was. It was fun. No commitments, just the joy of being together."

"It is joyful?"

"It can be."

Phoenix looked at the smooth metal surface of the table. He placed his hand on it and felt the cool smoothness of it against his skin.

What would it be like, to lie with a woman you love . . . ?

"How is it that I know about something like love, when I have no memories and it's something I've never seen?"

I am your sanctuary.

"Love is not something one forgets. You must have had it in your past to know it now," Laylon said.

"But I was so young," he said.

"Nothing more than a boy," Laylon agreed. "A very independent one, I might add." Her hands found his chest protector. "But you must have had a family at some time. You were obviously educated."

"I was?" He stood, took off the loose shirt he wore, and replaced it with one that fit tightly against his skin. He picked up the thick leather boots and yanked them on, then adjusted the tops over his kneecaps.

"Yes. You know things that most of us don't. When you talk it's quite evident you have an education. And you'd had physical training. Or else you would not have survived this long."

"You would think that someone would have searched for me, then. If I did have a family."

"Never, ever underestimate the power of the Circe," Laylon said. "I don't know what happened to you or your memories. I do know there is nothing you can do about it either. All you can do is survive. That's how you beat them. They sent you here to die, yet you've survived this long."

"But what about my healing? Shouldn't that make me recognizable to someone, if someone was looking for me?" He raised his arms for Laylon.

"If it was known," Laylon said. "But it's not."

"They keep it secret," he said in realization. "Some tale to keep the fans screaming in their seats."

"Part of the mystique of the pits," Laylon said as she buckled the protector into place. "Go now," she said.

He went to relieve himself and came back to find her smiling wistfully again.

"I just thought of something," she said. "The one we helped. The one the Circe hated?"

"Yes?" he asked to let her know he was paying attention.

"His name was Phoenix. Shaun Phoenix."

The name meant nothing to him. Nothing more than a title he abhorred. But it was a strange coincidence.

"What happened to him?"

"He and his woman disappeared so the Circe couldn't find them."

"Sounds like a smart man," he said as Laylon fastened his thigh protectors into place over his thick boots. She handed him the cup and he slid it into place. Next came his armbands, thick polished silver. They fit over his upper arms, a small comfort against a blade strike.

She handed him the thick leather gloves and he pulled them on. Then she brought him the blades.

He held his arms out and she fastened them on, one at a time, using her fingers to feel each buckle to make sure none would come loose. To do so would be his death. He spread his arms wide and bent over so she could place the mask over his face.

She stopped just before she slipped it on.

"What do you look like?" she asked.

"Why?"

"I want to know." She reached her hand up and tentatively touched his cheek, brushing her fingertips over the bristle of his beard. Her hand searched onward and upward until it ran into the fall of his hair over his forehead.

"What color is it?" she asked.

"Dark," he said. "Not really black, but almost."

Her fingers trailed down his forehead and found the bridge of his nose.

"And your eyes? What color are they?"

He shrugged, amused at her sudden curiosity. "Gray," he said. "Pale gray. Like there's no color there at all."

The door swung open. "It's time," the guard said. "They're waiting on him."

Laylon stood, as if frozen, her fingers still touching his nose.

"Laylon?" he said.

She moved then and placed the mask over his face.

"Is something wrong?" he asked.

"No," she said and gave him a quick smile. "It's time to do battle."

CHAPTER TWENTY-FOUR

Elle spun the Sai in her hands without thought as she watched her father and grandfather talk on the balcony below.

No doubt they were talking about her upcoming nuptials.

The Sai were second nature to her now. Her excellence with them was beyond measure. No one could compete with her. No one wanted to.

It was all about the power.

Her father looked up at her. He was not happy with her at the moment. Or maybe it was more he was not happy with her choice for a husband. He agreed with her logic that it was best for the people of Oasis. Just as her mother did.

If only he knew what her real plans were.

Her intended was scheduled to arrive tomorrow. Her family was going to the capital this afternoon. Moving to the palace where she would stay until she left to go to Senate for her wedding.

There were too many memories in the villa. Memories that would not go away.

Elle smiled at her father when he looked up. She quickly went back inside to finish her training. It was easier to let him think everything was fine.

It was more important than ever that she be perfect with the Sai. Fear was a great inhibitor. If people feared her, then they would not challenge her.

Just as they did not challenge the witches.

Bella's invitation to study on Circe had become an open one. Every communiqué that arrived from the Senate held the request that Elle come to Circe to be trained. Her parents ignored them and attributed them to just another way to haunt them about Zander, but Elle was seriously considering taking her up on the offer once the ceremony was over. It was as good an excuse as any not to live with her husband-to-be.

She was confident that her intended would go along with her plans. Especially since he did not know that she controlled his mind. Especially since he did not want to marry her any more than she wanted to marry him.

Elle moved to the middle of the floor and gracefully lowered herself into a cross-legged position. She placed her feet upon her knees and then placed her hands, still holding her blades, upon her ankles, palms up.

She took a deep cleansing breath and closed her eyes. Without thought her fingers spun the Sai, nimbly working the trident handles as if they were extensions of her hands.

"Don't think," she told herself. "Don't think about the marriage. Don't think about the Circe. Don't think about Mother and Father. Don't think about Zander. Don't think about Boone."

Don't think. She might as well have told herself not to breathe.

Elle was very good at pretending but she was smart

enough to know that now was the time to get better at it. And to get stronger. So she could have more power. Power to start the new chapter in her life. The chapter where she was the victor. And everyone who had caused her and her family pain was punished.

If only she could stop thinking about it. Everything she did in her life was an effort to block out the memories, to block out the pain, but nothing seemed to work.

What would life be like if things were different? If only our parents had told us of the threat of the Circe. If only Zander had been patient for one more day and not run away. If only Boone and I had not been distracted by the wild urgings of our bodies. If only I had not blamed him.

If only for that, then she would at least have Boone. They could have comforted each other. They could have moved on. They could have loved.

If only she wasn't such a spoiled selfish gank.

The saying went that with age comes wisdom and she was wise enough now to know that she was as much responsible as Boone was for almost giving in to the desire. And she was also wise enough to know the Senate was treacherous enough to pump something into the atmosphere to cause such poor judgment.

It was the only explanation for the two of them nearly losing their heads. They both loved Zander. They both would have done anything to save him.

She shouldn't have blamed Boone. It was her fault he was gone. She deserved to suffer. She deserved to be miserable. Her mother was worried there would be no happiness for her. Why should there be when she caused so much unhappiness for so many people?

Boone's family. Tess, Ruben, Zoey. They were devastated by his loss. And it was all her fault.

The realization had come on the heels of Boone's disappearance.

There was nothing she could do to bring back Boone. Or bring back Zander. But she could stop the

Circe and the Senate from manipulating people's lives. From their treachery. From having all the power.

It was all about the power.

Elle gripped the Sai and gracefully rose to her feet. She began her Kada, going through the steps without thought, thrusting and slashing with her blades in different positions as if she were performing a dance instead of contemplating death. She spun and she twisted. She flipped through the air and the blades remained in her hands the entire time, an extension of her being.

She landed a particularly difficult aerial in a crouched position, ready to defend, ready to attack, and saw her father standing before her.

"You amaze me," he said. His handsome face showed his pride and love, his vulnerability, where his daughter was concerned.

It was a powerful gaze. One that she could not stand to look upon.

Elle moved to the weapons rack, put her blades away, and picked up a towel.

"You always said training was the key," she said as she wiped the sheen of sweat from her face and neck.

"It's evident that you listened," he replied. He crossed his arms and leaned casually against the stone arch that anchored the door, as if he were waiting for something.

It was impossible for her to breeze by him as if she had something urgent that required her immediate attention. Obviously she could not fool him as easily as she did her mother. Or as she pretended to fool her mother. And her mother pretended to let her.

"I never see you in here," she said. "Have you given up training altogether?"

All she had to do was look at her father to know that to be untrue. He was still as fit and strong as he'd been as far back as her memory went. Still solid, still commanding, still as handsome, although the dark hair was now tinged with gray.

Would Zander look like him now, if he was still alive, if he'd had a chance to mature?

The flash of pain that ran across her father's face let her know that he read her thoughts. It was hard to remember that she must keep the wall up at times like this.

"I come in the mornings, before you wake," he said. He moved to the weapons rack, picked up an Escrima, and spun it, just to show her that he could still keep up.

Elle knew the hours that he kept as the Sovereign Nicholas of Oasis. It was a wonder he slept at all.

"How are things with Oasis?" she asked. She knew she should be more a part of the day-to-day running of the government. Her father's method placed all the decisions into the hands of representatives of the people, which usually meant endless debates and posturing for individual recognition. It mostly bored her.

But she was the heir. The only one left in a royal bloodline that had sat at the head of Oasis for eons.

It should have been Zander.

"Oasis is fine. If only all the planets in our universe were as conscious of conservation as we are."

"The Senate is worried about our universe?"

"Some planets are experiencing water shortages. The seas are infected with a virus of some sort."

"Can't they contain it?'

"They're trying. And they want us to help with the restoration."

Elle laughed. "Does the Senate actually ever do anything?"

"Great politicians know how to delegate," Shaun said with his own laugh. "Especially when it comes to blame or credit."

"Father," Elle asked. "Would you be doing this, running Oasis, if you had a choice?"

"What do you mean?"

"You weren't raised to be sovereign. You spent your entire life thinking you were one thing and then found out you were another. You could have walked away. As far as the people of Oasis were concerned you were already dead. You could have gone on and lived your life the way you wanted to."

"This is the way I wanted to live my life," he said. He looked thoughtful for a moment. "With some exceptions."

Elle knew he was thinking of the Circe threat.

"Besides, your mother would never have allowed me to walk away," he continued.

Elle smiled. Her mother did have a great sense of diplomacy. But that was what she was raised to do. To be. The Princess of Oasis, ready to sacrifice her life for her people.

Then she sobered as she thought about where her mother's life had led. Would it have changed her mother's path if she'd known that she'd have to sacrifice her son's life? She'd been ready to sacrifice her own happiness—she was willing to do that before she met her father. But Zander?

It was all such a conundrum. However, there was one thing Elle was sure of, thinking of all the pain. Love would never play a role in her life again.

"Does this have anything to do with your decision, Elle?"

Her father's question brought her back to the present. "My engagement?"

"We never wanted you to marry for anything other than love." Shaun dropped the Escrima back into its slot and turned to face his daughter. "Can you honestly say that you love Peter?"

"I don't pretend to love Peter."

Shaun placed his hands on her shoulders and Elle had to admire the way he'd maneuvered her into a corner so she had no way to escape his touch, or the piercing pale gray eyes that mirrored her own.

"Then why are you marrying him?" he asked.

"Because it's the best thing for Oasis."

She didn't want to be touched. Not even by her parents. It made everything too personal, too close. "And it's as good a reason as any to marry someone." She shrugged her father off and moved away.

"Have I ever given you any indication that this is best for Oasis? Have I asked you to sacrifice your happiness for something that Oasis doesn't even need?"

"The Princess of Oasis married to the prefect's son? How could Oasis not benefit from this?"

"Elle, Oasis is fine and should remain so for a very long time. It does not need your sacrifice."

"It's not a sacrifice, Father. And it does make me happy."

"But he's a self-absorbed, sanctimonious gank," Shaun said.

Elle couldn't help it. She laughed.

"Don't hold back, Shaun, tell her how you really feel," Michael said as he walked into the room.

"Grandfather," Elle exclaimed. He was the one exception to her self-proclaimed avoidance of physical contact. She ran to him and gave him a kiss on the cheek and he gave her shoulder a quick squeeze in return.

"I found something on SSN that you might find interesting," he said to Shaun.

Her father looked at her, his mind probing, and then acknowledging her escape.

"What is it?" he asked.

"It seems the latest Murlaca champion has something in common with you."

Shaun arched an eyebrow at Michael. "What is it?"

"They call him the Phoenix."

Shaun grimaced. "Should I be flattered that the Senate's latest assassin carries my father's name?"

Elle knew he referred to the man who had raised him as his own, Ryan Phoenix. The man whose murder he avenged with murder on his own. Murders that put him on the path to meet her mother.

"I just thought it amusing," Michael said. "Apparently this one is unbeatable."

"So was Ram," Shaun said. "At the time."

"Mother told me that you fought the Murlaca," Elle said.

"Only once," Shaun replied. "And it's not something I ever care to do again. I can't even tolerate watching it."

"It's a vicious sport," Michael agreed. "If you could call it sport. Mostly it's a bloodbath."

"I wonder why they call him Phoenix," Shaun mused. "I've never run into another with that name. Could he be related to my father's family somehow?"

"The rumor is that he can't be killed. He gets injured one day and comes back the next as if he's never been touched."

"That's strange," Shaun said. "He must have a healer with him. A Circe."

"The Circe have those abilities?" Elle asked. "I know Tess is a healer but does she have the capacity to heal deep wounds overnight?"

"When I was injured your mother was able to heal me fairly quick. We think it was because we both were Circe. But I still felt wounds. And it was a while before I was fully recovered."

"We thought him to be dead for the most part when Ruben and I carried him back to the embassy," Michael said.

"You are never going to let me forget that, are you?" Shaun said. "Both of you . . ."

Elle realized that her father bit back the words about Ruben, the friend he barely spoke of anymore. The one man who shared the same pain as he because they both lost sons, yet they could not share the pain, or help each other through it.

Because of her.

The Circe were a curse. Even to those they loved.

"This Phoenix will eventually meet his end," Shaun said. "Just as they all do. Then another will come along and he will soon be forgotten."

"It will be hard since he can't be truly hurt," Michael said.

"Someone will find a way," Shaun said. "Someone will find his weakness."

Elle took advantage of their conversation to slip away with a puzzling thought nagging her mind.

He can't be hurt.

If the Circe had the ability to heal that quickly, then she needed to know about it.

It was all about the power.

CHAPTER TWENTY-FIVE

There were still those who considered him the Empowered One, even if his eyes were the wrong color. After all he had come to them in the same words of the legend. From the sea. Escorted by dolphins. If only they knew that the Empowered One was killed before he ever set foot on the planet.

If he'd only had the sense to believe that before he came here, then his life would be totally different.

But what difference did that make without Elle? And he was even a bigger fool now than when he first took off on his hopeless mission. A fool because he still loved her.

I'm cursed. Boone ran his hand over his recently shaved head, a necessity with the coming heat of summer.

Boone was smart enough to know that hope was a good thing, even if he had none, so he did not tell the rebels all the facts about Zander. And it could be Shaun they talked about when they told their tales around the fire late at night. He never mentioned him either. Hope was one thing, hopelessness another. Shaun knew that he could not fight an entire planet and the Senate.

With age comes wisdom. And there's nothing more foolish than a boy in love. Unless it's a grown man in love with a memory.

Boone picked his way through the scattered fires and makeshift shelters on his way to Sagan's cave. He felt the eyes of the women upon him. He heard the whispers. Before he was always self-conscious, about his scar, about their questions, about their stares. But now he knew, thanks to Sagan, what the questions were about.

He had to laugh when he thought about how easily Sagan had gotten his secrets from him. And learned his sexual preferences.

And it had been a long time since he preferred anyone. Longer than he liked to think about. Was it wrong of him to want some relief? Would it be a betrayal to lie with a woman?

She betrayed you.

Elle's final words still haunted him. Yet they were the ones that had driven him to this place. Should he blame her? As she blamed him?

Should he give up hope? Should he give in? It would be easy enough. There was one who had made it obvious she wanted him, even with the scar.

It wasn't as if he were going anywhere. At least not in the long term. But at the moment he had someplace he was supposed to be. And his musings on the beach had him running late.

There was a meeting tonight of all the rebel leaders. A risky venture to have them all in one place but Sagan had a plan.

And it all depended upon the collars failing.

They looked up when he came in with the same look he still received every time they saw him.

Why aren't you the one? The Empowered One. Why are you here?

They knew him to be Sagan's nephew. It was obvious to anyone who saw them together. Because they shared the same blood they shared the same heritage.

Yet they resented him because he was not their savior.

"Boone," Sagan said. He pointed to an empty stool close to his side, but a little bit behind the circle.

Still not quite a part, even after the years he'd spent fighting by their side. And he had the scars to prove it. Scars beyond the one on his face. Scars that would fade over time but never go away.

Maybe you should quit wishing for the stars.

A woman served him from the tray and her eyes were encouraging. Boone took the drink with a slight smile and watched her as she moved into the shadows and waited to see if anyone else required anything. Boone felt her eyes upon him.

It could be mindless. It could be physical. It could be something just to remind him that he was really alive.

Maybe it was time he gave up living in the past and wishing for things that would never be. Maybe it was time he looked to the future, even though there was none. Maybe it was time for him to grab some sort of happiness, however brief it may be.

Hope was a cruel mistress, Boone realized as he forced himself to pay attention to the conversation going on around the fire.

"What guarantees do we have that what you say is true?" It was Amberly. Always the skeptical one. Always the one with the questions. He never took anything on faith. Maybe that was the reason he was still alive.

"It makes perfect sense," Sagan said. "The liquid form is breaking down. Turning into the gas."

"But we still don't know if that makes it ineffective,"

a woman said. Boone did not recognize her. She was either from a distant region or else a new leader, replacing one who had been killed or captured.

"It's easy enough to find out," Sagan said. "We just capture one of them."

"And have the entire guard after us?" another one protested. Petree. The coward.

"We can get one alone," Sagan said. "Draw him out. Overpower him. Disarm him. Talk to him."

"And if your plan fails, then he will call in the guard to capture us."

"Not all of us," Sagan said. "Just a few. A few volunteers."

"I'll go," Boone said.

"No," Sagan said. "You can't." His words were emphatic, his tone stern.

Everyone seemed surprised at his protests. Boone was simply confused.

"We have need for you," Sagan said. "Later, if it all goes according to plan."

"What value does he have?" Petree asked. His eyes on Boone were almost angry. Boone recalled that he had lost his son to the slavers in a vicious battle a few solars back. He had reason to hate him if he thought Sagan was protecting him from the same fate.

"He's the only one of us who can fly," Sagan said simply.

His chest hurt. The thought of flying again nearly suffocated him. To once more know the freedom, the joy, and feel the power and the yoke in his hand. To have the sky eternal before him.

To escape this hellhole of a planet, this useless existence, this misery, this eternal longing.

Boone realized that everyone around the fire was looking at him. Considering him. Seeing him for the first time. All but Sagan. Boone looked at his hands and they actually flexed as if he were about to grab the yoke. Instead, he stuck one in his pocket and closed his fist around his toy, gripping it so tightly that he felt the painted metal digging into his palm.

To fly . . .

"If we can turn the guard on-planet," Sagan said. "We will need a defense against the guard in the sky. They would never expect an attack from above."

"We'll have to steal a starship," a man said from the outer extremes of the circle.

"We'll need a Falcon," Boone said. He was surprised he could speak. "One with weapons."

"They never land," Amberly spouted. "They stay in the sky or on the satellites."

"One will if they suspect trouble," Sagan said. "You forget the Circe's weakness."

"They have none," Petree again.

"Yes, they do," Sagan said. "They are overconfident. They think we are beaten. Occasionally they send the guard out to round up the rebels and sell us as slaves, but for the most part they ignore us, unless we insult them."

"Like seducing one of the witches?" the new woman said. She grinned at Sagan, who returned her smile with an easy one of his own.

Boone realized it had to hurt him. To have his love treated so casually. But he didn't show it. He was a good leader. And a wise one.

"We could do it," the woman said. "My men and I."

And just that easily Sagan had his volunteer. He had made the woman feel welcome among the men and since she was one woman among many men she had something to prove.

A wise leader. Sagan knew his people. He knew their talents. He knew their needs.

I'm going to fly.

CHAPTER TWENTY-SIX

Phoenix kept his eyes on Laylon as the lift began its ascent. He should be looking inward. He should be concentrating on the coming match. He should make himself ready in case whoever was waiting above him took advantage of the temporary blindness that would come with the lights.

She had been strangely quiet as they moved toward the match. Distracted even. And it had something to do with the way he looked.

Was there something wrong with him? Something he did not realize? And how could she, a blind woman, perceive it?

She stood as she always did by the lift, listening to the hiss of released pressure as the hydraulics did their work.

The floor of the arena split and opened to allow his passage up. He saw the lights flashing and heard the crowd chanting his name.

"Phoenix. Phoenix."

He was not the first with the name to fight here. It didn't matter. The name was borrowed. Not his own. Never his own.

The floor above him rocked. Whoever was waiting must be stomping on it. Trying to draw his own fans into the fray, no doubt.

"Laylon," he said. He was above her head now. The ascent was four times the height of the ceilings. A long way. Enough time to talk. He moved to the edge of the platform so he could look down at her. He felt the need to say something. To do something. She was troubled.

She turned her head upward as if she were looking at him. He opened his mouth to speak and the lift suddenly jolted. He felt his balance go and looked up to see his opponent staring down at him with a malicious grin on his face.

One of the chains holding the lift was broken. The man had slashed it with his blades. The lift tilted at a crazy angle as the other three chains kept working. He was sliding and there was nothing to catch his fall.

Nothing but Laylon, who still looked upward, confusion plainly written on her face.

"Move!" he yelled as his body tumbled. In desperation he tried to bury the blades into the floor of the lift. They caught and spun his body around so he dangled with his feet hanging over the side. The floor was light, made to give and bounce when someone landed upon it, and the harsh metal tore through the fibers, splitting it like skin.

"Laylon! Move!" he yelled again. The distance between him and the floor was thrice his height. He knew once he started falling he would have no control.

She moved back against the wall. Part of the lift fell away where his blade had shredded it and crashed to the floor in front of her, blocking her escape. His arms ached with the effort to bury the blades deep and keep from falling. The edge loomed closer. The blades reached the end and he flew out into the air with nothing to stop his descent and nothing to stop him from cutting his own body into pieces.

His arms and legs flailed through the emptiness as he sought to catch himself on something, anything, but there was nothing there. He had no control over his body until he felt himself land on something soft. Something giving.

Laylon.

He heard her sharp intake of breath, then a hiss. Phoenix pushed himself up and realized that he was covered in blood.

Laylon's blood.

"Laylon?" He moved his arm. The one that curled between him and Laylon with the blades buried into her abdomen.

"Uhhhh," she gasped.

"Laylon?" He wanted to touch her. Pick her up. Comfort her. But he was afraid he would do her more damage. And there was no one to take the blades off. He held his arms out and tried to touch her face with just his hands.

He heard the pounding of footsteps, he heard the shouts of the guard and the questioning shouts of the crowd. He even heard his challenger laughing at him from above.

Her hand moved up, touched his mask. "I . . . know . . ."

He bent closer.

"I . . . know who . . . you . . . are," she gasped.

"Who am I?" His heart raced. How could she know? How could she have kept it from him all these years? What was happening?

"You're . . . sh . . . sh . . . Phoenix," she said. Her hand fell away from his face.

"Laylon? *Laylon?*"

Blood trickled from her mouth as her throat rattled. She was dead.

The roar started deep within his gut and echoed off

the walls that surrounded them. Hollow emptiness rushed in where once before there was warmth.

Somewhere in his subconscious he heard the guards around him, heard their questions, then their shouts as he jumped up and grabbed the empty chain that dangled against the wall.

Phoenix pulled himself up the chain, his blades scraping the wall as the chain swayed with his weight. Through the opening above he saw that the arena was dark and heard the restless buzz of the crowd.

Somehow he knew that what he was doing was foolish. But what difference did it make. What was the worst thing that could happen?

You could die.

Then let it happen. Let it happen now, this moment. Let it all be over with. The endless questions, the endless dreams, the endless torture of his mind, his body, and his soul.

But before he died he would take someone with him. And then he would do his best to kill the woman who'd violated him.

Because the only person who cared about him, the only person he cared about, was dead.

His hands found the edge of the arena. He knew the blow would come that would take his fingers off and he clenched his hands against it as he swung his body up onto the floor.

The blow did not fall. Two guards had his opponent pinned into the corner with their prods. The lights that usually brightened the cage flashed above their heads.

The crowd, quiet with apprehension and curiosity, erupted into screams when he gracefully came to his feet and the lights found him.

"Let him go," he said, so calmly it surprised him, and he crossed his blades in challenge.

The two guards smirked and backed away as Phoenix moved around the opening in the floor.

My floor. My ring. My arena. My victory.

As they slipped through the gate he slung an arm after them, striking the latch as they pulled it shut, and jumped to the floor beside the ring, both quickly turning around so as not to miss anything between the two combatants.

No one noticed the gate, so focused was everyone on the coming match.

"Did you have a problem on your way up?" his challenger asked as he postured his way out of the corner.

"Did you fear to face me on equal ground?" Phoenix said. "Do you think to cripple me so you can beat me?"

No one outside the ring could hear them. But the crowd quickly realized the open hostility in the ring. This was more than just another match. This had become personal. The audience buzzed over what exactly had happened in the pits below and rumors quickly circulated in the ring.

"This is the Murlaca," his opponent said, as they both ignored the noise around them. "Whatever it takes to win."

"Another challenger from another planet," Phoenix said. They were circling each other, around the hole, cautiously looking for a weakness, an opening. "Soon the universe will run out of challengers."

"Do you think to live forever?"

"Didn't they tell you?" Phoenix sneered. "I can't die. You can slice me into infinity and I will be back to fight again tomorrow."

"Not after I finish with you."

"Then please do," Phoenix said. "I'm tired of the talk."

The challenger feinted left. Phoenix did not give him a chance to go right. Instead he dived across the hole and hit the man full in the chest with his head and his arms coming down onto his shoulders, instantly crippling him.

As they hit the mat, the man landed on his back with his arms flung useless at his sides.

Phoenix buried a hand in his hair and lifted his head. With a slash of his arm he cut his opponent's throat.

The crowd gave a collective intake of breath, so quickly did it happen, and then erupted into a roar.

Phoenix jumped to his feet and went to the gate. The guards looked aghast when he kicked it open, his eyes scanning the crowd for his next victim.

She saw him coming. The dark-haired woman screamed and fought her way through the crowd to get away. Her scream alerted him to exactly where she was and he jumped into the crowd. Some tried to move away, others attempted to touch him; all wished to avoid the dangerous blades that he chose to ignore as he moved through, not caring if he injured anyone in his path.

The arena was chaos. Phoenix kept his eyes on the woman as she struggled up the steps. He could cut across and reach her. His boots hit the benches and he leapt from one to the next as bodies scattered out of his way, most diving underneath the benches for protection.

His hands curled in anticipation. He didn't know if he should choke her or slash her. It wasn't until he felt the shock from the prod hit him that he realized he might not get to her in time. Another one rocked his body, along with a blow, and he roared his frustration as he stumbled. Another shock came, then another, yet he moved forward, his eyes focused on her screaming face as she moved farther out of his grasp.

It wasn't until his head exploded from a heavy blow that he gave up the attack as redness overcame him and then the blessed darkness.

As he hit the ground he wondered if they would kill him.

CHAPTER TWENTY-SEVEN

Elle willed her hands not to clench the rail of the balcony that overlooked the city as she watched the parade celebrating her engagement. The celebration was magnificent. The people were out in great numbers, all to show their love and support for their beloved leader, the Sovereign Nicholas, his consort, Princess Lilly, and their daughter, Princess Arielle, whom they had only seen a few times since her existence was announced.

Streamers decorated the crystal air with bright colors, adding a festive feel that was desperately missing on the balcony. The sunlight of midday danced off the gemstones set in the stone of the buildings and dazzled the eye. The time of the parade was not an accident. It was carefully planned to show the prefect and his Circe advisers just how special Oasis was.

And to remind them that they couldn't have it.

It was almost exactly the same as her mother's bridal parade, over twenty-five solar years ago. Elle researched the entire thing carefully, watching the dige in the historical archives over and over again. She'd been amazed that her gentle, diplomatic mother told the people of Oasis to fight for their freedom. And they had, which brought about the defeat of the Ravigans, the restoration of her father to his rightful place on Oasis, and put the Circe and the prefect in an indefinite bad mood. It was a beautiful thing to watch but Elle had no aspirations for the same thing happening to her. After all, her handsome hero was long gone and there would be no last-minute battle for her hand.

Boone would think that funny. If he were here. If he were still alive.

And she had no one to blame but herself. Her stupid, childish, impetuous self.

Yet she couldn't help but think the decision she'd made about Peter was just as childish.

It would take a while for Peter's vanguard to arrive, so she might as well indulge herself in the fantasy of having Boone arrive at the last moment, blazing across the pristine blue of the sky in the Firebird and declaring his undying love for her, after he defeated Peter in battle.

The image of Peter in battle, much less handling a weapon, was enough to send her into laughter, which she wisely bit back.

Or maybe it was just the insanity of what she was doing, threatening to overflow.

Her mother and father seemed calm enough. No hysterical laughter simmering under the surface. Her father's mouth was set in a thin line as he prepared to be civil to the prefect. Luckily they were so high up that the crowd did not notice the pretense. But they had to know.

Surely some of them had been present at her mother's parade.

Her mother, the very definition of elegant grace under pressure. Lilly waved graciously to the crowd, a beautiful smile on her serene face.

Elle, on the other hand, wanted to throw off the heavy, ornate robes she wore and disappear into the crowds. She longed for the sight of the ocean and the simple company of the dolphins. How long had it been since she sought the solace of the water with the simple innocence of youth?

There would be no ocean, no dolphins, and no breeze freshened with salt air on the Senate planet.

But she would find her escape from its confines.

If only she could go back, if all three of them could go back to that last, wonderful, innocent day.

It's about the power. This is what you wanted.

"Elle!"

A moment passed. A memory stirred. Happiness . . . contentment . . . as if . . .

Elle looked around in confusion. Was the voice in her head, or did someone call out her name? Someone who knew her intimately instead of as Princess Arielle? But who could it be? Only her family called her that.

"Down here!"

Elle looked down. A tall young girl with vivid blue eyes and long dark curls stood directly below waving wildly as the crowd looked at her with disbelief at her faux pas plainly written on their faces. A huge black newf stood at her side as a sentinel, persuading those who thought to chastise her to wisely keep their tongue.

"Zoey?" Elle asked in disbelief.

The girl nodded and smiled broadly up at Elle.

"Get up here." Elle leaned over the rail, totally ignoring the proper protocol of the day. She felt, rather than saw, Michael behind her and quickly straightened up as he cleared his throat.

"It's Zoey," she said as explanation and grinned

when Michael leaned over in the same undignified manner.

"I'll take care of it," he said and Elle saw the guard quickly jump to do his bidding.

"I wonder where Ruben and Tess are," Lilly said.

They should be here, Elle mused. But then again they should be celebrating her marriage to Boone instead of to the bridegroom that was quickly approaching.

"They must be close," Shaun commented. "I can't imagine them turning Zoey loose in this mob."

"They were invited," Lilly said. "They should be here."

They should be here.

So her parents had invited Ruben and Tess to the celebration. Even though they hated her. And why shouldn't they?

"Here we go," Shaun said and Elle was grateful for the interruption. Her memories seemed to be haunting her more this day. Her self-control was not as she wanted it to be. Which meant she would have to train even harder.

Elle's face did not reveal her inner turmoil as she looked over the parade route, waiting for Zoey to arrive. The prefect's hoverpod was in view and weighed down with everyone who felt they deserved to ride with the ruler of the known universe.

It was easy enough to spot Bella's ridiculous headwear and the prefect's silver-streaked hair. But the sight of two blond heads close together made Elle's lip curl in disgust.

Calvin.

Peter never went anywhere without Calvin. His assistant, Peter called him.

Calvin, who always watched Peter closely and Elle more so, as if she were planning his demise.

More likely it was the other way around. Elle had no illusions considering Peter's sexual preferences. It was another reason why she chose him. No expectations. No complications. No pain.

Peter had made a formal inquiry to her availability, and she had feigned boredom with his request. Elle was certain the inquiry had come at the urging of Bella and his father, who still lusted after the riches Oasis had to offer. After that it was just a matter of waiting for his injured pride to make him show up in person and then convincing him that their marriage was all his idea.

Calvin hated her. She might have to do something about him, eventually, if he made things difficult.

"Elle!" A set of arms came around her waist and Elle was amazed to see that Zoey's head was level with her shoulder. She impetuously hugged her without thought.

"I can't believe you're here," Elle exclaimed. "You've grown. Let me look at you."

Zoey, half her age, was nearly as tall as Elle, which made sense since both Ruben and Tess were tall. Her eyes were the vivid blue of her father but her face looked more like her mother's. Kyp stood beside her, his tail beating a swath among the bodies crowded on the balcony.

She looked like Boone. Elle's heart squeezed inward upon itself as she looked at the innocent face.

No pain. No pain. No pain. . . .

How could it still be so fresh, after all these years?

"Where are your parents?" Elle asked and wondered if she actually did sound like her mother.

"Somewhere," Zoey said carelessly. "They didn't want to get in the way."

Elle rolled her eyes. "They're our friends. They would never be in the way."

"It's hard for them," Zoey said. "They talk about how things should be. Not how they are. They don't think you should be doing this." When had Zoey become so direct? And fearless? Where was the bubbly little girl who used to follow her around?

"They're not the only ones," Elle said and felt like a rebellious teenager once again.

"And they were wondering . . ."

"About Peter?" Elle asked.

"Yes," Zoey said. "They wanted to know who took Boone's place."

Elle felt her heart crunch again.

How could Zoey sound so casual about Boone? He was her brother, gone, just like Zander was. Didn't she have a hole in her heart too?

"No one can take Boone's place," Elle said. The cheering of the crowd was louder now. The hoverpods were quickly approaching the staircase that led to the balcony.

"He's not dead," Zoey said in a matter-of-fact tone as she peered curiously toward Peter's pod. "And I know you don't believe he is dead."

"Zoey," Elle said. Now was not the time to get into an in-depth conversation with her. Zoey was still a child and if it gave her comfort to believe Boone was still alive, out in the universe, somewhere, then it was not her place to disillusion her. But eventually Zoey would have to face the facts. And besides, her fiancé was coming.

"You still wear his necklace," Zoey said, pointing to the silver chain that showed beneath the sheer neckline of her dress. "You know he's coming back."

Elle's hand went without thought to the gem that hung between her breasts.

It was a childish fantasy, nothing more. Nothing more than the hopes and dreams of a child, who missed her brother.

Zander . . .

Did Zoey feel as incomplete as she did? And did she feel this way because Zander, her twin, was gone, or because Boone was gone?

And what difference did it make now?

It was all in the past. And it would remain there.

So there would be no pain.

Elle pasted a broad smile on her face as Peter followed his father up the staircase. Bella and Calvin trailed beyond them, both of them keeping their faces pleasantly political.

Zoey and Kyp moved back into the shadows, gently guided by Michael as Elle moved closer to her father.

Keep your friend close and your enemies closer.

She knew what her father was thinking without reading his mind. It was the same thing she was thinking.

Everyone was thinking it. Except Peter, who was totally oblivious of the undercurrents on the balcony.

His only thought was how he could keep Calvin from leaving him.

Elle suppressed a smile when she saw her usually serene mother arch an eyebrow. Apparently she had slipped into Peter's mind and quickly figured out where his interests lay. Elle was certain her mother would renew her attack on her later when they were alone.

Not that it mattered. Her mind was made up. Peter was the quickest route to obtain what she wanted.

The power . . .

Bella seemed smug. Calvin looked terrified and Elle quickly realized that it was Kyp he was afraid of when he skittered behind one of the guards with an undignified yelp.

"Stupid gank," her father said in her mind.

Elle concentrated on keeping the serene smile on her face as the two families joined together at the balcony rail.

Apparently Kyp felt the same about Calvin. There was no mistaking the sound of his growl and Zoey calling him down as Calvin nearly climbed over Michael in his haste to get away from the beast.

They smiled and waved to the crowd. It was such a farce.

What if Boone is alive?

CHAPTER TWENTY-EIGHT

The plan was simple enough. Just wait to get one of the guards alone and then take him before he could raise an alarm.

So why was he so worried?

Boone knew he would feel better about the whole thing if he were the one involved. Being told to stay put was not exactly what he wanted to hear, especially when the success of the plan made the difference between whether or not he could fly again. It made him feel like a child again. But he realized the wisdom of it. He was the only one of the rebels who could fly.

If only the Firebird wasn't lying at the bottom of the sea.

Boone looked out the window again. Every time before when he'd been to the capital city with Sagan he'd felt comfortable and was able to blend into the ebb and flow of the city without any problems. This time he felt claustrophobic.

Probably because so much was riding on this trip.

If he looked at just the right angle, he could see the lights of the small spaceport that faced the ocean. The approach reminded him of flying into Crater Lake on Oasis.

Elle . . .

"No sign?"

Amberly. The man watched him as if afraid he would betray them. What had he done to make the man think that way?

It's what you haven't done.

"Nothing," Boone said. Waiting was always the hardest part.

Which was all he had done since he came to Bali Circe. Waited.

He didn't belong here and everyone knew it.

"Chanice worries me," Amberly said. "What do we really know about her?"

"Sagan seems to like her," Boone said. It wasn't a secret. Chanice had volunteered her men for the mission and apparently volunteered to warm Sagan's sheets.

Was twenty years long enough to mourn for a love that could no longer be?

"I've heard she has a sister that was taken by the slavers."

"Doesn't most everyone here have someone like that?"

"I've also heard she'd do anything to get her back," Amberly said. "Which would include trading us for her."

At least the waiting would be over.

"Sagan trusts her," Boone reminded the man.

"Sagan trusts too easily," Amberly said and stomped away.

Boone watched him go. He wouldn't put it past Amberly to turn him in if it suited his needs. But Amberly was a worrier so it was just his way.

He turned back to the window.

The streets were deserted. It was long past curfew.

Anyone caught on the streets would be arrested without question.

And those who waited would have no way of knowing what happened to their friends. They would simply disappear.

What would he do if Sagan was captured? Boone looked toward the spaceport again. If only he could get a ship. But without help, without a plan, it was suicide. The port was impossible to get to without walking through hundreds of people, most of them Circe witches, or the guard.

They would read his intent before he could take a breath.

The only way to get a ship was to get a Falcon to land on-planet somewhere.

A movement caught his eye, nothing more than a shadow, and he turned, willing his eyes to pierce the darkness as if he could see.

Like Shaun . . .

It had to be them. Boone counted six figures skittering in the shadows, and two of them were dragging someone in between.

"It's them," he said quietly. He heard Amberly come up behind him.

"Are you sure?" the man asked. "It could be a trap."

"Or they could have succeeded," Boone said. The neon glow of a collar showed on the man they dragged and Amberly nodded in surprised appreciation.

In a matter of seconds they were all inside and very short of breath as two of Chanice's men lowered their captive into a chair. He was easily recognizable as one of the planetary guard. He was dressed in all black, carried a stunner that someone had removed, and was collared. Everyone's eyes immediately went to his neck. The collar blinked bright pink under a face that showed the lines of middle age.

"Any problems?" Amberly asked.

"Not until they realize he's missing," Sagan said.

"We caught him taking a piz," Chanice said with a salacious grin.

"They actually let them do that?" Amberly asked.

"Better than having them piz themselves, I guess," Sagan said. "He was part of the nightly patrol. No Circe around that we could see, so it will probably take them a while to raise the alarm."

"Because none of his friends want to admit that they messed up," Boone said.

"Or take the punishment for losing him," Sagan added. "We should have plenty of time."

As if on cue the guard's head lolled and he let out a soft moan. Sagan nodded at Amberly and the man jumped in with some rope and tied the guard to the chair.

"Rebels!" the guard said when he finally realized that he wasn't where he was supposed to be. His face revealed his fear as he looked at the group that surrounded him

"Yes, we are," Sagan said. He pulled another chair up before the guard and sat down to face him. "And we're hoping to bring you over to our cause."

The guard immediately shook his head to the contrary. The whites of his eyes showed his fear. "You don't know what you're saying," he said. "Let me go and I won't tell anyone about you."

"You won't have to tell," Chanice said. "Your handler can find out just by looking inside." She touched the side of the guard's head for emphasis.

"What's your name?" Sagan asked.

"Bry . . . Bryant," the guard stuttered. "Please let me go," he said. "You don't know what they'll do to me."

"You can join us," Sagan said. "And we'll make sure they don't find you."

"They can always find me," Bryant said. "As long as I wear this. And there's no way to take these off. Unless you have the key."

"I think you're overestimating the power of that collar," Sagan said. "What is your first order should you become separated from your troop or find a rebel?"

"Report," the guard said. He seemed stunned by the proceedings. Shocked that anyone would dare to cross the Circe.

Sagan crossed his arms and leaned back in the chair. "Yet here you sit."

"I'm tied up!" the guard said.

"You haven't even tried to escape," Chanice pointed out. "And you're talking to us. Without anyone telling you to."

"I'm allowed to speak," the man said indignantly. "I am a Circe Guard, not a slave or a prisoner." He spoke as if it were a high honor to be a guard.

Boone laughed. "You wear a collar that needs a key. The prisoners get temporary ones, don't they?"

He had no answer for that.

"The collar you're wearing," Sagan said. "How long have you had it?"

"I've been in service for twenty-eight years," the man said proudly. "They will let me retire in seven more."

"Do you have a wife?" Sagan asked. "A family?"

"It is not permitted," he said.

"Do they allow you women?" one of the men asked.

Sagan raised an eyebrow at the questioner and looked at the guard.

"We get rapture women for a reward . . . sometimes."

"Sometimes . . ." Amberly sneered.

"How would you like to have a normal life?" Sagan asked. Boone was glad to see he ignored the jeers from the men in the circle. "A happy life?"

"As a rebel?" Bryant asked incredulously. "You don't know what you're saying. If you're lucky they'll just sell you off when you're captured."

"Instead of sending us to the Murlaca?" Sagan asked.

"How is it you know of the Murlaca?" Bryant asked. His indignation had turned to caution.

"We know plenty of things that happen off-planet,"

Sagan said. "Which proves that they do not control everything."

Boone knew Sagan was bluffing. The rebels had heard of the Murlaca. Sagan knew his father had suffered that fate because they taunted him with it when his family was captured. But none of them knew what it was until Boone told them. Everything they knew of the universe came from Boone.

"You are insane," Bryant insisted. Boone saw the fear in his eyes.

"No," Sagan said. "I'm not insane. But I am determined. We can defeat these women. We can throw off their yoke of oppression. And I can prove it to you."

"How?"

"The collar you wear," Sagan said. "How long have you worn it?"

"Since I was chosen for the guard," he said.

"They've never changed it?"

"No. They always remain on. Since . . ."

"Since my father stole my mother away from the Circe and started the rebellion," Sagan finished for him.

The look in the man's eyes was almost reverent. Almost. Perhaps there was some hatred there also. Boone could practically see the wheels turning inside Bryant's head.

How long had it been since the man had thought for himself?

"The reward for you is great," Bryant finally said.

Boone took a step closer to Sagan. Just in case anyone was tempted. He had a serviceable blade in his pocket. Nothing like his father used but one he knew how to handle if the need arose.

"Freedom is the greatest reward of all," Sagan replied. If he was worried about treachery from any in his band he did not show it.

The silence in the room stretched as if each one was weighing the choice. Boone's eyes darted between the assembled as he tried to figure out who had the guard's stunner.

"Let me show you how," Sagan said gently. "Do you wonder why you're not trying to get up from the chair, even with the bonds in place? Do you wonder why your mistress isn't searching for you? Do you wonder why you're sitting here talking to us about the rebellion when you know you should be trying to escape because your mistress's will controls you?"

Bryant's eyes widened. Boone did not have to be a Circe to know what the man was thinking.

Sagan touched the collar with the tip of his finger. "This no longer controls you," he said. "And the color certainly does not become you."

Bryant flushed a brighter pink than his collar and his hand went to his neck.

"The Perazine has broken down," Sagan explained. "It's as ineffective as the gases in our atmosphere."

"Are you sure?" Bryant whispered reverently.

"There's only one way to find out," Sagan said and he nodded to Amberly, who quickly produced a set of cutters from his pocket.

"No!" Bryant almost shrieked. "To remove it means instant death."

"Only if they control you," Sagan said. "Only if you believe the Circe still controls your mind."

Bryant struggled against his bonds then. "She's looking for me," he gasped. "I can feel her." His eyes bulged as if he were in great pain.

"Get if off him," Sagan said.

"No!"

Two of the men slammed Bryant down firmly as he tried to rise from his chair. They held his shoulders while Amberly went for the lock with the cutters.

"Try to keep him quiet," Chanice barked out as Bryant let out a yelp. Another man grabbed his head from behind and kept him from moving by squeezing his face between his hands.

"This is going to take a while," Amberly said.

"Look at me," Boone said to the struggling Bryant. His face showed his panic.

"Right here," Boone said, pointing to his eyes. "Repeat what I say. It will protect you."

"Noooo," Bryant said. "You don't know. You don't know."

"My mind is my own," Boone said. "Repeat it!"

"My mind is my own."

"No other may possess it."

"My mind is my own . . ." Bryant said.

"Listen to me," Boone insisted. "My mind is my own. No other may posses it. I will keep my mind and use it to overcome my enemies."

"My . . . my mind is my own . . ."

"Believe it," Boone said. "You must believe it."

"They're coming," Bryant said.

"We better move," Chanice said as she moved to the window.

"Do you see anything?" Amberly asked.

"Nothing," Chanice said. "But they've got to be close if he can feel the witch."

"We're not leaving without him," Sagan said. "And the collar stays here as a sign to the rest of them."

"Say it with me," Boone said to Bryant, who looked as if his head were about to explode. He leaned in close to Bryant, his nose inches away from the other man's face. "My mind is my own . . ."

Bryant repeated the words, and then fell into unison. He closed his eyes, squeezed them tight. Boone closed his eyes also, trying with all his might to reach out to Bryant, to calm his fears, to become one with his mind as he'd seen Elle do so many times.

If only he had the power. If only . . .

Concentrate on Bryant.

"My mind is my own. My mind is my own. My mind is my own . . ." Over and over again they said it.

"Got it," Amberly said and flung the collar against the wall.

Bryant's hands went to his neck and the men released him. Boone sliced the bonds with his knife.

"You're free," Sagan said as Amberly, Chanice, and the rest of the men silently filed out of the back door. "Now you can choose. Do you want freedom?"

Bryant appeared to be in shock as he looked up at Sagan. "I can choose?" he said.

"You can now," Sagan said.

"Best make it right now," Boone said. There was no mistaking the sounds outside on the street.

"Take me with you," Bryant said.

CHAPTER TWENTY-NINE

"Come with me," the guard said as he kicked him awake.

Phoenix blearily rolled from his cot.

Would today be the day they would kill him? He hoped so. He was tired of the waiting, tired of the wondering, tired of just existing from day to day as he waited, alone, for his fate.

He did not even know how many days it had been since Laylon died. Since he lost his mind in the ring. Since they beat him senseless and threw him in his cell to heal so they could drag him out and do it all over again. And again.

At least the guards were enjoying themselves.

He followed along as ordered, wearing nothing but a torn pair of bloody pants, and was surprised when the guard led him to the bath. More so when he shoved him inside and slammed the door behind him.

He looked around the huge tiled room to make sure he was totally alone. Steam rose from the glass-blocked shower. Beyond it the shallow pool seemed cool and inviting. The table was set with real food instead of the compacted protein that was pitched into his cell three times a day.

Phoenix circled the room to make sure no one was hiding. Not that there was any place to hide; the room was empty except for the table and chairs and an armoire that held thick towels and several different soaps. The door on the opposite side was locked from the outside, as was the one he entered through.

If he was to die today, then he would do it clean and well fed.

Clean was his first desire. He still wore the pants from the day of Laylon's death. They were drenched with blood—Laylon's, blood from the last man he fought, his own, and most likely some innocent blood from the crowd. Although somehow they did not fit his ideal of innocence.

Where did you learn such concepts?

The questions were one part of living he would not miss.

He dropped his pants to the cool tile and kicked them into a corner before he entered the shower.

The water was hot enough to give him pause and he briefly wondered who had turned it on before he bent his head and let the water pound against his back. He found the soap and took a moment to inhale its fresh, spicy scent.

A vision passed before him. Something so quick and elusive that he could not name it but he recognized that laughter was attached to it. He smelled the soap again and was rewarded with nothing more than a sneeze.

As he scrubbed his body from head to toe, he figured that at least he could die with a brief moment of contentment.

When he felt himself finally clean he left the shower and walked naked to the pool. The water was cool, comforting, and vaguely familiar against his raw scrubbed skin. He sank into it and let his body drift until he was on the bottom.

He closed his eyes as he held his breath.

Was it hard to drown? Would it be easier than whatever death awaited him? What did they plan for him?

If he could just stay here and let the water take him. Death had to be better than life. His life. Or was everyone's existence this miserable?

How long would it take?

He kept his mouth closed, and compressed his chest. He was determined to find out. He would stay this way until his lungs burst and the water rushed inside and took his life away.

It shouldn't be too much longer. The desire to breathe was great but his will would be greater. It had to be.

His head protested. His lungs screamed. His heart pounded in his chest. He kept his eyes tightly closed and willed his mind into submission.

Lights flashed before his closed lids. Tiny pinpricks that exploded into stars as the blood pounded in his temples, begging him for relief.

He would not give in. He would die now, this time, this place, at his leisure. How much longer would it take? How much longer could he hold on? How much longer until he passed into oblivion?

Then he saw the dolphins. His mind's eye did not recognize them but his brain identified them as so. If he reached out his hand, he could touch them. They smiled at him in invitation.

Take me. Take me to the next world. Surely it is better than this one.

They nodded in agreement and moved before him as if leading the way. Beyond them he saw two forms moving gracefully in the water. A girl, slim, on the brink of womanhood, and a young man, younger than he was now, whatever age that might be. The girl's hair, light and smoky in the water, floated around her. She turned to him and waved and he saw her eyes were the same color as his own.

The touch of a hand to the top of his head brought him streaming back to the present. His instincts took over and he grabbed the arm above and flipped the owner into the tub as he exploded to the surface, drawing in a long gasping breath.

It was a woman. A very petite woman. He pulled her up by the arms with one hand and smiled in amusement as the water sluiced off her dripping wet form as she dangled from his grip.

She gagged and choked and slung her pale blond hair out of her face with a shake of her head. She stared up at him with wide amethyst eyes.

"Was it your intent to drown me or yourself?" she asked when she found her voice.

Phoenix stared at her in amazement and let go of her as if she were contaminated. She stumbled and fell back into the water, going under again. He stood and watched as she fought her way back to her feet.

"Who are you?" he asked. He paid no attention to the water that poured off his body, or the fact that he was naked. He placed his hands on his hips and looked at her, the woman who haunted his dreams.

"I am Mara," she said. "I'm to attend to your . . ." She stopped in midsentence and stared at him, open-mouthed.

Either he was seriously lacking in some department or she was a total innocent. "Have you never seen a man before, Mara?"

She still stared at him as if she didn't hear him and he realized that strange voices whispered at the edge of his consciousness. He turned away from her in confusion and found a towel lying by the edge, obviously put there by Mara. Phoenix wrapped it around his waist since she seemed so shocked by his appearance.

She was younger than he first thought.

She snapped her mouth shut and moved to the steps that led out of the pool. She was dressed simply, nothing more than a linen tunic over pants, both without dye or ornamentation and now, soaking wet, entirely transparent. Her hair, pale as he recalled in his dreams, hung past her waist in long wet snarls and droplets of water clung to her dark lashes.

She bowed her head submissively when she stood on the tiled floor. "I did not mean to interrupt your bath. My only intent was to alert you to my presence."

Phoenix burst out laughing and the strange voices in his head scattered. Her words were in complete contrast to her earlier attitude.

"Who are you?" he asked again, when he was able to speak. "Are you a slave?"

"Yes," she said. She seemed confused by his laughter.

"A slave for a slave?" he said.

Her confusion became obvious on her face.

"Would you like to continue with your bath?" she asked as she forced her face back into a calm mask.

"Yes," he laughed. "I would."

He dropped the towel and settled back into the pool, resolved now to enjoy himself. If it was a trick, and it had to be one, then let it come.

His only question was how they knew about his dreams. How did they know what she looked like?

"Is he the man I see in my dreams?"

He turned with a start. Had she spoken? He heard her voice as if she were sitting beside him whispering in his ear, yet she stood by the table with her teeth chattering as if she were waiting for his whim.

"Don't just stand there dripping," he said when he realized he was staring at her. "Dry off."

"I have nothing to put on," she said softly.

"I fear him."

Why was it he could hear her speak with two separate voices? Was he still in his cell and once more locked in a dream?

Phoenix stretched out his hands before him. The water felt real enough and his skin was wrinkling from it. The food smelled tasty and real.

Yet every dream he ever had of her was before the ocean.

How did he know the ocean when his only memories were of the pits?

She stood as before, shivering and wet.

"Use the towels," he snapped, his confusion making him strike out in anger.

She jumped and her fear hit him as if she had struck him. She dashed to the armoire and hid behind the open door as she stripped and wrapped one of the towels around her.

It's almost as if I can read her mind.

She was furtively watching him as she changed and different thoughts bombarded his mind.

"His eyes . . . who is he . . . what will he do to me . . . how can I escape this place . . . his eyes . . . he said he is a slave too . . . his eyes . . ."

"Enough!" He erupted from the water, startling her again, so much so that she jumped and hit her knee on the armoire door.

She hobbled around, one hand rubbing her knee as she held up the towel with the other.

"What is it about me that frightens you so?" he asked, then smirked. "Beyond my reputation, that is." He stood in the pool with the water lapping around his thighs, watching her nervously scramble around.

"Your reputation?" she asked. The towel was much too large for her petite frame and she tucked the end of it under her arm so that she wore it as a shift.

"Don't you know who I am?" he asked.

"I know that I am to serve you," she said. "They did not bother to tell me your name."

"That is easy enough since I have no name," he snarled.

She paused, apparently taken aback, before she spoke again. "How can you have no name?" she asked incredulously.

"Ask those that sent you here, if they are the same that sent me."

She shook her head in confusion. "All I was told was to make ready the room for you and to serve your needs."

"All my needs?" he asked as he came up the steps out of the pool.

Her face flushed scarlet.

"He thinks I'm a whore. How can I tell him I've never . . ."

"You're food is growing cold," she said.

It happened again. Her mouth speaking one thing and his mind hearing something else. Phoenix touched his fingers to his temple. Perhaps they had drugged him in some way? This could not be a dream.

"Mara?" he said just to make sure he wasn't losing his mind.

Her head bobbed.

"Where do you come from?"

"Bali Circe," she said.

"And where is Bali Circe?" he asked.

Her face once again showed her confusion to his questions. "Out there?" she said hesitantly, pointing toward the ceiling.

"Another planet?"

"Yes."

"And why are you here?"

"I was brought here," she said hastily. "By the slave traders."

"And sent to attend to my needs."

"Yes."

"Did they say what my needs are?" He wrapped the towel around his waist and went to the table.

"They said you fight and I am to clean your weapons, arm you, feed you, and see to your needs."

"Please. Not that."

She hid her fear well. She uncovered the dishes with a steady hand as he sat down at the table.

"Sit," he said. He needed time to think. And it had been a while since he'd had a conversation. His last was with Laylon.

She was Laylon's replacement. The realization washed over him more fiercely than his cool swim, and chills moved over his bare chest and down his spine.

So I am to continue to fight the Murlaca. I am not condemned to die.

Mara jumped up from her seat, ran to the armoire, and returned with two towels. She tentatively placed one over his shoulders.

"You are cold," she said simply.

He looked up her. Somehow with all her fear, she still felt compassion. It was an odd combination. If she feared him she would have ignored his chill. As a slave she should have waited until he told her to get him a towel.

He would try not to be so intimidating. Laylon never found him so.

"Tell me about Bali Circe," he said in an even voice as he began his meal.

"What do you want to know?" She perched on the edge of her chair after she wrapped her hair in the towel.

"What does it look like?"

Her face was dwarfed by the size of the towel on top of her head. She seemed all innocence, her eyes huge and deep against the pale color of her skin.

Her teeth caught the edge of her lip for a moment and a vision hit his mind. A mother and daughter, it had to be so because they looked so much alike, and both of them chewing their lips and laughing because they realized the daughter was exactly like the mother.

He caught the entire gist of the scene but could not grasp the when or the where.

Or the why.

Did it come from her mind or from his? Was it a memory?

"It's a planet, much like any other," she said. "Except for this one."

Did she not see what he saw? If it came from her, then she must see it.

"What about this one?" Perhaps if she talked there would be more to it. An explanation. He needed to know why he experienced it. For some reason she had to be the key.

"The domes," she said. "Everything is under domes. I saw them from the sky."

He had not realized it. In all the time he could remember he'd never left the pits.

"Do you have an ocean?" His visions of her always included an ocean.

"Several," she said. "More water than land."

"But no domes?"

"Our technology is not that advanced," she said. "And our government does not allow visitors on-planet."

"Yet they sell off its citizens?"

"I did not say our government was perfect," Mara said.

A slave with spirit . . . How long before they subdue it?

"How long have you been a slave, Mara?"

She looked over her shoulder and he leaned to see what she was looking at and realized she had a brand there. Two linked circles as if they were part of a chain.

"All my life," she said quietly, almost submissively.

"When did they brand you?"

"When I left the school for orphans. I was twelve."

He felt compassion. A strange feeling for one who killed so frequently. He saw her then, skinny, pale, frightened. Her eyes huge in her childlike face as unknown hands held her down and branded her with the mark.

Was the entire universe a cruel place? Why did people tolerate it? Or was everyone as imprisoned as he was?

"Do you know why you are a slave?"

"Because I am not a Circe."

Laylon spoke of the Circe. The Circe sent me here. His heart quickened at the thought that this poor little slave . . . waif . . . might have the answers to his questions.

"Who are the Circe?"

"How can he not know about the most powerful beings in the universe?" her voice said in his mind.

"I don't know," he said.

Any more than I know how I can read your mind.

Her eyes widened in shock and Phoenix leaned back in his chair with his arms crossed, waiting and watching to see what would happen next.

"His eyes . . . he is the Empowered One. How else can it be?"

Her thoughts came at him as plainly as if she spoke them.

"Who is the Empowered One supposed to be?" he asked.

She looked at him then and Phoenix watched with fascination as her face seemed to change. It took on a peaceful countenance, one that was familiar to him from his dreams. Her eyes darkened to a deep purple hue and she blinked, as if the wind were in her face. It wouldn't have surprised him in the least if her hair rose up about her as if the wind caressed it, but it was trapped beneath the towel. "There will come, someday, a man with forbidden eyes that will have more power than the Circe women." She spoke as if she were someone else. As if someone other than her were speaking, using her voice, her mouth as a vessel. "The Empowered One will come from the sea escorted by the dolphins. The dolphins will join him in battling the Circe Witches and when it is over all people on the planet, woman and man alike, will finally be equal."

"And you think I'm this . . . Empowered One?" Phoenix asked incredulously.

"You have the eyes," Mara said simply.

He laughed then. A deep hard laugh that started in his gut and overflowed. He put his head back and howled until his eyes watered and he could not draw a breath. Never in his memory could he recall laughing as he had.

"He's insane."

Mara looked at him with her eyes wide and an expression of fear on her lovely face.

"I am," he agreed with her, his amusement fleeing as quickly as it came.

Why did her fear irritate him so?

He stood so fast that his chair overturned and Mara jumped in her seat. He walked around the table in a few quick strides and lifted her by her arms from her chair. Her towel fell from her hair and it tumbled down her back in a thick tangle of silver snarls.

Phoenix jerked her as if she were a cloth doll and the towel around her body fell to the floor as he pressed her up against the cold tile of the wall. He held her arms over her head with one hand as his other moved over the soft, silky skin of her body.

"This is the only thing I'm empowered to do," he said into her ear as his hand closed around her throat.

Her eyes were wide, huge in her face, and they turned on him in horror.

"I kill. And that's all I do."

"Will you kill me?" she whispered, as if she were afraid that her words would end her life.

He released her as quickly as he had grabbed her and stepped back. Mara stayed pressed against the wall, shivering against it.

"You haven't seen to my needs yet," he said and cast his eyes over her body.

She looked down and he felt her fear again. It was

nameless, terrible, and he felt a moment's pang of guilt for causing it.

But only a moment.

"What would you have me do?" she whispered again.

He reached out his hand and brushed the back of his knuckles across her cheek. Her eyes flashed up to his face in fierce rebellion, even though her body trembled in fear.

Her lashes were incredibly long.

He could take her. He was ready. He throbbed with the thought of it. The only thing that separated them was his towel and the scant inch of space between his erection and her naked form.

And her innocence.

"Tell the ones who sent you that I only have one need," he said as he turned away. From the corner of his eye he saw her quickly dip and pick up her towel.

They already knew his weakness. Somehow they had found her in the flesh.

"I need to kill," he said.

CHAPTER THIRTY

She was swimming with the dolphins. Perhaps it was her subconscious just yearning for peace. Elle did not care. She let her mind go, dropping her barriers as the dream took her away.

The water felt cool and soothing on her skin. More so than any luxurious pampering she'd enjoyed. She moved gracefully through the water with the dolphins by her side.

They were guiding her, leading her. One would tap her shoulder with its snout if she became distracted by a piece of coral or the sunlight dappling through the water. Another would motion with its fin, which she knew in itself was not possible, but she knew it for a dream so she let it happen.

Even though she'd been underwater for quite a while, she did not feel the need to breathe. She smiled at the thought and even checked her outstretched hands to make sure she had not taken on the form of a dolphin for the purpose of the dream.

"Come on," the dolphins said in the language that she shared with them. "We want to show you something."

Why were they rushing her? Didn't they know that she missed them? Why couldn't she just enjoy the peace and tranquility of the water and their companionship for a while before she had to get back to the real world?

The world she hated.

They insisted so she followed along, her body gracefully undulating from her head to the tips of her toes in an effortless motion that carried her along at their side.

The water was clear and bright and it was easy to see another dolphin in the distance. He swam in a circle around a dark form suspended in the water.

Elle stopped. For some strange reason she did not want to go any farther and she treaded beneath the water in indecision.

The dolphins refused to let her stay. They nudged her with their snouts and bumped her arms with their dorsal fins until she finally grabbed hold of one and let it take her on.

The sun broke through the water as if clouds parted above. It shone down like a beacon on something.

It was a man. His body was held suspended beneath the water by chains. A band circled his wrists, his ankles, and his neck.

Elle thought at first he was dead but the trickle of bubbles that led to the surface let her know that he was breathing.

But how?

The dolphin led her around as the one who circled him backed off and joined the pod that had brought her there.

When she was facing the man her escort scooted off to join the others and Elle shook her head at their strange behavior.

Her hair scattered out around her and she smoothed it away from her face as she turned to look at the man.

He seemed to be in great pain. His eyes were closed and dark lashes caressed his cheek. His nose was straight and proud and his jaw was covered with the shadow of a beard. His hair was dark and long enough that curls floated about his ears. His body was heavily muscled and he seemed to be tall.

Elle smiled. He reminded her of her father in a strange way. But he was much too young.

A dolphin nudged her spine and she turned with a questioning look.

The dolphin tossed his snout toward the captive man.

Elle turned back and found eyes the exact same color as her own looking straight at her. They bored into her mind as if he was trying to tell her something.

Something important.

"Zander."

Elle woke with a start and wondered if she had actually spoken her brother's name aloud. The cryo state made her groggy, disoriented. She shouldn't be awake yet. Should she?

Elle's eyes scanned the luxuriously appointed stateroom of the official Prefect Transport. The prefect, Peter, Calvin, all slept, their monitors peacefully blipping their stats to let the Senate Cryo Coordinator know that all things were as they should be.

But what of Bella? Elle barely turned her head and saw the woman reclined in her chair, her wristband still connected and her monitor signaling that she was as she should be.

Her ridiculous hat sat on the table beside her and her dark blond hair hung in two long tails over her shoulder. It was a surprising contrast, the youthful style of the hair against the stark darkness of the robes. It made Elle wonder what Bella had been like in her youth. What made her so driven? Could she look back on her life and point to the exact circumstance that brought her to her position of power?

But more importantly, had Bella planted the image of Zander in her dream?

"Mistress?" a soft-spoken voice inquired. One of the cryo techs noticed her wakening. "We have several hours left. Would you like to be reactivated?"

"No," Elle said. "I would like to move about."

The tech released her wristband and handed her a bottle of water. Elle drank it gratefully as she stretched her muscles to get her blood flowing properly. She quietly rose from her chair and her mind could not help but recall the last time she woke from cryo.

Boone . . .

In the years since the day of Zander's death she had not dreamed of him once, although Boone seemed to haunt her dreams, especially as she drifted off and then again upon wakening. But never Zander.

So why now? Why when she was far way from home and totally alone for the first time in her life? As she wanted to be.

The wedding was to take place on Senate. It would be the celebration of the millennium. A celebration of the union between the two greatest powers in the universe. Elle chose to travel with her bridegroom. Her parents would come later. Right before the ceremony. It was all of the Senate her father could stand.

Keep your enemies close.

Was it a sign? Was she not as successful as she thought she was in eliminating all emotion from her life? Was it her subconscious longing for past times, past lives, past happiness?

Zander was not happy in her dream. He was a prisoner. He was trapped.

What did it mean?

The ship she was on was huge compared to the compact craft she had traveled on before. There was a lounge of sorts on a lower deck and she made her way there, hoping she'd find it empty.

It was.

Her dream made her feel vulnerable. Weak. She needed time to center herself. To regain her strength.

There was no doubt in Elle's mind that she would need every bit of strength she had for the coming days.

For the rest of your life.

Elle knew exactly what she was in for. She was moving headlong into the heart of the enemy camp. Her constant companions would be the very ones who sought to destroy her family. Their greatest prize would be the conquest of her home planet. They had already murdered her brother.

And she was willingly going into their midst.

So I can learn more. So I can have the power.

Into the fire where there would be no comfort. No love. No one to lean on. No one to give her strength.

Elle had no fantasies about her marriage. It would be in name only. Peter could barely stand to kiss her and she was certain he was physically unable to consummate their marriage.

And even if he were physically capable, she would take steps to make sure that it didn't happen.

At least Calvin would be happy. He could have Peter all to himself.

The thought of what she was about to do overwhelmed her so much that she realized she'd best regain control of her emotions before Bella saw her weakness.

Or was Bella the cause of her weakness?

Elle went to the corner of the lounge where a set of deep couches were attached to the hull. Tempting as it was to stretch out on one and sleep off the Cryo, she instead sat on the floor before them and moved her legs into her meditation position.

As always, when she longed for peace, she concentrated on the ocean. She centered her being into the cool waters. The only sound in her ears was that of waves.

And Bella.

"If only all of our novices were as dedicated as you are," the witch said.

Elle opened one eye and saw Bella standing before her with a pleasant expression on her face. She briefly wondered how long it had taken her to stuff her hair up under her hat.

She also blocked her thoughts from Bella's mind, as she was sure the witch was doing with her.

"I'm hardly a novice, Mistress," Elle said. "My mother has given me the highest training."

"Even your mother, with all her training, all her power, all her breeding, has not learned all there is to know about our abilities," Bella said as she carefully arranged her robes and sat on one of the sofas.

Elle saw that her moment of peace was over. She rose to sit across from Bella. Her father had taught her the importance of staying on the same level as her enemy. Sitting on the floor put her in a submissive position to one she swore she'd never submit to.

"Because she never trained on Bali Circe," Elle said.

"Yes," Bella said with another of her sanguine smiles.

Elle had to admit the witch had perfected that art. Her face was a serene facade.

"With Lilly's bloodlines she had the potential for greatness."

"Bloodlines?" Elle asked. This was something her mother had never mentioned.

"Your mother is the grandaughter of Honora, my predecessor," Bella informed her.

"And therefore the mother of the woman who murdered my father's mother and my father's uncle," Elle said, just to let Bella know she was not totally in the dark about her heritage.

"Zania," Bella said. "She sacrificed greatly for our cause."

Was this woman so enraptured by herself and her abilities that she did not realize who she was talking to? Elle carefully arranged her features so that no hint of her disgust would show.

"I've heard you mention breeding several times," Elle said, deciding that it was best to take on another subject. "Do you find that important?" She also wondered how Bella would react, given who her father was.

Bella's smile was almost genuine. "I am so pleased that you wish to discuss this," she said. "It is the very thing that I wish to discuss with you."

"Oh?" Elle said.

"I must say first of all that I am extremely happy

with your choice of husband," Bella began. "Peter is exactly who I would have chosen for you."

"Because you only have my happiness in mind?" Elle said.

Bella placed her hands inside the sleeves of her robes. "Let us not pretend that you have any feelings of kindness with me due to the unfortunate circumstances of your brother's sudden disappearance," Bella said. "But rest assured that I do want what is only best for you."

Unfortunate circumstances? Elle fought the urge to send a blazing torturous thought into Bella's mind. Instead she concentrated on presenting a peaceful facade to the witch in hopes that she would reveal something to her. Something Elle could use against her.

"I see no need to dwell on the mistakes of the past," Elle said. "The only thing it accomplishes is denying the future."

Bella raised an approving eyebrow and smiled benevolently.

"The only problem I foresee," Bella continued, "is Peter's rather eclectic tastes."

Elle smiled. "It's not a problem for me," she said. "I find Peter's tastes"—she acknowledged Bella's delicacy—"are what makes him so endearing to me."

"How fortunate for you that you do not have to put up with the more distasteful part of marriage," Bella said.

"Indeed," Elle said as she firmly repressed the memories of Boone kissing her, Boone touching her, Boone making her insides tremble.

Things she knew she'd never feel again.

"But for every good thing that happens, there is also a bad," Bella said.

Elle realized the witch was about to make her point.

"Some women find it joyful to have children." Bella was unable to disguise the curl of her lip, as if she found the entire idea disgusting. "How do you feel about the subject?"

Elle saw it all so clearly, as if Bella had laid out a plan before her.

They wanted to use her for breeding.

"It is a decision I have decided to put off for now," Elle said diplomatically. "After all, this is all so new to me. The coming marriage, a new life away from Oasis, the opportunity to learn more about my abilities . . ."

"Are you considering my offer to study on Bali Circe?" Bella said.

"I consider all offers that come my way," Elle said and wondered how long she'd be able to continue to talk to Bella without turning her upside down.

"Excellent," Bella said. "And don't worry about Peter, or the prefect, not wishing you to go," she said. "I'm sure we can arrange everything to *our* satisfaction."

I already have.

"I'm sure they will agree with whatever decision *I* make," Elle said.

It was all about the power.

CHAPTER THIRTY-ONE

Everyone was in place. The plan should work.

Boone touched the toy in his pocket, as if it were a talisman.

"Please let this work," he said under his breath.

He felt a hand on his shoulder.

"Remember what I told you," Sagan said. "If things don't work out the way we planned on I want you to get out of here. If you get on the ship and find there's nothing you can do, then ... what were the words you used?'

"Turn and burn," Boone said, repeating the slang used at Academy.

"Turn and burn," Sagan said with a lopsided grin. "Go back to your family. Tell my sister about me and tell her what I told you about our family. Tell her I was happy for a brief while. Then go find your woman, if she'll have you."

"She's probably forgotten all about me by now," Boone said.

Sagan squeezed his shoulder. "Then it's her loss, Boone."

Boone shook his head. He didn't dare think that far ahead. The first thing he had to do was get a ship. Then he had to remember how to fly.

His hand closed over the toy in his pocket.

He remembered how to fly, the same as he remembered how to breathe, walk, talk, eat, drink, live . . .

"One more thing," Sagan said.

"I'll tell them," Boone assured him. "I'll tell everyone I know what's going on here."

"Do you think it will matter?" Sagan asked.

"It will to some," Boone said. "But there's no need to worry about it. Everything's going to work out. This is what you've been waiting on. By this time tomorrow there will be a new government on Circe."

"Maybe I should put you in charge of public relations," Sagan said.

"Just let me be in the air guard," Boone replied.

There was an awkward pause and then Sagan pulled Boone to him in a rib-cracking hug and thumped his back.

"Safe stars," Boone said. It was time for him to go.

"Safe stars," Sagan said after him.

Boone moved off with a few others into the darkness. They hid beneath some bushes on a small rise on the outskirts of the city, close to a wide roadway.

A perfect place for a Falcon to land.

In the distance the lights of the city winked beneath the heavy cover of Perazine gas that hung over the rooftops. Visibility was low tonight, something that would favor the rebels.

A series of attacks were coordinated for a certain time in different parts of the city. If the Circe stayed true to form, the air guard would fly over to dissuade the rebellion, but this time they would find most of the fighting taking place from the shelter of buildings so they would not be able to fire upon the rebels.

But most of that depended on the hope that the rebels in the city would be able to turn some of the guard.

It was Sagan's plan to lure one of the Falcons to the ground by using Bryant's com link. The bait was Chanice disguised as an injured Circe Witch. The hope was that Bryant would be able to convince one of the pilots that the witch needed immediate medical attention and that the rebels had them pinned down.

Risky and desperate. The best and only plan they could come up with.

Watching and waiting was the hardest part.

Boone had participated in plenty of battles over the years. Raids for food, medical supplies, to rescue those taken by the slavers, a number of small raids that resulted in tiny victories or major defeats and some injuries through the years. He bore a scar over his ribs, the result of a blaster burn. He'd spent the good part of a solar flat on his back when his leg was broken in several places from being trampled by some cattle.

It was an incident that still made him laugh in spite of the pain he felt. He was the one who'd suggested it since he'd had some experience with cattle. Chasing a drug-crazed heifer when he was a boy was a bit different than stealing an entire herd, he realized as he went under the thundering hooves.

None of the battles he participated in and none of the training he received at Academy prepared him for the stomach-churning anticipation he felt now. This was the big one. This was life and death and honor all mixed into one. This was a way out, a way back, a way to possibly fix all the things that he'd broken when he left without a word all those years ago.

If Elle would let him.

A series of perfectly timed explosions rocked the darkened city. Boone's eyes went to the spaceport. The lights of the approach shimmered beneath the surface of the water as they led into the bays protected by the mountain.

Just like Crater Lake. Just like home. He watched as five Falcons hurled into the night sky with their engines screaming from the quick burn.

He wanted it so bad he could taste it. He could feel the yoke in his hands. He could feel the g-forces slamming him back. He could feel the power of the engines as they thundered through the night sky.

Please let it work.

There was fighting in the city. He heard the report of blasters ripping through the streets. Fires burned in the distance. There were shouts and screams as explosions blasted into the night.

Boone shifted in his hiding place and felt the others with him do the same.

Waiting was always the hardest part. They could only hope that the battle came their way.

Sagan, Chanice, Bryant, and the men with them took up their positions in the road. Chanice lay on the pavement in her bloody and torn robe. The rest took up defensive positions around her while Bryant used the com link to call down one of the Falcons.

Boone barely dared to breathe. Instinctively he ducked, even though he was well covered by underbrush, as a Falcon hovered over the road and shone a spotlight on the group gathered there.

Sagan waved his arms and pointed at Chanice, who still lay upon the ground.

If the Falcon decided to fire upon them they were all dead.

One of the rebels who was stationed on the opposite side of the road fired wide of Sagan's position in an attempt to let the pilot know that he was the injured Circe's only escape.

"Move," Boone said quietly as the Falcon turned and fired a blast toward where the shot had come from.

The Falcon slowly and steadily lowered to the ground. The engine whine was deafening and the exhaust from the engines threatened to blow every bit of cover away. Boone covered his eyes to keep flying debris from striking him until the blast abated.

The Plexi shield rose and the pilot climbed out.

"Let's go," Boone said and the group dashed from their cover toward the back of the Falcon.

Sagan held a blaster to the man's cheek and the rest covered him as Boone ran around the Falcon.

"What are you going to do now?" the pilot asked nonchalantly. "Fly away?"

"Yes, as a matter of fact I am," Boone said. He stuck his toe in the step and launched himself into the cockpit. Within a heartbeat he had the shield closed and the engines once again screaming to life.

He saluted Sagan through the Plexi as the Falcon rose and the pilot watched with his jaw hanging open. Boone couldn't resist a wide grin as he urged the Falcon up in a hover until he knew he could blast into the sky without hurting anyone below.

He let out a whoop as he kicked it into full throttle and the g-forces threw him back against the seat. He did a quick turn and then a flyby with the belly of the Falcon nearly scraping the treetops close to where the rebels shouted in victory.

"Get out of here, Boone," Sagan said over the com link.

Boone looked down and saw the rebels rushing into the underbrush. One man remained on the road. The pilot.

An alarm went off on the com. He was locked.

Boone rolled off to the left. Two Falcons were coming for him. The other two were flying low, after the rebels.

The pilot who landed must have signaled them somehow.

The pilot was not wearing a collar. There was no way they could operate with the split-second decisions that flying a Falcon required.

Boone knew the mind-set of the pilots. He was one

himself. It was all a matter of pride. One of their own had been taken.

A blast went wide to his right but he was still locked. His more immediate concern was the forces on the ground. If the Falcons opened up with strafing fire they would be done for. He pulled the Falcon straight up.

"Come on, baby," he said as the two on his tail blew by beneath him. The Falcon vibrated with the effort but Boone was confident the structure would hold. His main concern was that the engine would flame out. If he'd been flying his Firebird . . .

"Did you see that?" one of the pilots exclaimed over the com link. "That guy is crazy."

"Where did he learn how to fly like that?" another said as Boone rolled out of the climb.

"There's an entire universe out there," Boone said as he came up behind one of the Falcons. "You should see it." He fired a blast and it skimmed off the tail of the Falcon.

It was enough to put it out. The Falcon peeled off with smoke pouring from one of its engines.

The other two ignored him. They were after the rebels. They flew low and fired several blasts toward the underbrush.

Boone headed straight toward them. He had to draw them off Sagan.

He flew directly at the two Falcons. His com pinged again and he knew the one behind him was locked.

He couldn't stop. He had to give Sagan enough time to get away. He heard the excited chatter on the com from the other pilots.

"Pull up. Pull up. He's going to take us out!"

Had they ever had anyone fight back? The Firebird was unarmed when he'd flown it into the atmosphere above Bali Circe. They'd shot him down without even giving him a chance to surrender. Would they do the same tonight?

He had to make sure Sagan was safe. He would not back down.

Boone gripped the yoke. A roar started deep in his chest and he bellowed it out in an explosion of sound that rocked the pit as the two Falcons peeled away a nanosecond before they would all collide.

But he still had one on his tail.

"Turn and burn. Turn and burn," Sagan screamed into the com. "We're safe, Boone. Get out of here."

Go. Boone checked the fuel tanks. Nearly full. Definitely enough to get him to a hyperport.

Still, there was one thing he needed to do.

Boone went through a series of rolls and slides to shake the Falcon on his tail. He didn't have much time and he was betting that the pilot behind him couldn't keep up. How many times did the Circe air guard actually chase someone down before they fired upon them?

"Just try to keep up," Boone said. He headed for the city and the tall conclave of buildings. He kept the Falcon low, secure in the knowledge that its wingspan was narrow enough to get him through. The fires that still burned in the streets gave off plenty of light as he wove his way between the buildings, making split-second decisions on which route to take with his destination ever forward in his mind.

Boone saw a narrow passage and he turned the Falcon on its side and skimmed between the two buildings. The air pounded around him and he gave out a shout of victory when he caught the reflection of flames in the windows.

The Falcon behind him was gone, pieces of it flung all over the streets.

Boone shot straight up over the city and headed directly for the spaceport. He punched a button on the com and the targeting screen lit up. He aimed for the roof and punched the fire button on the yoke.

Three missiles fell off the belly of the Falcon, one after the other, and headed straight for the hangar. Boone was rewarded with a heavy blast as he pulled the Falcon up and kicked in the thrusters for deep space.

There would be no more launches from the planet. From now on everything would have to come from the satellites above. That should give the rebels time to accomplish something.

Elle . . .

"Let's go home," he said to himself, punching up the nav. It would be nice to have ELSie to talk to. To plot the course. But he knew the coordinates for Oasis. They were branded into his mind next to the images of his mother, his father, Zoey . . . and Elle.

The alarm went off on the com. He was locked again. Boone did a quick scan. Five Falcons surrounded him.

"Surrender," came over the com. "Prepare for landing in Bay five four."

"Can we talk about this?" Boone asked. The hyperport was just ahead. He could see it. "Let me go and I'll never come back. I swear it."

He could beat them. He knew he could. All he had to do was hit the port and they would never catch him.

A warning shot flew over the nose of the Falcon.

"The next one is up your exhaust," came over the com link.

Did he want his life to end this way? Shattered into millions of pieces over the planet Circe?

Elle . . .

A Falcon came up before him and he saw the shadow of one above him and one on either side. He was surrounded. There was no place to go.

"My mind is my own," Boone recited as the Falcons herded him toward the satellite.

"Just let me keep it," he added as he shut down the engines in the satellite bay.

The entire Circe air guard was waiting for him. Or at least it appeared that way. Boone stood with his hands raised before he stepped out of the Falcon.

They wanted to kill him. He could see it on their faces. After all, he had killed some of their comrades.

I deserve it.

He blocked the first punch that came at him, managed to land a solid one on another, but quickly fell beneath the numbers.

"Enough!"

He wasn't sure how many hands hauled him to his feet. His face felt swollen and bruised and he was certain a rib was cracked. None of that mattered, however, because he found himself standing face-to-face with a Circe Witch. Her face beneath the stupidly ornate hat was narrow and pinched. Almost haggard. Yet definitely familiar.

And her eyes . . .

"You know me." Her words coiled around him. They slithered through his bones and snuck into his mind. A chill ran down his spine and the men who were gathered around grinned in anticipation.

"My mind is my own."

"You know the litany." Her eyes were pale and empty. "And how to fly." Not empty . . . hollow . . . evil. She moved, no, glided, until she stood right before him, her pale eyes, the same color as Elle's but not the same, staring up at him. "How?"

There was so much he knew. So much he couldn't betray. So many lives that could be lost.

"My mind is my own."

She laughed. A hollow, empty laugh.

"Someone else said that at one time," she said. "A young man, much like you."

Zander . . . Is she talking about Zander?

What happened to Zander?

"We took his memories and left nothing but a shell." She walked away a few steps and then turned as if she were trying to be coy. Trying . . . "Should I do the same to you?"

Elle . . . Would he be better off to never think of her

again? After all, it was the curse of the Circe men. To love once and forever no matter what.

"No." He said it simply. Firmly. It wasn't a protest or a plea. Just a statement. *I choose no.*

One of the men holding him jerked his head back. Boone jerked his arm away in response and the Circe smiled at him. This one was more genuine than some. As if she was impressed with his spirit. She gave a slight nod and the other man released his hold, leaving him to stand before her on his own.

He knew then why he recognized her. It was the woman who captured Zander. He had only seen her for the brief moment before he disappeared into the crowd with Elle, but it was her.

Arleta was her name. Shaun and Lilly had undermined her quest for power. Capturing Zander had restored it.

What did she do to Zander?

"Where is he?" Boone asked. "The one whose memories you stole."

A sense of silent shock filled the room from the pilots and flight techs gathered around. How dare he question a Circe Witch?

Boone had been around the Circe his entire life. They were women. Just as he was a man. Each had talents. Each had a will. Each could kill. He knew how they could travel in his mind. Elle had done it enough. With and without his consent.

Arleta tilted her head as if to see him better. Her eyes glowed with a sense of excitement and recognition. Did she enjoy the challenge?

"He's serving our will," she said. "Just as you will."

Zander's alive.

The realization filled Boone with a sense of righteousness that he had not felt in years. Belief that Zander was alive was what brought him here. And if what she said was true, if the Circe had taken his memories, wouldn't that erase his connection with Elle so that she would truly believe him dead?

Zander's alive.

"Where is he?" It wasn't a question. It was a demand. Arleta's nostrils flared and a gut-wrenching pain filled Boone so suddenly that he fell to his hands and knees on the flight deck. He gasped for breath and tried to fill his mind with the litany.

Arleta laughed.

"Men," she said in disgust. "You think you are so strong but you are weak." She cackled. "Weak."

"My mind is my own."

Boone knew it for a trick. The same as when he'd teased Elle when they were children and she responded by sending him a quick searing pain. But this was different. This was devastating. How could it be a trick when he felt as if his insides were being squeezed out of him? He rolled onto his side and curled his body up in an effort to protect himself but to no avail. There was no protection from this assault.

"Please . . ." he finally gasped and Arleta released her hold on him.

She nudged his side with her toe. "Weak," she said in disgust. "Your litany is nothing, just as it was nothing for your friend."

Ben was right.

He couldn't fight their power. He wasn't strong enough. There was nothing he could have done to stop them from taking Zander. Anything he would have tried would have resulted in his death.

And here he was, years later coming to the same end.

The pain started again. It rolled through his insides and squeezed until all he could do was grit his teeth and try to hold back the scream. His body contorted, his legs twisted, his arms flailed in an effort to make it stop.

The men on the flight deck backed up and gave him plenty of room, as if they were afraid he was contagious.

Let me die.

Arleta laughed.

Elle.

An image filled his mind even as the pain filled his senses. Elle standing over him, dressed in the robes, wearing the stupid hat, and watching him as he begged to die. Her beautiful face, once so alive, was blank. Her dark-lashed, pale eyes, once so sparklingly beautiful in their intensity, were empty. She watched him suffer without emotion.

"She's one of us now," Arleta said. "That's why I've asked you no questions. I already know your answers. She told them all to me."

"No!" The word projected from his mouth in a howl as the pain intensified until his mind and body could take no more.

Then the blessed darkness came and filled his mind even when the witch tried to deny it.

Elle . . .

CHAPTER THIRTY-TWO

The door slammed shut behind him, the clang of it more jarring than the roars from above.

They were still chanting.

"Phoenix. Phoenix. Phoenix."

Calling for him.

"Phoenix. Phoenix. Phoenix."

His ears rang with the sound.

"Phoenix."

They wanted more blood.

He wanted to wipe the sweat and gore from his face but he didn't dare. Not as long as he wore the blades. At least he had the satisfaction of knowing that none of it was his.

Not mine . . . not now . . . not since she came . . . Before it was his strange ability to be able to heal quickly that had saved him in the games.

Now they never touched him. He was too fast. He was too deadly. It was said that he anticipated his opponent's moves.

He knew better. It was not anticipation, nor was it wisdom learned from many battles. The fact of the matter was he now knew what his opponent was going to do before he did it.

He was reading the minds of the men who were sent to battle him.

How?

He heard the clink of chains and the bang of a door.

Mara . . . It had all started with Mara. Ever since she came . . .

She kept her eyes down as she walked behind the guard. No wonder. He knew that he frightened her. Why shouldn't he? He scared himself.

I don't even know who I am.

"Your bath is ready," she said.

The guard unlocked the door of the cage at the bottom of the lift and stepped back so he could step through. He clenched his hands into fists and noticed the gore was still present, dripping off his blades. He felt the fear tremble inside the guard as he walked by.

They no longer beat him, just to watch him heal. They no longer jabbed him with their prods.

Yet they watched him every second with their weapons ready. They were instructed to kill him if he tried to escape.

They feared him because they thought they could not kill him.

Someday they would find a way. But it wasn't the thought of his death that frightened him. It was something worse. They could maim him. If he lost a hand, would it grow back? A leg? His eyes?

Fear comes from the unexpected.

Phoenix followed Mara, their footsteps ringing on the stone floor, his eyes focused on the crown of her pale blond hair.

If only he could touch it. Let it sift through his fingers like fine silk. His fingers twitched beneath his heavy gloves. And a vision of his hands leaving a trail of gore among the tresses sickened him.

If only he could stop thinking of her. She had become his obsession. Because of her his life was different.

What else was there to think about? His past? He had none. His future? He had none. His life? That consisted of the killing and the waiting to kill.

And the dreams he had now. They left him more confused, more frustrated, more agonized than before. Nameless faces, places he could not remember, and through it all was Mara and the sea.

And she held no answers for him. She didn't know him. She was terrified of him. He saw it all in her mind.

They entered the bath chamber. The shallow pool welcomed him beyond the steam rising out of the shower.

He put his arms out automatically as he heard the door close behind them. They made sure he was cared for. After all, he must fight again another day. How else would they make their credits?

Mara unbuckled the armor from beneath his arms and lifted it over his head. He bent to give her easier access as she eased it over his body. In a short time they had learned each other well.

As he flexed his muscles, free once again from the confinement, he felt her amethyst eyes scanning his skin, looking for wounds. There would be none of course. There hadn't been any in a long while. That was one need she never had to see to.

He sat on the stool and she pulled off the heavy boots that protected his calves, and then unbuckled the thigh protectors and placed them to the side. Her hands shook as she reached for the waist of his pants and he grabbed them. She sucked in her breath at his touch. In fear.

"I'll do it," he said, looking down at her.

She nodded in agreement, color flushing her cheeks, and as always avoiding his gaze as she quickly moved away. The sight of it tore at his insides, cutting him

deeper than the blades would have, if ever they penetrated his armor . . . his protection.

He watched as she gathered his armor and placed it
on the table for cleaning. She shouldn't have to do that.
She shouldn't have to touch it. She shouldn't be here in
this place of death.

Mara turned back and her eyes widened in panic
when she saw how he watched her.

"Your water will chill," she said and quickly turned
away to arrange his towels.

Phoenix nodded wearily and stood. He peeled off
the thick leather pants that fit him like a second skin
and kicked them aside. He walked into the shower
and let the water pour over the ridges and slopes of
his body.

Clean now, he walked into the pool and felt the cool
touch of the water on his body as he slid beneath. He
stayed under as long as he could, then came to the surface and settled his back against the side. He leaned
his head back with his eyes closed.

If only he could wash the pictures of the destruction
that rattled in his mind away as easily as he washed
away the blood and gore. If only he could stay under
the water long enough to make the screams of the
crowd and the death gasps of his conquests go away.

Mara changed him. Just by coming. Just by being
sent to attend to his needs.

"Do you hurt?" Mara asked.

She always asked. He always answered.

"No."

There was no pain. Not visibly. Not inside. Not on
his skin. Not in his muscles. Not in his organs that continued to work like a machine, taking the blows and
then mysteriously healing at almost the same pace that
the wounds were inflicted.

Like a Phoenix rising from the ashes.

Was she looking at him? If he opened his eyes,
would he see her deep amethyst gaze, looking down at

him, looking into his? Would she see his soul? Could she tell him what secrets were locked up tight inside?

"I see their memories now," he said. The water was still and he concentrated on not moving so as not to disturb the quiet calm. "The men I kill." His back was to her but he sensed it when she stopped her movements. She remained silent. He knew she listened.

"As they die, their memories flash before them," he continued. "Most of them are criminals, some worse than me. Others . . . others have done nothing more than make someone in power angry."

"It's the way of most worlds," Mara said finally. "Those with power use it over those without."

"I wonder when I die if I will see all my memories," he said. "Will I then know who I am?" He flexed his hands beneath the surface of the water, amazed to see that the blood was gone.

"Who you are is more than a name," she said.

So what would he see when he died? Endless bodies? Oceans of blood? A slave to the whim and will of others?

He drew in a ragged breath. He was a machine. They created him. They took a clean slate and made him into a monster. It did not matter what he was before. All that mattered was what he became.

And what Mara saw when she looked at him.

No wonder she feared him. No wonder everyone feared him. He was the incarnation of evil.

She said he was the Empowered One.

He was nothing.

"Your food is ready," she said.

Phoenix let out a long shudder. The thought of food disgusted him.

He disgusted himself. He had spent long years wailing at the injustice, blaming the woman who sent him here, hating the crowds, hating the guards, hating the system.

And fell right in with their plans.

"A fitting tribute to his father," the woman who sentenced him had said.

A father he could not remember. And if he saw him, if he realized who his father was, would he turn away in disgust? Would he kill him as he killed all the other men who had stood before him?

He needed to kill.

He rose from the pool and his body felt heavy. Fatigued. He felt old, and even though he did not know his age he knew he could not be as old as he felt. His legs felt like lead as he dragged them up the steps and out of the water.

Mara held a towel for him . . . as always.

"Something troubles you," she said.

He laughed. There was no joy in it. It was a vile thing inside him that needed to get out.

The laughter kept coming. This was not like the first time he was with her. When he got some strange humor out of the circumstances.

And then he realized that he could truly be insane.

That he most likely was.

The laughter changed to a horrid sound and became strangled as he felt moisture on his cheek.

Tears.

He touched his cheek and looked at the drop on his finger. He looked at Mara in wonderment.

"Where did this come from?"

He saw the fear behind her eyes. He saw it in her mind. It was ever present; every time she was with him the fear came along also like an unwelcome chaperone.

This time fear bought a companion.

Pity.

Mara did not answer him. Instead she took his hand in her own. He was amazed that she touched him voluntarily. She led him to his chair and he sat because he did not know what else to do.

Then she put her arms around him, settled into his lap, and took his head against her breast.

And he cried.

How long it took he did not know. The tears subsided and all he knew was a heavy weariness that left him too weak to lift his head from her breast. He felt her cheek move against his hair as if she stroked him.

"Why am I still alive?" His voice was hoarse, his throat sore, his speech no more than a whisper.

"You have a higher purpose," Mara said.

"I don't understand."

"You are the Empowered One."

He felt his frustration rising again but was too weary to give in to it. Her answers did nothing but give him more questions. Yet she sounded as if she truly believed what she said.

Or was she just part of the madness that was his life?

Phoenix wearily lifted his head. He felt Mara tense so he grabbed her hips to keep her on his lap. Her amethyst eyes, on level with his, widened with fear when he looked into her face.

"You talk as if I'm some sort of savior, yet you fear me," he said.

She cast her eyes down to her lap and folded her hands. She did not answer.

"You fear me." Phoenix jerked his knees beneath her to shake loose a response. He knew he could just look into her mind and see everything but the thought sickened him.

"Yes," she said. "I fear you."

"I will not hurt you."

A smile twitched at the corner of her mouth but she quickly suppressed it.

"You think that's funny?"

Mara shook her head no. "I think that we have two different ideas of what hurting is."

He had no answer for that and she managed to slip off his lap and busy herself with his forgotten meal while he considered her.

"Have I ever given you a reason to fear me?"

He had. The first day she came he threatened her and he frightened her. But since then . . .

"You have not hurt me," she said. She did not look up from the table as she rearranged his food, stirring it to bring back some of the heat.

"But you still fear me." He stayed in the chair so as not to intimidate her. She had a way of keeping the table between them when they talked, yet she had just held him in her arms as if he were a baby.

"Yes."

"Why?" He took a deep breath and carefully controlled his frustration. "Don't say because I am the Empowered One."

She stopped what she was doing and looked across the table. Her eyes glistened with a strange light as she studied him.

Phoenix gripped the arms of the chair to keep himself from moving. From scaring her.

"I fear how you make me feel," she said. "You stir something within me."

He felt a jerk close to his heart at her words. If only she knew what she stirred within him. She evoked feelings that he dared not release.

Mara pressed her fingertips to her temples and closed her eyes. "I see you in my dreams. You've always been there but you were never in this place. I don't know why except to say you that you are the Empowered One. You are the legend whispered about for years on my planet. You are the one the Circe fear above all."

"The legend . . . You said in the legend the Empowered One will come from the sea escorted by the dolphins?"

"I did. It is the legend."

Phoenix stood and swept his arm out to show the room. "There is no sea. No dolphins. There is only a prison. This is not Bali Circe."

"You are alive," she said. "Circumstances can change."

"What? They're going to let me go? I've tried to escape. The only escape for me is death." He laughed. "But first they have to find a way to kill me."

"You say you don't know why you are here," Mara said.

"I don't know anything before *here*." He felt the familiar rage boiling beneath the surface once again. The frustration. The anger. The helplessness. His hands curled into fists.

"The Circe sent you here?" Mara gripped the edge of the table as if it would keep her locked into place.

"Yes. You know they did."

"Why?" Her eyes were wide and innocent. There was no fear there. Not this time. She seemed to be earnestly trying to figure out his dilemma.

Phoenix could not help himself. He slammed his fist on the table and she jumped as the dishes rattled. "I. Don't. Know. Why." How many more times must he say it?

"But you do." Her voice was earnest. Her face compassionate . . . hopeful . . . as if the answer was right in front of her.

Phoenix opened his mouth to speak, then clamped it shut.

You are the Empowered One. . . .

"They fear me."

His body trembled. Phoenix collapsed into the chair as the realization washed over him.

All these years he thought he was being punished for a crime he did not remember. He thought he deserved his sentence. He considered himself unworthy of anything beyond survival.

He scrubbed his hands over his face and through his hair.

They fear me.

They sent him here because they feared him. Because he fit the description of the legend that was whispered about on their planet. But he was hardly more than a boy when he came here. How could he have been a threat? What did they think he would do?

You have power.

He could read minds. His body was practically indestructible. But these things had developed over the years. More so since Mara came.

Mara . . . She still stood across the table, watching, waiting . . .

"Tell me about the Circe."

He ate while she spoke. She told him the entire history of her planet as she knew it. He recognized the propaganda for what it was—the Circe were portrayed as great beings. Mara knew it too but when he questioned her on it she just shrugged her shoulders.

"This is the way it was taught to me," she said. "The legend I learned from whispers and secrets."

"So these women can control the minds of anyone they choose?"

"Yes."

"And no men have the power?"

"Men are not permitted to have the power," she said. "The male babies are killed if they show eyes the color of yours."

Eyes his color. Had he ever seen anyone with eyes his color? In all the men he killed, in all the women who used him, in the faces of the crowd, only the woman who sent him here had eyes the color of his.

Laylon had asked him what color his eyes were. It was a shock to her when she found out. She knew who he was but she died before she could tell him.

"Do you think my parents are Circe?"

Laylon never spoke of knowing a Circe except to say she'd tweaked their noses with her friend Ruben.

"It could be," Mara said.

"But how come I survived if they kill the male babies?" Could he be the result of such a union? How did he survive if he was? And what happened to his parents?

"I do not know. There are rumors of rebels on the planet. I have seen the results of the attacks but it is forbidden to speak of such things."

"I could have been one of the rebels?" He liked that idea. But it didn't make sense in his mind. "Why didn't they kill me when I was captured? If I'm such a threat?"

Mara shook her head again. She had as many questions about his history as he did.

"How do they control the minds?"

"They just do. It's because of their eyes. If you have the color you are a Circe. If not, then you are a servant. If you defy them, then you are a slave."

"When did you defy them?" he asked. She must have. She was branded with the mark.

The smile teased the corner of her mouth again. What would it be like to see one blossom across her face? To watch as she laughed with delight? To see her simply happy? "Since I can remember," she said.

Phoenix pushed his plate away. He was done and he was not sure how much longer he would have before the guards came to take him back to his cell.

"Tell me about your life," he said as he pulled on the loose pants and shirt that were his usual wear.

"I was raised in a home for orphans. I have no memory of my parents but the staff whispered that I was rebellious, like my mother. I always imagined her as one of the rebels. They also said I was a disappointment so I felt that I had nothing to lose since I was already lacking. From the beginning we were taught to be servants to the Circe. But I chose to run away every chance I got. One time I got as far as the sea before the Guard captured me. That was when they branded me and sold me as a slave."

"How old were you?"

"Fourteen. I was brought by a Chatelaine. A Circe who sees to the distribution of wares for the populace," she explained when he looked at her in confusion. "I was lucky, I could have been sent to be a rapture whore," she said with a slight reddening of her cheeks. "But I kept running away until my mistress sold me to a slave trader and he sold me to the master of the games."

"You kept running away."

"I did," she said with some satisfaction.

"What did they do to you when you ran?"

"Beat me," she said.

"But why didn't they just control your mind?"

"They couldn't," she said simply. "They could for a while but as soon as they stopped telling me not to run I ran."

He shook his head, amazed at the spirit within her petite body. "Where were you running to?"

"The sea. I always ran toward the sea. I guess that's why it was always easy for them to find me."

He will come from the sea.

"Where do you go when you leave here?"

"A cell. Close by."

"You haven't been outside since you came?"

"No."

The rattle of keys and the turn of the lock announced the guards coming to take him back to his cell.

"Did you make good use of your time?" one guard asked with a leer. They were always hoping to catch him with her. He would never let that happen.

Mara jumped to her work, scraping the plates, folding the towels, straightening the mess.

Phoenix resisted the urge to wipe the leer off the guard's face. Instead he tried a different tact.

Drop the keys. . . . He concentrated on the thought and smiled inwardly when the keys slipped from the man's hand.

The guard hastily snatched up the keys while the other held out his prod as if Phoenix had designs on going after them.

He didn't. He found out what he needed to know.

Now he needed time to think on all he had learned.

CHAPTER THIRTY-THREE

Elle stalked the halls of the prefect's palace, her mind open to any who passed her. She kept a slight smile on her face as if she were thinking about her coming marriage instead of filing away the different thoughts revealed to her as she made her way down to the training room.

The palace, like the Senate, was a place of secrets and shadows, whispers and innuendos, plots and pretends. It was not a place where you could let your guard down, even for an instant.

Elle hated it. She was her father's daughter, after all. But where her father chafed and stormed and refused to be a part of the politics, Elle did her best to blend in.

She knew that with knowledge came power. There were more secrets to be heard in the shadows than out in the open. There were those who were more willing to talk to a pleasant face, than one shuttered off in anger.

But forefront on everyone's mind and tongue was the conspiracy coming from the Murlaca pits. Elle

stopped in a common area where some of the servants
and staff were gathered around a large dige screen
watching an extraordinarily beautiful woman make a
report.

"Phoenix, the greatest Champion of the Murlaca in
this millennium, continues his refusal to fight," she
said. "Last night was the fifth match he has missed,"
she continued. "And Murlaca officials have no com-
ment on the situation. If this keeps up the games will
continue to lose revenue. Inside sources say that the
master of the games is at a loss as to how to convince
the mysterious Phoenix to make an appearance at tonight's match."

Elle had heard the rumors. It meant nothing to her
that the man refused to fight. If he didn't want to, then
more power to him for spoiling their fun. The report
was not what kept her eyes on the screen.

The broadcaster stood in the very spot where she'd
last seen Zander. She found herself totally unprepared
for the onslaught of memories that washed over her.

My mind is my own. She could not show weakness.
Elle forced her face to remain pleasant, impassive, in
case someone was watching.

There was always someone watching.

"Tonight's games are of special interest," the woman
continued. "Even without the presence of Phoenix
they are expected to be a sellout as they feature the
current champions from Bali Circe."

Elle, composed again, looked at the screen skeptically. She didn't have to live a lifetime on this planet to
know what the broadcaster was really saying.

"The rebellion on Bali Circe is getting out of hand,"
one of the staff murmured, giving voice to Elle's
thoughts. The man stood in front of her and did not
seem to know she was there. "The rumor is the current
Circe champion is responsible for destroying half of
their air guard."

"I heard that Mistress Bella is livid over the Phoenix matter also," his companion whispered back.

Why?

Somehow the staff members sensed her presence and immediately stopped their discussion.

Fools. Just because she did not dress as a Circe did not mean she was powerless. Elle jumped into the man's mind without hesitation and plundered his thoughts.

For a quick moment she felt guilt. She was no better than the Circe Witches. But if something was disturbing to Bella, then she needed to know about it.

Knowledge was power. Especially on this world.

Why did the Circe care about the Murlaca? Except for its use to execute their criminals. And who was this champion-prisoner that destroyed half their air guard?

She must not know.

The man was terrified that Elle would find something out. Which meant that he must have some affiliation to Bella, because she would know if he betrayed her.

What was it? Elle delved deeper into his mind and the man shifted on his feet.

It wasn't the man thinking it. He was merely recalling what he overheard Bella say. All she could glean was snatches of a conversation between Bella and another Circe. Bella seemed ecstatic yet cautious.

"She must not know." Who must not know what? *"We will find a weapon to use against him."*

"What kind of weapon? He has no one. He has no attachments."

Elle's victim rubbed the back of his head, hastily excused himself from his friend, and took off down the hallway. Elle moved away also but toward a balcony that overlooked the Senate building. She needed a moment to sort through what she'd heard.

The walls of the domes were visible from where she stood on a balcony high above the city. No matter how immense they made them, they could not disguise the fact that they were all enclosed in a bubble of breathable air. What would happen if the dome cracked? Would they all go spinning out into space or would the deadly gas from the atmosphere leak in and kill them silently?

The vanity of man knew no bounds. The planet did not want life yet they came here and made it the way they wanted it.

The power was the cause.

Below her the spires and balconies of other places beckoned to any who cared to look. Elle had no trouble identifying the Oasian embassy with its pure white granite winking in the artificial light. It would shine much brighter in the natural light of Oasis.

How long would it be before she saw her home again? How long before she breathed deep of the clear, clean air?

When she left she knew it would be a long time before she returned. There was nothing left for her there. No reason to go back. No reason to linger. No reason to remember.

"No time for melancholy, Elle," she reminded herself. Was it just seeing the place where she'd last seen Zander that brought back the memories? Or was it the fact that seeing Zander's face in her mind also brought Boone's face to the forefront?

She would never forget the look of pain on his face when she blamed him, no matter how hard she worked her body or how much she willed her mind.

Think of something else.

Her eyes wandered to the Senate building, where politics and posturing won out over any real good that could be done for the inhabitants of the galaxy. The problems with the water viruses were getting worse and the Senate was looking to her father to help since they seemed unable to come up with a solution.

This was the world she'd chosen. With her choice came all the intrigue and the subterfuge. She knew what she was getting herself into.

Why is Bella so concerned about the Murlaca?

Her mind went back over the things she'd heard. They were keeping it secret from someone. Who? Why were they so desperate for the champion to fight? What kind of weapon would they use against him? Who was this prisoner from Bali Circe who single-handedly destroyed half of their air fleet?

Boone was lost over Bali Circe.

Elle gripped the rail of the balcony with white-knuckled tension. Could it be? It was six solar years since Boone disappeared. Could he have survived?

She suddenly felt sick to her stomach. So sick that she was in jeopardy of losing its contents over the side of the rail. Elle hung her head over the side as she willed her rebellious stomach back to its usual calm state. Her hair tossed in the constant circulation of air that was stronger at this height. It wasn't the same as the fresh wind of home but it helped somewhat. She straightened her body and took a deep cleansing breath.

What if Boone was alive? Was it possible? Or was her mind just scrambling for some reason to escape the prison she'd created for herself?

Boone . . .

She had to find out who the prisoner was. But how? If she just went to the games it would be too late.

She realized just how alone she was. There was no one to talk to, no one to trust, no one to help. She finally had exactly what she wanted, But she also had the power. And it was time to use it.

Elle took off at a run for Peter's chambers. If anyone knew their way around the underbelly of the Senate planet, it was Calvin. He was always coming up with creative ways to keep Peter entertained and thus keep

Peter interested. She slowed down when she got close and slipped silently inside the door.

Elle calmed her racing heart and reached out with her mind for Peter and Calvin. The last thing she wanted to do was walk in on them in a compromising position. It was one thing to have a secret lover. It was something else to flaunt it in front of your betrothed.

If she'd arrived a few moments earlier she would have interrupted them. Calvin walked past the open door to Peter's bedchamber with his shirt off and Elle could not help but observe his well-cut physique. He must work as hard as she did at training. There wasn't an ounce of fat on his body. Peter could take a few lessons from him. His overindulgences would soon give way to fat if he wasn't careful.

They were talking and it was a simple enough matter for Elle to listen in.

"I heard the Phoenix will fight tonight," Calvin said.

"But SNN says he is still refusing," Peter said. Elle quickly cast her mind into his. Peter was sprawled on his bed appreciating the same view that she had just witnessed.

She just as quickly withdrew. She could hear them without invading Peter's mind.

"How many times do I have to remind you that my sources are much more reliable than SNN?" Calvin said with a laugh. "Not only is the Phoenix fighting tonight, but I've arranged for us to have a special visit after the match."

The delight in Peter's voice was obvious but still he asked, "What do you mean by special?"

Elle heard the creak of the springs and the low growl of Calvin's voice. "I mean that as soon as the Phoenix is victorious they will take him to a room and strap him down to a table with his blades still on him. And you can do whatever you want."

Elle covered her mouth to suppress the gag that

threatened to erupt. She felt a moment of compassion for this Phoenix, whoever he was.

"And remember," Calvin added. "They say he heals almost instantly."

"We could see firsthand if that's true," Peter said. He sounded awestruck.

Do they not realize this is a human being? Even if he is an assassin.

Was her betrothed so spoiled that he would resort to such depravity? What kind of world had she come to?

But then again, maybe the Phoenix deserved it. It seemed that he killed without discrimination and had done so for years.

Could Boone possibly be his next victim? She had to find out. So far all she had was information on how to get in afterward. She needed to get in now.

"How are they getting him to fight again?" Peter asked after a long silence.

"Apparently there's a woman that he cares for," Calvin said.

"A woman? Really?"

"Yes. She's a slave that attends him. My source says he's grown quite fond of her. So they've taken her away."

Calvin had a source. Perhaps one of the guards?

It grew quiet again in Peter's chamber. She didn't want to see what they were doing but she had to find his source. If she found the source, then she could use it. Elle prepared herself for what she would see, then quickly jumped into Calvin's mind.

She was not where she thought she'd be. Calvin was moving. Creeping up on someone. What was he doing?

The blow hit the back of her head at the same instant her hand went for the Sai strapped to her hip. As she staggered forward and slumped to the floor she heard Calvin's tsk. . . .

"You're just like the rest of them," he said. "You think all men are fools." Through the haze she felt her

arms being jerked around behind her and bindings
strapped around them. A silk scarf was stuffed into her
mouth and tied around her face.

Stay awake.

"What are you doing?" Peter asked as Calvin shoved
her into an alcove and pulled a curtain around her.

"Bella wants to make sure she doesn't show up at
the pits tonight," Calvin said. "The visit with the
Phoenix is my reward for making sure that doesn't
happen."

Elle fought against the darkness that threatened to
overtake her. She had to stay awake. She had to know . . .

"She's going to make you suffer when she wakes
up," Peter said.

"When she wakes up she'll be on Bali Circe,"
Calvin said.

"But what about marriage?" Peter asked.

"It will be done by proxy," Calvin said. "You didn't
really want to marry her, did you?"

"You know I didn't."

"Then it's all for the best. Your father gets what he
wants, Bella gets what she wants, and we get what we
want. Everyone is happy."

"Everyone but Elle."

Everyone but Elle. . . .

"Her father—" Peter started.

"Can take it up with Mistress Bella," Calvin said.
"Get ready, we need to go."

"But—"

"It's taken care of. . . ."

Elle heard their voices trail off and then the firm
closing of the door as they left.

The blow to the back of her head brought back the
nausea that she'd fought into submission earlier. The
gag made it worse and she worked her jaw against her
shoulder until the slick silk moved down and away
from her mouth and nose.

Every move she made shot pain through her head.

The light in the alcove was dim at best and the red haze that covered her brain did not help matters. She concentrated on her breathing, hoping it would clear her head.

She had to stay conscious. It would be so easy to slide into the darkness.

There could only be one reason why Bella did not want her at the games tonight.

Boone was alive. How much longer would he stay that way? She had to escape. How long did she have before someone came to take her to Bali Circe?

Calvin was right. She'd underestimated him. When her parents finally talked to her about the Circe her father said over and over again that their conceit was their worst enemy. Her own had certainly led to her downfall. All these years she'd spent developing her powers and the first time she'd really tried to use them she'd fallen into the same trap.

All she had to show for her power was a headache and a one-way trip to Bali Circe to become the mother of a pawn of Bella.

What good was the power if she couldn't save Boone? All she ever wanted it for was to beat the Circe. To cause them as much pain as they caused her.

As they still intended to cause her.

Boone was alive. There could be no other explanation. Everything that she tried to deny, everything she tried to suppress, everything that she was determined not to feel was there. It was a part of her. She loved Boone. She always had. She always would.

She had to escape before they came for her. Elle rolled onto her back and slid her arms down and her legs through until her bound arms were before her. It was a simple matter to slice the bindings with one of the Sais strapped to her hip. Her blades were sharp enough to cut through the strongest substances.

"Who's the fool now, Calvin?" she mumbled as she pitched the bindings in the corner. "I'm sure Bella will be pleased when you explain to her that you left my weapons."

The sound of footsteps alerted her to someone coming, undoubtedly her escort to Bali Circe. Elle slipped from the alcove and into Peter's bedchamber just as the door opened.

A black-robed witch and four Circe Guards came into the room. One of the guards held a collar. There was no doubt in Elle's mind who it was intended for.

The witch's eyes scanned the room. Her nostrils flared as if she were scenting Elle's trail.

Arleta . . .

The witch responsible for Zander's death. Elle's hands jerked toward her Sai just as Arletta yanked open the curtain on the alcove she'd recently vacated.

"She's still here," Arleta said. "Find her."

Could she take them? Four armed men and a powerful witch? She ached to try. But once the collar was on all would be lost. Escape was the better tactic. Elle ran on silent feet to the balcony.

The height was staggering. But to Elle it was nothing more than the villa back home on Oasis. She gracefully rolled across the balcony rail and slid down the ornate balusters until she dangled beneath the platform. She hooked her feet into the carving on the support and formed her body to the shadows of the arch.

Elle felt the vibration of footsteps above her. The air currents swirled her hair around her as they sought their path through the curves and dips of the palace walls.

"She's not here," one of the guards said.

"Fools," Arleta spouted. "You've missed her. She's here. I can *feel* her."

Unless one of them hung upside down by his heels or climbed down they would not see her. Still, Elle started the litany in her mind. She willed her body and mind to be invisible. Let them search the villa. Let them think she was somewhere inside.

"Not here. Not here. Not here."

Elle felt as if she were made of stone. A carving on the building, nothing more. It was not difficult. She'd been made of stone ever since Boone left.

Arleta was growing more frustrated by the minute. Elle felt it flowing from her.

"She must not go to the games. All will be lost."

Elle moved her head back and looked at the lights below her. She'd only been to the pits the one time. It was several domes over. But she knew she'd have no trouble finding the place. All she had to do was follow the crowd.

She dropped gracefully to the balcony below, and then slid off the side. Arleta had her guard searching the entire floor that housed Peter's quarters.

Just stay inside.

Elle dropped down to the next balcony. It was a long drop. But she could do it. It was just like climbing the cliffs at home.

CHAPTER THIRTY-FOUR

The fear was evident. Each man knew he faced a death sentence. It was automatic for any and all rebels captured on Bali Circe. From the moment they woke up on Senate with the collars around their necks and been herded into the chambers beneath the pits, all the prisoners knew it was just a matter of time.

At least they gave them the dignity of removing the collars so they could fight. One of them might possibly survive the night to die another day.

Amberly was one of the prisoners that Boone knew well enough to talk to. The rest regarded him with awe. It didn't take long for Amberly to spread the word that Boone had struck a devastating blow for the rebellion.

He could die with the knowledge that he'd done something right. It was some small comfort.

None of them except Boone knew what to expect. He advised them the best he could. He'd only seen the games a few times. The most they could hope for was a quick death. He touched the toy spaceship in his pocket. It was the only thing left that would say he was here. It was a miracle that they didn't take it when he was searched. It had no value to anyone but him.

It was not long before slaves came to arm them. The real tragedy occurred when one of the prisoners recognized one of the slaves as his wife. The reunion was short and bittersweet. The men were herded out as the woman wept and her companions did the best they could to comfort her. The men were taken to the pits.

All except Boone.

"You're to remain here," the guard said.

"Why?" He was fully armed, even more so than the others. He wore a chest plate, thigh protectors, thick gloves, and heavy boots over the clothes that he'd been wearing when captured. They started to place a mask over his face, but the Master of the Games took one look at the scar that ran over the left side of his face and put it aside.

"You're the Circe champion," the guard said with a wolfish grin. The screams of the crowd drifted down.

"I've never fought the Murlaca in my life," Boone protested. He knew what was happening above. The men were forced to fight. Jabbed with prods that shocked their bodies. The only way to escape was to join the melee.

The guard shrugged. "Not my problem," he said. "All I know is you're to fight the Phoenix."

"Who is the Phoenix?" Boone asked. The screams were louder, combined now with shouts from the men.

The guard looked at him incredulously. "How could you have not heard of the Phoenix?"

Boone returned the look with one of his own. "How could you not know how things are on Balli Circe?"

"Like I said," the guard had to yell over the noise. "Not my problem." His eyes moved up to the ceiling where the screams were now accompanied by heavy thumping.

Just what Boone was waiting for. His slashed his arm across the man's chest. Blood spurted and the guard fell to the floor like a stone. Boone hopped over him and went out the door.

It was hard to run with the blades. He needed to get the contraption off but there was no way he could do it himself. The buckles ran up under his arms and there was no way to reach them without doing serious damage.

Which way did he come in? He'd been wearing the collar. He'd tried to focus but the twists and turns of the tunnels were difficult to remember when your mind was not your own.

Get out. Get to a com link. Get help.

Elle . . .

There was hope. He was on Senate. He was close. It was just a matter of finding someone to help him. Stefan. His uncle Stefan usually came to the games. He used them as a cover. If he was on-planet.

"Going somewhere?"

He was caught. Four guards with prods surrounded him. He wouldn't stand a chance in the battle if they shocked him. He needed his wits about him.

Because maybe, just maybe Stefan was up above.

It was a slim chance at best. And the only one he had at the moment.

"Time to go," a guard said. Boone raised his arms as best he could with the heavy gauntlets and turned in the direction they indicated.

He was helped on his way by a poke in the kidneys with the blunt end of a prod.

He stumbled forward.

"Gank," Boone hissed under his breath.

"That ought to feel like a kiss compared to what you're in for," one guard said.

"Did you see it the night the Phoenix ripped that guy's head off?"

They all grinned and laughed.

"That will be nothing after tonight," one said. "He is one angry champion. They took away his woman."

Boone got another "kiss" in the back. "How about you, Circe Champion? You got a woman?"

Elle . . .

"No," Boone said. He wouldn't give them the satisfaction. "I've got several."

"Well, I hope you told them all good-bye." They came to a lift. Blood dripped from the sides and Boone caught sight of a body being dragged around a corner.

"No survivors tonight," the lift operator said.

He felt a moment's compassion for Amberly and the man who'd just found his wife. They all deserved better than this.

The ceiling vibrated with the noise of stomping feet. Boone looked up as he was pushed onto the lift. Lights flashed above a long chute that led up to the ring.

"Time to die, Champion," someone said as the lift started its ascent.

His stomach lurched as he rode up. Fear chased around his insides but he could not give in to it. As long as he was alive there was hope. He was closer now than he'd been for the past six years. He would not give up as long as there was life in his body.

The light was blinding. The floor was wet and slick. Boone took a deep breath as he was prodded off the lift. The lights flashed around and above.

Was Stefan here? Would he recognize him? Had six years changed him beyond the scar that marred his face?

Boone walked the perimeter of the cage and his eyes scanned the crowd. It was hard to see. Faces were covered with blood and contorted with screams and yells. Stef wouldn't be a part of that. He'd be a sea of calm in the madness.

How much time before the Phoenix appeared? Not

until the crowd was in a frenzy. They were nearly there now.

He ignored the calls and the drink and food flung at the cage as he kept walking, kept searching, kept willing his uncle to be there. To see him.

"*Stefan!*" Boone yelled it as loud as he could.

There was no way he'd be heard. He could barely hear himself.

The announcer's voice rang out and echoed over the crowd.

"And now . . . your champion . . . Phoooeeeeeeenix!"

Boone stepped back as he felt the floor lurch with the advent of the lift. The lights spun. He was blinded when he came up. Would it have the same effect on the Phoenix? There was only one way to find out.

He'd seen the matches. He knew there was posturing by the champions. It was all part of the act. Give the people what they want.

Tonight they would get something different.

Boone watched the lift closely. A black form appeared and Boone realized the champion wore a crested mask that gave him the look of a bird of prey.

Perhaps he should have worn the one they provided him.

Boone took a step so he would be behind Phoenix. The head turned and the eyes glittered strangely in the slits of the mask.

A massive set of shoulders appeared, then arms heavy with the hooked blades that bounced the light as it spun around them. Boone took another step and the head followed.

It was strange. The eyes should be dark, lost in the black of the mask. Instead they glowed with a strange pale light.

There would be no surprise attack.

"Stef, if you're out there, now would be a really good time to show up," Boone muttered as the man before him grew.

He could see why the man was champion. He was huge. Muscular. He held his arms easily out and away from his side while Boone's shoulders screamed from the effort.

He was as good as dead.

The platform stopped and the crested hood turned toward him and looked him full in the face. A disturbing smile stretched across the features and Boone knew it didn't reach the eyes.

The strange eyes.

"He serves our will now."

A feeling of dread moved through Boone. There was no way this could be.

"Zander?"

He couldn't hear him. The crowd was too loud. Yet the man looked at him as if he just discovered he was standing there. It was as if he were studying him.

"We took his memories and left nothing but a shell."

Phoenix rocked up on the balls of his feet, bounced three times, and cocked his neck to the side. Boone could only imagine the pop of the ligaments sliding across the bone.

"Zander!"

The head came down and the eyes glowed like coals.

"So you think you can trick me?" he said. "You think you know me?"

How could he hear him? The crowd was so loud he could barely hear himself. Then Boone realized. He was talking inside his mind.

Was it Zander? Could it be? The man who slowly paced around him was huge, but six years would do that. Zander was nothing more than a boy when last he saw him. Shaun was tall, wide, and muscular. The build was certainly the same.

"Who is this Zander?" The man crossed his arms and jerked his blades. Sparks flew off his arms and the crowd screamed louder.

"My friend. My best friend. The Circe took him. Six solar years ago."

The man stopped.

"They took his memories."

The head bowed for a moment.

Boone took a long deep breath.

The head came up and the man charged. Boone threw his arm up for defense and found his body pinned against the wall of the cage. His arm was buried in the man's chest and blood dripped down. He tried to look at the wound but couldn't.

His opponent's blades were at his throat. Any move he made would rip his throat out.

"You can't kill me. But I have to kill you," he said. "Because that's the only way I'll see her again." His voice was full of pain. "They took her away."

"They did the same thing to you." He didn't dare speak. He felt the warmth on his throat and knew he bled. *"You have a sister."*

"You love her."

Boone swallowed and felt his throat press against the blade.

"Who am I?" The blades backed off enough so that he could speak.

"Alexander Phoenix. Son of Shaun and Lilly. Brother to Arielle. Prince of Oasis. The Aberrant of the Circe."

He laughed. "You forgot, the Empowered One."

How would he know that? How could he know the legend?

"That too." Boone was conscious that the crowd screamed but it seemed very far away. They wanted blood. His blood. And they would very soon have it. There was nothing to stop him. Nothing at all.

He looked into the eyes that glowed within the mask. The shape was familiar. The color haunted every moment of his life. Yet there was nothing there he recognized.

"When you find Elle again," Boone said, "tell her that I loved her."

Phoenix roared. Boone jerked his head back at the sound and the man released him. Boone's arm hung in the chest protector and Phoenix jerked free.

Phoenix's chest swelled as he flexed the muscles across it and Boone watched in amazement as the torn skin that showed beneath the scars in the armor miraculously closed.

The crowd was berserk.

"I need time." Boone saw Phoenix's mouth move, knew he spoke, knew it was impossible to hear him, yet he did, inside his mind.

Zander never had those abilities. Could he be wrong? Was it possible that there was another, just like Zander?

If only he could see his face he would know.

If it wasn't Zander, then he surely was a dead man.

Phoenix raised his arms and shook them at the crowd. How did he do that? Boone's arms felt like leaden weights and he was yet to strike a blow. The crowd screamed and Phoenix moved to the other side of the cage to give the opposite side a chance to revel in his greatness.

"You have doubts now?" Phoenix questioned in his mind. He wasn't looking at him but Boone knew that he anticipated his every move. How could he not? He read minds.

"I don't want to die."

"Tell me something I don't know." Phoenix's voice in his mind dripped with sarcasm.

"You didn't have this ability when they took you." Boone was desperate. *"I'm betting it just happened."* He recalled the pain in Phoenix's voice. *"Since you met her."*

Phoenix turned to look at him and Boone once again felt strangely unsettled. Was it because of the hooked crest on the hood he wore?

"Mara?" Phoenix's voice whispered in his mind.

Boone's mind filled with a vision of a petite woman with silvery blond hair and huge amethyst eyes. He shook his head to clear it. There was something remotely familiar about her. This was not the time to figure it out.

The guards who circled the cage moved in close with their prods. The pit master was not happy with the way the match was going. Apparently the crowd was unhappy also. The sides of the cage were being pounded with drinks and food.

"Kill him!" a woman screamed right next to the cage.

"You must fight me," Phoenix said.

"Yeah," Boone replied. "I'll get right on that." He rolled his shoulders to relieve some of the tension. "How 'bout instead we go to a nice tavern and talk about old times?"

Phoenix actually grinned at him. White teeth flashed pleasantly beneath the mask. "Sure, why not?" he said. "Now we just got to get past all of them."

"Hey, you're the killing machine. Do your thing."

"Unfortunately these blades aren't very effective against their shock wands. And there's the little matter of getting through the cage."

"Phooeeeeniiix . . ." The announcer's blaring voice interrupted their conversation and instantly quieted the crowd.

"Our champion needs some encouragement to fight!" the broadcast echoed around the pit. "Let's give him some!"

"Yes!" the crowd roared. The lights spun around the arena once again and then settled on a platform in front of the booth where the prefect and other high-esteemed guests usually sat.

The crowd immediately got quiet and Boone turned to see why the skin beneath the mask on Phoenix's face had suddenly gone pale.

Boone recognized the flowing robes and ridiculously ornate hat of a high Circe Witch. She had to be the Sacrosanct Mistress. Beside her stood a petite woman with silvery blond hair. She was dressed in the drab linen of a slave and wore a collar around her neck. Her face was ghastly pale in the light.

It was the same woman Phoenix revealed in his mind.

"Mara," Phoenix said.

"How about we see if this slave can fly?" the announcer asked and the crowd roared its approval.

Boone knew that the witch would command the woman to jump and there would be no way she could refuse. And all Phoenix could do was watch from his place in the cage.

Unless he decided to kill Boone instead.

"What will it be, Phoenix?" the announcer said. "You get to decide." As his voice echoed off the stands the crowd got strangely quiet and watched, their eyes jumping between the cage and the two women high above the ring.

Boone knew the answer. He could no more watch her take a dive off the platform than Phoenix could.

No one was coming to help him. If Stefan was here he would have shown himself by now.

He gave it one last chance. "They'll never stop using you," Boone said. "Or her."

Phoenix's eyes remained on Mara. "Don't you think I know that?" He turned to Boone and once more crossed his arms so that sparks flew from the blades. "You're going to have to kill me," he said.

An impossible task. How do you kill someone who heals immediately? Boone shook his head. "I can't kill you." How could he kill his best friend?

Phoenix ripped off the mask and raised his chin to reveal the vulnerable skin of his throat. The crowd gasped as one as the flashing lights settled on a face he thought he'd never see again. The lean jaw was now covered with a thick dark stubble and the eyes were full of pain, but the face held a familiar wistfulness that struck Boone to the core.

"You can," Zander said. "If you ever were my friend, then I beg you, please do it."

CHAPTER THIRTY-FIVE

Elle threw off the robe that she'd used to disguise herself as she traveled through the tunnels that connected the domes. She stood at the top of the pits and looked down on the cage.

Two men fought. Both had dark hair but where one was lean and quick, the other was huge and relentless. Both had the agility of dancers. They dodged, twisted, spun, and flipped away from the deadly blades. They were too far away for her to see their faces.

The lights spun and the crowd roared and through it all she sought a quiet place in her mind so she would know.

"Boone?"

The lean man jerked his head. It was so slight that anyone watching would have missed it. Elle didn't need to see him. All she had to do was feel.

"Elle?"

The large man roared and swung his arm toward

Boone. Boone ducked and the blades glanced off the cage and sparks flew out into the crowd.

She had to get down there. She had to help him. It was too far, there were too many people, the pits were covered with guards, and Bella stood on a platform overseeing it all.

Impossible odds. None of it mattered. Boone was here. He was alive. How long would he stay that way?

Get to Boone.

Elle took off at a hard run and when she ran out of the room she launched her body into the air with her arms outstretched.

Get to Boone.

She soared over the screaming crowd. If she could move an unwanted suitor with her mind and turn him upside down in the air, then why couldn't she do it with her own body? A man held his fist in the air and thrust it downward as if he were wielding the blades and he brushed her thigh as she flew over him.

Elle stretched out her hands and her fingers gripped the metal of the cage as she slammed into it. In the next instant she held a Sai in her hand and she slashed at the metal beside her. The cage gave way and she spun inside with her other Sai drawn and crouched down in the ready position, both Sais spinning in her hands.

The warriors stopped and looked at her with their chests heaving. Blood dripped from Boone's upper arm and a thin red line crossed his throat. In the blink of an eye she took in the lean line of his jaw, the scar across one side of his face, the short clip of his hair, and the surprise and wonder in his eyes.

But it was the other man who held her attention. One move and he would die. She would slash his throat before he could blink. The realization that he looked exactly like her father would not stop her for an instant.

"It's Zander," Boone said. He stood beside her. "He doesn't remember us."

"Zander?" Elle gasped out her brother's name. How could it be?

"Get these blades off of us," Boone said. Boone, always practical, always steady, always thinking ahead to counterbalance her impetuous nature. He raised his arms and Elle cut the straps. The blades fell to the floor with a thunk.

"Boone," she breathed as he flexed his shoulders.

"Zander," he said as he looked at the man who was supposed to assassinate him.

The guards, momentarily shocked by her abrupt arrival, circled the cage with their prods armed.

Zander grinned wolfishly as he held up his arms for Elle to cut the straps. She gazed into his eyes and saw nothing familiar, nothing that would say he shared a life with her, a womb, a home, a family.

There was nothing there but pain.

He didn't say a word. As soon as the blades fell he leapt through the opening. One guard moved to jab him with the prod and Zander ripped it from his hands. It became a weapon. Zander used it to beat back the mob and shock the guards who rushed him as the crowd panicked in their attempt to escape. They shoved their friends in his direction to keep him away from their route. They clambered over the benches and drove bodies in to the hard surface of the floor in their frenzy.

"Let's go," Boone said. He touched her arm, so quickly, so gently, that she could have imagined it as she watched him slip through the slash in the cage. "Are you ready?" he asked as he stretched out his hand toward her.

They would have to fight their way out of the pits. Then what? Where would they go? How would they get off-planet? Unfortunately she had not thought of anything besides finding out if Boone was alive. She'd given no thought at all to her attack on the cage. She'd just done it.

"Zander's alive." How long would he stay that way? He tore through the crowd but for some strange reason he was going for the platform. Why wasn't he trying to escape?

Elle stood inside the cage and looked at the melee around her. It was as if time had stopped for her. Everything moved so slowly that she saw droplets of sweat fly from Zander's check as a guard landed a blow. His arm came up and struck the man away as if he were nothing more than an annoying ibi that buzzed around the fields back home. The crowd parted before him as if he were tearing silk apart with his hands.

Above, on the platform, Bella was livid. Why wasn't she attacking Zander's mind? The slave girl was held by two Circe Guards on either side of her. Bella pointed down at Zander, who seemed determined to get to her and did not give a care as to who got in his way or what happened to them.

The image of Zander in flames, as he was the day he disappeared . . . the day he disappeared, not the day he died.

She had to stop Bella before she got into Zander's mind.

Elle spun her Sai and slipped through the opening. Boone held a guard against the cage and rained punches on his face and gut.

"Zander," Elle screamed above the noise. She pointed in Zander's direction.

Boone nodded. He dropped the guard and picked up his prod.

More guards poured down the steps. These wore the uniform of the Senate. Reinforcements had arrived. As they ran toward Zander, Boone touched his forehead with his fingertip.

"Speak in my mind."

Elle jabbed her Sai into the gut of a guard and jerked

it out. She kicked the body away with her foot as Boone used the prod like a club and hit another man in the jaw.

Elle saw one thing in Boone's mind as they fought their way toward Zander.

"Save him."

Zander was at the platform. He grabbed on to one of the supports and jumped up. His back and legs were covered with hands trying to pull him down. Someone used a prod and Elle felt the jolt go through her body. Zander tried to shake them loose but there were too many.

Elle sliced with her Sai and then thrust as Boone shoved several attackers back. The moves he used were reminiscent of her father's training, but there was also a new edge to him. A dangerous edge. He fought for their lives yet he remained calm and unaffected by the madness around him.

Elle gathered the calmness that emanated from Boone and took a deep breath. She concentrated with all her strength and then sent a command to the men pulling at Zander. They all flew away from his body as if Zander were the prod that held the charge.

"Did you do that?" Boone's voice rang in her mind.

"Yes."

"Let's go."

No time for reflection. No time for amazement. No time to realize she was doing things she did not know she was capable of. She followed Boone as he charged up the steps.

Half of the crowd was gone. The rest were trapped against the exits, kept inside by the Senate Guard who was trying to determine exactly what was going on. Some of the attendees cowered under their seats while others lay in agony on the ground, the victims of the stampede or Zander's rampage.

Lights sliced through the sky. Hoverpods! The rapid

fire of piercers blistered the ground behind her feet
and she dived for cover under the platform. Boone
landed on top of her and covered her body with his.

The hoverpods kicked up a sharp wind, and trash
and debris from the crowd swirled around. They both
raised their heads to see what was happening. One of
the pods bumped up against the platform while the
other gave cover. Bella, the guards, and the woman
jumped aboard and the pod took off.

Zander was nearly to the top. When the pod lifted
off he launched himself from the support and grabbed
on to the step rail. He swung precariously as the pod
tilted. He roared in pain, rage, fear, all of it as he tried
to claw his way onto the pod.

Bella looked down at him as he hung on to the side
and Elle knew she was gathering herself for an attack.
The Senate Guard were just below, waiting for Zander
to hit the ground, and the other pods held their
weapons ready. He would be either killed or captured.

"No!" Elle screamed. She jumped to her feet and
stared up at Bella. Her hair flew around her and she
felt Boone beside her, ready to defend or attack,
whichever way she went.

"You will not take him again."

"He's already mine." Bella's tone was condescending
but Elle saw the fear in her eyes.

Elle stretched out her arms. *"You will not take him."*
She felt Boone move behind her and his hands settled
on her waist. Elle closed her eyes and gathered her
power. She saw it coiling inside and a vision flashed
before her of her father shattering the doors and windows in the embassy the day Zander disappeared.

She expelled all her rage, all her anger, all her loneliness in a scream. She felt the force of it flow through
her body and out her fingertips. It hit the hoverpod like
a blast of wind and the occupants were flung to the
side as Zander fell back to the ground.

Elle stumbled back and Boone steadied her. She

looked at the pits in amazement. Everyone they had fought lay about as if hit with a proton blast. The hoverpods spun precariously as their pilots fought for control. The one with Bella scooted away after bumping into the platform and nearly getting snagged on a line of banners that surrounded the pits.

Zander stood on the ground howling his rage at the skies.

"We've got to move," Boone said. "We can't fight all of them and we don't know how long it will take them to recover."

Elle took a deep breath and nodded. "Where do we go?"

"The port," he said as he leapt down the steps toward Zander. "Stefan."

"Zander!"

Zander whirled when Boone called his name. The look on his face was tragic. Heartbreaking. What did they do to him? There was no time to find out.

"We've got to go," Boone said.

"She's gone," he said.

Boone cautiously reached out a hand and put it on Zander's shoulder. Zander looked at it as if he'd never seen a hand before and shook it off.

"We've got to run," Boone said.

Zander nodded. Then he looked directly at Elle.

There was nothing there. No recognition. No memories. Nothing that Elle could use to reach out to him.

"Who are you?" he asked.

Boone shook his head. "Let's go."

The men lying about were stirring as they bolted up the steps. They jumped over bodies that were scattered over the steps and the bleachers. Elle focused her power on the gates and they swung open as they reached the top and ran through.

Elle recognized the SNN broadcaster at the edge of the pavement that surrounded the entrance of the pits. They certainly would have a show tonight. And the fact that her face could be broadcast across the universe nearly made her laugh. Or maybe not. They ran away from the broadcaster as the crowd once more parted around them.

I wonder if Peter and Calvin were here.

"We can't use the transport," Boone said. "They'll be watching. Unless you think you can blast our way through everyone all the way to the ports."

Elle shook her head. She wasn't even sure how'd she done it. She just knew she needed to do whatever it took to save Zander, who looked at both of them skeptically.

"How do we get there?" she asked.

"The access tunnels beneath," Boone said. "This way." He took off toward the transport exchange where people were lined up to escape the madness of the pits. He ducked behind some shrubbery and seemed to be hunting for something.

Elle turned. Zander was not with them. She heard a scream and saw Zander with his hands around a woman's neck. She heard a snap and the woman's head dropped to one side of her neck. Zander released her and she fell to the ground. She was obviously dead. Her black hair was flung out around her and her transparent dress lay rucked up around her waist, revealing her lack of undergarments underneath.

"Zander," Elle said. "What did you do?"

He didn't speak. He didn't even turn around when the crowd realized what had happened and once again mounted into hysteria. They screamed as if Zander was personally on a quest to murder all of them with his bare hands. But he just stood waiting patiently while Boone opened a hatch and motioned for them to go down.

Elle jumped down into the tunnel behind Zander. Boone came behind her and fastened the hatch into place. Zander had already stripped off his chest and thigh protectors and prowled down the long length of the tunnel. Boone stopped to remove his own body armor.

"Did you see?"

"I saw." Boone's voice in her mind sounded resolute. He wasn't one to judge. That much hadn't changed. *"At least now we have a diversion."* He ripped off the edge of his shirt and Elle helped him tie it around the wound on his upper arm. It needed attending to but now was not the time.

"Why did he kill that woman?"

"We don't know what he's been through, Elle."

Zander turned and looked at the two of them. Was he reading their minds? Zander couldn't . . . could he? His eyes looked strange in the darkness. They almost glowed, resembling her father's when he took them into the tunnels back home. Did her eyes look like that? Could Zander see in the dark like their father? How much had he changed since he'd been gone?

How much had they all changed in the years gone by?

Elle's thoughts were as confusing as the directions they took, but Boone seemed to know where they were going. He told Zander where to turn and he did without hesitation.

Elle was tempted to look inside her brother's head, but the fear of what she'd see kept her from doing it. Now was not the time or the place.

Will there ever be a time? The walls around Zander were tangible. As if he were still inside the Murlaca cage.

He's the Phoenix. He'd been right under their noses the entire time. The same name that was granted to her father by a loving couple who found him. And all she'd been concerned about was his ability to heal as if she could use it as a weapon against the Circe.

She should have known. The last day they had spent together, a cut to Zander's temple healed soon after he received it.

She should have known he was alive.

Yet he was right in front of her and she could not *feel* him. She'd always known exactly where he was from the time she became aware of their entities as life. Even in the womb she'd known he was there.

His memories were gone. The essence that made him Zander taken away. Would it be possible for her to give them back? The shared memories they had?

They moved down a long chute and then moved up. As soon as they began their ascent they were greeted by a heavy rumbling above.

"We're under the spaceport," Boone said.

"How did you find it?" Elle asked. "I don't even know what direction we're going."

"I've got a built-in nav system," Boone said with a grin. "And a nose for speed."

Zander stopped in front of a ladder and looked at Boone, who pointed up. Zander moved up the ladder.

Elle reached for the ladder but realized she still held her Sai in her hands. "How did you know?" Boone asked as she placed them back in her belt. "You didn't know about Zander but you knew to come looking for me. What were you even doing here?"

Elle looked down at him from the first rung. The boyishness was gone, replaced by a steady resolve. Would he be the same if he had not gone? She took a long look at the scar that ran from his forehead, across his eye, and down his cheek. He was lucky he didn't lose an eye. The eyes were the same. Deep green, almost black in the dim light, and gazing upon her as if he'd never get enough of her.

Does he still love me?

"It's a long story, Boone. Six solar years worth." She laid her hand against his cheek and her thumb ran down the scar. "Your family is fine," she said in answer to his unasked question and moved up the ladder to where Zander waited.

CHAPTER THIRTY-SIX

Elle, here, beside him. He could reach out and touch her if he wanted.

But what did she want?

The three of them lay beneath a shuttle as Boone scanned the area, hoping to see the familiar lines of the Shooting Star. Luckily the port was divided into three sections, Government, Commercial, and Private. Boone knew where his uncle Stefan liked to dock but whether he was there or not was the question. The port was shut down, that much was obvious, and they were probably the reason for it. Were the three of them that valuable to the Senate?

Ships were stacked up on the launch pads, each one waiting for permission to take off. If they couldn't find the Shooting Star, then he'd have to steal a ship. Was Elle's power strong enough to convince the flight officers to open the portals in the domes and allow them to leave?

Elle's power. Where did that come from? How much

had she changed since he'd been gone? Outwardly it was obvious. The slim athletic physique was much the same, although he did notice a few more curves in her tight-fighting clothing. The biggest difference was how she held herself, with a determined resolve that seemed to place a shield around her.

The girl was gone. What was left in her place?

"We need to move to the other side," Boone said. "There's so many ships it's hard to see."

The place was busy with pilots, ground crew, and Senate Guard. The timing would have to be perfect for them to make it to the opposite side of the port.

"I wonder if all of this is for us," Boone said as a trio of Senate Guards walked by.

"Probably," Elle said.

"Why?"

Elle chewed on her lip. "I'm engaged to the prefect's son?"

Zander let out a grunt of disgust.

"What are you complaining about?" Elle said. "He was planning on visiting you after the match."

"Then he would have ended up like that woman," Zander said. "The one whose neck I snapped."

Elle rolled her eyes and Boone looked at them as if they were insane. Zander might not have any memories but he and Elle were bantering just like they always had.

"The prefect's son?" Boone asked. "Wasn't he a bit . . ."

"Yes," Elle snapped. "It was a political match, that's all."

"Shaun agreed to marry you off to the prefect's son?"

"His name is Peter and yes, he did."

Boone looked at her.

"So he didn't agree," Elle hissed. "Do we really need to discuss this right now?"

Zander looked at the two of them. "No wonder I forgot everything," he growled. "Is she always like this?"

"Let's go," Elle said. "I'll distract them."

It was impossible to see her do it but the Senate Guard suddenly decided to move away from their position. They were able to make their way unseen from cover to cover until Boone had a view of the rest of the spaceport.

"Maybe he's got a new ship," Elle said as they scanned the area from inside a tech hut.

"I wonder," Boone said. Stefan getting a new ship was not something he'd considered. Boone quickly dismissed the idea. Stef had loved the Shooting Star ever since the day his father gave it to him. It would take a lot to make him part with it. Something along the lines of crash-landing into an ocean on a forbidden planet.

If I only had the Firebird . . .

Boone was fairly certain that part of the fortune his father had amassed was due to a share in Stefan's slightly shady dealings. And no matter how many credits he had, Stefan would not part with the Shooting Star.

"If you recall I've been out of touch," Boone added to Elle's suggestion.

"Where have you been?" Elle dismissed his sarcasm as she always had.

"Bali Circe."

Zander turned his peculiar gaze upon him again. It was unsettling to have him look at him as if he didn't know him.

He didn't. "The champion of Bali Circe," Zander said dryly. "Were all of your opponents already dead?"

"I used to kick your ass," Boone said. He looked up and down Zander's broad form. "A long time ago."

"Not solving our problems," Elle said.

"Wait," Boone said. "There." He pointed to a large building. Just beyond he saw the nose of a large ship. "I think that's her."

They moved from the hut to the corner of the building and cautiously looked around. Boone's heart swelled at the sight of the familiar lines and the giant blue letters emblazoned on the side. It was almost like being home. Almost.

The ship was sealed and the Senate stamp was on it. A good thing. It meant it was already inspected and cleared for takeoff.

"Is there anyone inside?" Boone asked Elle.

"I don't sense anyone," she said.

"The engines are on," Boone said. "Stef has got to be close. Stay here."

Boone moved out, after making sure that no one was watching. The hatch was on the opposite side from where they hid. If Stef had not changed the code, then they could get on the ship.

Six solars was a long time not to change a code. Boone punched in the numbers but before he could finish he felt the cold barrel of a blaster pressed against his ear.

"Going somewhere?"

He could only hope that Elle and Zander were watching. He turned with his hands up and found himself looking into a very familiar face.

Stefan raised the blaster. "Boone?"

Boone nodded. He couldn't speak. Stefan grabbed him and crushed him in a hug as Zander and Elle charged around the nose of the ship. Elle held up a hand to stop Zander, who looked as if he was ready to toss Stefan across the port.

Boone closed his eyes, just for a moment, long enough to feel the loss and longing that he knew he had put his family through by his own impetuous act.

"I can't believe it," Stefan finally said. "You must be the reason why the port's closed down." Stef pushed a remote and the hatch slid open on the ship. "Get inside, now!"

They filed in and went to the bridge. Stef punched up a dige screen and an SNN broadcast appeared, replaying portions of the incident from the pits, but not all of it. Mostly it was of Zander's rampage. Then Elle's face was plastered on the screen with the tag KID-NAPPED beneath it.

"The entire planet's on lockdown," Stefan said. "They want you bad. I was already cleared for takeoff but they closed the portal so now everyone is stuck."

"Do they want all of us?" Boone asked.

"All of you," Stefan said. "You know too much about what's happening on Bali Circe. He's a violent murderer." Stef tilted his head toward Zander, who was deathly quiet. "And according to the Senate Guard, both of you kidnapped our princess here."

Elle let out a most unprincesslike snort. "Anyone who was watching knows that's a lie."

"They know what the SNN puppets tell them," Stef said. "When they kept saying the champion of Bali Circe I had no idea it was you. I usually go but I had some . . . er . . . business to take care of." Stefan took a long look at Zander. "It's good to see you alive," he said. "I should have known those Circe bitches would hide you in plain sight. But honestly, we thought you were dead."

"That was my fault," Elle said quietly.

"They took his memories," Boone explained as Zander remained silent. "There was no way you could have known it was him."

"We never gave up on you, Boone," Stefan said. "I tried every way I could think of to infiltrate Bali Circe but it's almost impossible."

Boone squeezed his uncle's shoulder. "I know. No way in, no way out, unless you get shot down into the ocean."

"Is that how you got that scar?" Stef asked.

"Yes," Boone said self-consciously. He was so accustomed to it that he'd forgotten the impact it would have on those who knew him before.

"It doesn't matter. Your mother and father will be so happy to see you she won't care what you look like. And Zoey . . ." Stefan shook his head and grinned.

"So how do we get out of here?"

"I'll have to bribe someone. Which is pretty much how you get off-planet when it's not locked down. Everyone here has a price and yours is one of the biggest I've seen in a while. We'll have to submit to another search but that's not a problem. I've got a place to hide you. It's over the reactors so the infrared won't sense you." He led them to the cargo bay and popped one of the floor grids. "It's going to be tight."

"Has this always been here?" Boone asked. In all the time he'd spent on the ship with his uncle, he'd never seen the hiding places.

"Since your dad," Stef said. "We figured what you didn't know wouldn't get me in trouble." Stef flashed a dazzling smile, then checked the hole in the floor. "Zander, in here."

Zander looked skeptically at the opening and then dropped down and wedged his shoulders through.

"Zander?" Elle said as he lay down as best he could in the narrow confines. He looked up at her with eyes that were full of pain but he nodded reassuringly.

"Help me move this," Stef said after he'd replaced the grid and Boone helped him shoved a palate full of boxes over top of Zander's hiding place.

"You two will have to share," Stef said as he moved to another grid. "The others are full of things that are . . . slightly illegal." The smile on his face reminded Boone so much of Ruben that he felt a jolt close to his heart.

Soon . . .

As if he read his mind, Stefan placed a hand on his shoulder. "I can't risk sending a message to Oasis. But I promise you, I will get you there."

"I know," Boone said.

"I can't wait to see the look on their faces," Stef said. "All of them." He included Elle. "It's been hell." He shook his head. "You first, Elle. It's going to be tight."

Elle dropped gracefully into the hole and Boone jumped in beside her. It was awkward, each one trying to get into a position where they could lower their bodies down.

An alarm sounded. "Company," Stefan said. He practically pushed them down with the grid and Boone collapsed onto the floor with Elle on top of him. They heard the screech of a palate moving on top of them and then the ringing of Stefan's boots as he walked away. It soon got lost in the hum of the engines.

Boone's eyes looked up as if he were following Stefan's footprints. When he could no longer hear him he brought his focus down and realized Elle was doing the same thing. Her head was turned toward the fading sound.

They were alone. He lay on his back and Elle lay stretched out on top of him with her arms propped on his chest as if she needed some distance. The feel of her was something he'd dreamed about for six long, lonely solars . . . longer, if you counted the longings of a boy.

Elle moved her leg and it hit him like a blaster. Every muscle from his chest down to his thighs jumped and she turned to look at him, her eyes pale against the shadows of her face. He circled her waist with his hands and her hair pooled on his chest. The familiar scent of lavender filled his senses. The scent of home.

Don't move.

She had to feel him. His need for her throbbed against her thigh.

The curse of the Circe men . . .

The scar on his face suddenly felt huge. He wasn't the same boy who foolishly ran off all those years ago. He turned his head away from her steady gaze.

What is she thinking? If only he could read her mind as easily as she could read his. She had yet to read his. At least he had not felt her inside his mind. It could be that he wouldn't.

She'd changed. That much was evident just from her appearance in the pits. It was unbelievable. It was as if she flew.

And the power she showed. The sheer force of it emanating from her was enough to strike terror in all those in her path.

It certainly terrified him. Where did it come from? How and when did she get so strong?

"Boone," she whispered and he turned back, both afraid and anxious of what he would see in her eyes.

She chewed on her lip. Something he'd seen her do more times than he could count. A sight so familiar that he thought his heart would burst. How quickly the little things came rushing back. She always did it when she was thinking . . . when something troubled her.

Without thought he reached up and pushed her hair away from her face, placed it behind her ear, and let his hand trail down the length of it. It was snagged on something around her collar and he tried to pull it free but Elle stopped him.

"Boone," she whispered. "Will you—"

The sound of several sets of footsteps overhead stopped her, and Boone's arms automatically went around her, pulling her down tight against his chest. Neither one of them dared to breathe. They heard voices and Stefan firmly stating that his ship had already passed inspection. The footsteps continued, along with the sounds of palates moving and boxes falling.

If this was his last moment with Elle, then so be it. If they were captured, then he would surely die and Zander with him.

At least he had this moment.

He felt her move and her hand crept up his chest and to his face. Her fingertips brushed across his scar and then they settled on his temple.

Boone closed his eyes.

She did not invade his mind. Instead she sent him one thought and one thought only.

"Forgive me."

Forgive her . . . Did she not know that he still loved

her? That he would never stop? That he couldn't stop? How could she?

"*Forgive me.*"

Her face was hidden, buried in his shoulder, resting beneath his chin, as if it belonged there. It always belonged there. Since they were children. It was how it was meant to be. He and Elle together since the first time he saw her. He reached up and grabbed her hand and pressed it against his temple.

He felt her sharp intake of breath as all his thoughts, his fears, his wants and needs poured forth from his mind into hers. Her hand trembled beneath his; then her fingers spread and gripped his head and her face moved up.

Boone grabbed the back of her head and guided her face toward his. He touched her lips with his and Elle gasped as he pressed her down, claiming her, devouring her, loving her, every bit of the past six solars told to her with the kiss. His other hand roamed down her back and pressed her body against his so there would be no doubt in her mind.

"*I forgive you. I love you. I never stopped.*" He said it with his mind and he said it with his kiss.

"*Boone . . .*" he felt her soft sigh in his mind.

The quarters were entirely too cramped but somehow he managed to roll them both over on their sides, mainly because he did not know how much longer he'd last with her body on top of his. They lay side by side and Boone cocked his leg over hers and rose on his elbow so he could look at her face.

"*I was such a fool . . .*" she said inside his head. "*It wasn't your fault. I never should have blamed you.*"

Boone touched his finger to her lips and quirked an eyebrow. "*It doesn't matter. We were both foolish, me more so because I left. I don't want to waste any more time, Elle. It's too precious.*"

She chewed on her lip and he could not help but wonder what she was thinking.

He knew what he was thinking and for the moment that was enough. He kissed her again, hoping that he would chase away any foolish thoughts that remained. Time was short. They could be taken. Stefan would fight to the death to protect them but if they were discovered there was nothing he could do.

Boone didn't want to live another moment without having her. So much time had passed. The last thing she told him, before the anger and the blame, was she needed time.

Was six solar years enough?

He needed to breathe but he didn't want to stop. His all-consuming need was for Elle. Who needed oxygen when he was kissing her?

She seemed more than willing herself.

Boone stopped and pulled back to look at her. Her incredible eyes glittered in the dim light as she looked up at him with her face full of longing.

Boone stroked her cheek. *"Have you had enough time to think about us?"*

"You're all I've thought about."

"What about your engagement?"

"He's a gank."

They both grinned and then hastily turned as they heard footsteps once again above them.

"It's Stefan," Elle said. "And he's alone. Everything is fine."

As Stefan opened the grid Boone shook his head at how close they had come to being caught in an embarrassing position.

"Don't worry," Elle said as she climbed out of the hole. "I would have sent him away."

Boone grabbed her arm in a mock attempt to pull her back down and she laughed. Stefan looked down at him with a cheesy grin on his face.

"Making up for lost time?" he asked as they went to free Zander.

"Yes, I am," Boone said.

CHAPTER THIRTY-SEVEN

They watched silently as they reached the hyperport. Senate battleships guarded the entrance and they watched them through the Plexi as Boone guided the Shooting Star to the gate.

Stefan manned the turret gun . . . "just in case," he said as he climbed up into the hold.

Elle stood between the chairs on the bridge and concentrated on being invisible. If she willed it, then perhaps the battleships would not see them. Zander watched everything closely through the Plexi as if he'd never seen the sky before.

Maybe he hasn't . . . that he can remember.

Boone punched in the release code when they were hailed and they were allowed to proceed.

"Everything is for sale," Boone said. "Even our escape."

"Both your fathers owe me big time," Stefan said. "It took me a year to earn the credits I parted with today."

"We're worth it," Boone said. "Besides, you know

both our mothers would kill you if they found out you abandoned us."

"Well, I do value my life a bit more than I value yours," Stefan said agreeably. "Get out of my seat."

Boone gave his uncle a crisp salute and turned over the controls.

"You two better hold on," Stef said. "Hyperspeed in five, four, three, two, one."

Boone wrapped an arm around Elle's waist and grabbed on to a clip that hung from the ceiling. He braced his legs wide and leaned forward. Elle felt the thrust of the hyperdrive and her body was slammed into Boone's, but he remained steady and unyielding against the g-forces that pummeled them.

Boone. Always steady.

The ship went soft as quickly as it had thrust and Boone's stance relaxed but he did not seem inclined to let go of her waist. With his arm flexed around her Elle noticed the wound on Boone's arm. "That needs sealing," she said.

Boone looked at his arm and grimaced. "I'd forgotten I had it," he said. "But now suddenly it hurts."

"There's a med kit in the lav," Stefan said.

Elle took Boone's hand and led him into the lav. The quarters were tight and Boone took off his shirt before he shut the door so they could access the cabinet that held the med kit.

He was nothing but lean muscle. There was nothing soft about his body. It was obvious that his life had been tough. It was a miracle that he'd survived it.

Yet here he was, sitting on the bowl while she cleaned the gash left by Zander's blades. He made a face when she poured the sterilizer on and then watched carefully as she used the liquid sealer to close up the wound.

"He wanted me to kill him," Boone said quietly as she worked.

"Why?"

"I think he thought it was the only way to save Mara."

"Who is Mara?"

"The woman on the platform."

"The slave woman?" Elle dabbed at the line on his throat and Boone sucked in air. He must have moved fast to escape the blade. If she had not gotten there when she did . . .

"Yes," Boone said. "He didn't want to fight me, especially when he realized that I recognized him. But then it was as if he didn't have a choice."

"I overheard Peter and Calvin talking about the match. They said there was a woman they were going to use to make him fight tonight. Apparently the Phoenix had been on a strike lately. It was very important to the Circe that he fight you tonight. It was also important to them that I not be there. That's when I realized that it could very well be you they were talking about when they said—"

"The champion of Bali Circe?" Boone said with a grin. "A dubious honor at best."

Elle grinned back. "No, what made me realize it was you was when they said you single-handedly wiped out half of their air guard."

Boone nodded approvingly. "And all with one shot." He looked up as Elle finished wrapping a bandage around his arm. "Pretty good shot, I'd say."

"Don't let it go to your head," Elle replied as she packed up the med kit. Boone grabbed her hand when she was done.

How easily he touched her. And how easily she let him after rejecting all signs of physical affection from everyone in her life. Every time he touched her Elle felt him claiming her as his. Elle rubbed her thumb across his knuckles and felt the strength in his hands.

"I thought he was going after Bella on the platform," she said. "Could it be that he's in love with her? Mara?"

"It would explain a lot," Boone said. "I always thought that it took a woman to trigger the male Circe's powers. And Zander definitely has powers now."

"There's only been two known male Circes in existence," Elle said. "Could it be true? My father certainly did not come into power until he met my mother." Elle looked toward the wall that separated the lav from the bridge.

"How did you know it was him? Didn't he always wear a mask?"

"The Circe who captured me on Bali Circe was the same one that captured Zander," Boone began.

"Arleta."

"Yes. When I tried to protect myself with the litany she laughed and said I was just like my friend, the one whose memories they took. And that he served their purpose now. Which basically was to kill me. When I was in the ring I noticed his eyes and then he did the thing he always did before he worked out."

"Jump three times and then crack his neck?"

"Yes. That. It all fell together. But then I thought maybe not, because I could hear him speak inside my head."

"I wonder how strong his powers are."

"I was wondering the same thing about you," Boone said. "Elle . . . the things you did . . . it was amazing."

"Ever since you've been gone, all I've thought about is the power. I wanted it so I wouldn't be hurt again. Boone, everything I've done since the day you left was an attempt to be more powerful than Bella and the rest of those witches. I didn't want to ever feel the pain again that I felt when we thought Zander had died and you . . . We really thought you were dead. We couldn't find anything about you other than the fact that a ship like yours was reported shot down over the ocean on Bali Circe. And there were no survivors."

"The rebels found me. And it turns out the leader is my mother's brother."

"Tess will be pleased to hear that."

"So you thought I was dead," Boone said playfully. "Is that why you were marrying Peter?"

"I'll have you know I could have had any man in the universe." Elle raised her nose with a superior air.

"And you chose him?" Boone said incredulously.

"None of them were you." She looked down into his deep green eyes. Could she be dreaming? Was it possible that she was in cryo and imaging how she wanted her life to be?

Boone closed his arms around her waist and pulled Elle next to him. He laid his cheek against her stomach and Elle rubbed the top of his head. The short stiff hairs felt bristly against her fingertips and she well recalled a time when it was long and silky back before he went to Academy. This was real.

"Does that mean that you missed me?"

"Every day." She reached inside her shirt and pulled forth the necklace he gave her. "I never took it off."

Boone touched the gem on the end of the chain with the tip of a finger. He smiled. "I never touched another woman the entire time I was gone," he said. "It's important that you know that."

"It doesn't matter."

"But it does, Elle. There's no one else for me but you." She saw the hope in his eyes, the vulnerability, the longing. Her mind moved back to the day it all fell apart, when he gave her the necklace and swore his devotion to her. "You've got to know that."

"I know it. I've never doubted it. But you've got to know I'm not the same girl you fell in love with. I'm afraid that you won't like what I've become."

"You did what you had to do to survive." Boone touched her cheek. "We all did. Including Zander."

Zander . . . What about Zander? Elle chewed on her lip.

As if reading her thoughts, Boone released her. "Why don't you go talk to Zander? I haven't had a hot shower since I left and suddenly I don't think I could live another moment without one."

Zander was in the cargo bay. Elle found him leaning his forehead against a stack of crates that were marked *Farm Equipment*.

I wonder what they really contain. Just like Zander, what's on the inside is hidden.

Elle knew it would be a simple matter to look inside her brother's mind. But for some reason that was a line she did not want to cross. She well knew the signs of a personal shield wall. After all, she'd perfected the art herself.

Zander did not want to be touched yet she could not help but reach out a hand and touch his shoulder.

He flexed his muscle to shake her off, then turned to look at her. It amazed her how much he looked like their father, but then again, she was the image of their mother.

"You are my sister?" he asked.

"Yes. Your twin."

His anger erupted and he shoved over the crates and stalked away. Elle jumped back as the crates scattered and splintered and the deck heaved at the sudden shifting of weight.

"Hey!" Stefan yelled. "Watch it!"

Zander turned back to where Elle stood. "Why don't I know you?" For some reason she expected him to yell but his quiet whisper was somehow more disturbing.

"Bella . . . the Circe . . . they took your memories."

"Why?"

"Because they feared you."

"He said I was the Aberrant of the Circe." Zander had yet to call any of them by name. "Mara . . ." His voice tripped over the name but he swallowed and recovered. "Mara said I was the Empowered One. That she'd seen me in her dreams on Bali Circe." He let out a short bark of a laugh. "She even quoted some legend. Is this why they fear me?"

"They fear you because you were not supposed to be

born. Neither of us was. Our father is a Circe who never should have survived and the Circe feared his union with our mother would create a powerful being. One they could not control."

"Am I supposed to be this powerful being?"

"Yes."

Zander clenched his fists and looked at them as if he'd never seen them before. "What power am I supposed to have?" He didn't let her answer but continued. "What is it I'm supposed to do? What weapons do I possess besides these?" He lifted his fists in the air. "*Why did they do this to me*?" he roared at last and Elle gasped back a sob in the face of his anger.

Zander stalked around the bay as if he were looking for something, anything to vent his frustration on. He finally stopped in front of Elle. "Where are you taking me?"

"Home. To Oasis."

He lowered his head and closed his eyes and Elle watched him carefully, not sure of what he was capable of.

"I can't see it. No matter how hard I try, I can't remember you, Oasis, none of it."

"What do you remember? What is your first memory?"

"I was in a room with two of the witches and some guards. They sent me to the games. A fitting tribute to my father, they said."

"Our father fought in the Murlaca once. To win our mother's hand."

"That's why they sent me there? To that hell? Because of our father?" He scrubbed his hands through his hair. "I think it would have been better if I'd never been born."

"Don't say that."

Zander grimaced. "Our parents. They are still alive?"

"Yes."

He looked at his hands once again. "I don't want to go there. Is there someplace else you can take me?"

"Why?" Elle asked. "They will be overjoyed to know you are alive."

He looked at his hands and then rubbed them as if they were covered with dirt. "Their son died a long time ago. What I've become is not . . ." He stopped, looked at his hands again, and then dropped them to his side. "I don't want to see them. I thank you for releasing me. But I'm not going to Oasis."

She knew she shouldn't touch him. But she had to. Elle quickly, quietly moved to where Zander stood and grabbed his forearms. She looked him in the eye and dared him to walk away. "I think I can help you if you'll let me."

"Help me what? Forget the past again?" He tried to turn away but Elle concentrated her will on him so that he would have to look at her. She was desperate to save him.

"Release me," he said.

"I don't know how to take away a memory," Elle said as she held on. "But I know how to bring one back. I did it before . . . we did it . . . a memory from our childhood. But you have to help me. You have to let me in your mind."

"That's a place you don't want to go."

"I love you, Zander. I always will, no matter what you've done. But it won't work if you don't want it to." She released her hold. It had to be his choice.

He turned away and stretched his arms out on a large crate. He leaned his head against the box and Elle could not help but marvel at the line of muscle that showed beneath the tight black fabric of his shirt.

He was remarkable. Everything a Prince of Oasis should be. Yet his life had been and would be wasted. If he didn't go home now, he never would. He'd really be lost to them forever.

He let out a sigh and finally turned. "What do I have to do?"

"Sit down," Elle said. She nodded toward the floor and Zander sat down. He automatically put his body in the pose that they always used.

It was amazing that the body would remember what the mind forgot.

Elle settled down in front of him with her own legs crossed upon her knees.

"I'm going to touch you," she said. "Here." She put her fingers to his temples and Zander obligingly bent his head. The pattern of his dark hair was so achingly familiar that she wanted to run her hand through it as she used to do when his dreams made his sleep restless.

He would not allow it. He barely could stand her touching his temples. She felt the resentment inside him coiling like a snake.

Like a Circe.

"You can see in my mind?"

He looked at her for a moment. His gaze was steady, disconcerting, as if she were guilty of some crime against him. "Yes." Perhaps she was. She believed him dead and they never searched for him. The Circe hid him in plain sight and they never even bothered to look. And all because of what she believed. Was it because of Bella? Or the fact that his memories were gone and the essence of what was Zander was no longer linked to her mentally?

There was no time for recriminations. Zander was right in front of her and needed her now. "Let me see in your mind."

"How?"

"Relax, Zander. Let me in."

Zander raised his head and looked directly into her eyes. It was strange, almost like looking in a mirror. Elle recognized the emptiness as something she'd seen in her own reflection many times.

"Think back," she said. "Go back over the day."

Elle saw the events of the day unfold in Zander's mind. They reeled before her in a series of scenes. As he concentrated she was able to slide into his mind.

"Go back . . . keep going."

She saw it when he begged Boone to kill him. He raised his throat and told him to take it. *Tear it out so I'll bleed to death before I have a chance to heal.* He wanted to die. He wanted an end to the hell that was his life.

Zander . . .

Elle saw it all then. Blood. Gore. Death. Hatred. Perversion. Despair. It was too much. The killing went on and on like he was a machine. It was all he knew. He had no choice. If he stopped they would torture him over and over again because he could not die.

She couldn't stand it. She had to get away from it. She tried to pull away but Zander grabbed her arms and kept her hands on his face.

"I can't." She sobbed the words as her hands and arms trembled. How could she stand it? How did he live with it?

Just when she thought she would pull away she felt a new strength flowing through her body.

Boone. He sat down behind her and wrapped his body around hers. "Be strong, Elle. Bring him back," he whispered in her ear.

"Can you see it?" she asked.

"I don't need to," Boone said. *"All he needs is you."*

Zander clenched her wrists so tight she thought they would break. She had to go back in or he would be lost in his memories.

She went back. The battles went on over and over again, each one undeterminable because they all started and ended the same. She saw his grief when he lost his friend, she saw his madness; then she saw his confusion.

It was the beginning for him. It was what she was looking for. Elle pushed deeper into his mind. She roamed the tunnels of his memories, opening doors, looking for something, anything that would bring him back to her.

The sea. He remembered the sea. The sea was their retreat. Their escape. Their celebration. It had always been that way. The three of them and the sea. She grabbed hold of his memory and brought him into her mind and showed him hers. She started with the sea and brought in everything else from their lives. Every moment of everything in her memory she showed him, starting at their first awareness and taking him to the last moments that she saw him.

He saw everything. She felt his awareness as if they were both struck with a prod.

"Elle?"

"Yes, Zander. It's me."

"I want to go home."

CHAPTER THIRTY-EIGHT

Boone left Elle and Zander alone after his memories came back. It wasn't long before she came to the bridge to find him. Stefan was bringing him up to date on Zoey, who apparently was keeping his parents on their toes.

"She's just like Ruben," Stefan said smugly. "A bit of an outlaw."

"A bit?" Boone asked with a grin. He snagged Elle's hand when she placed it on the back of the coseat. "How's Zander?"

"He's asleep," she said. "In one of the bunks back in the hold." She sat down on the arm of the coseat. "How long before we get home?"

"Still have over a day left," Stefan said. "I'm fine if you guys want to catch some sleep. Or I could put all of you in cryo."

"No," Boone said. He looked up at Elle, who shook her head also.

"Why don't you two go stretch out in my cabin,

then?" Stefan said with a wicked grin. "My bunk will hold two."

"Let's go," Elle said and pulled on his hand. Boone tripped over the seat in his haste to follow and left Stefan laughing at his reflection.

Elle led him to the cabin and shut the door firmly behind them.

She looked up at him with her extraordinary eyes. "I don't want to waste any more time."

Boone felt his heart skip a beat. He cupped her face with his hands and looked into her eyes. She seemed scared. He rubbed his thumbs over her cheeks and waited.

"I love you," she said.

She said it. She meant it. There was no doubt in her eyes, no confusion, only love. It was worth it. All the years of waiting and longing for this moment.

He opened his mouth to speak but she stopped him.

"And I'm the biggest fool in the universe."

Boone laughed. "Why?"

"Because I sent you away the first time you told me."

"You needed time. I understood that."

"Boone." He knew she was about to tease him by the way her eyes danced. "I didn't need this much time."

"So let's quit wasting it," he said and pulled her to him.

She met his kiss with an urgency that surprised him. Suddenly all the years of waiting and longing were too much. He had to have her now. His hands moved over her back and down and she jumped up and wrapped her legs around his waist. Boone stumbled back and crashed into the wall.

He pressed her body against his and Elle whimpered. He kissed her neck and she threw her head back as he moved his lips lower. When she moved her head she hit his and stars exploded, causing him to stagger. They fell to the floor of the cabin and landed with Elle on top.

She pulled on his shirt and whipped it over his head. Boone rose and met her lips again while her hands roamed his back. He bent his knees and pushed her back against his thighs as he fumbled with the belt that held her Sais.

She grabbed his hands. "I'm so used to wearing them I forgot I had them on." She gasped as she ripped the belt off her waist and thighs and flung it in the corner. She smiled saucily then and very slowly reached down for the tail of her shirt.

Boone moved his hands under her shirt and wrapped his hands around her narrow waist as she teased him, slowly pulling the shirt up until it reached her breasts. When she stopped he moved his hands up and cupped her breasts. He felt the star-shaped gem hanging between her breasts as Elle gasped and threw her head back. She pulled her shirt off as Boone's mouth found the place where his hands had been. She wrapped his head in her hands and pressed him against her as he moved his lips over her skin.

"Boone . . ." she whispered. "Please."

He rose and gently laid her back on the floor. He slid his hands down the contours of her stomach and her muscles clenched. Boone pulled off her boots and then removed the rest of her clothing until she lay trembling below him.

Elle reached for him, her usually graceful hands fumbling nervously as she sought to free him.

"Shhh," Boone said and moved her hands up to his waist. He slid out of his pants and slowly, carefully, stretched out on top of her.

Skin touching skin. He body stretched on hers. Her breasts caught against his chest, her stomach curving away from his, their thighs meeting until she spread her legs and wrapped them around his waist.

"I love you, Elle," he said. "It's the curse of the Circe men. To only love once and for a lifetime. There will never be another for me. Only you."

"Only you, Boone," she said and reached for him.

Slowly, carefully, achingly he entered her. He knew it was her first time. Her eyes glittered as he felt her close around him and he thought he might die from the sheer joy of it.

She had changed. She was no longer the girl he left behind but a passionate woman. She met him easily, willingly, and returned all the emotion that he gave to her.

Elle touched her fingertips to his temple and as he moved he felt the cabin of the ship slip away. He closed his eyes and felt the two of them surrounded by stars as if they were part of the sky. He was floating in space and the only thing that kept him from spinning away was Elle. He felt her inside him, at the very core of his soul, as he was inside her.

He felt her move with him, felt her rise to meet him, felt her passion inside him as her soul danced with his until they spun round and round and the stars became one continuous light that was so bright he was blinded by it.

He gasped her name and fell against her until he could see again. Then he wrapped her in his arms and rolled them both over on their sides.

Elle snuggled against him as if she could get closer. Boone was fairly certain there was no space left between their bodies but he obliged her need and held her tightly against him.

Then she giggled.

"What's so funny?"

"I guess this means my wedding to Peter is off," she said against his neck.

"Don't even go there," he growled. "I'll tell him myself."

"Oh, that should do wonders for the diplomatic relations between Oasis and Senate."

"Diplomacy be damned," Boone said. "You are mine and Senate can go blast itself."

"I'm not going anywhere," she said.

"Well, actually you are."

"I am?"

Boone moved to his knees and scooped her up in his arms and then deposited her on the bed. "Now you're not going anywhere," he said as he lay down beside her and pulled her into his arms.

Later, when their passion was spent and they basked in the comfort of just being together, she spooned up against him. Boone's finger traced the tattoo on her left shoulder. Three dolphins formed a circle, nose to tail. It was no bigger than his fist and intricate in the detail of the blue shades and shadows.

"When did you get this?"

Elle looked over her shoulder at the markings. "Soon after you left. It's a right of passage for Oasian Royalty."

"I knew Lilly has one, but does Shaun?"

"He said his scars are his markings."

"Why this? The dolphins."

"I got to choose what I wanted. Something significant to me. It's the three of us. The way we were as children."

"Playing in the sea with the dolphins."

"Yes."

Boone traced the circle round and round. "The Empowered One will come from the sea escorted by the dolphins."

"What is that?"

"It's the legend on Oasis. About the Empowered One." Boone quoted the legend as Sagan told it to him. "I didn't have the heart to tell them that the Empowered One was most likely dead. Then I thought maybe it could be Shaun but . . ."

"Now you believe it's Zander."

"It's too much of a coincidence not to be."

"He talked about Mara after you left. He wants to find her."

Boone wrapped his arm around Elle's waist. "I know

how he feels. And now that I've found you again I'm never going to let you go."

"Hold on tight, Boone," Elle said.

"I plan on it."

It was the shift of the engines that woke him. They were coming out of hyperdrive.

"We're home," he said as he kissed Elle awake. They quickly dressed and went to the bridge. Zander was already awake, and sitting in the coseat. His damp hair gave evidence of his use of the shower.

"I couldn't risk sending a message," Stef said. "In case they had bounty hunters waiting to ambush us here. I just told Ruben and Tess to meet us at the villa. It's all over the SNN that you've been kidnapped, but they're not divulging the identity of the kidnappers. It would make the Senate look bad to know that the missing Prince of Oasis has been right under their noses the entire time."

"Prince," Zander grunted. "That's going to take some getting used to."

"Don't worry," Elle said. "I'll keep you in your place."

"Thanks, Princess," Zander said dryly.

The sky brightened around them. The air was so clean and clear that Boone couldn't wait to inhale it. The planet below took form and his trained eye quickly picked out the familiar landmarks that meant they were close to the villa.

Two Oasian Fighters joined them.

"We were told to bring you in, Starfox," one of the pilots said.

"Thanks for the escort," Stefan replied.

"Any news on our missing princess?" the pilot asked.

"That's a negative," Stefan said. "Starfox out." He looked at the group around him. "I like surprises," he said. "They'd blab it before we got there."

The sunlight bounced off the ocean below and it

wasn't long before the lines of the ancient volcano that sheltered the villa were in sight. Stefan guided the Shooting Star over the craggy cliffs and the ship skimmed the silvery water of the lake.

Boone looked at the cave in the face of the cliff. He never thought he'd see it again. The villa was as much a home to him as the winery where his parents lived. But this was where his happiness was found.

Elle's hand slipped into his and a smile lit up her face.

"Home," Boone said and raised her hand to his lips.

Stefan shut down the engines and the hatch opened. Boone walked out and seriously considered kissing the ground as his feet hit the floor of the bay. The guard's jaw dropped open and he finally fumbled out a "Welcome home."

"Where are they?" Elle asked.

"On the main floor," he replied. "I'm to tell Master Stefan to join them there."

His face turned white when Zander ducked his head out of the hatch and looked tentatively around the bay.

"Don't tell them," Elle said. "It's a surprise."

"And a good one," he said as he looked in wonder at Zander. "And, Princess . . . your grandfather is here also."

"Grandfather?" Zander said. "Michael."

"Yes," Elle said.

Boone and Elle walked hand in hand through the tunnels.

Stefan led the way. "I want to see the look on their faces," he said as he stepped in before Boone and Elle. Zander came behind them. Elle kept turning around to look at him.

"He's frightened . . ." she said in Boone's mind.

"So am I."

They moved from the natural surface of the tunnel floor to the polished granite of the villa's floor. Boone saw them all on the balcony—his parents, Shaun and

Lilly, Michael. But before they turned he was knocked flat on his back by a bundle of fur that surely outweighed him.

"Kyp?" The newf whined and trembled as he sniffed Boone's face and chest. He sat up and wrapped his arms around Kyp's neck. "Yes, I missed you too," he said as he rubbed his hands through the ruff around the massive head.

He looked up and saw five sets of faces with jaws slack.

"Boone?" His mother. Did he do that to her? Age her? Her hazel eyes were etched with grief and she burst into tears as she threw her arms around his neck before he could stand. His father came up behind her and Boone reached for him and Ruben, enfolded both of them in his arms.

"Where's Zoey?" he was finally able to say when they let go.

"Here," a voice he did not recognize said. Boone turned and saw a tall, slim girl with dark hair and her father's eyes and the hint of what would someday be dangerous curves. She'd grown up.

"Who told you you could grow up?" he asked.

"Who told you you could leave for so long?" she replied.

"I guess we need to watch out for each other."

Zoey flew into his arms and he picked her up and swung her around as Kyp barked at his waist.

Zander . . .

Zander stood in the doorway watching the reunion. Elle's return had been a shock, even though they were certain she was the reason for Stefan's mysterious summons. Shaun and Lilly just now realized that there was someone else here.

Lilly held her hand to her mouth to stop the trembling.

"Zander?"

He nodded.

Lilly, always graceful, always perfect in her decorum, stumbled forward. Zander caught her arms before she fell and she burst into tears.

He didn't know what to do.

Boone looked at Elle. Tears streamed down her face as Michael held on to her as if he were afraid of falling over.

"Help him."

Elle nodded and Boone knew that she entered his mind when Zander slowly and tentatively drew his mother into his arms.

"Let's go outside," Ruben said as Shaun finally stepped forward to greet his son.

Boone and his family moved out to the balcony and found Stefan leaning against the rail with a drink in his hand.

"I love happy endings," he said with a big grin.

"Wait until they find out how much money they owe you," Boone said.

Ruben pulled Boone to him and hugged him. "It's worth every credit," he said. "Now do you mind telling us where you've been for the past six solars?"

"Bali Circe," Boone said. "With my uncle."

Ruben looked at Stefan, who shrugged his shoulders.

"Mema's brother," Boone said.

"My brother?" Tess said in amazement.

"What about Zander?" Ruben asked. "Where was he?"

Boone looked at the group inside. "He was in hell."

And still a long way to go before he leaves it.

Tess gently touched the scar on his face. "I guess we're lucky you survived."

Boone nodded. "Elle saved me."

As if she heard him mention her name, Elle came out to where they stood and slipped her arms around his waist. Boone kissed her forehead and drew her close.

"She saved both of us," he said. "It's a long story, one that everyone needs to hear. I'm not sure Zander is up to the telling."

"At least it has a happy ending," Zoey said.

"Ending?" Boone said. "This is just the beginning."

Our beginning.

EPILOGUE

Elle and Boone stood on the beach and watched as Zander headed out toward the water. Kyp bounced joyfully around their feet and chased a piece of driftwood that Boone flung into the surf. The sun hung on the horizon as if deciding whether it really wanted to turn away. Pinks, purples, yellows, and blues streaked from its orb, making promises of a glorious morning to come.

Zander stood in the last rays of the day and lifted a handful of water. He splashed it on his face and scrubbed it in. Then he did the same with his shoulders, his back, and his torso. His hands scrubbed at the smooth surface of his skin and rolled over the dips and planes of his musculature, all of it glorious in its perfection.

No scars marred his body, none like Boone carried. All of Zander's scars were on the inside.

Beyond him, a dolphin broke through the surface,

then another, arcing back and forth before him, as if they were waiting for him to come in.

He watched them for a moment, along with the waves that rolled into shore. He waded toward them and then he dived, his body slicing through the crest of a wave and coming up eventually in the distance, close to the dolphins.

They circled him, filling the air with friendly chatter, and he listened to them. One of them jumped and landed with a great splash, covering him with water, and when it came up again he swung his arm, pushing water toward the creature.

It became a game and Elle smiled as she watched her brother frolic and play.

"There will come, someday, a man with forbidden eyes who will have more power than the Circe women," Boone said. "The Empowered One will come from the sea escorted by the dolphins," he continued as he quoted the legend as Sagan had told it to him. "The dolphins will join him in battling the Circe Witches and when it is over, all people on the planet, woman and man alike, will finally be equal."

"Do you think it could be true?" Elle asked. "Do you think he could be the one?"

"As he is now?" Boone said. "I don't think so. He's lost. You said it yourself. How can he save an entire race of people when he doesn't know who or what he is? But maybe, given time, he could be. But that will be up to him. His decision."

"And when the time comes, we will go with him?" Elle asked.

Boone's finger traced the tattoo on her shoulder. "We will," he said. "The three of us together."